MIKE HODGKINS
BETTER RED THAN DEAD

To Sue.

Best Wishes

from Mike

MIKE HODGKINS
BETTER RED
THAN DEAD

DB
PUBLISHING

First published in Great Britain in 2012 by The Derby Books Publishing Company Limited, 3 The Parker Centre, Derby, DE21 4SZ.

ISBN 978-1-78091-078-9

Printed and bound by Gomer Press, Llandysul Ceredigion.

A Fireman to be successful must enter buildings; he must get in below, through panels of doors, through windows, through loopholes cut by himself in the gates, the walls, the roof.

He must know how to reach the attic from the basement by ladders placed on half burned stairs, and the basement from the attic by rope made fast on a chimney. His whole success depends on his getting there and remaining there and he must always carry his appliances with him as without them he is of no use.

Sir Eyre Massey Shaw 1830-1908.
Superintendent of the Metropolitan Fire Brigade

1

Mac peered through the windscreen into the rain-lashed night. The wipers skimmed the rain from the glass. The engine roared as the driver changed gear to take the roundabout. Mac's mind drifted back to the times when busy nights had made his heart pound with anticipation. He still loved the job, but the thousands of calls he'd been to over the years had taken their toll. He was tired; it had been a busy night. In the early days, being up all night at fires was what he'd wanted. The watch would play cards through the night between shouts. It had been fun, but now it had become routine and that was something he regretted. Fire fighting had been his life. It still was, but to a less intense degree than when he was younger. He sometimes envied the adrenaline shot the youngsters got from a fire.

'It looks like a job, Mac,' Taff shouted as they rounded the bend in the road. Over the rooftops of the factories in the industrial estate, a dull orange glow flickered, reflected off the underside of the low-lying rain clouds.

Taff pulled hard on the wheel, forcing the appliance into a tight arc close to the factory. Flames poured through the slate roof at one end of the old brick building.

'Right boys, get your sets started up, and get a jet onto it, quick as you like,' Mac called to Brian and Jock.

Mac scanned the scene, allowing a few seconds to compose himself before committing to the job. The crew were on with their jobs: they knew what to do. Taff, the pump operator, was chasing water up behind the BA team, ensuring that it was there when they needed it. Ray Swift – Mac's Number Two on the watch – had set up the BA entry control board, and – at a speed that belied his fifty-four years – had run to the hydrant to supply water before the tank on the fire appliance was drained.

Mac lifted the radio handset from its holder. '*Control from Alpha Zero One Zero, from Sub Officer James at Bright Lane Industrial site. Factory well alight. Make pumps four. TL required.*' Mac leapt from the appliance. Not waiting for a response from control, he called to Taff, who was operating the pump and filling out the information on the BA entry control board. 'When the next machine gets here, Taff, tell the OIC to contact me on the radio, and get another BA crew in the other end of the building.'

Dan Brogan stumbled across the dark floor of his bedroom. Control had informed him of the Bright Lane fire. *I'd better have a pee before I leave,* he thought.

This call was on Dan's patch. It sounded like a goer, so he would go and have a look. He'd decide which calls to attend and which to leave. Mac making pumps four was a shout he couldn't ignore.

He'd known Mac for all of his service. They'd trained together and been stationed with each other for several years. Eventually, Dan had gone for promotion, Mac preferring to remain as a fireman, content with his lot. It wasn't until he was pressured by Dan and by his wife, Val, that Mac finally took the exams, passed them and was soon promoted, and he'd never regretted the decision. He found, much to his surprise, that he liked the responsibility and had a natural instinct on the fire ground. He was a born leader, and was soon highly respected by his men.

'What have we got here then, Mac?' Dan Brogan said, as he approached Mac from his car.

'Can't you see, Dan?' Mac said, a broad grin creasing his face. 'A cracker of a fire,' he laughed, pointing to the building which was by now well alight. 'Single-storey factory. I've got two BA teams in: my lot on the left, a crew from Billing are in on the right. I've told them to stop it coming any further along, make a stop where it now is. When the next appliance gets here, I thought I'd get another jet in just to reinforce what we're already doing.'

'Have you had a look round the back?' Dan asked.

'No, haven't had the chance, yet.'

'OK, I'll do it, then, and have a chat with the boys on the way round.'

'OK, I'll see to this half, if you'll watch the back.'

Dan nodded. He'd had similar conversations with Mac many times before. The processes and procedures came almost automatically to them – none of the old formalities between trusted and experienced colleagues.

Brian and Jock had smashed their way into the side entrance of the factory, the large crowbar being the irresistible force, easily bursting the lock. They were rigged in breathing apparatus equipment, protected by anti-flash hoods and heavy leather gloves. Their tallies were on the board at the entry control point, the hose snaked out behind them, and with a cold aluminium hand-controlled branch ready to deliver a high-powered jet of water, they were fully prepared, both of them keyed up and ready to commit to the fire. Hit it hard. Blast it, before it gets you. The furnace-like torrent of scorching smoke surged over their heads. The fire growled its contempt: rushing air, crackling timber, splintering glass and the ever-present sounds of the building groaning under the impact of the fire.

Brian glanced over his shoulder at Jock, his heart thudding loudly in his chest. He gripped the branch tightly, his right hand forming a perfect arm lock on the hose. Jock nodded at him.

'OK, Jock, let's get in and give it some. Stay low.'

Jock slapped Brian's shoulder. No words were needed, just the physical signal that he was ready. Both of their hearts pounding, adrenalin rushing through their veins, giving them the drive and nerve they needed to go on, when every other sense is saying this is not a good idea. Fight or flight. Their only thought was to hit it hard and fast, their only way to win the fight.

The searing smoke at first failed to impact on them, protected from the heat as they were, no exposed skin to tell them of the furnace they were entering. The only outward sign was the blistering paint on the door as they entered. The smoke swirled over their heads as they crouched, the cooling wind driving oxygen into the fire, coming in low around their heavy rubber-booted feet.

Dan walked swiftly around the jumbled rear of the factory, the concrete yard littered with pieces of rusted steel, wooden pallets piled high, a store of empty oil drums and skips overflowing with the detritus of the factory. He stood back from the building and got a clear view of the problems they faced. Orange flames leapt through the roof, which in part had collapsed under the heat of the fire. The ridge line looked stressed and began to sag. His heart skipped a beat. He pressed the switch on his hand-held radio.

'*Mac. Are you receiving me? Over.*'

Brian and Jock crouched low, driven down by the heat. Everywhere they looked, they saw fire. Brian opened the lever of his branch and felt it recoil as the wide arc of cold spray disappeared into the flames; the flames subsided momentarily as the water absorbed the heat, turned to steam and descended in a stinging cloud around them. Jock leaned forward, pushing his facemask up close to Brian's head.

'Are yi all right there, big man? Let's get stuck in and kill the bastard.'

Brian turned his head. He could see the flames reflected in the heavy plastic mask on Jock's face. He hadn't heard the whole thing, but he'd got the message.

'Yeah, all right. Let's do it.'

Brian laughed above the sound of the high pressure air being forced into his facemask. Jock laughed back at him. Tough as it was, as unpleasant and dangerous as it was, they both enjoyed the adrenalin, a concoction which stimulated and sharpened their reflexes; this was what they were born to do.

Mac paced across the car park, watching the building, assessing the efforts of the crews. Another appliance pulled into the car park. Mac grabbed the Officer in charge.

'Get your lads with a jet into the right side of the building supporting the crew already in there. Help shore up the stop, OK.'

The crew quickly ran out another line of hose and disappeared into the factory. As a turntable ladder thundered into the car park, Mac spoke to the officer in charge.

'Set up in a central position. I don't want you working yet, but get ready if we need you.'

The driver manoeuvred the large machine into a position where the high-powered monitor could direct its jet of water onto the majority of the building without having to be re-positioned, its crew connecting to the hydrant. A fire fighter climbed awkwardly along to the head of the ladder as it lay horizontally across the back of the appliance, and using the massive hook on the belt he wore, clipped himself on to the heavy steel ring at the head of the ladder. The operator stood at its base and moved the levers on his consul and the head of the ladder began to rise slowly.

The crew from Billing were holding the fire, stopping it dead in its tracks. The second crew arrived and added to their efforts. They were confident that the fight was being won. Mac gathered another crew and pushed them in behind Brian and Jock, to double the attack on the fire, which, until that point, had shown little sign of being beaten.

'*Are you receiving me, Mac?*' Dan Brogan's voice spat out of Mac's radio. Mac heard the tension in Dan's voice.

'*Yeah, receiving you. Over.*'

'*Mac, I'm worried about the roof. It looks very dodgy. I'm not sure it'll stay intact much longer. I think we should move the boys out pronto.*'

'*Will do. Thanks, Dan. We'll whistle them out,*' Mac replied.

Brian and Jock were confident, they'd made good progress. The team behind them were watching their back and they could see that the teams at the other end of the factory were holding it. They had the fire in a pincer grip, it was just a matter of time now.

Jock peered up through the haze of smoke and steam. The steel roof trusses were just becoming visible and he saw with horror that the horizontal steel cross members, the pieces of the roof which maintained its stability, were glowing bright orange and were sagging wildly. He heard groans from the structure of the building as the strain of the fire began to take its final devastating toll.

'Look at that, Bry. What di yi think?' Jock called, unable to hide his concern.

'I think we'd better get our arses out of here fast. I don't like the look of it. Let's move it,' Brian shouted above the sound of the shattering glass and the screech of tormented roof joists.

In a second, large sections of the roof began to shower them. Shards of glass and hot steel bounced off the concrete around their feet. Neither said a word, their focus now directed inwards, survival paramount in their minds. They ran, Brian dropping the branch as he turned, Jock ahead of him, still keeping low below the layer of thick brown smoke as they climbed over collapsed piles of boxes. Jock cursed as he tripped over the hose, hidden in a deep puddle of water. Brian grabbed the back of Jock's BA set and, with his massive arms taut, he hauled Jock back onto his feet.

Mac began blowing his whistle with repeated short blasts, the signal for everyone to evacuate immediately. The roof began to collapse, the middle section first, and then the collapse slowly moved outwards along the building, the ridge turning inwards, driving massive showers of flame and sparks into the night sky.

Brian and Jock were moving fast. They could hear the sound of collapse behind them, and then they saw the branch of their support team lying abandoned on the factory floor. They heard the sound of whistles. The men outside had clearly spotted the danger and were trying to warn them. The whistles gave them extra impetus. The door – their exit from the building – was ten feet in front of them, and they could see men urging them out through distorted light. Brian felt a thump on the back of his head. The next thing, he was falling. The light went out.

Mac sprinted to the entry point of the factory. He could see that the crews at the other end had abandoned the job safely; his main concern now was the two crews who'd been fighting the fire at this end. As he approached, the back-up team sprang from the door, their coats smouldering, a fire fighter quickly covering them in a cold spray of water. Smoke and ash spewed from the door, driven by the pressure of the collapse. As Mac peered into the smoke, he could hear the sound of men moving at pace. He saw Jock approach the doorway, he saw a steel beam swing across their path and Brian flung into the wall before collapsing into the sodden floor of the passageway, instantly disappearing among the dust and debris of the collapse. Jock stumbled out of the door, exhausted, a colleague catching him before he collapsed.

Fear surged through Mac's chest. Without thought, he strode through the doorway into the hell of the corridor, debris pouring over him. Brian was lost from view; he'd fallen amid the dusty debris of the collapse. Mac groped around the floor, quickly locating him. He shouted: 'Come on, Brian. Let's have you out of here,' but there was no response. So Mac grabbed the back of Brian's BA set.

'Make a bit of room for an old bugger, Mac.'

Dan Brogan was now crouching beside Brian.

'Take an arm each. We'll have him out in no time.'

'Thanks, Dan,' Mac gasped, coughing and spitting dust-filled mucus from his mouth.

The fire fighter at the head of the turntable ladder signalled with his arm and the operator on the pump of the turntable ladder span the wheels of the deliveries and slammed down the throttle, water spat from the monitor like a cold bullet. The monitor swung from side to side covering the building with its vast cooling spray and flooding the dying building with thousands of gallons of cooling water. The fight was lost.

Brian dreamed of his daughter; he remembered that he was due to do his other job tomorrow.

I'll just sleep in till the alarm goes off, he thought. He felt something on his face; somebody was slapping his face. 'Go away, you bastards. I'm still tired.' He prised open his eyes. 'Who's she?' he thought.

A little over one hundred yards away, an interested spectator had watched in horror as the building had begun to collapse. He'd seen the panic on the faces of the fire fighters. This hadn't been part of his plan.

Brian prised open his eyes. A female paramedic was checking his pulse.

'What are you up to?' Brian asked, making a brave attempt to smile at the girl.

'You just lie still a minute. You've had a bang on the head, but I reckon you firemen must all have thick skulls. You seem to be OK.'

With the building lost to the fire, the plan changed. The aim now was to extinguish the fire without risks to anyone.

Dan, Mac and the other officers gathered together and decided on a plan of action for the remainder of the job. Mac's main concern had been Brian's welfare, but Brian was adamant that he was OK and insisted that he would carry on.

'Why would I want to go to hospital? It was nothing,' he said, convincing everyone that he was fine.

Over the next hour, the crews worked hard to kill the remnants of the fire, as some appliances were returned to their stations. Finally, at two o'clock a relief appliance came and Mac took his crew back to Graveton; maybe then they would get a couple of hours sleep.

'Right, boys. Service the sets, dump and re-stow the hose, and let's get in and have a nice cuppa,' Mac said, feeling cheered. The incident with Brian had scared him; he felt mightily relieved. They sat on the mess deck, everyone tired now, the absence of adrenalin, now gone, had left them feeling weary. They sat quietly, drank their tea and one by one sauntered off to their beds in the dormitory.

By three o'clock, the relief appliance reported that the fire was out and they were returning to their home station. The appliance drove out of the car park, leaving the area in darkness. All that remained was the burned-out building, wisps of steam still pouring from the still-warm debris and the smell of charred timber and plastic hanging in the air. The appliance disappeared into the distance, its red rear lights finally disappearing from view.

One hundred yards away, James McEvoy – security guard, aged twenty-five – looked at the darkened pile of debris. This was more than he had planned. Feeling both fear and guilt, he jammed his hand into his pocket, felt the box of matches and shuddered.

What have I done? He thought.

2

Dan Brogan hauled himself out of bed. He'd had a disturbed night and the Bright Lane fire had been the highlight. Dan had never been much of a sleeper: as a young fireman, he'd often stayed up all night, reading a book or studying for his exams, the men on his watch thinking he was mad and often telling him so.

He lived alone in a comfortable semi-detached house on a small housing estate, about four miles from his base at divisional headquarters. Over the five years he'd been making the journey from home, it had become such a mundane routine part of his everyday life that he would sometimes arrive at the HQ unable to recall any of the journey, a journey usually taking twenty-five minutes, if the traffic was kind.

He stretched, yawned as he looked in the mirror. *'You're getting too old for this game, Dan, my boy. Time you gave it up,'* he thought to himself. He shaved, had a shower and was soon feeling human again. He quickly drank a mug of tea, had a slice of toast and he then he was on his way.

Today was the day of the monthly meeting, bringing the officers from the Division together. Divisional Commander Ian Blain would be in the chair. He hadn't been in the job long: tall and slim, aged thirty-one, his career had begun in the Surrey Fire Brigade at eighteen years of age. He was bright and ambitious and this was soon recognised, he studied and was promoted and was soon on the fast track to further promotions and high level management. A command course at the college soon followed. The next phase began, as Divisional Commander 'A' Division South Yorkshire Fire and Rescue Service.

Brian Parks was tired, his head ached, a lump and bruise visible from the events of the previous night's escapade. Brian found the prospect of a day working for a local furniture removal company not ideal. He'd been doing this kind of work for years: it helped to fund his life – buy the things he needed – and he had a low boredom threshold, quickly become unhappy when he wasn't occupied with something. At forty years of age, he was beginning to feel that it was time to give it a rest. He didn't need the money and he was single. He had a child from a relationship seven years earlier: a little girl called Bill, the real love of his life. Jane, Brian's ex-partner (and Bill's mother) disliked the name, a cause of friction between the two parents.

'Her name's Jill, and I'll thank you for using it. She's a little girl, not a boy.'

Brian took little notice; he didn't much care for his ex-partner, just doing enough to keep the cart on the wheels. He didn't want any problems with access to his beloved daughter. He tried to be a good father. He never dodged his responsibilities, always paid the maintenance – sometimes more than required – without complaint. It was his duty and he was happy to do it. The two most important things in his life were his daughter and then the boys on the watch.

Jock Mclean got home, kissed his wife, who was just on her way out to her job at the supermarket, then, after a cup of tea, he fed the cat and went to bed. He needed his sleep. Later he would be doing his other job as a doorman at a local nightclub. He enjoyed the work, the job suited him perfectly, the pay was good, and he loved the camaraderie with the other doormen. The money was useful, too. Jock was a proud Scot, but over time his accent had mellowed and sometimes a hint of a Yorkshire accent would emerge. He'd lived in Sheffield for so long he felt this was where he belonged, though that was something that, if asked, he would never admit. He liked the fact that he came from somewhere else: it made him feel a bit special. Jock fitted in, he identified with the rough and readiness, and the unselfishness of the people. In many ways, they were similar to the people he'd grown up with in Glasgow.

Mac arrived home, Val made him a cup of coffee, and then they chatted for a while about the events of the night. Val was always interested to find out what had gone on at his work.

'Let's go for a walk shall we?' Mac suggested. 'It'll knock some of the cobwebs out of my head.'

'That sounds good to me. I'll throw some stuff into the rucksack,' Val called from the kitchen.

They liked to walk along Froggatt Edge, with its glorious views and bracing breezes; that's what they would do today – something to help Mac to relax after a busy tour of duty.

Soon they were heading out of the city in the reliable old Volvo that Mac couldn't find the courage to change for a newer model. They turned south, the road cutting across wild moors which stretched for miles. Glancing to her right, Val called to Mac: 'Look over there. The stags are on the move with the deer.' On the horizon of Big Moor they could make out the shapes of a large herd moving slowly through the gorse.

Fifteen minutes later Mac pulled into the car park close to the start of the walk. Mac threw the rucksack (stuffed with their equipment and food) over his shoulder, grabbed Val's hand and set off up the rocky, eroded track.

The day was warm with just a gentle breeze as they made their way up the first steep incline which brought them on to the top of the escarpment. The trail, an old coach road, later used to transport millstones by pack horses and sledge, was dry but rough underfoot, but they walked easily.

Mac always counted it a blessing to have such an area close at hand. As they walked they were frequently distracted by the views over the valley below, with its lush green fields separated by lines of trees and dry stone walls, and the river in the valley bottom, glistening in the bright sunlight. Across the steep-sided valley, in the deep grooves created over millions of years by the movement of water, villages had grown. Further along the valley floor lay the village of Grindleford, many of its fine houses anchored to the steep wooded hill side. This was the target today. After some discussion they decided to call at the railway station café a unique place and one of their regular stopping points, renowned for its quirky style of service.

They headed west at an easy pace, chatted about family, work and the plans for their next holiday. To their right, the land rose steadily to White Edge. The track they were walking wove along the top of a series of steep grit-stone crags, a rock-climbing paradise.

It was evident that there was plenty of activity today; climbers sat perched on the edge of the crags, legs dangling into space, but their bodies firmly anchored by ropes to large rocks. They could occasionally hear snippets of conversations between the climbers.

'Take in the bloody slack will ya or I'm gunna fall off.'

'Yurra wuss. Get yerself up. You've fell off harder stuff than this before,' came the unsympathetic response from the man on the other end of the rope. Seconds later there was a gasp, a clinking of metal on rock and loud shrieks of laughter.

'I said I was gunna fall off, didn't I?' the climber shouted in mock anger, trying to contain the laughter in his voice.

Mac chuckled to himself. He could easily identify with the climbers: madcap, brave, enthusiastic, just like the guys on his watch.

They wandered comfortably, eventually descending through dense woods, crossing a metalled road, then steeply downwards, eventually emerging at the café which in earlier times had been the railway station's waiting room. As always, there were cars parked nearby, this being a convenient spot for some excellent walks. They pulled open the door into the café and were met by a blast of warm air, carrying with it the aroma of freshly-cooked bacon.

'What can I get you my love?' the attractive middle-aged woman asked from behind the old counter.

'Bacon sandwich, beans on toast and two mugs of tea please, love?' Mac replied-both he and Val ignoring the fact that they had sandwiches and a flask in the rucksack. Over the years they had walked in this area and it had become a routine, part of their ritual. Thirty minutes later, refreshed, they headed off, deciding to return to the car via White edge. This would take maybe an hour and a half at a steady pace.

The first twenty minutes was a struggle after their lunch, a steep climb was not the ideal. However, they soon cleared the woods and headed up past an old derelict stone lodge onto White Edge. To the right the land fell away, giving views of the route they had walked earlier, and along the Derwent Valley to the left, there were extensive views across vast tracts of heather-covered moorland.

The weather had cooled, the sky had clouded over and the breeze had turned and now came from the north, so they stopped briefly to put on an extra layer of clothing and then continued walking.

The day was perfect. A few other walkers and a fell runner had passed them, going in the opposite direction. They walked and talked; within ten minutes they'd warmed up and were walking smoothly back towards the car.

'What do you reckon that is, Val?' Mac said, looking along the path ahead into the distance. Mac quickened his pace, sensing a problem. Ahead of them a group of people had gathered and were crowding around a figure collapsed on the path. As Mac and Val approached, there was obviously a problem. Mac began to jog towards the group.

Lying unconscious on the path was an elderly man, equipped for a walk; the small gathering looked confused, unsure of what to do. Mac asked them what had happened, and a young woman spoke.

'He was walking just in front of us. He staggered and then collapsed.'

The man's skin was grey, his lips were turning blue, and Mac knew he had to be quick, 'You,' he called, looking directly into the eyes of a young man. 'Have you got a mobile phone?'

'Yes,' the youth replied, 'but there's no signal up here.'

Mac looked at him, instantly assessing him.

'Right. Get your phone and start running, that way, until you do get a signal. Then call for an ambulance tell them that we're about one mile east of White Edge Lodge and we have a male casualty collapsed and possibly having a heart attack. Get yourself into gear and do it.' The young man, jolted by the instructions, turned and sprinted away at speed, looking anxiously at his mobile phone.

Mac knelt at the side of the old man and removed the rucksack from his back, lifted the man's chin to clear his airway and then checked to see if he was breathing. He then jammed his fingers below the man's jawbone, feeling for a pulse, but he could feel nothing.

'Right. You,' Mac said, pointing to a man in his thirties. 'Get your phone and run that way, until you get a signal and make the same call as the other lad.' The man, pleased to help, jogged away, looking at his phone for any sign of a signal.

Mac knew that speed was vital. He pinched the old man's nose and placed his mouth over the elderly man's mouth and blew air into the inert body. Then he pressed down on his chest. A sense of urgency now pushed Mac into the rhythmic C.P.R. mode that he'd recently had refresher training for.

'Twelve, thirteen, fourteen, fifteen.' Mac leaned back, taking a couple of deep breaths, and then blew two more breaths into the mouth of the old man. The group of bystanders watched in silence. Mac was working hard. After five minutes of sustained effort he was beginning to tire.

'Look, I need some help here,' he said. Several people moved towards Mac. He picked the most capable-looking among the volunteers to assist him.

'You've seen what I've been doing. Can you copy that?'

'I'll try,' the man replied.

'Right,' Mac said. 'The second I finish blowing air into the man's mouth, you press fifteen times on his chest, the way I did, all right?'

The man looked terrified.

'OK,' he replied. 'I'll do my best.'

'That's all I can ask. Give it your best shot,' Mac said. '. . . And thanks.'

Twenty minutes later they were both tiring, but they persisted. The size of the crowd grew; Mac heard voices coming from the crowd.

'I reckon he's a goner,' he heard one young man say. Mac glowered at him, the young man looking away embarrassed.

Mac wasn't listening now: he was tired, on the edge of exhaustion, and it was taking all of his energy and concentration to keep both himself and his helper going.

They heard a faint buzz in the distance; it gradually grew louder. Then one of the group said: 'Thank God. I think that's a chopper.'

Within a minute, the buzz became the distinctive clacking of the rotors of a helicopter. They could hear the wailing of sirens, in the valley below, as an Ambulance struggled through traffic. The crowd of onlookers waved furiously at the helicopter as it approached them. The crew of the helicopter could see them; it circled for a few seconds before picking a safe place to land nearby, the group of onlookers ducking down low in an attempt to avoid the downdraught created by the rotors, as it landed.

The two men returned with their mobile phones, Mac sparing a second to thank them.

'Well done. This guy will be forever grateful to you.'

The Doctor, aided by Mac and some of the bystanders, secured the man onto a stretcher and quickly loaded him into the helicopter.

'Well done, you did a good job. I think he'll survive because of you,' the doctor called to the crowd as he climbed back into the door of the vibrating helicopter.

The engine of the helicopter roared as its rotors sliced through the air, their speed increasing. The crowd on the ground braced themselves against the blast of the downdraft. The helicopter rose slowly into the sky, flattening the bracken and grass around them, then turned steeply and headed rapidly in the direction of Sheffield just a couple of minutes flying time away.

The incident had lasted no more than half an hour, but Mac was exhausted. After the disturbed night, then this, he felt completely drained.

'Come on, love,' Val said. 'Let's have a steady stroll back to the car.'

The younger of the two men whom Mac had dispatched to make the call offered to carry Mac's pack.

'You were great,' the young man said, with a look of admiration directed straight at Mac.

'So were you, young fella,' Mac replied.

'Mind if I walk with you?' the boy asked.

'Of course you can, love,' Val replied, sensing that the boy was keen to talk to Mac about what had just happened.

'Where did you learn to do all that?' the boy asked.

'It's just part of my job,' Mac replied.

'Are you on the ambulances then?' the boy asked, as they walked slowly along the rutted track.

'No,' Mac replied. 'I'm in the Fire Brigade.'

The boy looked at Mac, a wide-eyed expression crossing his face. 'I didn't know you did that sort of stuff. I thought you just went to fires and car crashes.'

Mac was tired but spoke to the young man all the way back to the car park, prodded on by the boy's obvious enthusiasm.

'Well, young man, we'll have to go. It's been nice meeting you,' Mac said, as they walked into the car park. '. . . And thanks again for your help.'

'That's OK' the boy replied as he turned to walk away.

Mac and Val were half way to the car, when the boy turned again and said: 'Could I join the Fire Brigade then?'

Mac stopped and asked: 'Where do you live son?'

'Dronfield,' the boy replied.

'And how are you getting home?' Mac asked.

'I'm getting the train from Grindleford,' he replied.

'But that's four miles back in the direction we've just walked from,' Mac said, realising the boy had put himself out to help them. 'Get in the car. We'll run you home. It's not out of our way,' Mac lied. There was something about the boy that Mac liked; he didn't know what, but something.

The drive to Dronfield was slow; the roads were busy.

'How old are you?' Mac asked the boy.

'I'm eighteen next month,' he replied smiling sheepishly.

'Have you got a job?' Val asked.

'Yeah, but I don't like it,' he replied.

'What do you do?' Mac asked.

The boy brushed back his hair, and wiped the perspiration from his forehead.

'I work on a building site' he replied.

'Right, what do you do on the site then?' Mac asked.

'I'm a labourer. The pay's not bad, but I want to do something a bit more interesting. When you said you were a fireman, and seeing what you just did, I thought that's great; I think I'd like to do that.'

Mac looked at the boy. He could feel the boy's enthusiasm. It seemed that he'd found something that had inspired him, something to look forward to, beyond toiling on a building site.

'If that's what you want, then give it a go,' Mac said with a smile on his face.

Twenty minutes later, they drew up outside a neat terraced house in Dronfield.

'Thanks,' the boy said.

'Likewise,' Mac replied.

'What's your name?' the boy asked.

'Call me Mac. That's what my friends call me; I think you just about qualify. What's yours?' Mac said.

'I'm Jake. Well Jacob, really. My mum's the only one who uses it. Everybody else calls me Jake. I prefer it,' he said.

Mac smiled at the boy 'Well, Jake. Thanks. Good luck. I'll look out to see how you do.'

Val leaned across the car.

'We both will,' she shouted to him through the open window of the car, as they turned round and drove away.

'I like that boy,' Mac said, a smile crossing his face.

'Yes, so do I,' Val responded.

Ena was outside, hanging out the washing when Taff arrived home from work.

'You look tired, love,' she said. 'Have you had a busy night?'

'Yeah, we were up and down a bit. Even when I got to bed I couldn't sleep,' he replied. He'd slumped into one of their comfortable armchairs, and was closing his eyes and beginning to drift.

'I'll make you a cuppa, and we can have a chat before we go to the hospital,' Ena said. Today was a big day; they were booked in to see a specialist in the next phase of their attempt to get onto an IVF programme.

They'd wanted to have a family from the early days of their marriage, but nothing seemed to happen. After a couple of years of fruitless trying to get Ena pregnant, it had started to become a problem. As a result, Taff felt guilty and a little inadequate. Ena understood how he felt, and had always made light of it, even now, when they were in the final stages of the treatment.

Clive Botham dismounted from his mountain bike. After twenty miles of off-road biking, he was pretty tired. The ride was only intended to be a quick burst up a few hills to get him sweating, but as usual he forgot himself and was soon miles away from home. *Why do I always do this?* he thought to himself. He smiled. The last hour had been great, away from it all. He was hot and sweating, but high above the city he looked around and all he could see were hills and moors, covered in the pale green bracken and the faint purple hue of the heather covering the nearby hillsides. He was single and fancy free: he didn't have to operate to anyone's clock. He could do what he liked, when he liked, and the bike ride was just that: exactly what he wanted to do.

Clive loved all of the boys on his watch, but above all he loved Mac. In the early days of his service, Mac had been like a second father to him through some difficult times. If Mac wanted him to run through a wall, he'd give it his best shot.

In another couple of days he was due back on duty. He'd been on annual leave for two weeks, and couldn't wait to get back. He'd read about the factory fire on Bright Lane. He hated missing the good fires, and cursed his luck at missing that one.

Tony Ellis sat with his head in his hands. He was in the second week of a course at the brigade training centre. Tony was keen and working hard for promotion, but he was frustrated, feeling that he should have been promoted long before now. He was a good operational fireman, had lots of experience and a good knowledge of the job. If he had a weakness, it was his performance at interview: he didn't come across well when he became tense, he developed a stammer, and this had undoubtedly stalled his efforts to become a junior officer. Everyone who knew him rooted for him, and all the reports showed he was capable; he'd volunteered to leave his beloved watch, to sample temporary promotion in the fire prevention department, and he'd spent some time in the training centre, becoming involved with recruit training in an attempt to increase his chances of making the first step up the promotion ladder.

Despite the disappointments, he never gave up, but kept trying, with a single-minded dogged determination to do better – something his watch and many of the officers within the brigade admired.

'It will happen one day,' he would say to himself. Mac understood how desperate Tony was to be promoted and had spoken to him many times, impressing on him that he should keep at it, that he was good enough.

If Mac thought he was up to it, then that was good enough for Tony.

Jim McEvoy turned the ignition of the car for the third time.

The engine fired and spluttered, throwing out a cloud of black oil-rich smoke into the wet night air. He was sick of the car; it had always been difficult, even after it had scraped through the last MOT. Since then he'd spent eighty pounds for a local amateur mechanic to replace the points and plugs, and yet the car still struggled to start and run smoothly. He was beginning to think it was on the last leg of its inglorious life as he slammed the gear lever forward and jerked out into the stream of evening traffic, heading for yet another night of monotony.

His patrol began at three thirty precisely. This was the routine: it had to be that way. There were people who were paid more than he was to ensure he carried out his duties. The boss was a stickler for routine. The job, menial as it was, still had to be done to a rigid standard, and Jim resented this fact. His life was controlled by a man who was probably fast asleep in his warm bed, in his large house, in the comfortable suburbs of the city.

His patrol was a slow half mile stroll around the outside of the main building, checking that doors had not been tampered with and that there were no potential intruders lurking around the perimeter of his domain. Next was a patrol of the four floors on the inside of the office block, isolating alarms and re-activating them when he'd checked the area. This was his routine, his mind withering from the lack of stimulation. Nothing had ever happened on his patrols, but he knew that if he neglected his duty, the boss would know and he would be out on his ear.

Sometimes his mind would wander, he'd imagine what life could be like if he'd done better at school, maybe got a trade or a qualification in some skill. His life could have been so different. It would have been easy; all he'd have had to do would have been to face down the cretins in his class who'd made life a misery for anyone who'd shown interest in learning, but he'd have become an outcast. He wished now that he'd done that, taken the chance to do something with his life. He always felt that he had more to offer life than this, but now it was too late: twenty-five years old and given up on life already. He imagined what it would be like to have a girlfriend, what it might be like to have someone he liked, someone that liked him in return. How would it feel to kiss a girl or maybe more than that? He'd read about love, even felt it in a small way – he thought he'd loved his grandmother – but he was sure that was a different feeling to the feeling of love you got with a girl. He thought about his grandmother a lot. She'd brought him up from the age of thirteen, after his parents had been killed in an accident on the nearby M1 motorway.

He was on the second patrol of his night shift, a trip he'd made hundreds of times. He hated the job and his life; there was nothing to relieve the mind-numbing monotony. His was a solitary existence; the repetitive nightly tasks were soul-destroying. If he could live without the money, he'd give it up. The thought that this was his lot for the foreseeable future sent a shiver through his skinny body. Forty minutes after the patrol began it was over, the same dull routine completed. He removed his uniform jacket and hung it across the back of his chair, lit a cigarette, and settled back to watch late night television, on the small portable set on his desk, next to the CCTV monitors.

He was restless. He stubbed out the remnant of his cigarette, and paced around his small office, biding his time until the next patrol. The sky outside his office was black, with just the odd streetlamp shining from across the valley to break up the dark canvas, reminding him that there was life beyond the fences of his present incarceration: people had lives, they had wives and husbands, kids, jobs and they had social lives, had friends, went to the pub, made love, had fun. This all seemed a long way from the life he was living. He felt totally isolated from the world outside, an outsider in his own town.

3

The day was cold, dull and overcast, but it was a special day. Jacob Higgins was eighteen years and one day old. Three weeks before, he'd travelled into the city, and then he'd walked the half mile from the bus stop to the Fire Brigade Headquarters building. In the foyer, he'd met a smartly dressed middle-aged man.

'Can I help you?' the man had enquired, having noticed that Jake looked unsure where he should be.

'I hope so. I'd like to join the Fire Brigade. Who do I need to see?' Jake had asked, anxiously.

'Just hang on a second,' the man had replied, a smile crossing his face. 'I'll get someone for you. It's not my department, you see. Just hang on there a minute.'

He'd left Jacob standing in the reception area.

For a few minutes Jacob had been alone. He'd looked around the foyer. On the walls were an array of large photographs; firemen involved in fighting fires. One picture in particular had caught his eye. The picture, in black and white, showed a child being passed from one man to another at the base of a ladder, the rescuer anonymous, his face obscured by a breathing apparatus face mask. It showed a fire in a terraced house, similar to the house he lived in. Steam poured from the body of the rescuer as he stood on the snow covered pavement close to the house. Jacob had glanced at the other man in the picture. The face was familiar. As he looked closer, it had begun to dawn on Jake that the man in the picture was the man he knew as Mac, Jake had recognised him although the picture had been taken years before. He'd told Jake to run, make a phone call, a vital call that helped to save a life. That was the reason he was here today. He knew this was exactly where he should be.

The middle-aged man had soon returned with a young lady in her early twenties.

'Right young man, I have to go. I'll leave you in Sue's capable hands. She'll tell you all you need to know . . . and good luck.' The man walked through the front door of headquarters, the door swinging closed behind him.

'That's a good start for you,' the young lady had said.

'What do you mean?' Jake had replied.

'That was the Chief Fire Officer,' she'd said, smiling.

Jake hadn't known what to say. Soon he had forms he needed and a small wad of pamphlets, giving information on life in the Fire Brigade.

'Thanks for your help,' Jake he'd said to the young woman. 'By the way, do you know that man is in this picture?' Jake had asked, pointing to the picture on the wall.

'Of course,' Sue had replied. 'Everybody knows Mac. He's bit of a legend in the brigade. He's done more rescues and got himself hurt more times than you can count. But he's not one to make a fuss about it. He's one of the really good guys.'

'I know,' Jake had said, proudly. 'I met him in the Peaks. He saved a man who'd collapsed. I thought he was great. Thank you for your help.'

Jake had gathered up the forms and strode out of the Headquarters building, like a man on a mission.

I'll fill in the forms, and as soon as I'm eighteen, I'll apply to join the Brigade, he'd thought to himself, walking quickly away towards the bus stop.

Jake had filled in all of the forms and returned them to the headquarters the next day. His mother had been delighted by the fact that her normally morose son had suddenly developed a spark and had a spring in his step. She'd mentioned it to him and he'd told her what had happened on his last trip into the Peaks, then surprised her by saying: 'I'm going to try to join the Fire Brigade if I can.'

Within a week Jake had received a letter from the Brigade, inviting him to attend Headquarters for a preliminary interview.

Jake's Mum had taken him out and bought him a suit. He'd felt strange; he'd never worn a suit and tie before. His mother had emphasised: 'It's important that their first impression of you is a good one.' Jake had agreed. He was determined to get into the brigade. Wearing a suit was worth it if it gave him a better chance.

Jake walked self-consciously through the main doors. This was his first time in a suit and his first ever interview.

He sat in an ante-room on the third floor, along with three other men, all there for the same reason. Two of the men were in their early twenties. One had very long hair and looked unkempt. The other was shaven-headed, tattooed and wore a scruffy looking black tee shirt. Jake wasn't impressed with either of them. The third man was much smarter. Jake spoke to him briefly. He told Jake that he'd recently been demobbed from the Navy; he'd done fire-fighting on board ship, so this seemed an obvious choice for him when he left. He'd tried to join several Brigades, but South Yorkshire were one of only a few Brigades who were recruiting. So he'd travelled up from Kent the previous night and stayed in a bed and breakfast, to ensure he was on time for the interview. Jake was impressed.

They talked for a while, Jake doing most of the listening. He introduced himself as Mark Devonshire, born and bred in Kent. He told Jake of his time in the Navy; how he'd been an ordinary seaman, and had travelled extensively around the world, he was married to Trisha, and they had a baby boy named Josh. Jake had never met anyone so travelled, or spoken to anyone from the south of England before. Mark was twenty-nine years old and followed Arsenal Football Club. Jake imagined that that would go down well in South Yorkshire.

They talked for about twenty minutes until the door to the ante-room swung open, and a smart young man in uniform entered.

'Right boys, I'm Sub Officer Porter, Staff Sub Officer. I just need to confirm your details. The interviews will be starting in a couple of minutes.'

Jake began to feel nervous and it must have shown.

'Don't worry, you'll be OK,' Mark said. This somehow made Jake feel better.

'Thanks,' Jake replied.

A few minutes later the interviews began. The first two candidates had their interviews, and returned to the ante-room to pick up their belongings. Neither looked as if they had found the process a comfortable one.

Mark was called next. He walked smartly out of the room behind the Sub Officer.

'Good luck,' Jake said as he walked past him out of the room.

After what seemed an age, he returned, beads of sweat on his forehead, but with a confident look about him.

'How did it go?' Jake asked.

'It went well, I think,' he said. 'They didn't ask me anything I couldn't answer. Lots of stuff about me. 'Who are you?' type questions. So I just told them. You've nothing to worry about. Just be yourself.'

Jake was nervous, but what Mark had just said made him feel better.

I'm OK. I've never been in much trouble, he told himself. He wondered if Mac knew what he was doing, what he would say if he knew Jake was here, trying to get in the Brigade.

The door swung open again.

'Sorry to have kept you waiting, Mr Higgins. It's your turn now,' the Sub Officer, said apologetically.

They walked together down a long blue carpeted corridor, passing several doors, eventually arriving outside a conference room door. Jake felt the palms of his hands becoming hot and damp. Questions flitted in and out of his head. Was he doing the right thing? Would he be good enough? Did he look stupid in the suit? At that moment, he was wishing he was anywhere but here.

The Sub Officer knocked on the door.

'Come in,' a voice said from within the room. He opened the door and introduced Jake to the interview panel.

'Come in and sit down, Mr Higgins. Make yourself comfortable. I'm Divisional Officer Price and these are my colleagues, Mr Handscombe, and Mr Bryce. The lady on my left is Mrs Jane Harvey. Just try to relax. This isn't an interrogation, but a chance for us to meet you, and find out a bit about you. Do you mind if we call you Jacob?'

'No, sir,' Jake replied.

'OK then Jacob. Take a couple of minutes to tell us about yourself.'

Jake shuffled on his seat and pulled himself up until his back was straight. His mother's words came into his head. 'Remember, Jacob; first impressions count.'

Prior to the interview Jake had mused over the questions he could be asked. This was a question he had anticipated. He'd practised what he would say.

'Well, sir, I'm Jacob Higgins. I was eighteen yesterday. That's why I'm here. I live in Dronfield with my mum. Dad died, so mum brought me up for the last few years, on her own,' Jake said, trying to sound confident. 'What are you interested in Jacob?' one of the officers asked.

'I enjoy being outside. I sometimes go out to Derbyshire and walk. I've tried rock-climbing, but I couldn't really afford the equipment. I just like to be out in the fresh air, so I go out as often as I can,' Jake said, beginning to feel a little more relaxed.

'Tell us about your work Jacob. What do you do for a living?'

'I'm a labourer on a building site,' Jake replied.

'Do you enjoy the work?'

'No, not really. It gives me a wage, which is important; it helps me and mum out. I've always done it since I left school. I didn't know what else I could do,' he said, almost apologetically.

'So you thought you'd try the Fire Brigade?' the most senior officer said. 'What made you think of the Fire Brigade as a career?' he asked.

'Mac,' Jake replied. 'I met Mac.' 'Mac? Mac who?' they asked.

'I don't know his name really. I met him and his wife out in Derbyshire. A man had collapsed and Mac was giving him mouth to mouth. He asked me to help,' Jake said. 'That's how I met him. He told me he was a Fireman. I asked him about joining the fire brigade and he said to give it a try. That's why I'm here today.' 'Tell us what happened,' one of the officers asked.

Jake then related to them the events of that most remarkable day in his short life.

'I was just so impressed by him. He just seemed to know what to do. Everyone else stood back, not sure what to do. Then Mac came along the path and sorted it all out. He gave us all a job. I had to run off with my mobile phone and call an ambulance. He was fantastic.'

Jake's enthusiasm was bubbling over, his nerves had gone. The Panel sat quietly, whilst Jake described in great detail what had happened, relating that Mac and his wife had taken him home, and then encouraged him to try to become a fireman.

'So you've met Mac. You're a lucky young man. Mac's a good fireman.' The officers were writing things down on the sheets of paper they had on the desk in front of them. Jake wondered what they would be writing.

'All right, Jacob, that's all we need from you at the moment. Is there anything you want to ask us?' they asked.

'No thank you Sir.' Jake replied.

'Right, that's all. We'll contact you again soon, and thank you for telling us about your experience with Mac.'

Jake left the room, his heart pounding: he'd got excited again just relating to those people the events of his day in the Peaks. He grinned and thought to himself: 'That's not so bad after all.'

As Jake passed the ante-room, Mark was still there, waiting. He came out of the room.

'How did it go Jake?' he asked.

'It was fine, just like you said. Anyway, what are you still doing here?' Jake asked.

'I was just interested to see how you got on. Was it OK?' '

They stood in the corridor for several minutes, chatting about their interviews.

'Well, I'd better be off,' Mark said. 'I've got a train to catch. I hope to see you at the examinations . . . if they've accepted us,' he stressed.

'It's good to meet you. Hope you're through to the next phase. It would be nice to meet up again,' Jake replied.

'Sure would. Bye then,' Mark said as he walked off towards the railway station, his overnight holdall slung across his shoulder. He turned again and shouted: 'Good luck.'

Jake was elated: he felt confident and relieved that he hadn't disgraced himself. He'd managed to tell them about his one great moment with Mac, and he'd made a friend. It had been a very satisfying day. Suddenly he felt that the suit fitted him perfectly.

Tony had finished his course at the training centre. He'd given another two weeks of his life to the pursuit of his ambition. He'd done more courses, and time gaining experience in other brigade departments than any one he knew, he was still working hard to pass his station officers examinations, but he was getting frustrated, feeling that the recognition of his efforts was long overdue. When he got back on station he would have another chat with Mac about his prospects, he knew Mac would put him right.

4

Ray Swift climbed into his car. He felt tired: he hadn't slept well for a couple of nights. He started the car and waved goodbye to Mary (his wife of thirty-two years) before he reversed out of his drive. He wondered what was on the agenda at work today.

Ray had been the Leading Fireman on Red Watch for fifteen years, and he'd spent most of his service working with Mac. They were friends from way back, and had seen most things between them. They shared a strong bond of friendship and mutual trust, forged over years of working together in some very dangerous situations. He was content, he'd found his niche, he was happy. In the coming months he'd be thinking about his retirement, which was due to happen in the summer next year. He'd sat with Mary and planned what they'd do when he did finish work.

He had mixed feelings about it all. He loved his life in the brigade: he loved the work and most of their friends were from a Fire Brigade background. The other side of the coin, however, made them both think it was getting towards the time to retire. If the watch had been busy, especially during the night shifts, he would come home shattered. Mary had noticed that he would still be tired four days later, when he had to go back on duty. She worried about him. He was a veteran now, not as young as he used to be. She realised it was very much a younger man's job, and she was also ready for a change in their life. They planned to travel, once he had given up work; maybe buy a camper van and tour around Europe. The more she thought about it, the more convinced she was that Ray should retire soon.

He was recovering from a cold, so when he began feeling hot on his way to work, he assumed that it was the remnants of the cold making him feel rough. Driving through the traffic along his familiar route, he noticed shops and houses where over the years he'd fought fires, or rescued a cat from a tree. He noticed a small flood of water flowing across the road and made a mental note to check that it wasn't the hydrant leaking. He'd mention it to Mac when he got in to work.

Ahead of him, he saw the drill tower of the station. He slowed at the pedestrian crossing to let a woman with two children cross. Still feeling hot but thinking nothing of it, he pulled the steering wheel of his car to the left and drove the twenty-five yards up the drive into the fire station yard.

The buggers, he thought. They'd not left much space for him to park, so he pulled onto the grass at the end of the row of cars that were filling the designated parking bays. He'd move the car when the night crew went off duty. He opened the door of his car and climbed out, and then, leaning back in to grab his sports bag, he grasped the leather handle.

A stabbing pain hit him like a sledge hammer, paralysing his body. He gasped, clutching his chest, and stumbled against the car, his vision blurred. He could hear someone shouting in the recesses of his head, but couldn't understand the words. He saw the floor coming up to meet him. Feeling nothing but the pain in his chest, he tried to shift his body to relieve the pain, but his body wouldn't respond. His head became fuzzy: everything within his vision had become blurred and grey.

Ray suddenly realised what was happening to him. He felt scared, and breathing was painful. He struggled to bring his thoughts into focus, convincing himself that he was going to be all right. Then he drifted into unconsciousness.

Clive Botham had just arrived at the station, chained his mountain bike to the smoke house hand rail and he now stood talking to Brian Parks. As they spoke they glanced across the drill yard and saw Ray drive into the yard and park his car. They shouted 'Morning Ray' across to him but he didn't reply. He was leaning against the car with his back to them.

'What's the old fart doing now?' Clive said. 'It looks as though he had one too many last night.' They watched in horror as Ray tumbled face first onto the grass bank. They sprinted across the drill yard; Clive was the first to reach him. He could see immediately it was serious

'Go, Brian. Call an ambulance, and tell Mac. He'll be in the office by now.' Ray's face was grey and rigid from the pain in his chest. Clive leaned over him.

'It's Clive, Ray. Don't worry. Help's on the way.' Clive loosened Ray's collar and spoke to him whilst checking the pulse in his neck: it had become faint and erratic. Clive felt close to panic. It was different with a friend. He'd done this before and it hadn't been a problem. He heard voices and footsteps running; it was Mac with the rest of the crew, along with most of the night crew, all coming to lend a hand.

The pain in Ray's chest was easing: he could hear familiar voices and he could hear the wailing horn of the Ambulance. He thought of Mary. What the hell would she think? Then he faded back into the darkness.

The siren wailed through the traffic, as Mac felt the ambulance lurch from side to side; he watched as the ambulance paramedic inserted tubes into Ray's arms and planted a monitor on his chest.

Mac, ignoring the fact that he was just coming on duty, had asked the Officer in Charge of the night shift to cover for him, and, against the wishes of the Ambulance technician, had climbed aboard.

'Don't argue,' Mac had said. 'There's no way he's going to hospital without me, got it?' The ambulance man saw the look in Mac's eyes and said: 'OK, but don't interfere. Keep quiet and leave me to do what I've got to do.'

Dan Brogan had been in the headquarters building for about twenty minutes. He'd arranged for one of the girls to make him a cup of tea, when his pager operated. He strolled across to the nearby phone and called control.

'What's up?' Dan asked, casually.

'Just to let you know, sir, we've been informed by the duty crew at Graveton that Ray Swift has been taken into hospital with a suspected heart attack.'

'Which hospital has he gone too?' Dan asked.

'The Northern General, sir, and one more thing, sir: Sub Officer Wilson is riding in charge. Sub Officer James has gone off in the ambulance with Ray'

'Right, thanks, I'm mobile. Has anyone spoken to Ray's wife yet?'

'No, sir. We've only just been informed.'

'Right, I'm off to see her. Will you inform the Divisional Commander?'

'Yes, sir. Will do,' the control operator replied. Dan walked quickly to his car.

Mary Swift had just put another load of washing into the machine. She felt strange, as she brushed her brow with the back of her hand. Something wasn't right. There was no logic to the feeling, but the feeling persisted. She'd give Ray a call at dinner time and ask him to bring another box of washing powder in for her to save her having to lug it across town on the bus. She wished that she'd learned to drive. Ray always said: 'Don't worry, love. You know you wouldn't get a cheaper chauffer anywhere than me.'

She heard the door chime sound and instinctively knew something was wrong, as she walked down hall to the front door. She recognised the colour and shape of a fireman's cap through the frosted glass of the front door and froze for a moment, before, having gathered herself, she turned the latch to open the door.

'It's Ray isn't it? I just had a feeling,' she said, clutching her hands to her chest. Dan stood there silently for a second. Put off by Mary's statement, he struggled to get the words out.

'Let's go inside, Mary.' Dan put his arm around her shoulder and walked her into the lounge. 'Ray's been taken into hospital. He collapsed at work, but he's OK, I think. I just thought it should be me who told you. Can I get you a drink?'

Mary sat quietly for a time, and then asked: 'Will you take me to see him, Dan?'

'Of course I will. Get your coat. We'll get straight over there. Is there anything else I can do?'

She didn't reply: her face was strained, as she fought to hold herself together.

'Come on. Let's get off,' Dan said, and gently led her to his car.

Mac sat on a chair in the reception area close to the Intensive Care unit. When the ambulance arrived at the hospital, two nurses were waiting. They whisked Ray straight inside. Mac shouted to him as he went through the door.

'You hold on, you old bugger. You still owe four quid to the tea swindle.' Then Ray was gone, taken by two nurses and a doctor through the plastic swinging doors.

5

Daytime television's rubbish, he thought to himself, having just sat through yet another boring programme. He clicked the remote control and turned the set off.

Jim McEvoy was unsettled and time was dragging: bored at work, bored at home. Life was a pain. How to pass the time until he had to go to work tonight?

Thinking about work gave him no pleasure. He pushed himself up out of the old brown cloth armchair, put on his trainers and the old green bomber jacket he'd been wearing since leaving school nine years ago: he never seemed to have the time or motivation to go and buy a new coat. He decided to walk to go to the precinct half a mile away and buy a paper. Recent events had scared him: he was sure his crime would be reported in the local paper and the thought made him flush and feel heavy with guilt.

The precinct was busy: old folks, some in wheelchairs, were out doing their weekly shop, young mums were struggling to carry bags of groceries and control their children. One walked close by him. She was having some difficulty. He thought for a second that he might ask her if she needed some help, but he couldn't summon the courage to speak to her. He'd thought about offering help before, but lacked the confidence to speak. Today was no different.

He walked into a general store and, bypassing the daily papers – there was nothing there to interest him – he picked up the local paper and began thumbing through it until he found what he'd been looking for. The headline read:

LOCAL FACTORY BADLY DAMAGED IN BLAZE.
Fire Brigade Suspect Arson.

There was a photograph showing the outside of the badly damaged building, along with the local reporter's summary of the events at Bright Lane. James flushed and felt an overpowering sense of guilt. He bought a copy and then walked quickly out of the shop, desperate to get back to his flat and read about the fire.

'Crews. Crews, 'shun.' Both Red and White Watch came to attention. 'White Watch, fall out. Red Watch, stand at ease.' Sub Officer Alan Wilson, covering for Mac, whilst he was at the hospital, watched his own crew file away out of the appliance room.

'Right. Duties for the day. Fireman Parks, driver. Fireman Ellis and Fireman Mclean, you'll be BA today. Fireman Botham, mess duties.' The Sub Officer paused for a second. 'Mac just called in. Mary's at the hospital. Ray's poorly but he's stable. He'll be back soon. In the meantime do the routines, and let's have a cup of tea, mess man.'

Brian Parks stowed his fire gear in the appliance and climbed aboard the Dennis Water Tender Ladder. He would check the fuel and ensure that all the equipment was stowed and in order. Twenty minutes later, he'd finished his checks and recorded it in the watch room log book.

'Did the night watch have anything?' Brian asked, casually.

Taff looked in the log. 'Yeah, a couple. Nothing much. Just an AFA at Boots and a rubbish fire.'

The two BA men for the shift, Tony Ellis and Jock McLean, checked their breathing apparatus sets, a task they performed meticulously. They knew it was a matter of their life or death having a serviceable set to wear. Their BA set was their lifeline, their self-contained atmosphere. Without it, they couldn't function. This job was always done one hundred per cent: their lives depended on it.

Mac returned from the hospital around ten thirty. The watch were keen to know what was happening with Ray.

'He's OK. He's had a mild heart attack and he'll be off the run for some time. Mary's still there. We'll pop round in the appliance later this afternoon,' Mac said, looking relieved that his friend was going to be OK.

'I'm sorry this got dumped on you, Alan. I owe you one,' Mac said as Alan got changed to leave the station.

'No worries, Mac. Ray's a good guy. If there's anything more you need my watch to do, just give us a shout. We'll probably go round to see him and take the piss in a few days. It should help speed up his recovery.'

'I'm sure they'll both be happy to see you,' Mac replied. 'Anyway, Al, I'm grateful. Couldn't have done it without you.' Alan waved back to him as he walked across the drill yard to his car.

The station tannoy sounded, as Mac's voice was transmitted around the station.

'Duty crew, meet me in on the mess deck in two minutes.' The crew made their way from various parts of the station over the next few minutes. They found Mac standing in the mess room, looking out over the drill yard.

'Sit down boys. Let's have a chat,' Mac said, a serious look on his face. 'Ray's going to be fine, so the doctors say, but he's going to be off for a while. I've spoken to the Station Commander and he's agreed that, for the time being, we need someone to step up until he gets back to duty. Who wants to do it?' There was silence. Tony sat tight-lipped, desperate to speak up and offer his services, but worried what the boys would feel about him replacing Ray.

'Well, somebody's got to do it,' Mac said, a mock look of confusion on his face. 'If nobody volunteers, then we'll have to get somebody from another watch to do it. Come on, who wants it?'

There was silence, and then Jock spoke.

'We all know who wants to do it. We all know who should do it, and if he dunna speak up soon, I'm gunna stick a hose reel up his jacksey.' Everyone laughed, with the exception of Tony, who sat uncomfortably in his seat. The watch realised this was his chance. They also understood his reluctance to appear too keen to jump into Ray's boots. Tony had waited long enough, and nobody on the watch was prepared to stand in his way.

'Well, Tony. It looks as if all those years of coaching from the boys has finally paid off. You've got the job. Get the rank markings out of the office drawer, and the insulating tape is in the consumable cupboard. Get that stripe put on your helmet.'

Tony grinned, overcome by a feeling both of gratitude and excitement. All he could think of to say was: 'Thanks, lads.'

He thought to himself: *These are a special bunch of blokes.* The watch could see the relief in Tony's face, and they were happy for him.

'Right, you lazy lot. Let's have you out of here. You've been sitting about most of the morning. Things are gunna change around here,' Tony shouted, a broad toothy grin splitting his face. The boys laughed, and looked forward to what the coming days would bring.

'You'll see,' he said 'Things are about to change. Isn't that right Mac?' This was the happiest moment of Tony's life.

'If you can change this shower, you're a better man than I am, Gunga Din,' Mac replied. This had made a difficult day much better.

Mac always said: 'If you can laugh when things are bad, things will only get better.' The boys agreed with that philosophy.

6

Jake stood with one foot on a pile of house bricks, his elbows leaning heavily on the handle of the shovel he was supposed to be using to load the cement mixer. He stared vacantly into space, his mind in other places. He'd already been told off by the bricklayers for not keeping them supplied with cement and bricks.

Jake didn't care much: mentally he was no longer a labourer; he was going to be a fireman, a fire-fighter. These words revolved around his brain. Who knows, I could be a hero, save people's lives. He couldn't wait for the letter, which would hopefully launch him into his new world.

He noted every siren that passed the building site. He would strain to get a view of the passing vehicles. Earlier that morning he'd seen an ambulance screaming past, though Jake hadn't known it was on its way to the Fire Station, coming to the aid of Ray Swift.

I wonder what Mac's doing? Jake thought. He really hoped he would meet him again and he was sure that Mac would be happy that he was trying to join the brigade.

'I think you're doing the right thing,' one of his workmates said. 'It's a great job. One of my dad's mates was in the Fire Brigade in Doncaster. I think he was a leading fireman, although he's retired now. He's getting on a bit: he must be about fifty. My mate reckons he retired with a good pension.'

Jake had told most of the men on the building site about his experience on White Edge, and how it had made him want to change his job and become a fireman. They all thought it was a good idea, although a few said there was no way they'd be blowing into someone's mouth and doing CPR.

After the lunch break Red Watch gathered in the appliance room.

'Right, lads. We're going to test a few hydrants. Then we'll get off up to the hospital and visit Ray. Tony, this is your chance to beast the boys. You organise the inspections. I'll stay on the appliance. I've got some paperwork to do. Don't let them slacken off,' Mac said, a smile creasing his ruddy face. 'And don't take any lip. If they give you any grief, give some in return.'

The boys groaned. 'Oh no, not more hassle. We'd better behave then,' they laughed. Both Mac and Tony knew this would be an interesting afternoon.

Testing a fire hydrant is a routine but important part of a fireman's job; it ensures they are serviceable when needed in an emergency, and also keeps the crews up to speed on their location. The appliance sped up the City Road and turned into a large council estate. 'OK, boys, let's get off here. Get the standpipe key and bar off,' Tony ordered. The crew didn't respond, pretending they hadn't heard him.

'Come on, you lot. Let's be having you,' he said, attempting to insert some authority into his voice.

'Letsby? This isn't Letsby Avenue, this is Vanguard Drive. Letsby Avenue isn't round here,' Brian Parks said, giggling. Mac smiled. He'd heard this routine a dozen times before.

Tony raised his voice.

'Right, you sods, if you don't get off, I'm gonna get a proper grip of you all. Then you'll wonder what's hit you.'

This was the signal for Jock and Taff. They grabbed Tony. Brian pulled on the handbrake of the machine. After a short but violent struggle, Tony's trousers were removed, and he was bundled onto the pavement. Brian drove the appliance a couple of hundred yards down the road.

'You bastards,' Tony shouted. As he cowered, attempting to hide behind a privet hedge.

Mac looked up from his paperwork and said: 'How's it going, boys? Tony's not driving you too hard is he?'

'No, he's fine. He's really got a grip on us,' Jock replied.

The radio crackled.

'*Control calling Alpha zero one zero. Over.*'

Mac grabbed the radio handset.

'Control *from Alpha zero one zero. Go ahead. Over.*'

Brian gave a short blast on the appliance siren.

Tony sprinted towards the appliance. An elderly couple pushing a pram laughed at the site of Tony's thin white legs sprinting along the pavement towards the fire appliance.

'*Alpha zero one zero. Proceed to the junction of Kelling Lane and Whitehole Road. We have a report of a car fire following a collision, persons reported. Over.*'

Tony clambered into the back of the appliance, quickly retrieving his trousers. The rest of the crew were already getting rigged into their fire gear.

'What have we got?' he shouted above the roar of the engine,

'Persons reported, Kelling crossroads,' Jock said, grimacing with the struggle to get into his fire gear.

'Sounds like it could be nasty,' Taff said, a grim look settling on his face.

Mac leaned across to Brian.

'Give it the gun, Brian. I don't like the sound of this one.'

Brian slammed the accelerator to the floor: with sirens wailing and lights flashing, the traffic cleared a path and they sped back towards the town. Over the radio they could hear other appliances being mobilised. Mac heard Dan Brogan's call sign, booking mobile to the incident.

Things must be looking up, Dan remembering to use the radio. Mac thought to himself.

The appliance swerved violently as Brian nipped to the left to pass a queue of traffic at the lights, then swerved to the right and took the roundabout on the wrong side to avoid yet another queue of stationary traffic. Mac looked to his left as they passed rows of shops: he could see the flashing light of the appliance reflected in the shop windows, and then he heard Brian curse when a motorist panicked and stopped directly in front of them, just leaving sufficient space for him to break heavily, drag the wheel violently to the right, then sharply left again, feeling the mass of water in the tank sloshing, affecting the stability of the appliance as it danced around bollards and through traffic lights.

As they rounded a bend, ahead of them, about a quarter of a mile away, a plume of black smoke climbed above the blocks of flats. Adrenalin surged through the veins of the crew of Alpha Zero One Zero.

Jackson Ecklan was proud. He'd worked and saved for two years to buy his new car, depriving himself of many of the things his friends had. He wanted a Jag: it would be loved and cared for and would be with him for years.

To most people it was just an old Jag, but to Jackson, it was his dream come true. He had his girl by his side, the soft top down and the wind blowing in his face. He was truly happy. He hadn't noticed his speed.

On the road into town the traffic was light, so he trod heavily on the accelerator of his car, as he flew up Franklin Way, overtaking a couple of slower cars. The road ahead was clear, but damp from a shower about twenty minutes earlier. In the distance he could see that the traffic light at the crossroads had just changed to green. He reasoned that he could easily get through the lights before they changed colour again forcing him to stop.

Approaching the crossing, heading southwards, was a refuse lorry, filled with the city's rubbish and heading for the landfill site. The driver adjusted his speed to time his run, to reach the lights as they turned to green.

Fifty yards before the lights, Jackson was approaching the crossing at around fifty miles an hour If the driver of the lorry timed his run to perfection he would hit the lights perfectly.

Forty yards to go and he was committed to crossing the lights. The lights turned to amber, so he accelerated to over sixty miles per hour. He glanced to his right and saw, with horror, the refuse lorry coming through the lights at green. The lorry driver saw the Jaguar and braked heavily, pulling hard to the right on the steering wheel. He heard the screech of tyres.

Jackson gripped the steering wheel hard. His foot jammed down hard on the brake pedal, smoke erupted from the tyres of the Jaguar. Jackson's girlfriend put her hands across her face and screamed.

The front of the Jaguar ploughed into the rear wheel of the Refuse lorry, the bonnet of the Jaguar crumpling, the pressure on the engine mountings forcing them to snap, the engine being pushed back into the driver's space. He felt the weight of hot smoking metal crush his feet and legs. The impact sent the car spinning to the right, before turning onto its roof and bursting into flames. Jackson's final thought was: *What a bloody stupid thing to do* as the flames from the ruptured petrol tank engulfed him.

Ian Blain was in his office, catching up on some long-overdue paperwork when he got the call from control.

'OK, control. I'll make my way there, thank you.' Ian had a strong urge to delay; the gory side of the job had never been his forte. At times like this, he sometimes wished he did something more mundane to earn a living. Ian was a career Fire Officer, well aware of his shortcomings in the operational side of the job. Given his time again maybe he would have done things slightly differently. But he was proud of what he'd achieved and he enjoyed the kudos that came with the position. He was confident, too, that given time, he would be promoted further, to positions where there would be much less requirement on him to attend fires. *Every organisation needs chiefs as well as Indians,* he said to himself, unconvincingly.

The closer he got to the incident, the more anxious he became. Ian secretly hoped to hear a message from the incident that it was under control, and therefore he wouldn't be required to attend. But when he saw a plume of smoke rising in the distance above the tops of the houses, he knew it was a forlorn hope.

Ian arrived at the crossroads, his stomach churning; the fire in the car was virtually extinguished – just grey smoke and vast clouds of steam remained, created when the cold water hit the red hot metal that had once been the Jaguar belonging to Jackson Ecklan. The crew still poured water into the burned-out relic of what once was a car. He saw lines of hose being rolled up and debris strewn across the road. Some of the crew were blackened by the smoke from the fire, pinching their noses and blowing, to get the filth and stained mucus from their noses, some rubbed their eyes, sore from the effect of the acrid smoke. He saw Mac leaning into the cab, picking up the radio.

Mac was about to send the stop message to control when he noticed that the Divisional Commander's car had arrived. He thought, as a matter of courtesy, he would see him before sending the message, so he replaced the handset in the cab and walked briskly over to the DC.

'Hello, boss,' Mac said. 'Nice to see you. Do you want to see the job?'

'Good morning, Mac. I'll just book in and I'll be with you.' He called Control and then, rigged in his pristine fire gear, said: 'OK, Mac. What's the score?'

'The police have asked us not to move the car for a short while,' Mac said. 'They've to do some calculations. It was a stinker of a fire. It seems the car shot the lights. Not a lot the driver of the bin lorry could do to avoid it. The girl passenger was thrown clear. Didn't have her seat belt on, apparently. She was very lucky. The driver: well, he's still in there. When the police have finished we'll get the wrecker to move the car and we'll clear up.'

Ian saw that here was a man who knew his job. He was impressed. Mac seemed very comfortable in his skin, a man very much in command of his job.

'I don't think you needed me here, did you Sub?'

Mac looked at the DC and smiled.

'I would never say that, sir. It's nice to see an Officer come out to jobs. If you don't come, the lads think you don't do anything,' Mac said, with a faint smile on his lips. 'It gives us a bit of a boost to know you're bothered. Will you hang about whilst we remove the body?' Mac had guessed that the DC would, if given the choice, disappear. 'It would be good if you stayed. The lads would respect that.'

Ian gulped: inwardly he was in turmoil; he wanted to go, unsure of his ability to appear in control. On the other hand, he had the overriding feeling that he should stay.

'Of course I'll stay. I've got nothing much to do,' he said.

Mac was pleased. He could tell it would be a trial for the DC but he was sure it would be good for everyone there.

'I was going to send a stop, boss. Shall I send it from you?'

'No from you, Mac. It's your job.'

'*Control from Alpha Zero One Zero. Over.*'

'*Alpha Zero One Zero. Go ahead. Over.*'

'*Control from Alpha zero one zero stop message.*'

'*From Sub Officer James. Stop for Kelling crossroads, two vehicles in collision, one motor car destroyed by fire, one male casualty, code one, two hose reels and one FB5X, one female casualty taken to hospital by ambulance, one fireman with minor burns to face, dealt with at the scene, message ends. Over*'

'*Your message received and acknowledged. Control Out*'

The police soon finished their work. The ambulance had taken the girl to hospital and most of the debris had been cleared from the road. The police were now keen to see a swift conclusion to the incident, which was creating traffic chaos in the city, so that they were keen to get it over and done with, and the road cleared.

'Bring it back, a bit more.' The wrecker was poised to get chains onto the Jaguar and manoeuvre the vehicle back on to what remained of its wheels. 'A bit more, whoa, stop. That's fine.' The recovery vehicle was in position: the driver pulled down the Jacks and then lashed chains around the car, with the help of the fire crews.

Ian motioned to Mac.

'Let's get some sheeting up before we disturb the body. We don't want pictures being taken by the public.'

'Sure, boss. I'll see to it.' Mac grabbed Tony's arm. 'Tony. Get the boys and rig up some sheets. We don't want to upset the public'

'Right, lads. Get back a bit,' the driver said, as he operated the small crane on the rear of the truck. As the car was lifted, charred debris fell from the car onto the road, then, with a thump, the blackened remains of Jackson Ecklan tumbled from the wreckage.

'Can you swing the car away, mate?' Mac shouted. The driver pushed a lever and the car swung away, exposing the charred remains in the road.

'Jock. Get a salvage sheet over him, will you?' Mac instructed, keen to maintain as much dignity for the dead driver of the car as possible.

An Ambulance had been standing by to remove the body, but only after a doctor had been called and, after a cursory look at the body, pronounced Jackson dead at the scene.

Mac was careful to pick the men needed to put the remains into a plastic body bag. He knew the ones most suited to the task: Brian and Jock got the job. Ian Blain stood back, letting Mac and the crews get on with their task. He was impressed by Mac's control and the professionalism of the crews and, surprisingly, his own performance. He was glad he'd stayed.

'Do you want to come back to the station with us, boss?' Mac asked. 'After dirty jobs we usually have a cuppa and a chat about things. It'll be nice for the boys to have a chat with you, too.'

Ian thought for a moment. 'I'll do that. A cuppa would be very welcome. I'll just have to inform Control that I'll be delayed for a short while.'

'Control *from Alpha Zero One Zero. We are mobile to home station.*'

7

Jim McEvoy sat in the public bar of the Nags Head in Edale. He'd driven aimlessly for about half an hour, noticed that his fuel gauge showed that his tank was almost empty, so he'd stopped at the next garage and put petrol into the car. As he'd driven on, he'd noticed the sign for Castleton. He hadn't been there since a trip from school had taken him there along with his teacher and, he remembered a steep descent underground and a trip on a boat along an underground river. He remembered how damp and eerie it had all felt. The memories of his childhood came flooding back to him. The emotions it stirred within him came as a surprise.

Jim sat, immersed in his thoughts, remembering days from years ago, when he came out to Derbyshire with his grandmother on the train, in the days when she was mobile. She was the only person he could remember showing him any affection in his life. He missed those days.

The pub had filled up since he'd arrived. Several groups of people, men and women, some old some young, weighted down with heavy rucksacks had poured into the pub. He caught snatches of conversation.

'It's nearly three hundred miles, you know.'

'They reckon this first bit is the worst; fifteen foot bogs, people getting lost for days.'

The voices betrayed trepidation, and excitement. Jim assumed that they were about to embark on the Pennine Way walk – a walk which would probably see them struggling for the best part of three weeks northwards along the spine of the country culminating in Kirk Yetholm, across the Scottish border.

'Excuse me,' a light voice brought Jim back to reality. 'Do you mind if I squeeze in next to you?'

Jim gulped, surprised, dragged out of his reverie back to reality. The young girl was small and pretty, James was taken aback, unsure how to respond. He struggled to expel a coherent sound.

'No, that's all right. Hang on a minute. I'll move up a bit,' he blurted, glancing up at her again. She was small, less than five feet tall, he reckoned, and very pretty. His first impression had been correct. Jim clammed up, and looked down at his beer. He sensed beads of sweat forming on his forehead; he could feel his heart beating loudly in his chest.

'Are you on your own?' the girl asked. 'I've never been out here for years. Isn't it lovely?' she continued. James nodded his head, but couldn't force himself to look at her, 'Have you been here before?' she asked.

'Yeah, a few times,' Jim replied, mumbling self-consciously.

'I wanted to go for a walk,' she said quietly. 'But I don't know which way is best. Do you know the walks around here?' she asked.

'I'm not an expert,' Jim replied, nervously. 'But there's a walk I did with a friend about five years ago.' Jim picked up his beer and took a long swallow, gathered up his courage. 'Can I get you a drink?' he asked.

'Yeah, thanks. Can I have orange juice, please?'

Jim made a determined effort to smile.

'Course you can. I'll go and get it.'

Confused and breathless, he quickly made his way to the bar and ordered the drink. *Is she chatting me up?* He asked himself, quickly reasoned that she wasn't. 'Why should any girl want to chat me up?' he thought. Anyway, he was glad she had spoken, given that he wouldn't have thought about chatting to her. He returned quickly to the table with the drink.

'Thanks,' she said. 'When we've had this drink, do you fancy showing me this walk you know?' she asked, looking at him straight in the eyes. 'You seem like a nice man.' James blushed. She noticed his discomfort. 'I'm sorry,' she said. 'I'm not normally this chatty, but you just look like someone I can get on with. Do you mind?'

'No,' Jim spluttered.

'My name's Madeline, but people usually call me Maddie or Mad, which is probably the name that suits me best,' she laughed. 'What's yours?' she asked.

'James or Jim,' he said nervously, trying to look at her, but finding that his eyes kept being pulled down towards his feet.

'It's nice to meet you, Jim,' she said, and held out her hand. Jim took her hand and shook it gently. He noticed her hands were cool and very small. He let go reluctantly. He was surprised at the effect touching her had on him. He could feel his heart beating loudly in his chest, and the touch of her hand on his, made his skin tingle.

Jim didn't understand what was going on, but he felt glad and excited. He couldn't believe his luck.

They soon finished their drinks and left the pub together. Turning right, they walked up the gently rising road, Jim looking upwards at the mass of Kinder Scout as it rose up before them, its steep slopes covered in dark brown and bright green foliage. They walked through the village, soon leaving the neat stone built houses behind them. Then they crossed an old packhorse bridge over a stream; they were walking the first half mile of the Pennine way.

From the bridge they entered a wide valley, with steep slopes to both sides of the path. Ahead was the well-worn track which followed the line of the stream, the most popular route onto the Kinder plateau the highest point of the Peak District. They talked breathlessly. The walk so far, although short, was steep, and they were surprised at the effort it needed just to walk this short distance.

'We turn right here,' Jim said, pointing to an ill-defined path zigzagging steeply upwards to their right. 'Have you got a map?' he asked.

'Yes. Do you want to look at it?' Maddie replied.

'Yeah. I thought I'd show you the route on the map while we have a breather,' he said. Jim opened the map of the Dark Peak and, after a couple of minutes of scouring the map, he located their position.

'We head up there. You see the zigzag path?' he said, pointing it out. 'Then we go round that small cliff face, and beyond that is Golden Clough – see there on the map.' He pointed.

'What a lovely name,' she said and moved in closer to him. Jim could smell her hair, see the small beads of perspiration on her forehead, he could feel the warmth of her body. His mind raced. Suddenly he noticed everything about her: he saw her eyes were brown and soft, he noticed the marks in her ears, where at some time she'd worn earrings, he noticed a small faint scar on her chin. He looked again at her eyes. She noticed and looked back. Jim wondered if this was really happening to him.

She looked up at him and winked.

'I hope I can trust you out on these wild moors with a strange man,' she said.

Jim blushed again.

'It's OK,' he said timidly. 'We head up there and then onto Ringing Roger.'

Maddie giggled.

'Ringing Roger! That's a strange name. Where did that come from?' she asked, a broad grin creasing her pretty features.

'I've got no idea,' he replied, 'but when we get up there it's beautiful. I remember when I went up the last time. I saw a Mountain Hare; it was white, with a gold streak down its back. It just ran out of the gorse in front of us. It was fantastic.'

Maddie looked at him and smiled.

'Right, we'd better get a move on. Are you OK?' Jim said, concerned that neither of them were properly equipped for an expedition up on to the plateau.

'I'm fine, but I've never been up this high before. Its hard work and I'm out of training,' she said.

Forty minutes later they emerged from the stony track onto the rocky plateau.

'I'm whacked,' she said. 'Can we stop and have a rest for a minute. I'm puffed. Hang on. I've got a bar of chocolate in my bag. Do you want some?' she said, breathing heavily as she rummaged through her bag and brought out the chocolate.

'Thanks,' Jim replied, breaking off a couple of squares. They sat in the sun for ten minutes, looking across the valley, hardly speaking. Below, they could see several walkers slowly making their way along the track alongside the stream hundreds of feet below them, all aiming for the plateau. They sat silently, absorbing the scene, neither wanting to break the spell.

'Come on, we'll take root if we sit here any longer,' Jim said at last, as he forced himself onto his feet. He reached down.

'Give me your hand. I'll pull you up.'

'Thanks,' she said, as she grasped his hand. Jim pulled lightly and she rose easily to her feet. He felt the warmth of her hand, which made his body tingle; then he reluctantly forced himself to release his grip.

'Thanks, 'she said, keeping hold of his fingers, and looking directly into his eyes – a look that Jim had never had from a girl before.

'This is great,' she said. 'You were right. It is beautiful up here. Thank you for bringing me.'

'That's OK, it is lovely, and so are you,' Jim blurted. He'd spoken without thought, immediately regretting the words, truthfully expressing his joy, but unplanned, and probably inappropriate at this time, he felt. 'I'm sorry,' he said. 'I shouldn't have said that.'

'Don't worry, it was nice of you,' she replied. 'I was just thinking how nice you are, too.'

Jim was once again lost for words. In his life, bereft of affection and love, he'd never acquired the verbal skills to communicate on such a personal level.

'Where do we go from here?' she asked, smiling.

'We just follow this track. It goes right around the rim of the valley,' he replied. 'We just do the horse shoe . . . look over there,' he said pointing enthusiastically into the distance. 'Then we descend back into Edale . . . over there,' he said, his hand mapping out the route before them.

'Yeah that's great, it's lovely, I've enjoyed every second of this afternoon, but where do we go from here?' she emphasised. 'I'd love to do this again, with you. I can tell you like me, and I like you, and we've had a nice time, so can we do this again?' she asked enthusiastically, once again staring into his eyes and touching his shoulder lightly with her hand. Jim wasn't sure what to say. Every molecule of his body yelled that this girl was from heaven, but this was new territory for him; emotionally it was beyond him.

'I don't know. What do you think?' he said, struggling to find the words.

Maddie thought for a few seconds.

'I think we should meet again, maybe next weekend, out here. We could have another walk. How does that sound?'

Jim's mind raced. He'd never imagined in his wildest dreams that a girl like this could become part of his life. He was finding it hard to put a sentence together; connecting his brain to his lips was proving to be a problem.

'That would be great,' he said eventually, the words tumbling from his mouth, failing completely to remain cool. 'That would be absolutely really great,' he called, punching the air, he set off walking along the rim of the valley with Maddie chasing along behind him, laughing.

8

Ray Swift lay in his hospital bed, surrounded by his wife and the whole of Red Watch. Dan Brogan had also arrived. They kept him up to date with what was happening and spoke about the job at Kelling. The nurse had said he could only have two visitors, but they'd managed to bribe her with the promise of a ride on the fire engine, if she came to the station when they were on nights.

'Will you lot keep the noise down?' the nurse said. 'The other patients need to get some sleep.'

'I think she's serious. Look, she's not smiling much when she tells us off, is she?' Brian said aloud.

The nurse turned around and, placing her finger over her lips, she said: 'Shhhhhhush. Be quiet or I'll have to throw you out.' She turned away, smiling to herself.

'OK, matron. We'll be good,' Brian said in a whisper.

'How much longer are you going to be in here for, Ray?' Mac asked.

'Well, they reckon they need me to be here another couple of days under observation, and all being well I'll be home by the weekend. But I've to take it easy, so I may be away from work a little while.'

Dan looked at Mac, both knowing what the other was thinking.

'Well, Mary, we'd better get off. Our public awaits us,' Mac said, putting his arm around her and kissing her cheek. 'Give us a call if you need anything, and you be good, Ray. By the way, young Tony here is doing your job for a while. He's really cocking it up, but you know us; we've lived with you doing that for years.' They all laughed.

'Don't you sods make me laugh. The nurse says I mustn't get too excited. It's not good for me . . . And thanks for the fatty chocolates you didn't bring,' Ray said, smiling broadly.

They left Mary alone with Ray. In the corridor, Dan grabbed Mac's arm.

'Hang on a minute, Mac. I need a word.' Mac had a pretty good idea what Dan was going to say, and told the crew to get back to the appliance; he'd be with them in a minute.

'I've been chatting to the DC,' Dan said. 'He reckons it's going to be difficult for Ray to come back on operational duties, but I think we know that, don't we? He reckons the Brigade Doctor will give Ray a medical discharge.'

'Yeah, I thought pretty much the same, but you don't like to even think about it. Poor old Ray's lived for the job all of his life I'm not sure how he'll take that,' Mac said, a resigned look crossing his face.

Dan looked thoughtful for a minute.

'Look, I'm going back to the ward. I'm taking Mary home in my car. If it feels right, I'll broach the subject with her,' he said.

'Sounds good to me,' Mac replied. 'I'm not sure how she'll take it, though.'

The shift had been quiet; there'd been no calls to disturb the routine station tasks. The crew washed and tested the dirty hose from the previous day's fire. They'd checked the appliance inventories and found that they were two lengths of hose missing, and a hydrant spindle had disappeared, along with a hay fork. The view was that it was those thieving sods over at Billing who'd nicked them.

'Right, Tony. Get on and earn your corn. Get in touch with Billing, tell them what we're missing, and sort it out, OK?' Tony looked nervous. 'Well go on, give them a ring,' Mac said, realising that Tony was not normally the confrontational type.

'What if they say they've not got the stuff?' he asked nervously.

'You use your authority; you're a junior officer now. Get it sorted,' Mac told him, with a hint of firmness in his voice

At Billing, the watch room telephone rang.

'Hello. Billing. Sub Officer Henry.'

Tony's heart sank. He knew Henry and they'd crossed swords in the past when Tony, as a fireman, had done a couple of tours of duty there, to cover manpower shortages. He never really got on with him.

'Oh hello, Sub, this is Leading Fireman Ellis at Graveton. We've checked our inventories and find we, we, we we're a c-c-coup, coup couple of b-b-bits missing.'

Henry interrupted.

'And you think we've got them Leading Fireman, do you?' The aggression in his voice knocked Tony off balance.

'Well, we were both at Kelling Crossroads yesterday. I thought you may have the b-b-bits we're missing,' Tony replied, meekly

'We haven't got the bits you're missing, Leading Fireman Ellis, all right,' he said, with venom in his voice, and put the phone down.

Tony walked through to Mac's office; he was sweating and breathing heavily.

'He says they h-h-havvven't g-g-got our th-things.'

Mac looked at Tony.

'Did he give you a hard time? I presume it was Henry,' Mac said, looking annoyed. 'Sit down,' Mac added, pulling across a chair. 'You're a Junior Officer now. Sometimes difficult things come to us, but, because it's our job,' Mac underlined, 'we just have to do it.'

Mac pulled his collar loose and stretched back in his chair.

'This is my philosophy. It's worked for me, so take out of it what you want,' Mac said. 'This is what I do and think. If it's any use to you then help yourself.'

Tony wondered what Mac was going to say. Mac looked at Tony.

'You know you shouldn't feel inferior to people. You've got this job on merit, because you're qualified and because you're good enough,' Mac said, putting his hands behind his head. 'To be an officer you don't have to be unpleasant.'

'You don't have to be an arse, but there are times when you have to be hard, and stand your ground, even with senior officers. You don't have to kiss arse. They'll respect you more if you stand by your view. But just be sure you're right, OK?' Tony shuffled in his seat. 'Secondly, we haven't had a chance to have a proper chat since you got Ray's job.' Mac sat forward in his chair. 'I have a rule that I always stick to.' Mac swivelled his chair round to face Tony. 'I picked this up in my early days from some of the old-time officers.

Have you ever noticed what I do when we turn up at a job, particularly if it's a going job?' Mac said quietly.

'Can't say I have,' Tony confessed, feeling that maybe it was something he should have spotted. After all, Mac was his role model: he looked up to him. He'd need to keep a closer eye on him in the future.

'When we go to jobs, watch. That's how you learn. See what I do. You may find it helpful. It's something I always remember. I've used it and I find that it works. Watch what I do when we arrive. You'll see that I don't dive straight into the job. I'll tell the lads what to do to get started. It may be, to get a jet run out or a hose reel.' Mac shuffled in his seat. 'Then I'll sit for a few seconds, give myself some thinking time before I get off the appliance,' Mac said casually.

He continued: 'Once I jump off the machine, and I'm running, my thought process can become erratic. Have I assessed the job properly? I may have missed something. Those few second of peace let me look at the job from a distance, get my head straight, calculate if I'll need more pumps, or how to attack the job. Maybe I need to send a message. Should I send a first informative message? It's too late if I'm off and running. There's no point me trying to do all of that whilst doing a hundred miles an hour around the building, do you see that?'

Mac looked at Tony and smiled.

'You deserve this chance. Give it all you've got, and you'll be fine . . . and if you have problems come in the office and we'll talk about it.'

'I sure will, and thanks,' Tony said, a smile now on his face.

'Now, get back on to Billing. Tell Sub Officer Henry, from me, that he'd better find that gear now, or after dinner I'll be over there and I'll stick that hayfork up his backside.'

Tony turned round and headed off to the watch room to make the call.

'No. Hang on a minute,' Mac called to Tony as he walked out of the office, suddenly realising it was unfair to put him in a difficult situation, 'I'll make the call myself.'

Tony breathed a sigh of relief.

The station phone rang. Tony picked it up. It was the Leading Fireman from Billing.

'Hello Tony, its Les Harding. Just to let you know, we've found those bits. Seems they were put on our motor by mistake. Sorry for the trouble. I'll drop them off when I come past on my way home tonight.'

Tony smirked.

'That's fine, Les. Thanks for your help. Cheers.' Tony hung up the phone, and went to see Mac with a spring in his step and a smirk still on his face. 'I don't know what you said, Mac, but they've found the gear. They're bringing it back tonight,' Tony said smiling broadly.

'See what I told you, Tony. Be reasonable, but be firm: it works,' Mac said with a big grin stretching across his face.

Ian Blain sat in his office: his in-tray was stacking up, which was unusual for him, because he took pride in being on top of his paperwork. His out-tray was also pretty full. June, his secretary, would keep him clear of a lot of the mail. She worked as a filter for him, often diverting mail into some of the ADO's trays, but she was away on maternity leave. He had a temporary secretary who was unfamiliar with his office doing the job;

hence the backlog. He took comfort in the fact June would be back to work in a couple of weeks' time.

Since attending the car fire at Kelling Crossroads, something had changed; what he'd seen had shocked him. Before, he'd been insular, focused on his career. Outside influences had never been allowed to interfere with his ambition. He'd always felt that he was a competent fireman, but also realised that, in his pursuit of promotion he'd neglected some of the basics of the job, it had always been a secondary consideration. He'd always had an eye on the ultimate prize, to be a Chief Officer: that was his dream ... to have ultimate power in a brigade. But now, the Kelling experience had altered his view of himself and the job.

He couldn't get a handle on it, explain or rationalise it. Was it the trauma of the incident, the violence which had brought about such devastation to the young man, now sadly lying in a Sheffield mortuary, or was it something to do with the men at the job? Maybe he'd seen things in them that he admired or recognised in himself from the days when he rode the appliance to fires, when being a part of a cohesive operational team was the most important thing. Maybe he'd deceived himself into believing that promotion was it, the be all and end all. Maybe he was mistaken. The only thing he knew for certain was that something had changed. He didn't know if it was a change for the better, but he was sure in his mind that he was going to react in a positive way, and perhaps be better for it. Maybe this was the itch that he could never scratch; perhaps he just needed a bit of time to evaluate his thoughts, to decide on his next step. He would run it by his wife: she usually supported him. He was sure she would see through the fog engulfing his mind and give him her unbiased opinion on the way ahead.

He thought he had always given credit to the operational crews, had always given them the respect they deserved; but now it was different. Kelling had affected him in a way he would never have imagined possible. He'd been blinkered for years. He decided that it was a lesson for him, and he was sure going to learn and act on it. The actions and attitude of the crews that day had somehow got into his head. From now on, he'd approach the job in a new way.

This tour of duty had been quiet; they'd attended a couple of shouts to small jobs. An elderly woman burning papers on her coal fire had set fire to her chimney. Believing that calling the Fire Brigade would cost her money, she'd sat, listening to the chimney roaring, with glowing embers of soot falling into her hearth, until her neighbour, smelling the smoke, had gone outside and seen tongues of flame and clouds of smoke pouring from her chimney. She'd promptly called the fire brigade, before knocking on the door to see if her neighbour was OK.

Red Watch came and quickly put out the fire, cleaned up the mess the fire had made and then made the lady a cup of tea, explained to her that the service was free and she should never delay calling them, that they were there to help her.

They'd been called to a dog with its foot caught in a metal grill. Its owner had been more upset than the dog. The crew, managing to avoid getting bitten, had soon released the dog, cutting through the grill with a hack saw. Later in the day they had had two malicious calls and one automatic fire alarm actuating in a block of offices close to the fire station.

After their final night shift they fell in for parade in the appliance room opposite the oncoming day watch. At times like these, there was always banter. Today, Green Watch was being slated. They were a watch of youngsters, so the older hands on the Reds found it simple to wind them up. The banter continued until the officer in charge of the day watch called them to attention, and then fell them out.

'How's the house coming on, Jock?' Tony asked, as they walked across the yard to their cars.

'It's doing OK, but I've not done much for a couple of weeks. I'm in the midst of a financial crisis,' Jock explained.

'Why's that? Not been doing your bouncing, lately?' Tony enquired.

'Yeah I'm still doing that. It's just I'm spending more than I'm earning. The house is costing a bomb and I'm still paying for last year's holiday: and the boy, Fraser . . . well, he's costing me as well.'

Tony mused for a second.

'You know the lads on the watch will give you a hand, Jock. If you need any help, give us a shout. You want a wall knocking down, I'm your man, you want some crap plastering done, Mick's your man. We'll help, don't forget.'

The drive home for Tony took about ten minutes. When he got home Alice, his wife wanted him to go shopping with her. She could drive, she had her own car, but she liked to get Tony to help her. She said she couldn't manage the bags on her own. What she really wanted was to have him with her.

The past couple of years she'd found it hard. Tony had been engrossed in his work and study, almost to the point where she felt that she didn't recognise him as the man she'd married just two years ago. Tony had been married before: it hadn't lasted long. He'd found out quite by accident that she was having a fling with a work colleague, fifteen years older than she was. Having found out, he took every possession she owned and placed it neatly on the pavement outside their rented house one day, whilst she was at work. Her arrival on the doorstep prompted a loud and violent outburst, culminating in her leaving Tony. A divorce soon followed. Tony had been glad to see the back of her

Jock arrived home. He quickly got changed and, after a short conversation with his wife, he got on with building their new kitchen extension.

Mac arrived home to find Val dressed for a trip to town.

'I'm off to meet the girls. Do you want to come?' she said, almost as though she already knew the answer.

'What's it gonna cost me?' Mac replied.

'You can have the pleasure of taking me and our two daughters for lunch in John Lewis,' Val said, smiling.

'I don't mind the lunch, but can I skip the shopping. I'll meet you in the restaurant at one o'clock. There are a couple of things I need to do first,' Mac said.

'And what's so important that you don't want to come shopping?' Val retorted with a mock scowl.

'I think I'll go and visit Ray and Mary, see if they're OK.' 'All right, I'll let you off this time. Give them both my love, and don't forget: John Lewis, one o'clock,' Val said, and left to drive to town.

9

Jim McEvoy felt sluggish after two night duties, but his demeanour was light. He'd spent much of his time thinking, running the events of the previous weekend through his mind. The chance meeting with the girl, and the feelings it had created within him, the chemistry he felt. He'd always had these feeling, but they'd been private, closed off in his head, but now these were a reaction to a fact of life. He couldn't believe his good fortune and was desperate for the next meeting with Maddie.

They'd arranged to meet on the bridge outside the railway station in Grindleford. Since meeting Maddie, his enthusiasm for life had been rejuvenated; he'd bought walking magazines, a map and a guide to the Peak District and he'd devoured them all avidly and found a walk that he thought they would both enjoy.

Jake moved quickly across the drill yard. This was the final phase of the tests to join the Fire Brigade and he'd found the theoretical part tough: lots of maths and writing, spelling and intelligence tests, designed to see if he was bright enough to join the Brigade. He'd struggled: his marks were OK, but not great. The examiners had recognised something in him, though, and so pushed him through to the next phase.

At each level of the tests, some fell by the wayside, the remainder moving on to the next phase.

The examiners decide who should go and who should stay. Mac understood this: he'd been to see the Instructors, two of whom had previously served with him. Mac was well known in the Brigade and was respected. He'd had a word with them, told them there was a lad he knew, coming up for testing. He'd told them that he thought the boy had what it took to be a good fireman, and told them the story of White Edge, how the boy had something special about him. The instructors of course couldn't make exceptions, but they said they would look out for him.

Jake and Mark sat slumped against the tiled wall of the appliance room, along with fifteen other hopefuls. They were in the midst of a very physically hard session.

Before the main practical tests began, an instructor took the group – which included two young women – through a series of warming-up exercises; then, accompanied by the instructor, they did a gentle run of about one and a half miles, before they had to demonstrate their strength by lifting one end of a ladder above their heads, followed by a series of runs at speed whilst carrying a fellow candidate on their shoulder. At this stage, one of the girls strained a muscle in her side and had to pull out. The remainder sat with their Jackets off, steam rising from their bodies, the instructors passing them liquids with 'a magic potion' in it.

At every phase the instructors urged them to greater efforts: 'Come on, faster, you can do it, keep going, nearly there, well done.' Jake found the encouragement useful. What he lacked in speed and fitness, he made up for in dogged determination, and this didn't go unnoticed by the instructors. They heard Jake swearing at himself, urging himself on: *'Come on Jake, do you want this? Come on.'* He gave every last ounce of effort; the instructors noted that this was a very determined young man.

During the rest period, Jake sat alongside Mark. They were both breathing hard and sweating heavily.

'We're half way there, Mark. They're not going to fail us now,' Jake said, but Mark looked physically drained. 'Are you OK?' Jake pressed him.

Mark turned his head wearily.

'You know, Jake, I don't know if I'll finish today. I'm absolutely knackered. I think this afternoon is the hardest bit. They reckon they lose more candidates in the next session than any other.' He looked at Jake. 'I don't know. I really want this but I'm not sure. I don't feel too good.'

Jake put his hand on Marks shoulder.

'If you can get through to dinner time, you'll get a rest, you can grab a kip. That'll probably help. You won't fail. You've put too much into getting this far. You'll do it. Failing isn't going to happen.'

'I wish I could be as determined as you. I'll do my best,' he said unconvincingly.

'You'll do it. If I can do it, you can. You've just got to keep going. I'll be with you.'

The instructors walked into the appliance room.

'Right, folks, up on your feet.' The instructor was middle-aged, balding and stocky; his appearance was perfect, he gleamed. His trousers were creased to perfection. He'd said earlier in the day: 'They're not pressed, laddie. They're sharpened. I'm Sub Officer Pearson. The next phase is very physical. Is everybody OK? Anyone got any injuries? Speak now or forever hold your peace.'

Jake looked at Mark, and winked.

'This is the last bit. Then we'll be in for dinner.'

The instructor looked at Mark.

'Are you OK, sonny? You look a bit rough.'

Mark pulled himself up to attention.

'I'm OK, Sub,' he said, trying to convince himself he was all right.

The Sub Officer continued: 'This next test will tell us if you have the determination to keep going long after you want to stop: this is one of the qualities needed to be a fireman. I'll demonstrate what you have to do. Watch me carefully,' he stressed. Picking up a length of rolled hose, he uncoiled it onto the floor, describing what he was doing. 'Having rolled the hose out, you must then rewind it like this.' He picked up one end of the hose, and gave it a few cursory turns: he then put it on the floor and with his hands on the lugs of the female coupling, crouching low, he ran quickly. In seconds, the hose was fully rolled back up to its original neatly-coiled condition.

'That's how it's done. Now each of you get a length of hose and have a couple of minute's practice.'

The recruits tried to replicate the action the instructor had just demonstrated so easily. Most of the recruits slipped, tripped or got the hose tangled. It was more difficult than it had looked when the Sub Officer had done his demonstration.

'Let me give you all a tip,' the instructor said. 'Start off slow and gather speed as you go. OK? And remember: keep going.'

The group were already sweating: having to perform such a task in full fire fighting kit, including boots and helmet, was proving tough, and the test hadn't started yet.

'How are ya doing, Mark?' Jake asked.

'I'll be OK, if I'm not sick,' Mark replied, looking pale and sweaty.

'Right, all line up here,' the instructor said, pointing to a white line painted on the ground. 'When I blow this whistle, all you have to do is run out the hose and then roll it up again. You keep doing that until we tell you to stop, or until you run out of time. This is hard, but we're looking for the people who can keep going when it gets tough.'

Jake's nerves jangled. He'd heard about this test and he wasn't looking forward to it. Mark stood next to him.

'Come on, Mark. I'll race you.' Mark gave a weak smile; realising Jake was trying to motivate him.

The whistle blew. Jake ran forward. Picking up a length of coiled hose, he moved smoothly forward, the hose streaming out behind him. He noticed several recruits had gone off fast, but he focussed his eyes on the ground in front of him; nothing else mattered, he wouldn't stop for anything. He turned, grabbed the coupling, took a couple of turns, started to roll up the hose in front of him. Soon he was at the other end of the yard. He picked up the hose and started to repeat the process. He looked at the other candidates and noted he was second from last: only Mark was behind him. He ran again, turned again. It became a blur of running and turning. He saw sweat running from his nose, but he felt no pain. He was focussed on the tarmac, which was a foot from his nose in front of him and he could make out the heavy breathing of a man to his right.

Jake moved without thought, just pure focus on the job he had to do.

'OK. Stop, son. You've done your runs. Well done.' Jake turned, he saw that everyone else was still running, some had dropped out, others were on the point of collapse, and were being closely watched by the instructors who urged them to keep going.

He could see Mark was still moving, but only just.

'Come on Mark,' Jake shouted. 'Keep going.'

Mark stopped momentarily. Standing up, he retched, vomiting on his hose, but he got back down and continued rolling the hose, slowly. When he reached Jake, he said, between heavy gasps of breath: 'I'm almost done, Jake.'

'You're not,' Jake shouted. 'You can't stop now; stop and you're finished, stop and you fail. Come on, Mark. Follow me.'

Jake picked up a length of rolled hose and stood alongside Mark and began running his hose.

'Keep up with me. You're not a quitter, you'll do it.'

Two of the instructors watched in silence.

'Come on, Mark, you've come a long way for this. It'll soon be over.'

For the next few minutes Jake coaxed and cajoled Mark through the remainder of the test.

The instructor blew his whistle.

'OK, all stop now. Well done, all of you. Go to the appliance room, get a drink and relax for a few minutes.'

Mark put down the length of hose with a sigh and collapsed into the sitting position against the wall.

'I wouldn't have done that without you pushing me,' Mark said, his face showing the strain of his exertions.

'That's OK. One good turn deserves another. You helped me at the interviews, remember?'

'That's it for the morning. Get a shower, then up to the mess deck. Have a lunch and a rest. There's more to come this afternoon,' the instructor said.

Jake noticed several candidates were being taken to one side; it seemed they had failed the test; he was relieved to see that Mark wasn't among them.

10

Mac peered through the frosted glass of the door. He could make out the figure of Mary walking up the hall to answer the doorbell.

'Hello, Mac. Come in. It's good to see you,' she said, giving him a peck on the cheek.

'How's Ray doing?' Mac asked.

'Better in health than temper; sitting about, reading the paper. That's just not Ray,' Mary said, with a smile.

Mac walked into the lounge where Ray sat, feet up on a stool, reading a book.

'Hello, you old sod. What you been up to?' Mac asked.

'Hi ya, Mac,' Ray said extending his hand out to Mac. 'I've been half expecting you for a while. How are the boys? Are they managing without me?'

'You know Tony's doing your job? Well, he had a bit of a run in with Henry the other day. He did OK, but yeah, we're missing you.'

'Henry? He's a prat. The sooner he retires the better,' Ray retorted.

They chatted for a while before Mac asked: 'What do you thinks' going to happen? Would you want to come back?'

Ray thought: 'Typical Mac. No beating around the bush.'

'Do you know, Mac, I'm surprising myself. I always dreaded the thought of retiring. I've always loved the job.' He paused, 'Mary and I, we've been talking. I'm not sure I will come back. I mean, even if I wanted to, I'm not sure they'd let me back.' He looked at Mac with a pained expression.

'Ray, I've been on to the DC and Dan Brogan. Their view is, if you want to go, they'll make it happen.'

Ray looked relieved.

'You know, mate. We're the last of the old timers. Some think we're dinosaurs, and they're probably right. You can't be replaced, you, we: we're unique; we come from a different time. If you want my opinion, which you're going to get any way, I think you should retire, move on and do the things you and Mary haven't had time to do.'

Mary came into the room with a tray of tea and biscuits.

'I heard that Mac, and thank you. I've been telling him that for ages.'

Inside, Mac felt sad: this was the start of a process that would end with his closest friend leaving the service.

Mac's mobile rang. 'Hello, where are you, Mac?'

'Sorry, love. I'm at Ray's. We got chatting. I don't know where the time's gone.'

Val laughed.

'Look, love. We're in the restaurant in Lewis's. Shall we wait for you?' Mac thought for a minute.

'No, don't do that. You carry on. Give the girls my love. I'll see you later. Get a taxi home.'

'Well, I'd better get on. Places to go, people to see. I think I'm in the doghouse now,' Mac smiled.

'Blame us,' Mary said, putting her arm around Mac's waist.

'Nah, she's all right. If she's got the girls with her, she doesn't need me. She knows I hate shopping,' Mac said with a grin.' Anyway, you two, I'll get Val to ring you. We'll have you round for supper . . . and, oh, Ray, I'll have a talk with Dan about what we've just been talking about. Don't you wear him out, Mary; he's getting to be an old man now you know.'

Mary laughed.

'Tell me about it. Grumpy old man would be more accurate.'

They all laughed. Mac climbed into his car and headed into town.

The instructor walked into the changing room where the remnants of the day's candidates were sitting, waiting for the final part of their tests. There were six of the originals left – five male and one female – the others having been rejected at various points during the day.

'Right, this is the final part of the test,' the instructor said. 'Can I congratulate you all for getting this far. You've all done well. This afternoon's test is the shuttle run. You either pass or fail, there's no in-between. Do you all know what the shuttle run is?' he asked. They all nodded, having been briefed earlier in the day.

'Right, just to dot the tees and cross the eyes' he said, with a smile, attempting to reduce the tension, 'I'll run through it for you, just so there is no misunderstanding.'

'*Beep. Level one,*' the voice boomed from a tape recorder, instructing them that the test was about to start. The six candidates began running at a slow jog, all moving comfortably as they reached the line twenty yards away and turned, running easily to their start positions.

'Piece of cake so far,' Jake called, looking across to where Mark was running effortlessly.

'*Beep. Level two.*' They turned again. The runners continued between the two lines painted on the drill yard. Jake sensed that the time between the beeps was less at each level, forcing him to move faster to get to the line as the beep sounded.

'*Level three.*' The group was still moving well. Jake could feel his body getting warmer by the minute. The time passed and the beeps continued. Almost before they knew it the machine announced level seven. They were now running quickly between the lines, some not getting to the line when the beep sounded and having to sprint to make up the lost ground.

'*Level eight.*' At this point two men stopped, and almost immediately collapsed. They were quickly aided by the instructors and taken from the drill yard.

'Piece of cake,' Mark shouted across to Jake. Jake was feeling the pace. He sucked in air, filling his aching lungs, gritted his teeth and turned his mind off the pain. He looked across at Mark, who was going well; the other two candidates were struggling.

Jake shouted: 'Come on, you lot. You've done too much today to let this beat you,' belying the fact that he was tired. 'Right, you bugger,' Jake shouted at himself, then sprinted at full speed, arriving at the line well before the bleep. 'Come on, Mark. Nearly there.'

The instructor blew his whistle. 'Well done, folks. Get yourselves into the appliance room, get a drink, and I'll come for a chat in a minute.'

Mac was standing in the station office, looking out onto the drill yard. He'd arrived ten minutes ago, spoken to the officer in charge and had just watched the shuttle run. The instructors came past the office and spotted Mac peering through the window.

'Hi ya, Mac. What are you up to?'

Mac turned and recognised the men.

'Hello, just thought I'd just come and see for myself how you beast the recruits. How's this lot doing?'

'We've only got four through from today's batch, but they're good. The boy you said to look out for, he's been excellent, very determined. He seems to have what we want. He was even bollocking the others for not trying hard enough. He'll be fine.'

Mac smiled.

'I thought he would be. Thanks for looking at him for me.' He turned and left the office, a smile crossing his lips.

Jock switched off the electric cement mixer; he'd do just another hour's work on the extension and then he'd have to stop. Tonight was club night and he was on the door.

Jock enjoyed these nights – mixing with youngsters, having a laugh with the other doormen – and the extra money was handy. The job had got pretty strict lately. There'd been some trouble at a nearby club: a doorman had got into a fight, the police had been called, the two lads had spent an uncomfortable night in the police cells, complaining that it was a mistake. When they'd been released, they'd accused the doorman of attacking them: a messy legal had process ensued. Jock's boss got his men together to discuss the situation. He installed a CCTV system to record the area around the doors and gave instructions to the doormen that there would be no situation that would, in future, justify them getting involved in a fight. At six fifteen, Jock got into his car and drove to town.

11

Ian Blain pulled his car into the only space available at the rear of Brigade Headquarters. Since his recent experience at the fatal car fire, he'd become unsettled, his mind often drifting back to the scene at Kelling crossroads.

After the fire, he'd gone back to the Fire Station with the Graveton crew, sat and drank tea with them and seen the tight bond that existed between the men. He'd noticed some of the crew were boisterous and others were quiet. He saw how Mac spoke to the crew about the job, how he told them where they had done well, and given light-hearted rebukes to the ones who might have done better. They talked about the job for ten minutes, when Mac asked: 'What did you think boss?'

Ian, who was practiced and confident at speaking in public, was taken aback; suddenly words were difficult. He'd been to fires before, many of them involving loss of life. Previously he'd remained detached, he'd never seen the incident as his main function; he could drive away, let the guys do the dirty work. But this one was different; somehow he'd been dragged into the lives of the crew and the victims and begun to realise that he'd been unprepared for the trauma of Kelling crossroads.

'What do I think? Well,' Ian paused. At this moment he wasn't sure what he thought. 'Well, lads, when control informed me of the incident, my first thought was that I don't like this kind of job, never have, but I came.' He paused again, struggling to find the right words. The crew looked at him. Mac sat quietly.

'When I joined the job I was at a quiet station that wasn't very busy; a good house fire was a major event. After a while, I decided to get my finger out and go for promotion and move away from the operational things. Lately it's become clear to me that operations are the most important part of the job.' He paused again. 'When I arrived at Kelling, I expected that it would be sorted. I thought I'd just show my face, then back to the office.' He turned and looked at Mac. 'But you do you know, I found something in myself I hadn't realised was there. What I saw was a rotten job being dealt with by a good crew. I saw you working together, giving each other support, especially when the job was really messy. I also saw compassion.' He paused again for what seemed an age. 'What I saw made me glad to be a fireman. I was glad I was there. You all did great, including Brian who, despite his best efforts, managed to give young Tony there a good soaking.' They all laughed. Suddenly the ice was broken, Ian felt at home.

'Y-y-yes B-B-Brian you b-b-bastard, that's another one I owe you,' Tony said, attempting to look serious.

'Well, boss: thanks for coming. It lets us see that you officers are human after all,' Mac said. 'You're welcome here when the reds are on any time. Shouldn't come when the others are on duty: they're not up to the same standard.' The crew gave Mac a small round of applause for this minor assault on the other watches.

Ian smiled. It reminded him of his time as a fireman, when attacking the other watches was par for the course.

'Right, boys. Thanks for the tea. I'd better get off, or my secretary will give me what for. You think you get it tough; you should try working at Div HQ.'

Mac walked with Ian to his car.

'Thanks for that, sir. It means a lot to the lads.'

'You're welcome, Mac. You've got a good crew there. I think you'll be seeing more of me in the future . . . I mean that in a good way. Well done, all of you.'

Ian got in his car and drove out of the station yard.

Ian knocked lightly on the Chief Officer's door.

'Come in,' a deep voice called from within. The Chief sat behind a large oak desk, piled high with papers and files. Ian sat down opposite him.

'Good morning, Ian. How's everything with you? You said you needed to see me?'

'Yes boss, I've had a bit of a re-think about the job.' Ian then spent a while talking to the chief about how recently his attitude had altered and now he wanted to give up the pressure of constantly pursuing the next job.

Over the next twenty minutes Ian related to the Chief how the Kelling car incident had affected him, how his thinking about the job seemed to have altered.

The Chief studied him for a few seconds.

'You know, Ian: promotion isn't compulsory. You've done well since you've been here. I understand what you say and I think we all go through that to a greater or lesser degree. However, I'll put it into the back of my mind for a while, think about it. If anything changes, let me know.'

Ian spoke again.

'You know Mac, the sub at Graveton? He's impressed me a lot. I don't think I've met one like him before. I've watched him and he's excellent at his job, he runs a tight ship and his lads love him.'

The Chief sighed.

'You're right, he's been outstanding for years. All his old bosses have tried to get him to take the next exam. He'd make a good officer, but he won't hear of it. He says he's happy, so why change things?'

Ian got up from his chair.

'Thanks for listening Sir.'

The Chief looked at him and smiled.

'Think on, Ian. We're in a great job. Only recently I met a young lad in the foyer who wanted to join the job: he reminded me of myself thirty years ago. You're right, we shouldn't forget what this job's all about: it's about boys becoming men. They do that by watching us, their peers . . . in fact that reminds me, that young boy – Jacob something or other – spoke to Sue from admin. She said that he'd met Mac out in the Peaks. Apparently he saved some old chap's life. Have you heard anything about that?'

Ian gave a quizzical look.

'No I haven't, but I'll see what I can dig up about it.'

Ian left the Chief's office and made his way along to the Admin office.

Janet Clark prised her eyes open; the radio had bored its way into her head and roused her from her coma-like state. It wasn't her type of music – indeed, no music at all would have been the perfect start to this particular day. At this time of the morning, after the night she and her husband had had, with friends and too much of her favourite tipple – a few lagers to start the evening off then several glasses of red wine – a sore head was the inevitable outcome of her pre-birthday celebration.

She forced her head from the pillow and glanced blearily at her husband, Duncan. He was sprawled across the bed, oblivious of anything, his head buried beneath a pillow. He wore only a bright red pair of boxer shorts and a black sock with a cartoon of Bart Simpson on his left foot. It was at times like this she cursed her commitment to the ranger service. Today, her routine was a fifteen mile patrol on foot, a day which would probably bring some form of hassle. She reluctantly climbed out of her warm bed and stumbled across the polished floorboards to the bathroom.

Janet and Duncan lived in a remote farmhouse, a building they'd spent years restoring. They kept a few sheep and chickens, mainly as pets. They also had two sheepdogs which, although trained in the theory of rounding up sheep, lacked the practical application. The house being remote, the dogs gave Janet a sense of security, serving as a deterrent to anyone who wandered along their lane uninvited.

After a quick shower, Janet felt the life flowing back into her body. Duncan was in awe of his wife's ability to recover after a heavy night out; he would suffer for most of the following day.

Janet packed up her rucksack stuffed with food drink and clothing for the day; she ate her toast and a plate of corn flakes, and was ready to go.

'Bye, love. See you tonight,' she shouted up the stairs to Duncan. Duncan grunted, falling back into semi-consciousness. She loaded her rucksack into the back of her four by four and headed down the mile-long dirt drive which led to the main road. Twenty minutes later, she turned into the Ranger station. Passing Grindleford Railway Station on her way, she could see from the number of cars parked along the roadside that today, her patrol would be busy.

12

It was a beautiful morning. The trees were bursting with leaves and wild flowers sprang up from amid the dirt and grime of the roadside verges. The trees cast dark shadows across the road, the sun bursting through, creating a dappled effect on the black tarmac.

Jim McEvoy drove steadily out of the city, emerging into the wealthy suburbs with their huge houses lining the road, the road rising steeply. He could see the dark hills and purple heather clad moors ahead: that was where he was heading and he was both excited and happy. He was going to meet Maddie again – the girl who had ignited his life for the first time.

The previous week had been a shock to him: the unexpected had happened. He'd dreamed about it all week and he couldn't contain his excitement. He'd told his work colleague, about it, and sat for hours thinking about it, unable to get the vivid image of Maddie's lovely face out of his mind.

Maddie sat on the train listening to the clatter of the wheels as they crossed the points in the rail; it was only a short journey from Sheffield railway station to Grindleford. This week she'd prepared. She'd shopped and bought a pair of hiking boots, a waterproof coat and a small rucksack. She'd filled a flask with tea and made some sandwiches, enough for both her and Jim. She sat looking out of the widow, considering the events of the previous week, a gentle smile set across her features. Jim wasn't her handsome prince; he was skinny and scruffy, but she connected with him in a way that she couldn't explain, and she was aware of the impact their unplanned meeting had had on Jim too.

The road into the Peaks was busy, with lines of cars filled with families venturing out for the day. Jim wondered where they were all heading. Sundays were always busy, he remembered. Two high-powered motor bikes screamed past him, powering away and cutting in sharply, avoiding cars travelling in the opposite direction. He regained his concentration, and, glancing to his right, he got the first sight of Higgar Tor, a prominent hill, its summit lined with high gritstone crags, the slopes of its hillside displaying an array of green and golden colours. Below it lay the old Bronze Age fortress Carl Wark, a honey pot for visitors, with many of its ancient walls still standing. Jim planned that sometime today they would walk over this impressive hill.

Maddie breathed a sigh of relief as the train emerged from the tunnel: it seemed to have taken forever to travel the four miles from entry to its ending at Grindleford Station. She'd arranged to meet Jim here at ten o'clock. She stepped from the train, pulled the rucksack onto her back, tying her coat sleeves around her waist, then made her way from the platform up on to the road.

Jim slowed to almost walking pace. The turn into the station access road doubled back on itself and descended gently down to the station about three hundred yards away. He could see that it was busy, so he pulled the car into the roadside at the first available space. Groups of people were unloading gear, putting on boots and rucksacks and walking down to the station and beyond for the start of their day's adventure.

Jim had also prepared this time: he'd bought some sausage rolls and a couple of cans of Coke, and jammed them into his coat pocket. His boots were the old ones he'd used at school and he felt lucky they still fitted him. He set off on the two hundred yard walk to find Maddie.

Stan Gregg had been a Ranger for what seemed all of his life; he had an unkempt beard and weathered skin. Brunt's Barn was his station and he insisted that every aspect of his station ran as it was meant to do. A stickler for punctuality, he ran a tight ship, frequently testing his team in various ways; usually when they least expected it. He liked things to be right, but lurking beneath the hard crust was a soft-hearted man who loved his job and his Rangers, but most of all he loved the Peak.

The shift of six Rangers sat in the room with their customary cups of tea, all dressed for the outdoors. Alongside was a stranger: a young man, a trainee. Today he was to accompany a ranger on patrol, as part of his training to learn the many aspects and skills required to join the service.

Stan got up from his seat at the end of the room.

'Right, you lot. Listen up. Today's jobs.' After some discussion the rangers were allocated their patrols, each one making careful note of the details of the other Rangers' patrols – normally straightforward, but today Stan knew it was Janet's birthday, and he had a plan.

'Right, Janet, I want you to do the Froggatt White Edge circuit. Come back via Longshaw, all right?'

'Thank you, leader. Piece of cake,' Janet replied, with a laugh in her voice.

'Well, just to make it interesting,' Stan said 'along the way find GR 2624 7410, then walk on a bearing to GR 2677 7536, then you may find something of interest. Record it and let me know when you get back, OK?' Stan's face had a badly-hidden smirk crossing his rugged features.

Janet grinned, having written the grid references in her note book.

'OK, leader, no problem. I'd better get going or I'll still be out after dark.'

With that she lifted her rucksack and threw it smoothly across her shoulder and walked out into the bright sunshine.

Stan grinned as she left and began lacing up his ancient walking boots. He would do a walk today. The paperwork could wait another day.

Ernest and Doris Galloway had driven out from Sheffield on their regular weekly jaunt; something they had been doing for over fifty years. Ernie who now suffered from mildly arthritic shoulders, struggled to turn the wheel of his old Morris Traveller into the approach to Grindleford station. It was busy, but as they approached, a car had pulled out leaving a space some forty yards from the railway station. After a couple of minutes they emerged from the car. Ernest was wearing knee-length khaki shorts. He looked hot and was perspiring heavily. Doris emerged much more gracefully, a smile stretched across her face, in contrast to Ernest, who looked as though he would rather be at the dentist having his teeth removed.

'I don't know why you're scowling, Ernest. I told you to get the car serviced. There's no way we should have to drive out here with the heater permanently on; not on a day like today, anyway.'

Ernest looked at her. 'Doris, why don't you stop mythering? I've told you, it'll get fixed when I get some brass. Until then, we'll have to manage.'

Doris stood on one leg, her other foot on the chrome rear bumper of the car tying the laces of her boots.

'Do you know, Ernest? You're a tight old sod. You don't complain about the price of the beer at the pub.'

Ernie made no reply, but fiddled about in his rucksack, pulled out a light scarf and tied it loosely around his neck. The flat cap perched on his head had seen better days, despite Doris's attempts to get him to buy a new one.

Jim strained his eyes. Looking towards the bridge, he could see Maddie, who was leaning casually against the bridge wall. She hadn't seen him yet. He walked quickly, feeling an almost overwhelming pressure rising in his chest. He was twenty yards away when she turned her head, glancing back up the drive towards the main road. At first she didn't recognise him, but then it dawned on her that he was here. She smiled broadly.

The elderly couple, stood close by, saw a young girl laugh and begin waving her arms. Then, as they looked on, they saw a scruffy young man walking quickly towards the girl, a smile splitting his gaunt face.

'Just look at that, Ernest. Isn't it lovely?' she said, with a nostalgic look on her face.

Ernie looked at his wife and winced.

'Looks like a soft bugger to me, our Doris,' he said, sure in the knowledge that it would provoke a reaction from his wife.

'Do you know what Ernest? You've no romance in you; you can carry the rucksack today,' she rebuked him. 'Now get them boots on, you old misery, and let's get walking.'

Ernie controlled the urge to smile 'You know I can't get down to tie my laces,' he said, a pained expression clouding his face. 'You'd better give us a hand, or we'll never get off.'

'If you don't buck your ideas up, Ernest, I'm gonna trade you in for a newer model. Now lift your foot up so I can reach it.'

Maddie looked at Jim's face. She noticed the beaming smile and the remnant of a tear on his face. 'Hello again,' she said, brushing his arm lightly with her hand.

Jim tried to look calm, pretending he had something in his eye; he wiped his face with the sleeve of his jumper.

'Hello, it's good to see you,' Jim replied, looking at her, unable to contain his smile. 'Shall I carry the bag' he said, while wanting desperately to say: *Can I touch you?*

'Of course you can, but can I have a hug first? I've missed you.' She moved up close to him and put her arms around his neck. 'I've really been looking forward to today,' she said, kissing him gently on the cheek.

The old couple walked slowly by.

'Did you see that, Ernest? That's what you used to do to me, back in the Forties,' Doris said, looking lovingly at the young couple.

'I'd do it now, Doris, but you know, I'd never get my arms round ya,' he said in his broad South Yorkshire accent, a smirk moving across his lips.

'You're a cheeky old man Ernest Galloway. Just you wait till I get you home tonight,' she scolded.

'Can't wait,' Ernie replied as they meandered slowly past the railway station towards the woods.

13

'How many more times have I got to tell you, Brian? Stop it. Her name's Jill. Use it, will you?'

Brian looked at his ex-girlfriend: he saw an attractive woman, her name was Jane. He always used to call her Janie, a term of endearment he used when they were together. For some years she'd been a pain in the neck. Since their relationship had broken down, Brian had suffered. He felt guilty about the split, the fact he'd not been around to support Jane at the birth of their baby. He also felt anger at the obstructions she'd put in his way when he wanted to see Bill (as he'd insisted on calling his daughter), and pleasure when he saw her, but most of all he felt regret at the failing of the relationship. He never doubted that he'd loved her.

When Jane gave him the occasional smile, he felt twinges of regret at having deprived Jill of a normal upbringing, albeit he'd moved heaven and earth to be fair to Jane. If he was honest, he couldn't criticise her in any way over Jill's upbringing. The fact they weren't together wasn't Jane's fault. The fact she became pregnant wasn't her fault either. Brian accepted the blame for all the negative things that had brought about the split.

'I'm sorry, I know it winds you up. I'll try to stop it,' Brian said, looking pensively at her.

'What's the matter with you, Brian? You're not normally so apologetic. Are you sickening for something?'

He looked at her again and was shocked. For the first time in a long while he saw the pretty woman he used to love so much; maybe a bit older and a bit time worn, he thought. Not surprising, having to manage as a single mother, bringing a child up on her own.

'How are you, Jane? Are you OK? You look tired. Is everything all right?' he asked.

She looked back at him, *the same old Brian, the joker in the pack, still tall, slim and good looking ... lost his hair though*, she thought. She reckoned it made him look five years older.

She got up from the kitchen table.

'I'm tired. I'm up early to get Jill off to school, then down to town. My job's not so easy these days. Then after school I have to take her to this place and that place. I'm shattered most of the time; there's never a minute's peace'

Brian stood there quietly for a minute. 'Can I help?' he said. 'If I can, I will. Just say the word.'

She looked at him. 'If you could take her to school a couple of days a week, that would help, you know, when you're off duty. But then you couldn't do that. You've got your other job,' she said, remembering the days before, when Brian seemed to be always working at one job or the other, also realising that he only did it to make ends meet when times were hard.

'I just do that job to fill my days, give me something to do,' he said, earnestly. 'If you want help, tell me what, and when. If I'm off duty, I'll do it.'

She smiled. Brian realised just how attractive she was; he hadn't seen her smile for a long time. 'That would be a big help, and Jill would like that too. When she comes in, we'll tell her.' Quite spontaneously they were smiling at each other.

Brian opened his mouth to speak. He couldn't believe what he was saying. It seemed as if his mouth was operating independently, that this had not been planned. He found himself feeling pleased at what was emerging, *maybe all along I've had, feelings I've been ignoring*, he thought to himself.

'You know the next lot of school holidays, well I wondered if you'd let me take Jill?' he emphasised. 'I've been thinking of having a few days at a cottage in the Isle of Wight. I wondered if you'd let Bill come with me ... sorry ... let Jill come with me?'

She tried not to smile. It was a while since she and Brian had had a serious conversation about anything.

'Of course, she's ten years old, she deserves a holiday. All of her pals are off on their holidays: Spain, Cyprus. Her little friend up the road's going on holiday to Canada. There's no way I can afford to take us on holiday,' she said.

Brian unexpectedly felt a twinge of pain in his chest. 'When did you last have a break?' he said.

'Three years ago. My Mum had Jill, while I had a long weekend with my sister in Scarborough,' she said with a rueful smile. Jill walked into the room.

'Hiya, Jill. Where've you been? I've been here ages.'

She walked up to Brian and put her arms around his waist. Brian leaned over and planted a kiss on the top of her head, noticing that she was hot and sweating.

'Are you OK, my lovely? You're very hot.'

She looked up at Brian. 'I know I'm hot. I'm sweating. Me and Kirstin, we've been skipping.'

Brian gave her a squeeze. 'Oh right,' he said. 'Your mum used to be really good at that ... Come on, mum. Show us how it's done,' Brian joked. Reluctant to do so at first, Jane eventually gave in to her daughter's pleading.

She began to skip, steadily at first, then, as her confidence grew, she tried a series of complicated manoeuvres. Eventually she collapsed onto the grass, gasping for breath.

'Brilliant, mum,' Jill shouted excitedly as she ran over, diving onto her mother as she lay on the grass. Quite suddenly they were all laughing.

They sat around the kitchen table, the conversation moving easily; they talked about school. Jane spoke about her work at the surgery. Brian mentioned that Ray Swift had been taken into hospital, following a heart attack.

'You never mentioned anything about that before,' Jane said. 'I liked Ray. He was a nice man, and his wife ... what's her name? ... She was nice as well.'

'Mary. Her name's Mary. She's been pretty cut up about it, but at least he's survived. I think he'll retire soon. He'd nearly done his time, anyway,' Brian said.

Jane glanced at Brian. 'Shall I tell her or will you?' Jane said.

'What do you want to tell me?' Jill said, looking questioningly at Brian.

'Go on. You tell her,' Brian said.

'Well, Jill. Your dad wants to take you on holiday with him, on a boat, across to the Isle of Wight. How do you fancy that?' she said.

Jill's eyes widened. 'What, you and dad and me, on a holiday. I'd love that,' she said, beaming, her face still glowing from the skipping.

'No,' Jane said.

Brian found himself saying: 'Well yes, if your mum can find the time, and if she wants too, then yes, we can all go.'

Jane looked bemused; this hadn't been their intention.

'Look I'm going. Lots to do. Have a think about it. I'll give you a ring tomorrow and we'll have a chat, OK?' Brian set off to leave. 'And, Jane … let me know when you want me to pick her up, OK,' he said gently.

Jill took hold of Brian's hand. 'Great to see you, dad. I'm really looking forward to the holiday now.'

Brian picked her up, and noticed how much bigger she seemed. He kissed her on the cheek, realising how much they had all missed.

'See you soon, my lovely. I love you.'

'I love you too, dad,' Jill replied, squeezing Brian's hand.

Brian looked across at Jane. 'Think about it. I'll ring you. Bye.' He got into his car, waved at the girls and drove away. On the drive home he turned the conversation over in his mind; he couldn't understand the turn of events. The only thing he was sure of was that he felt really happy for the first time in years.

'Come on, Clive. Cheer up, I won't be much longer,' Helen said, smiling. 'You know how much I hate shopping; we've been here for hours.'

Clive Botham had been tricked into taking Helen into the city. It was supposed to be a quick call into Ian Lewis's to take back a pair of slacks, but it had somehow escalated into a shopping frenzy, or at least that was how it appeared to Clive. He didn't like shopping. Whilst acknowledging that some shopping was necessary, shopping as some form of pleasure or entertainment couldn't be justified, so he kicked his heels whilst his girlfriend perused the rails of clothing, none of which she wanted or liked.

'So what is the point?' he mumbled to himself. He could see that outside, the weather was perfect: he could go for a run, or do a few miles on his bike. In truth, anything would be better than standing in a shop, not wanting or needing to buy anything. This was Clive's version of true pain.

'That's it, all done. Let's get you out of here before you pass out.' Helen knew from long experience that Clive hated shopping. Normally she would exclude him: it was much easier and less stressful doing it on her own. However, today she had an agenda.

'I just need to pop through here, love. Shan't be a tick.'

'Clive noticed that they were entering the bridal department. His mind was several steps in front. It was becoming clear that it wasn't only the slacks she was interested in.

'Oh look at that beautiful dress, love. Isn't it gorgeous!'

Clive shuffled awkwardly. Words such as gorgeous were not part of his everyday vocabulary. 'Yes its nice,' Clive responded, sweat beginning to form on his forehead.

'Don't you think that a dress like that would suit me?' she said, looking pointedly at him.

Clive began to feel there was something he didn't know, so he muttered something inaudible.

'What did you say, love?' she said.

Clive replied: 'It's a nice dress, but you won't be needing one yet, will you?'

She looked at him with a look akin to the cat that had the mouse in its paws. 'I've been meaning to talk to you about that,' she replied. 'There's something I need to talk to you about.'

Clive looked back at her, unsure what was coming next, but he felt something was about to blow. 'What's that?' he said.

'Well you know you've always said you didn't think it was right for children to be born outside marriage?' She paused. Clive gulped. 'You're going to be a father. I found out this morning,' she said turning her head quickly, making her long hair swing gracefully.

Clive looked at Helen, not knowing what to say. He was amazed, excited, frightened. The revelation had hit him like a right hook.

'Are you sure?' Clive said weakly.

'Of course I am. I didn't want to say anything until I knew for sure, I've suspected it for a little while now.'

Clive's mind tumbled, unable to grasp what he'd just been told. 'How on earth did this happen?' Clive said, his voice emerging weakly from his mouth.

She smiled 'Well you know, when we go to bed together, and you let me take advantage of you, because you're tired, well that's how it happened. We're going to have a baby. You're going to be a father, I'm going to be a mother, and I'm sure our families will be happy for us. To answer your first question, yes, I will be needing one, a wedding dress that is,' she said, with a giggle in her voice.

Clive sat down on a nearby seat and put his hands over his face.

'Are you all right?' she said. 'You are pleased about it, aren't you?'

Clive took a minute to gather himself. 'Of course I'm happy,' he said, the words muffled by his hands. 'Let me have a minute,' he chuckled. 'I think I've got something in my eye.'

She sat down beside him quietly; she didn't say anything, but just held his hand. Clive couldn't say anything, for fear of making himself look stupid.

They sat quietly for a few minutes and then Clive said: 'Can we get out of here? I need to say something.'

They started walking out of the store. When they reached the car park, Clive took Helen's arm. 'There's something I want to tell you. I know I don't say much, but I'm happy we're going to have a baby, and yes I do think that dress will suit you. Whether or not we can afford it is another matter.' They got into the car. 'Now let's go and tell the families shall we?' Clive said, his voice filled with pride.

They drove out of the car park into the busy afternoon traffic.

14

Jim eased himself through the squeeze stile and stepped onto the sandy soil which formed the path leading through the woods.

'Are you OK, Maddie?' Jim said as she passed easily between the two vertically positioned stone posts.

'I'm fine. Stop worrying about me will you. I'm not made of china. Under this skinny exterior lies a bird that's as tough as old boots.'

Jim looked at her and grinned. He still couldn't believe his good fortune. She was his dream come true. The events of the previous week had made Jim come to a decision: he would stop smoking. He'd noticed her reaction in the Pub when smoke drifted across her face; she obviously didn't like a smoky atmosphere. When he thought about it, he decided to stop, not to impress her, but because he didn't want to do anything that would offend her. Suddenly things were changing for him and there was no one more amazed than him.

They entered the wood, the light dimmed, the density of the trees and the depth of the foliage cutting out most of the direct sunlight. They climbed gently upwards, listening for, and then hearing, the water from the brook hissing over the rocks twenty feet below. The path they walked on was heavily worn; thousands of booted feet had removed much of the surface soil and had exposed the tangle of tree roots. Walking the path was a pleasure but the roughness of the track required close attention, especially on the parts of the path which came close by the edge, which plummeted down to the side of the brook, flowing fifty feet below.

'Are you all right, Jim?' Maddie said.

'Course I am. What makes you think I'm not?' Jim stopped walking and turned to look at her.

'Well you seem a bit quiet this morning. I expected you to be full of it today,' she scolded him. 'Lovely day, pretty girl, tasty sandwiches in my lovely new bag, and you've gone quiet. What's up?'

Jim's mind raced over what he should say. There was so much he wanted to tell her, but he couldn't find the words. 'I'm sorry, I've had a lot on my mind and I've just stopped smoking, so I'm a bit uptight.'

She leaned forward and squeezed his arm. 'I thought there was something different about you. I can't smell smoke on you. You didn't stop on my account, did you?'

Jim thought for a second then said: 'Well yes, I did it for you. I've thought about stopping before, but could never find a good enough reason, so yeah, I did it for you, and thanks for being that reason.'

Maddie was surprised. 'You mean you gave them up for me? That's good of you, but really you shouldn't. Don't get me wrong, I hate cigarettes, I saw what they did to my granddad. I just can't stand the smell. They're horrible, but you didn't have to do that for me.'

Jim looked back at her; he couldn't believe how strongly he felt about this girl that he hardly knew. 'Look, if me stopping smoking is hard for you, I'll start again. I thought you'd prefer it if I didn't smoke.'

She wiped her eyes with her sleeve. 'You dumpling, of course I prefer you not to smoke. If you ever get round to kissing me it will be much nicer if you've not just finished a fag.'

The words '*kiss me*' bored their way instantly into Jim's brain, his heart raced, he thought about what she'd just said and couldn't quite understand the message it was giving out, his mind was saying: *Does that mean she wants me to kiss her, or not yet, but maybe sometime … flipping women.*

'Look, I've stopped, so it's got to be a good thing, hasn't it?' Jim said, trying hard not to say the wrong thing.

'Does that mean you want me to give you a kiss … or not …maybe later, when you know me and when I know you better … maybe then if you think it's all right, then perhaps we could, if you want …' Jim stumbled through the sentence. His mouth was operating at twice the speed of his brain and he felt embarrassed. 'I'm sorry. I don't know what I'm saying.'

Maddie laughed. 'Come on, you nut case. Let's walk.'

They strolled slowly for ten minutes, the trees thinning out and the sunlight pouring through the canopy. They descended a flight of steps hewn from the rock. All around lay a thick carpet of brown leaves from the previous autumnal fall, leading them to a timber bridge spanning the brook twenty feet below, the waters crashing now over huge boulders as it surged downwards before disappearing into the depth of the gorge.

'Let's stop here for a minute. I want to take a photo of you on the bridge, then you can take one of me,' she said. 'Stand there,' she ordered. Jim stood rigidly in the centre of the bridge.

Maddie walked downstream about thirty feet. 'Say cheese,' she called out. Jim smiled weakly. 'Come on, Jim. Relax. We're enjoying ourselves.' He tried to relax but he found it hard, relaxing in the company of this beautiful girl: just to look at her made his heart race. 'Right, smile.' Jim grinned. Click, the camera rattled. 'Right it's my turn. You take a picture of me,' Maddie called, excitedly.

Jim had never used a camera before. 'You'll have to show me how it works,' he said. Maddie climbed the timber steps on to the bridge; she walked up close and leaned against him.

'Right, this is what you do.' Maddie moved up closer. Jim could feel her warmth through his jacket, her hair smelling of flowers. She was talking but he didn't hear what she was saying; he felt hot, his mind raced.

Without thinking, he leaned forward and kissed her forehead.

'Well it's about time,' Maddie said, taking his face in her hands and kissing him gently on the mouth. 'I thought you'd never get round to it. That was nice. Now come on and take my picture.'

Jim's face stretched into a wide grin. 'I'm sorry,' he said. 'You'll have to explain how the camera works again.'

Maddie leaned back against the rail of the bridge. Jim stood back a few feet and filled the viewfinder with her face, then clicked the camera shutter.

'When you get those developed, will you let me have a copy?' he asked.

They walked from the bridge, hand in hand. The path rose sharply again: steps had been formed up the hillside, and they were deep in mud. They made their way upwards trying to avoid the clinging mixture of clay and soil, but it was impossible. When they reached the top of the steps, their boots were plastered in the clay-based concoction, making their feet feel heavy.

'Can we stop at the top, Jim? I'm puffed. I could do with a drink of tea.'

Jim slowed. He was also breathing heavily, but trying hard not to show it.

'Of course we can. When we get up, we'll find a rock and have a rest.'

Just along the path the old couple sat close to a shallow stream which meandered downwards into the gorge. They'd stopped for a break. Doris was pouring tea from a flask, while Ernie struggled to remove the sandwiches from the cling film.

'Eee look at them, Ernie. She's just given him a kiss on the bridge' she said

'Well I suppose it's better than kissing him on the lips,' Ernie chortled.

'You're a cynical old sod, Ernest. I don't remember you being like that when you kissed me on that bridge before the war … Come here, you soft old man. Give us a kiss.'

She leaned across, grabbed Ernie by his collar, pulled him to her and, despite Ernie's struggle, gave him a kiss on his forehead.

'Don't do that, our lass. There could be somebody watching.'

Doris chuckled. 'I hope they are, Ernest. They might learn something. Any road, I love ya, even though you're a cantankerous old sod.'

Having reached the top of the steps, and puffing freely, Jim and Maddie trudged slowly upward, looking for a place to stop for a drink.

'This is a lovely walk, Jim,' Maddie said as she peered over the edge of the gorge and retraced with her eyes the route they had just walked. Further along the track they saw an old couple getting ready to have lunch.

As they approached, the old lady said: 'Hello, mi lovelies. How are you?'

Maddie said: 'We're fine. Isn't it a lovely day!'

The old lady said: 'Why don't you sit here for a minute, take a break. It's hard work coming up that bit of path isn't it!'

'You can say that again,' Jim said, wiping the beads of sweat from his forehead.

Ernie said: 'Its hard work coming up that path isn't it.' He grinned and dodged the back of Doris's hand as it came at him from his left side.

'Oh shut up, you daft bat,' Doris said. 'Excuse my husband. He used to be sensible you know, before he started losing his marbles.' They all laughed.

'Come on, sit down: it will be nice to have a chat,' Doris invited them.

For the next twenty minutes, Jim and Maddie were entertained by Doris and Ernie, who talked to them about their younger days in Sheffield, and how they would travel out into Derbyshire on the bus and would walk miles in all weathers. It was their escape from the grime of the city.

'Do you know what, love?' Doris said. 'We were watching you down by the bridge. I said to Ernest that I thought you were a lovely couple, didn't I, Ernest?'

Ernie blinked, surprised that he was being allowed to speak. 'You did, Doris. You went all soppy when you saw them kissing.' He started to fumble with the rucksack.

'Do you know what? If ever I start talking about love and romance, my Ernest goes all coy. Heaven knows how we ever got married. All he was interested in was football. He's been a Blades fan since his dad took him to Bramall Lane when he was six months old. Isn't that right, Ernest?'

Ernie was starting to look bored. He said: 'Doris, why don't you give it a rest? You've had that sandwich in your hand for twenty minutes. It'll be that hard by the time you get to eat it, you'll probably break your teeth on it. Get it down you. Give your tongue a chance to cool down a bit.'

The youngsters laughed and enjoyed the stories of the two oldies, Maddie realising that this was just their way; it kept their relationship fresh and funny.

'Don't listen to him, luvvie. He's daft. You two carry on. It seems to me that the pair of you will last a lifetime. I can see it written all over you.'

Maddie was surprised. She said with a smile: 'Well thank you. We've not known each other long, but I hope it lasts.'

15

Janet walked steadily up the rough lane leading past the railway station. She could see today was going to be busy. There were several groups of walkers heavily laden, ready for a day out in the hills, and this often meant the rangers' problems multiplied. She picked up her pace, turning right into an ancient bridleway which lead her steeply uphill, through an area of large houses. Maintaining her pace, she quickly left the houses behind and headed up into the woods. The sun was warm on her head and she was perspiring freely, soon emerging from the trees into strong sunlight, stopping briefly to remove her jumper. Over the radio other rangers spoke with their bases. She called her base to confirm that her radio signal was being received. After a further four hundred yards of strenuous climbing, she was pleased to reach the top of the slope and begin the serious business of walking and meeting the public.

There was a cloudless sky, with just a light breeze coming from the south. Below her, in the valley, the roads were filling up with traffic and she could see in the distance ant-like figures making their way up onto the plateau. Janet was happy. She was in her element, her headache was purged.

Janet walked strongly, greeting other walkers along the way with a cheerful 'Good Morning, lovely day.' She'd covered the car parks, recorded the number of cars and passed the Grouse Inn. She glanced upwards and could see already that there were several people walking along White Edge. She turned right, down the Tarmac road and soon passed through the gate leading on to the Western end of Froggatt Edge. She felt comfortable: this area held no fears or surprises for her, it was familiar territory. She passed on through the woodland comprising large numbers of immature silver birch trees. A small group of children sat in the centre of an ancient stone circle close by the path. She called across to them: 'Good morning, how are you all today?'

The older of the girls looked around. 'We're fine, thank you.' Janet smiled; she remembered sitting in that same spot years ago when out in the peaks on a school geography project.

The track was busy, with several small groups of walkers, some old, some young, the occasional jogger or individual walking a dog.

Maddie and Jim left the old couple and headed further up the gorge. The foliage of the trees was dense and where the sunlight broke through it created intricate patterns of light and shade, highlighting the rich greenery surrounding the track. They chatted easily as they made their way upwards, Maddie frequently stopping to examine a flower or cooing when a bird flew close by.

'I reckon that we need to learn a lot more about birds and plants. There's so much around here that I don't know about. I think I'm going to buy some books for when we come out again. What do you think?' Maddie said, enthusiastically.

Jim smiled. 'I agree. I'd like to know more myself,' he replied, pleased that Maddie was enjoying their walk.

They strolled along easily, eventually emerging from the wood alongside the stream which flowed fast over tangled piles of gritstone boulders. Along the bank, families were picnicking, fathers with their children, building dams in vain attempts to block the stream. The land before them rose gently. Bracken and heather-covered moorland topped in the distance by the impressive flat topped Higgar Tor, standing guard over the beautiful Burbage Valley.

'That's where we're heading,' Jim exclaimed. 'We're going up here to the left. That gouge in the ground is called Hollowgate. It's an old track made by the quarry men who brought millstones down from the quarries, on horse-drawn carts.'

Maddie looked at him, quizzically 'I'm impressed. Where did you learn that?'

Jim smirked. 'I bought a book and read about it. I knew we were coming this way so I thought it would be more interesting if we knew a bit about where we are,' he said, a smug look crossing his face.

'Well you were right. It is interesting. I look forward to the rest of the lecture as we go round the walk,' she said, happily.

They headed up Hollowgate, the narrow track with steep banks on each side badly eroded after years of use; in places, the track had reached the bedrock, making the track under foot very rough. They crossed the road near the Surprise View car park and ploughed on to the top of the hill half a mile away where a massive boulder stood, proudly overlooking the valley below.

They reached the top. Maddie was breathing heavily, and Jim, who was sweating profusely, said: 'I think we'll stop here, have a drink and a bite to eat.'

Maddie said: 'I love it when you're masterful. Climb up onto that boulder and let me take a photo of you.'

'No,' Jim said. 'You go up. You're the photogenic one. I'll unpack the bag and then I'll take your picture for posterity.'

'Okie dokie,' she said, enthusiastically, and scrambled easily up onto the top of the boulder and sat with her legs dangling over the side. Jim gazed up at her as she sat looking intently across the Hope Valley. He saw her beauty, her innocence and still couldn't believe that she'd selected him to be her friend. *She's just the most beautiful thing,* Jim told himself.

'Right, let's have a nice smile show me your teeth.' Maddie gave Jim her best film star smile and Jim clicked the camera.

'The views across the valley are breath-taking,' Maddie exclaimed. 'The most beautiful view I've ever seen.' She stood for a long time, staring at the countryside all around her. 'Do you know what, Jim? If I died now, I'd die happy. I think this is where my ashes should be scattered.'

Jim thought that was a strange thing to say. 'Come on down. I've poured you a cup of coffee. We can't hang about too long. We've still a long way to go.'

16

Doris and Ernie packed up their bag and set off a little stiffly at a gentle pace up the sloping track. Doris took hold of Ernie's hand, Ernie reluctantly allowing her to get away with this outward show of affection.

'You know, Ernest. I thought that young couple were lovely. Isn't it nice when you can sit with the youngsters and have a chat, and did you see how interested they were in us when we talked about our time as youngsters. I thought the girl was especially nice. I hope we see them again sometime.'

Forty-five minutes later they emerged from the gorge. This was a walk that was very familiar to them; they'd walked this area for nearly sixty years. Doris said: 'I feel like another break, Ernest. How about you?'

Ernie, though disguising it well, was also feeling weary.

'Whatever you wish, my dearest. Your wish is my command.'

They soon found a convenient grassy hollow close by the side of the stream. There were people picnicking, children paddling in the shallow water, dogs splashing around cooling off. The sun was high and the temperature was rising; it was getting very warm.

Ernest slipped off his jacket, Doris removed her light weight jumper, and they sat and drank a carton of orange juice.

'Let's stay here for a while, Ernest. I'm feeling a bit tired today. Must be old age catching up on me.'

Ernie was happy to have a prolonged rest, given that he was also feeling the heat. 'Whatever you wish, my sweet,' he said.

Doris chuckled to herself. 'I'm going to read my book for ten minutes,' she said, rummaging around in their bag. Ernie leaned back, rested his head against the grassy bank and was almost instantly asleep. From time to time Doris would nudge him, as he lay with his mouth open sending out intermittent snores, much to the amusement of passing walkers. Doris would look at them, roll her eyes and smile serenely.

She began to think back to the early days, before they were married. The day she met Ernie came clearly into her mind, a day she would never forget.

She'd cycled out to the Peaks from Sheffield and left her cycle at the Fox House Inn, and then walked the half mile down the road to sit by the stream to eat her lunch. There had been a group of young men larking about by the stream. Ernest stood out from the group; he was the only one who wore a tie, albeit it was twisted round to the side and appeared to have the remnants of his breakfast smeared across it.

Doris was not a shrinking violet. She'd liked the look of him so she'd moved closer to the group, attempting to catch his attention. One of the boys had noticed her, and had sworn at her. Doris had been upset and had turned to walk away. Behind her she'd heard a scuffle and turned to see a blur of movement. She'd heard a raised voice followed by a thumping sound and a yell of pain. She'd wiped her eyes and seen the youth who had abused her sitting on the ground, holding his mouth. Through swollen lips, he'd said: 'What was that for, Ernie?' Ernie had stood over him, fists clenched, anger etched on his face.

'Why did I hit ya? You know full well. We don't talk to lasses like that. It's a rule. How would you feel if I'd said that to your sister?'

The youth had looked humbled, as he'd stood up, turned to Doris and said: 'I'm sorry, lass. Ernie's right. I shouldn't have said what I said. I'm sorry.'

Doris had been surprised and impressed. Ernie had instantly become her hero. 'That's all right, I'll forgive you' Doris had said, wiping the tears from her eyes.

Ernie had come over to Doris and had said: 'There'll not be any more bother. Are you all right now?'

Doris had wiped her eyes again. 'I'm fine, thank you. My name's Doris. What's yours?'

Doris quickly came back to reality with a start. Ernest was snoring again. She prodded him, and he snorted and smacked his lips. She realised that the place they were sitting was the place where the unfortunate youth had landed after he had been punched by Ernie all those years ago. She smiled to herself. *Lovely memories* she thought to herself leaning back alongside her man.

She leaned across Ernest and looked into his face, now old and creased.

'You know what Ernest Galloway? You're a cantankerous old bugger, but when I got you, I got a good one,' she said, planting a kiss on his balding head. 'I think it's time we were moving,' she said, pushing herself up. As she rose her head began to swim: she staggered and fell back onto the grass. For a moment, she was startled but not overly concerned. *Old age creeping up,* she said to herself, taking a few minutes to regain her composure before she got up again. She gave Ernie a gentle shake. 'Come on, Ernest. Time to go.'

Ernest opened his eyes. 'No need to shout. I wasn't asleep; just relaxing,' he said, nonchalantly. He stretched out his arms over his head and gave out a loud yawn.

They gathered their equipment and stowed it in the old khaki rucksack and set off again slowly, crossing the stream on large grey boulders and then on up the hill towards Longshaw Park.

Janet had reached the first grid reference. It was located alongside the Eagle Stone, a prominent rock close to the main track across the moor. She opened her map and quickly worked out the position of the final grid reference point, the place she had to walk to.

She used her compass to calculate the bearing and the distance she had to walk. She figured it was almost two kilometres, comprising six hundred meters of rough boulder-strewn heather-covered moorland, then across two fields and a metalled road before she had to negotiate five hundred metres of marshland. Her destination was close by White Edge.

She took stock of her position, deciding to pace the walk: good practise when walking in difficult conditions. Through several years of practice she knew her pace was sixty-six double paces for every one hundred metres. However, crossing this type of terrain it would be more like seventy. *I'd better take a few back bearings,* she said to herself, *'just to make sure I stay on course.* She guessed it would take her forty minutes.

Knowing your walking speed was a vital ingredient of accurate navigation, and was hammered into everyone from the first day in the ranger service; a skill and discipline that was passed on to every trainee.

Thirty-one thirty-two: Janet counted her paces under her breath over the very rough terrain. At seventy paces – the theoretical one hundred meters – she would stop and check her route was accurate by taking a bearing back to her starting point. Sixty-nine, seventy: *That's one hundred metres,* she thought to herself. She held out the compass in front of her and, using the bearing and the arrow on the compass housing, determined in her mind a place on the landscape to her front that she should aim for. She turned one hundred and eighty degrees, took a back bearing and was glad to see that she was walking accurately on the bearing and was precisely where she should be.

She pressed on and was soon clear of the moorland. She crossed a couple of fields, checked the compass, checked the time: so far she was on schedule and on course, she was satisfied. She climbed over a dry stone wall, bringing her on to a narrow metalled road, crossing it quickly and was soon over the wall on the other side. Then she noticed what lay before her.

'Well thank you Mr Stanley Bloody Gregg,' Janet said to no one in particular. She'd looked at the map earlier and had noticed that this part of the walk was shown as marsh land, but she'd never walked this bit before. She smiled to herself. *You wait till I see you tonight you old bugger.* She ran through her mind several options to gain revenge, some of which required the removal of limbs.

The ground she had to cross comprised long clumpy marsh grass, forming unstable mounds. Sitting between the mini hillocks lay several inches of cloying oozing silt like mud. She soon realised that the next few minutes would prove difficult; pacing was going to be almost impossible, as was timing her progress. However, she decided that, despite the difficulty, she would concentrate everything on being accurate with the compass. Beginning slowly, she studied every footfall. Soon the water had found its way into her boots, and the soft mud was clinging to the textured soles of her boots, making them heavy and cumbersome. She stopped for a moment to check her bearing. The sod on which her right foot was standing collapsed, Janet stumbled forward, her hands disappearing into the clinging mud. The compass disappeared into a small pool of water. 'Stanley,' she shouted aloud, 'you bloody just wait. You're going to suffer.' She gathered herself up, recovered the compass and set off walking again, taking even more care than before. She could feel the cold water sloshing inside her boots; her hands and legs were stained the colour of peat. *You just wait,* she mumbled unhappily to herself.

For a few minutes she stumbled and grumbled through these impossible conditions. Halfway across the morass she saw in front, about twenty feet away, a piece of timber had been hammered into the bog. Attached to it was a plastic container. Janet approached the box, thinking who on earth put that here: you'd have to be mad to come here to put a piece of wood in the ground and attach a box to it. *'This must be the thing I was looking for,* she said to herself, with some satisfaction.

Balancing herself between two of the more sturdy-looking clumps of grass, she removed the box from the wooden stake; on the box was written: 'For the attention of Janet.' She carefully prised the box open. A card lay inside on which was scrawled: 'Happy Birthday, Janet. I hope you didn't get too wet. Love Stan.' She carefully removed the card beneath which was a baseball cap of the type she had promised she would buy, with a flap to protect the neck from the rays of the sun. *Thank you, Stan,* she said to herself. *'Why didn't you give it me before I set off? It would have been much easier.*

That's it then, Janet said to herself. *Job done. Let me get out of here.* She forged a route across the bog. After about fifty meters, she was clear of the mess, put the compass into a pocket in her rucksack and began the gentle ascent up to Swine Sty, an area just off the main track of White Edge.

In the distance, Janet could see someone sitting relaxed close by the track. As she approached, she began to recognise the figure of Stan Gregg.

What's he doing up here? She said to herself. As she approached, Stan got up, a beaming smile crossing his face. 'How's it going, lass?' he asked.

Janet smiled back at him. She put her arms around him and kissed him on his grizzled cheek. 'Thank you, Stan. It's just what I wanted,' she said. 'Now take that,' she said, wiping her muddied sleeves across his face.

'Well, you said you wanted one of those caps, so I got you one.'

Suddenly they were both laughing.

They sat by the track for a minute. 'You think you got mucky. You should have seen the state of me last night. I put it there in the dark. I got filthy,' Stan said, laughing loudly.

'And so you should,' Janet replied. 'I bet your wife was delighted with you, making her more washing. That's just what she needs.'

Stan looked at her, fondly. Of all the rangers he was responsible for, Janet was his favourite; she could take a joke, and she was good at the job.

They sat by the footpath, laughing. 'That was really nice of you, Stan. I've been going to get one of those hats for ages, but never got round to it. Thanks very much.'

'You didn't find it then?' Stan said.

'Find what?' she replied.

Stan smirked. 'When I briefed you, I gave you a start GR and a finish GR. I watched you all the way. When you found the box, you walked off course. You didn't go to the finish GR.'

'Well, no. I assumed that the hat in the box was it.' It began to dawn on Janet what Stan was talking about. 'You crafty old so and so. You tricked me into coming off course,' she said.

Stan gave her a knowing look. 'No, you took yourself of route. You were supposed to walk from GR to GR. I said you may find something along the way. That's no reason to abandon the route. This was a navigation exercise, and you fluffed it.'

Janet said: 'I feel awful now. That's a lesson learned, one that I won't soon forget.'

Stan smiled. 'Don't worry about it. It's only an exercise. If you hadn't learned anything, it would have been a waste of time, so let's finish the exercise. Do a quick resection and position us on the map.'

Janet got out her map and, using the compass, now covered in mud, she quickly plotted their position. 'Now, Mrs Clark, plot a course from here to the finishing point GR.'

Janet placed the compass between the two points on the map and soon calculated the bearing.

'Okie dokie, mon cherie. Let's go. Take me there,' Stan said, cheerfully.

Five minutes later, they'd reached the final GR.

'Just sit over there, will you?' Stan said, pointing to a spot a few feet from where he was going to sit. Janet sat on a small boulder. 'Now, Mrs Clark, if you look in the hollow beneath the boulder you're sitting on, mon ami, you may find something of interest.' Janet leaned forward: stretching her arm under the rock, she felt something, then a rustle of paper. She grasped what felt like a small parcel and pulled it out. Wrapped in shiny pink paper was a package. 'Come on now. Open it. You're getting behind schedule,' Jack said.

Janet smiled broadly. 'So this is what it's been all about is it?' she said, happily. She tore at the flimsy wrapping. Inside were a couple of pairs of thick red walking socks, with a note saying: 'From all Saturday B shift. Love on your birthday. PS. Hope you didn't get too muddy.' She stuffed the socks into her bag. 'Well, Stan , you crafty old sod. I'd better get on. Places to go, people to see. Thanks for the presents, thanks for the mud ... and, Stan, your French leaves a lot to be desired, mon petit pois.'

She threw her rucksack across her shoulder and, laughing, walked back along the track towards Longshaw Park.

17

Jim and Maddie struggled up the final steep section of eroded track leading to the crest of the flat-topped Higgar Tor. The top of the hill is covered heather and bisected by peaty tracks meandering over and around an array of large boulders. The southern section of the hill is defined by a steep escarpment of grey hard Gritstone and is frequented by the rock climbing fraternity. The northern edge is steep and has a mixture of bracken and rough grass.

Jim and Maddie walked slowly along the western flank; the views down into the Burbage valley were spectacular. Maddie stopped.

'Stand there, Jim. I want to get a picture of you with the view behind you.' The camera clicked. 'Thank you, sir,' Maddie said, happily. They strolled further: eventually they came to the crags on the southern extreme of the hill, where they could hear voices. Maddie looked over the edge and could see a group of about ten young men, all wearing shorts, bare-chested with belts around their waists adorned with immense amounts of climbing equipment.

'Let's sit here, have a rest and a bite to eat and watch the lads climbing shall we?' Maddie said, enthusiastically.

'OK, you unpack the sandwiches. I'll do the coffee,' Jim said in a matter-of-fact voice.

They sat watching the attempts of the climbers on the face of a huge overhanging crag. One by one, they all failed, running out of energy and falling off with a whoop or scream at the critical moments.

The heat was becoming oppressive, so Maddie stripped down to her sleeveless tee-shirt while Jim took his shirt off to get some sun, both noticing the other. Jim looked at Maddie's figure, filling out the tee shirt in a way she'd not previously revealed. Maddie noticed his glance and pushed her chest out even further. Jim's heart leapt with feelings he suspected he'd had but had never been in a position to experience before. He lay back and relaxed, but his mind was in a spin. The picture of Maddie's tight tee-shirt embedded in his mind. Something stirred. Jim felt embarrassed, so turned over onto his stomach and took the sun's heat on his back. Maddie understood and smiled to herself, taking it as a compliment, reasoning that if he didn't fancy her, it was all a waste of time. She noticed his pale skin and skinny frame and she wanted to hug him. He'd clearly not been taking care of himself. They lounged in silence for several minutes.

'Did you ever fancy having a go at rock climbing?' Maddie asked, looking at the climbers struggling up the rocks and laughing when they fell off.

Jim turned his head towards Maddie. 'Na. Never understood why anybody would want to do it. Can't see the sense in it,' he emphasised.

'Well, I think it's good. They're having fun and they're getting fit. Seems to me it's good exercise – better than those idiots who go around mugging old ladies or setting fire to things. They're seriously stupid.'

Maddie's words pierced Jim's chest like an arrow, the pain making him go rigid; out of the blue this girl had hit his weak spot. She'd unwittingly taken him from his wonderful present, back in to the nightmare of his other life, the life she knew nothing about.

Maddie sat for a minute. Jim was quiet. She turned and saw Jim's body was taut. He looked distressed, taking in huge breaths of air, like an asthmatic sufferer, trying desperately to get air into his lungs.

'What's wrong, Jim?' she said. Jim made no reply but kept sucking in air. 'Are you OK?'

Jim clenched his hands around his ears. 'Just leave me alone, will you? That's it. We'll go back. I can't do this.'

Maddie was shocked. 'What do you mean go back, and you can't do what?' she said, in a voice that cut through Jim like a sliver of cold ice.

He sat up, pulling his hands down and across his face.

'What is it? Have I said something wrong?' Maddie paused. 'I thought we were having a nice time. I thought you liked me. Where's this come from?' Maddie said, tears flooding her eyes.

Jim looked at her. Her reaction shocked him. The tears in her eyes sent a pain shooting through his body.

'You don't know me, Maddie,' Jim said, through wavering lips. 'There are things about me that you don't know. You haven't done anything to deserve me. You can do better. I know I don't deserve you. It's been good, but it couldn't last, I would have spoiled it sometime.'

Maddie walked across to him. 'Get up, Jim,' she said, in a determined tone. Jim looked up, as she stood over him. 'Give me your hand. Now!' Jim put his hand up; Maddie grabbed it and pulled hard. 'Let's walk a bit, shall we? Show me around the top of this hill.' Jim got to his feet, his face pale and blank. He'd somehow retreated into his other self. 'You say I don't deserve you and that you don't deserve me,' Maddie said, her voice hard and cold, displaying a determination to get to the bottom of the problem. 'I don't like anybody telling me who I should go out with. I know what I want and I know what and who I like. That just happens to be you,' she said, peering directly into his face. 'Fair enough, if you want to end it then say so, but don't go telling me I don't deserve you. That's something I'll decide for myself.' Jim heard the words but couldn't lift his face to look at her.

'Look,' he said. 'Meeting you was the best … the only good thing that's ever happened to me.' His voice cracked with emotion. 'I've never had a girlfriend. I've never been with a girl, if you know what I mean,' Jim said, his voice softening. 'It was just too good, too lucky. You don't know me. I'm just a lazy layabout. I live in a crap flat in a crap area, among crap people. You're the nicest thing I've known, but I don't think you know what I am.'

Maddie looked on while Jim struggled to express himself; she put her hand on his shoulder. 'I think that nobody is what they appear. These people in flash houses and cars, spending money like it was going out of fashion, we don't know if they're happy. Who knows? They're probably up to their necks in debt, having affairs, getting divorced, taking out loans to make sure that they appear well off, when in fact they're struggling to make ends meet.' She paused and ran her hand down Jims arm. 'So come on, we've all got secrets. You don't know me, we've only known each other for two weeks, we can't know each other.' She paused again, struggling to get the next words out. She looked at the ground and shuffled her feet. 'I've got a secret I don't tell people about' she said, in a quiet voice.

Jim looked up; he could see pain on her face.

They continued walking.

'Let's cut down there,' Jim said, 'towards the stream, we'll make our way back now.'

They descended sharply over a boulder-covered slope, not speaking, but just concentrating on moving safely down the hill. The base of the hill formed a natural cleft where a stream ran, crossed by an old stone packhorse bridge.

'Let's sit here a minute and talk,' Maddie said. 'I need to know what's happening. Half an hour ago we were happy, having a nice time. Now I feel terrible. I need to understand what's going on.'

They sat on the steep grassy bank close by the stream, Maddie waiting for Jim to speak, Jim feeling uncomfortable, not knowing what to say, feeling that the most positive thing in his life was about to disintegrate.

Maddie leaned across to Jim and put her head on his shoulder. 'You know, Jim,' she said, her voice light and shaking, 'meeting you was great. I know you've a pretty low opinion of yourself, you're not a smart arse, you're a bit scruffy, but there's something that I like about you.'

They sat beside the stream for a while, looking at the peat-stained water flowing rapidly by, neither of them saying a word, both unable to make the next statement, lest it brought about some point between them that they would have to confront. Maddie's mind was swirling with a confusion of ideas and thoughts. Jim sat blankly staring at the water, unable to get his mind beyond what Maddie had said. '*Idiots who set fire to things.*'

After what seemed an age, Maddie stood up, put the rucksack across her shoulder in silence and began walking quickly away. In her mind, she wanted to leave this pain behind, just get away: she didn't need this. She felt the dream had come to an end, but didn't understand why.

This sudden movement brought Jim back into focus. He saw Maddie walking quickly away from him and began to panic. He could see the end of this perfect friendship looming. If he was going to do something it had better be now. He pushed himself up, turned to retrieve his bag, tripped, half fell and half staggered into the stream. Maddie heard the shout and the splash. Turning around she saw Jim attempting to climb back up the muddy bank and couldn't help but smile. She jogged back, in time to see Jim pull himself up the last section of the bank.

Maddie laughed. 'I knew you were unhappy but I didn't expect you to try to drown yourself,' she joked.

Jim looked up, flattening his hair down onto his head, and gave her a sheepish grin. 'I just fancied a swim,' he said.

'Come here, you dope. Let's get your clothes off. You can spread them out. The sun will dry them in no time.'

Jim removed his shirt and socks. 'That's all I'm taking off. Let's sit and talk.' Quite suddenly the tension between them began to evaporate. Maddie took off her boots and socks and dangled her feet in the stream.

'Oooh, this is lovely,' she said, a broad smile splitting her pretty features. 'You know, Jim. We all have secrets; even me.' She lay back, closing her eyes against the bright sunlight 'You've got a secret, I've got a secret. It's normal. Nobody knows everything about everybody. It's life. If your secret's so bad it'll eventually get you, you've got to deal with it, sort it out. It's a bit like a debt, while ever it's there, it's a problem. Once it's been paid off, hey presto, no problem.'

Jim shuffled. The argument had resonated with him. He knew he'd have to open up to Maddie or they were doomed.

'What's your secret?' Jim said.

Maddie sat up and turned to face Jim. 'OK. Sit up and look at me. If I'm going to tell you everything, you'll need to listen.' Jim sat up, turning to look at her.

'You don't have to tell me, you know,' Jim said, his face twisted by indecision.

'I want to,' Maddie replied, firmly. 'Tell me. When you look at me what do you see?'

Jim didn't understand and looked confused.

'What do you see when you look at me?' she repeated.

Jim looked at her.

'I see you, Maddie,' he said, his voice betraying his confusion.

She looked again.

'Yes you see me, but what do you really see?'

Jim was still confused, not understanding what she meant.

'I don't understand what you mean, I look at you and I see you!'

Maddie saw the confusion clouding his face.

'Right,' she said. 'You sit there and listen. I'm going to tell you about me.' Maddie shuffled and changed her position. She sat close to him, looking directly into his face.

'When you've heard this you'll know me better, but it may alter how you feel. You may not fancy me much when I've told you.' Jim sat, transfixed by this girl he barely knew, but surely loved. 'I've been brought up in a nice area, I've got nice parents, I was a prefect at school, I got ten 'O' levels and two 'A' levels, my parents wanted me to go to university, but I declined, I just wanted to be a nurse. I studied to be a nurse, came out top of my class, and I love my job.' she paused. 'I've been to America, Spain, Portugal and Cyprus on holidays with my parents, I can ride a horse, I love the Beatles and folk music, and I've had a few boyfriends, none of them serious. I've had a nice life. I've got a good life!' she emphasised 'The last couple of weeks have been the best two weeks of my life, better than any holiday in Florida.' She paused again. 'Since I met you, I've got a new perspective on things. Being out here, seeing lovely views and being with you, with no strings, has been great.' She paused for a moment. Jim shaped to speak. 'Be quiet for a minute,' Maddie said, 'I've not finished yet.' She stopped and took a couple of deep breaths. 'I asked you what you saw when you looked at me. A girl, dark hair, quite small, a bit pretty maybe, but what you see isn't what you get with me.' She paused again and took great care about what she was about to say. 'A few years ago, I found a lump in my left breast. To be more precise, I found a malignant lump in my left breast. To cut a long story short, I had to have the breast removed.' Maddie put her hands on her head and her eyes welled with tears. 'You see, I'm not what I appear to be. Only my mum and dad and a couple of my close friends know, you need to know, need to understand. So now you know, twenty-two years old and that's me.'

Jim pushed up close to her, put his arm around her shoulder but couldn't think of a single word to say. He could feel her breathing as he felt a tear run down his cheek.

The minutes passed in silence. Eventually Jim got up, checked his clothes which were almost dry, and slipped them on, put on his boots, then looked at Maddie, who seemed to be deep in her thoughts. 'Time we were moving, mad woman' he said. This use of words made Maddie smile. She put on her socks and boots. Jim threw the rucksack over his shoulder and they began walking slowly and silently towards Longshaw Park.

Doris and Ernest strolled slowly through the main gate of Longshaw Park, they both felt a bit weary, Ernie's legs were getting painful. 'Let's head down to the fish pond, love,' Doris said. 'It's warm, so we'll have a sit and a drink before we get off down to the station.' Ernie loosened his grip on Doris's hand and stroked her hair. Doris thought *it must be my birthday.* It was so unlike Ernest to show anything remotely romantic, especially outside of the confines of their house.

'Are you all right, love? You're looking a bit hot,' Ernie asked.

'I'm fine. Just getting ready for a drink,' she replied.

Janet had made good time along the edge. There was little up there that required her to slow down. She stopped briefly for a sip of water from her bottle, then continued down and across the road, onto the track that led into the park. Among the trees she could see swathes of Rhododendron bushes giving a grand display with their luxuriant pink flowers contrasting against the darkness of the surrounding woodland.

Maddie and Jim came off the moor and headed up to towards the Fox House pub. They turned sharply downhill, heading straight for Longshaw. They walked between the stone gateposts, and on past the gatehouse.

Maddie had seen something 'Look, Jim. There's the old couple from this morning. Let's see if we can catch them up,' she said, a mischievous grin crossing her face. 'They were a lovely couple. I really enjoyed talking to them.'

Janet was walking comfortably along the limestone path, the area was busy: lots of families were out walking. This was what she loved, seeing people out enjoying the peak, as she did. She saw an elderly couple walking towards her, saw the man stroke his wife's hair and thought: *How nice of him.*

Doris was holding on to Ernie's hand. She felt very hot and unwell. She hadn't said anything to Ernest, knowing he would worry. She felt light-headed and faint. A pain erupted in her head. Suddenly everything was black. She dreamed of Ernie, the first time they met, of leaving school and her first job, she remembered her daughter, barely two years old, very ill in hospital. The dreams ended.

Ernie felt Doris grip his hand momentarily. Then he saw her fall away from him. It happened too fast for him to react and prevent her fall. He saw her hit the ground, her face driven into the gravel path. At first he thought she'd tripped, but quickly realised it was something more serious. She lay motionless on the ground.

Maddie and Jim were catching the old couple up, when they saw Doris fall. They were about twenty yards away, as they saw the old man attempt to lean over to reach her. Maddie instinctively ran towards them.

Janet was close by when she saw the lady fall. She ran forward and was the first to reach the couple. She leaned over the old lady. Ernie put his hand on Janet's shoulder. 'Will she be all right, love?' he asked.

At that moment, Maddie got to them. Leaning forward, Maddie said: 'I'm a nurse. Can I look at her?' Janet leaned away to make room for her. Maddie pressed her fingers into Doris's neck trying to find a pulse. It was clear to her that Doris was in a poor condition. Maddie pulled Doris on to her side, placed her cheek against Doris's lips to try to capture a sign that she was breathing. 'Come on, Doris. Come back, will you.' Doris's head lolled loosely, her eyes vacant.

Janet was on the radio, contacting base, and informing them of the situation as she knelt alongside Maddie.

'Hi, I'm Janet. I'm a peak ranger. Can I do anything?' she said directly to Maddie. Maddie turned.

'Yes, will you get her husband? His name's Ernest. I need him here'

Ernie came across to where Doris was lying. A look of bewilderment and fear flowed across his worried features.

'Hello, Ernest. Do you remember me from this morning?' Maddie said, hoping there would be a spark of recognition in Ernie's face.

Ernest stared at Maddie, trying to remember, amid the confusion of thoughts spinning around his head. 'Yes, I remember. We had a chat in the gorge.'

Maddie took his hand. It was cold and frail.

'Look, Ernest. Doris is quite poorly. Can you help me? I need you to sit here with her until the ambulance comes. Take this hankie, and keep her mouth clean. Stroking her hair will help, too,' she said. Ernest struggled to sit down, his joints being so stiff, but he eventually managed it. He sat and talked to Doris, gently running his hand over her head. 'Come on, Doris, it's not time yet,' he said in a voice he struggled to control.

The Ambulance siren wailed as it approached, both Janet and Maddie were relieved; Doris could now get the expert treatment she desperately needed. Janet stood by the gates of the park and waved the ambulance in.

The Ambulance crew quickly took over her care, checking her over, before placing her in the Ambulance. Ernie, in a state of shock, was helped into the back of the ambulance looking shattered. The doors of the Ambulance were quickly closed and it was soon leaving at speed with the siren blaring, heading for the city.

18

'Come in, Mac. Sit down. I need to speak to you about a replacement for Ray.'

Mac sat on a comfortable padded chair. Across the table sat the Divisional Commander and Dan Brogan.

'It's a difficult time, Mac. The ADO and I have been chatting about the situation on your watch. We think we know what should happen, and we've talked to the Station Commander, but thought you should have some input before anything was decided.'

Mac thought for a moment. He was never a man to say anything that hadn't been considered. 'The situation on the watch is fine, OK. I'm a man short but I'm hoping that will soon be sorted. I'd like to know what's going to happen about a replacement for Ray. Tony Ellis is doing it. He's earned his chance and personally I'd like him to get the job on a permanent basis. I'm not sure about the replacement for the shortage. Have we got anybody wanting to transfer over to Graveton?'

The DC looked at Dan Brogan.

'We've got two candidates who've already applied for a job there when one comes up. We're not sure if you'll like either'

Dan Brogan spoke up.

'Graveton's a station that people want to serve on, it's busy and got a good reputation, but we don't want to disturb the good balance there.' Dan scratched his head. 'To be quite honest, Mac, we wouldn't consider either of them, but you know how short of manpower we are in the Brigade.'

'Who are they?' Mac asked.

The DC raised his eyebrows. 'Pete Jacks and Justin Telfer'

Mac's face remained expressionless. 'If I remember these characters, Jacks is idle and scruffy and Telfer … well, we all know him don't we? Mister FBU, used to be a good hand until the Union got hold of him.'

'Spot on, Mac,' Pete said, 'but unfortunately that's the choice. Do you want to think about it a while?'

'No, I'll have Jacks. It'll be easier to clean him up than deal with militant Mr Telfer, and I wouldn't want to reward a trouble maker,' Mac said, wistfully. 'That will be a nice little project for Tony to get his teeth into.'

Dan Brogan raised an eyebrow. 'You surprise me, Mac. I would have taken money that you would have preferred the challenge of Telfer.'

Mac smiled. 'There was a time I would have loved it, but I leave the job soon. I wouldn't wish someone like Telfer on whoever takes over my job.'

The DC thought a second. 'Look, Mac. We appreciate your input. The ADO and I will have a chat about it, especially regarding Tony Ellis and we'll let you know in a couple of days.'

Mac stood up. 'OK, boss. I'll look forward to hearing from you.'

Dan spoke up. 'Just one more thing, Mac. What's this we hear about you saving some old fella's life out in the peaks a few weeks ago?'

Mac looked surprised. He'd put the events of that day into the back of his mind. Mac screwed his face up. 'The truth is, it was something that we stumbled on and didn't have any choice about.'

Mac then spent a couple of minutes relating the story to them. 'And that was all it was,' Mac said. 'How did you hear about it?'

Dan replied: 'Do you remember the young lad who helped by using his phone? It was him. It seems he mentioned it to the Chief and the interview board.'

'Yeah, he was a nice kid. Both Val and I took to him straight away,' Mac smiled.

'He did well in the tests. He'll get a letter soon to come for training. By the way, Mac, you've been nominated for an award by the humane society. Yet another medal for your collection.'

Mac gave a wry smile. 'Funny, isn't it? You just go out for a walk with your wife, and then all this happens. I suppose God was smiling on us all that day.' Mac turned and left the office *I'd better not let the boys know about this,* he though. *That'll be something else they can take the pee out of me for.*

Tony Ellis lined the crew up alongside the fire appliance.

'Today, gentlemen … that means you lot, for your delight and delectation …' he said, a mischievous grin crossing his face, 'we're going to do some practical training, designed to test, inform and improve your already very high level of skill. I've devised some situation drills to test your abilities as fire fighters.' He aimed a wicked grin directly at the boys. 'Also to educate you in a variety of crafts required to enable you to function as a cohesive unit in the event of a serious incident.'

The crew smirked, wondering what particular tests Tony had conjured up for them today. In truth, since Tony had been given the job replacing Ray on a temporary basis, he'd gone to a lot of trouble to make their training sessions interesting, and they appreciated it. They'd learned a lot, though that was something they would never admit, least of all to Tony.

'Right today, just to get you all nice and warm, we're going to do a basic drill. Remember the other day at Kelling Crossroads. The use of fast, effective jets at critical incidents. We're going to do something as basic as hitting a car on fire with someone trapped inside. I'll be the person in the car, the one over by the drill tower.' Tony paused a second for effect. 'So the drill is: one line of forty-five millimetre hose consisting of two lengths, with a diffuser branch fitted, to hit the fire at speed, as fast as you possibly can. A life may depend on it, OK.' He paused again and gave a leery grin. 'Then I want a second covering jet got to work, but what must we do gentlemen before we deploy the second jet?' he asked the crew, giving them a childlike smile. They all exuded a feeling of confusion, then, all together they said: 'We must supplement the supply from the hydrant, Leading Fireman,' their faces not betraying any emotion.

'Now, boys. This is important. This is basic. Let's do it and do it fast. Jock, for this drill you will be Officer in Charge. Taff, you're the pump operator. Is everyone clear about what I want?'

Once again in unison the crew said, with mock seriousness: 'We understand, Leading Fireman.'

Tony checked his watch. 'Right, I'm going into the car. Jock, you start when you're ready. I'll be timing this to the second that you hit the car with the jet.'

Tony strode off, setting the time counter on his watch, which was deemed to be waterproof to a depth of two hundred feet. He climbed into the driver's seat of the wrecked and rusty remains of an old Ford Escort and watched the crew mount the appliance. He waited in anticipation.

Mac made good time on his journey back to the station from Div HQ. As he turned the car into the drill yard, he saw that the crew were about to do a drill, so he stopped to watch from a distance, not wanting to disrupt the drill by suddenly appearing. *It was good that Tony was given a free hand to get in some practice at training the boys,* he thought.

Mac heard the roar of Jock's voice above the sound of the appliance engine. 'Crew, as detailed, get to work.' The crew spilled out of the appliance. Tony, sitting in the car, pressed the button on his watch to begin recording the time the drill would take. Mac noted the speed at which Taff got to the pump. Simultaneously, Mick Young was at the pump handing the coupling of the first length of hose to Taff. The action was blurred. Clive Botham had grabbed the hydrant gear and a length of seventy millimetre hose and was hurtling across the yard to set into the hydrant. Brian Parks was running out a second line. Taff was feeding water at speed, chasing the water down the hose, timing it to arrive at the diffuser branch as Mick plugged it into the female coupling of the first line of hose. The water crackled through the hose, twisting it as it lay slightly kinked. Mick reached the car, snapped in the branch, raised his right hand above his head and shouted: 'Water on.' Instantly, the water burst through the branch, a solid stream of water hit the car.

Sitting in the car, Tony looked at his watch; the first jet had hit the car in eleven seconds. *Brilliant,* he thought; he looked across and could see that the water from the hydrant was just being forced under pressure into the pump. Seconds later, Brian was relaying the order for the water to be delivered to the second branch. Tony was impressed: two jets on the car, the hydrant set in under forty second ... *absolutely brilliant.* Mac looked on from the vantage of his car and smiled. He sensed that something was about to happen.

Tony was looking at his watch, about to tell the crew to knock off and make up the equipment, when the door to the car sprang open. He heard Brian's voice. 'Casualty inside. Car well alight. Get the jets in.' Two wide sprays of water filled the passenger compartment in which Tony sat. He heard, through the rushing sound of the high pressure jets of water being poured into the car, 'Increase pressure.' The car was instantly full of fast-moving droplets of water, almost like dense steam. He could barely breath. The freezing water flooded down the collar of his coat, in his sleeves, and his boots were filling with water. He tried to tell the crew to stop. 'FFFFu g pack ittt in yyyyou bbbastards.' But the crashing of water inside the car rendered his voice inaudible.

After what seemed too long a while, Jock's voice could be heard. 'Knock off. Make up.' Instantaneously, the water was cut off and the crew began rolling up hose and replacing the equipment on to the appliance.

Mac sat in his car and watched the action. His shoulders were hunched up, lifting and falling spasmodically as he laughed, like he hadn't laughed for months.

The crew quickly re-stowed the gear and fell in a line at the rear of the appliance, Jock giving the order for the crew to stand at ease.

Tony was saturated; not a square centimetre of his body had escaped the deluge. He struggled to climb out of the car. His gloves were waterlogged and hung from his hands like pieces of chamois leather and his boots were filled with cold water. He got out of the car, water pouring from every part of him; slowly he sloshed his way back to the waiting crew, standing at the rear of the appliance, their faces not displaying any emotion.

Tony came to attention in front of the crew and looked at them. 'Well, crew that was absolutely excellent,' he said. 'First jet in under fifteen seconds, second jet under forty-five seconds, hydrant in. Fantastic, and you even managed to save me from an inferno. You have my undying gratitude.' He paused to take a breath. 'Now just a couple of points of criticism,' he emphasised. 'If you're going to go into the car with jets like you did, it's a good idea not to drown the poor bastard.' At that point the crew folded, shrieking with laughter. Tony pulled himself upright and said: 'Just one more point, lads. I don't know who thought that up, but I can't believe I hadn't thought that might happen. Good drill. Fall out. I've got to get changed.'

19

It was early. Jake sat at the kitchen table; he'd already had his breakfast and made a cup of tea for his mum. She'd been surprised, Jake not being the easiest person to get out of bed in the morning. She often had to shake him to get him out, long after the alarm clock had failed to spur him into activity.

Today was different: he was expecting a letter. It had been a few days since he'd completed the entry test to join the Fire Brigade and he was confident that he'd got through all right, even though, on the day itself, no one had given him any indication of how he'd done. The instructor had been non-committal and told all the participants: 'Thank you for your efforts today. You'll receive notification in a few days. You can sort out your clothing, get a shower if you want one, then you're free to go ... and good luck.'

Jake hadn't slept properly for a few days, his mind darting backwards and forwards, rerunning the events of the day through his mind. It had been tough but he'd loved every minute of it. He wondered how Mark had got on; he'd struggled with some of the tests. Jake had never mixed much with people older than himself. Mark had travelled and experienced so many things, they just seemed to click. He hoped that he'd made it.

Jake's trance-like state was interrupted by the sound of the letterbox slamming shut, followed by the crump of mail on the hall carpet. His heart leapt; the anticipation had built up inside him to the point where he began to dread the mail arriving and finding that he'd failed. He jumped to his feet and walked quickly to the front door, sweeping up the small pile of mail in one movement, quickly thumbing through it, dispensing with anything that looked unimportant. Amid the junk was a buff-coloured envelope.

Jake's mother sat up in bed, leaning back comfortably against the pillows that Jake had placed behind her. He'd switched on her radio. She sipped the tea from her favourite willow pattern cup, refusing to drink tea from any other crockery, it being one of the set her mother had left her.

'Nothing quite like a nice cup of tea from a bone China cup,' she would say to Jake as he ploughed through his mug, emblazoned with the Sheffield Wednesday motif.

She sat up rigid, startled by a series of whoops, she heard Jake shouting. She smiled broadly. *That can only mean one thing*, she thought. Seconds later, Jake entered her room, his face taut with relief and excitement. She looked at him and grinned proudly. She'd never known him want anything as much as he'd wanted this.

'I'm proud of you, Jacob. I knew you could do it,' she said, wiping the tears of pride from her cheeks. 'Here, let me read the letter.'

Jake passed her the letter. 'Read it to me, mum. I didn't read it properly, just the bit that said I'd passed,' Jake said, breathlessly.

'OK, Jacob. Sit on the side of the bed. Here, put my tea on the dresser for me will you?' she said, regaining her composure. She began to read.

> *Dear Mr Higgins,*
> *I am pleased to inform you that at the recent Induction tests you were successful.*
> *The recruit training course commences on 16th July1996. You should report to Brigade Headquarters on that date at 8.30 a.m.*
> *You will receive further communications in the near future*
> *Yours sincerely*
> *Henry Neville*
> *Chief Fire Officer.*

'There you are, son. You're on your way. I think it's wonderful. Now go and pour me another cup of tea before you go to work.'

20

Mac walked into the locker room. He saw Tony standing amid a pile of wet clothing.

'Nice one, Tony. I thought the boys did the drill spot on.'

Tony looked across the room at Mac, not sure what his reaction would be.

'I thought it would be a good idea to do that drill just to keep them sharp. After Kelling Crossroads, it seems to me we have to keep on at the basics. I thought the boys were great,' he laughed. 'It's a good job I've got a change of clothes here.'

Mac laughed. 'I thought you'd have known better than to expose yourself like that. I think hitting them with the basics is good, but ideally if anyone gets wet, it should be them. Anyway, no harm done. It's all good for morale, and it shows them that you're still one of them. Well done.'

Tony smiled with pride. Being complimented by Mac was indeed a thing to value.

'When you've got yourself dried off, come and see me in the office. I need to talk to you.'

Tony was putting his wet clothing into the drying room when the crew came into the locker room. They gave him a series of grins and chuckled light-heartedly between themselves. 'Well, Leading Fireman. That was a good drill. We need more of that,' Brian Parks said, his face giving no indication of the hilarity of what had just occurred.

Tony said, without turning: 'Don't worry, lads. We will. But it won't be me in the car the next time.'

The crew laughed. 'What do you want us to do, now drill's finished a bit early?'

Tony thought for a second. 'Go over to the tower. Have a look to see what needs doing. Just make yourselves scarce. I've got to go and see Mac about something.'

Ian Blain stood on the doorstep of Ray Swift's neat semi-detached house. As he'd walked up the drive he'd noticed the manicured lawn and the colourful array of border plants. Parked at the side of the house was a small camper van. Ian was aware that Ray had talked about touring Europe in a van when he retired from the brigade. He thought to himself: *Seems like Ray's got this holiday well into the planning stage.* A couple of hours earlier he'd spoken to Ray on the phone, asking if he could come across and see him, as he had some news that would be of interest to both Ray and his wife.

Mary came to the door. 'Hello, Mr Blain. Come in. Ray's up to his neck in something in the back garden. I'll get him.'

As Ian walked through into the lounge, he noticed pictures on the wall, one showing Ray and Mary posing alongside Mac and his wife, Val. It had been taken a few years ago: Ray and Mac were in both uniform and were wearing their long service and good conduct medals. Ian assumed the picture had been taken at Brigade HQ when they were both presented with their medals.

He looked around, scanning the room; this was clearly a home that they had shared for years, happily getting on with their lives. On another wall was a black and white picture, a replica of the one in the foyer at Brigade HQ. Mac was in the picture. Ian couldn't make out who the other fireman was, since he was wearing a breathing apparatus set, so that his face was covered. The fireman's body was partly obscured by a dense cloud of steam pouring through his Lancer jacket. Ian had seen the picture many times: he'd realised that Mac was in the shot, but had never thought about who the other man was. He moved up closer to have a better look and noticed that Mac had just taken the body of a child from the anonymous fireman's hands. He could see the compassion in his face, and he noticed that below the picture there was a medal and a small brass plaque. He read the inscription.

This medal presented by the Royal Humane Society of Great Britain to Fireman Raymond Swift for his courage whilst engaged in the rescue of a child, and receiving injuries in the process.

Signed J.C. Smyth. Brigadier General (Retired) Chief Executive, Royal Humane Society.

Ian heard footsteps coming through to the living room. 'Good morning, sir,' Ray said, smiling broadly and offering his hand to Ian, as he crossed the room. 'How's the brigade managing without me?'

Ian felt comfortable here. He returned Ray's smile. 'I think they're just about surviving. I think the watch are giving Tony Ellis quite a baptism, from what Mac tells me.'

Ray smiled, knowingly. 'I bet they are. Do you fancy a cup of tea? Mary's just putting the kettle on.'

Ray was looking fit again, Ian thought.

'That would be lovely. No sugar for me, thanks'

They chatted easily for a few minutes until Mary came in with a tray of tea and a plate of digestive biscuits.

'I see you've got yourself a camper van then, Ray,' Ian said, smiling.

'Well you know us, sir. We've always said when I left the job we'd travel, and that's the transport,' Ray said, with a laugh.

'I'm sure you'll have a great time. You'll have to send us all a postcard ... and, Ray, you can drop the 'sir' . I've got your date for leaving. One month from today.'

Ray sat quietly for a few seconds: suddenly he could see the end of the life he'd loved for nearly thirty years. His feelings were a mixture of elation, given that they could get on with their life, but a sense of loss and sadness at the end of something that he had loved. He picked up his tea and sipped it in silence.

Ian broke the silence. 'Of course, I'll inform your watch. I'm sure they'll have something planned for you.'

Ray sat there, his mind in a confusion of emotions: all he could think of to say was 'Thank you.'

'Can I ask you something, Ray?' Ian asked.

'Sure you can, sir,' Ray replied.

'The picture on your wall with the medal. Is that you, in the BA set? I've seen the picture many times at HQ but know little about it. I've often wondered.'

Ray shuffled uncomfortably in his seat; Mary took hold of his hand.

'I haven't talked about that job for years,' he said. 'It happened way back, nineteen sixty-eight I guess, middle of January. We got the call at Rocko.'

Ian interrupted. 'Rocko? Wasn't that the old central station, Division Street?'

Ray nodded, still looking serious. 'Yeah, it was called Division Street, but it was also on the edge of Rockingham Street. Everybody called it Rocko.'

Ray paused again and took another sip of tea. 'Mac and me were on white watch. In those days, we did a different duty system. The tour had been manic, the weather was bad, the roads were icy. On the night of the fire we'd had snow during the night, so we'd had to set about putting snow chains on the machines, and we'd had three or four shouts in the night. We eventually got our heads down about half past one.' Ray paused. 'At four o'clock, the bells went down. We got a call to a person reported at Tansley Street, just at the back of the station. As we turned out of the doors we could smell the smoke.' Ray paused again, his face blank: seemingly in his mind he was back on the machine. 'I was wearing BA that night with a fireman called Dick Blackburn. Mac was the driver. Bill Worsley was the officer in charge; in fact it was his last tour of duty before he retired. As we turned into the street you could see flames shooting out of every window in the house. The street was full of thick smoke. Bill had us getting rigged and started up ready to go. Mac was on the pump. An old woman grabbed my arm and said to me that she thought the whole family – two adults and three children – were still in the house. Somebody had got a jet going into the ground floor window. In my mind, I thought that they were all 'goners' . I couldn't imagine anyone surviving. We were outside the house and the heat was only just bearable.' Ray stopped again.

Ian said: 'It's OK, Ray. You don't have to say any more, if it's a problem.'

Ray looked across at Ian, 'It's OK. I've not spoken much about it. Mac and me, we've never mentioned it for years.'

Ian suddenly felt awkward. 'Well only if you're sure.'

Ray resumed the story. 'Bill sent me and Dick in ... told us to get in the back door, hit the fire hard and get up the stairs quick sticks. Somebody had broken the kitchen door down – a neighbour I suppose, trying to do something. Anyway, we went in low. The heat was horrendous, everything seemed to be on fire and there wasn't too much smoke. We just kept low, hit the fire as hard as we could, but all the time we were trying to get to the stairs. I suppose this happened in about a minute, although at the time it seemed a lot longer.' Ray paused and took a sip of tea. 'We got to the stairs. The house was only small, a two up two down terrace type. I was in the lead with the branch. Dick was just behind me, watching my back and feeding the hose to me as we went further in. We started up the stairs and halfway up we found the body of the mother. We lifted her up. In her arms was a small boy. They were both badly burned. We dropped the hose, I gave the baby to Dick, and I dragged the mother out. We left them both with people outside the back door. Then we went back in.'

Mary took hold of Ray's hand. 'You all right love?' she asked.

Ray gathered himself again. 'I don't know how we did it: there was a lot going on. There was nobody there to relieve us, because everybody was busy, so we just went back and got on with it. We got up to the top of the stairs and found the father. He was lying across the landing and he had another baby in his arms. We took them down the stairs. At the bottom we met another BA crew coming in so we handed these two to that crew and went back in again. I suppose at this stage we'd been going about five or six minutes max.'

Ian looked at Ray, he tried to imagine what they were going through: he listened intently to Ray as he spoke.

'Dick and me had a quick chat and decided that we didn't have time to fight the fire, so we'd leave the hose with its spray going and we would just search as fast as we could. As we started there was a crash. The heat got worse, sparks flew everywhere. We both hit the floor: I could smell the rubber on my face mask. It seemed that it was starting to melt, and my gloves had got wet and the water in them was scalding my hands. The staircase behind us had collapsed. The heat was unbearable and we knew we had to get a move on and try another way out, maybe jump out of a window. We got down on our hands and knees and felt every place we could get to. Everything was on fire. The window of the bedroom smashed in front of us, so the heat reduced a bit … and then we heard a cry, a baby's cry.' Ray's eyes began to fill with tears. 'It was difficult to work out where it was coming from: the only thing standing in the room was a wardrobe – one of those old oak ones. We scrambled across to it. It was on fire, but we pulled the door open, and inside was a rough pile of blankets. Under the blankets was a baby. One of the parents must have shoved her in there to try to save her. We grabbed her and got over to the window, which had been smashed by the boys, who'd slammed a ladder through it when they realised the stairs had collapsed, to ventilate the room and give us a way out.' Ray paused again for several seconds. It was almost as though he was back in the fire with his partner. 'I climbed out with the baby under my arm. Mac was at the base of the ladder, and he took the baby from me. I looked back up the ladder expecting Dick to be behind me but he wasn't there. Then we heard a crash. The bedroom floor had collapsed.'

Suddenly, Ray looked bereft; he stumbled through the next sentence. 'Dick's body was found in the debris a few minutes later.'

Ian looked at Ray, stunned at what he'd heard. He'd never been to a job where a colleague had been killed, and he'd never rescued anyone. Ray had never talked about it before. He could see that Mary was getting upset also.

'I'm sorry, Ray. I didn't realise.'

Ray looked at Ian. 'It's all right, sir. It's been at the back of my mind for years. It's about time I got it off my chest. Maybe today was the perfect time and there's a happy ending. The little girl we saved is fine and she's working at brigade HQ. More importantly, Mac and I are her godfathers. She's a lovely girl.'

Mary interrupted. 'That's not all though, is it, Ray?' Ray smiled. Mary continued. 'If you think Ray looked hot in the picture, well that was because he was burned. When he got out he was in pain, so they took him to hospital. He'd got severe burns across his back and arms, so he didn't come out of it as safe as I would have wanted.'

Mary stopped for a second. 'We've been lucky. Ray survived. Poor Dick's wife was in a terrible state, but the brigade did lots for her. The funeral was a big event done by the brigade. She gets the pension and a food parcel every Christmas and she still comes to the socials at the station. She's doing OK now.' She paused, a faraway look in her eyes. 'The brigade and Dick's old mates haven't forgotten. They still visit, but it can't have made up for the loss of her husband.'

Ian was surprised and stunned by the story. He'd heard odd bits and pieces about the incident, but it had occurred so long ago, most of the people who'd been involved had either retired and moved away or were dead. Ian decided that he must visit Dick's wife soon.

He moved across the room and shook Ray's hand. He saw Ray in a new light: he saw him as Ray Swift, a hero, an individual, a man who'd be missed when he retired. Ian hugged Mary. He wasn't normally demonstrative, especially with the men he worked with or their wives.

'Thanks again for the chat and the tea. I'd better get away.'

Ian walked down the drive to his car. Turning to wave goodbye, he saw Ray and Mary standing at the front door of their house, hand in hand, looking very content with life and the prospects for their future.

On the short drive back to his office, Ian reflected on the past hour and began to appraise his own life, success, and career. Promotion and kudos had been his watchwords: now things were changing. He wondered how the troops viewed him. Did they respect him? It surprised him that he could ask himself these questions, as previously it wouldn't have occurred to him. It wouldn't have mattered to him one way or the other.

What would his legacy be? Would they talk in hushed tones about him, his exploits on the fire ground or would he be one of those who, after retirement, just evaporated into the ether and was forgotten. Secretly, he hoped that he would be remembered as a good Officer who looked after his men, a man who could be relied on at a fire to make the right decisions.

21

Jim McEvoy felt different to the demotivated know-nothing individual he'd been a few weeks earlier. He knew why. The chance meeting with Maddie in the pub in Edale had turned his life upside down. Before they'd met, he'd struggled to think of a single positive facet of his life: he hated his job, he had no interest in anything, he was convinced his recent foray into the world of the arsonist was brought about because he felt no sense of belonging, or of being of any value to anyone. Now, good fortune had landed on his doorstep: he cared about someone, he loved someone, and even though he hadn't told her, he was sure she must realise how he felt. Most of the time he'd spent in her company he was overpowered by a sense of wonder that this beautiful girl was choosing to spend part of her life with him. She was all he thought about or at least she was central to everything he did or planned. He thought it was a miracle. She'd unwittingly rescued him from his pit of uselessness and he was grateful. This wasn't an opportunity he was going to let go easily. He'd change. He'd be different to the scruffy waster she'd met just a few weeks earlier.

Maddie had just come on duty in the Northern General Hospital. Since the walk with Jim and the trauma of their temporary falling out and then the awful incident with Doris in Longshaw, she'd not been able to clear the events from her mind. She was confused about her friendship with Jim. She liked him very much and was sure he liked her, but she had some worry about it all, including Jim's nervousness in her company. Despite his support when she'd told him about the cancer she wasn't sure how, ultimately he'd feel about it. In her mind, she adored the weekends with him, the beauty of the landscape and the freedom she felt, and Jim's simple naivety gave her a warm glow when they walked together. She hoped it would last.

The cancer and the deforming cure had somehow changed her view of things. Before, she'd always had an outgoing, carefree personality, always at the centre of things, bouncing with optimism. Her plan was a path through life which included marriage and children, holidays abroad, and a man who would enhance her life.

When she'd told Jim about her cancer she'd been as honest as she could, opening up to him more than she'd expected she could. What she hadn't told him was that at the time of her diagnosis, she'd been engaged to be married to a man she had been with for a few years. They had been due to get married within a couple of months. Most of the arrangements had been made, the reception arranged and the wedding dress bought. When she'd told her fiancé, about the cancer and the remedial treatment being suggested by the surgeon, he'd found it difficult. Within a week he'd told her that he couldn't handle the stress of it and left without warning or apology.

Today Maddie had worked non-stop, looking after the children on her ward. She loved her work, but it was hard, especially when one of her children succumbed to the illness. What made it particularly difficult was that she often became attached to her young patients. At the end of her shift, as she donned her cloak, she decided to go and see how Doris was getting on.

Ernest sat by the bed. Lying there was his beloved Doris, asleep but looking comfortable. He'd been overwhelmed by the kindness the staff had shown both to him and his wife. Doris lay quietly: a drip had been placed in her hand, but she'd not recovered consciousness yet. Ernie was sure she would. He'd use every particle of his will power to bring her back to being as she was before. He'd spent hours just talking to her, discussing the children, telling her how their son had just bought a new car, how the grandchildren were asking about her and that as soon as she felt better they were all coming to visit her, and he reminisced about their weekly walks. All the time he caressed the back of her hand, hoping that she would hear him and open her eyes.

'Hello, Ernie.' The voice from behind him brought him out of his reverie. 'How's Doris doing?' Ernest turned. He could see a nurse, either coming on duty or just going off, he surmised. It occurred to him that he nurses wouldn't be wearing cloaks if they were on duty.

'How is she, Ernest?' Maddie enquired, her face tinged with a sympathetic smile.

Ernest peered at Maddie for a few seconds before a faint sign of recognition began to cross his face. 'I reckon I know thee from somewhere. Have a seen you somewhere recently?' he said, with a slightly confused look. Maddie smiled again. 'Ernest! How could you forget me. I couldn't forget you. Remember yesterday walking up the Gorge? You and Doris sat and talked to a young man and a gorgeous young girl.'

Ernest grinned. 'I knew I recognised you from somewhere. I didn't realise you were a nurse. It was you and another woman that helped us, when Doris fell over.'

Maddie walked over to Ernest and put her hand on his shoulder. 'That was me,' she said. 'You know what, Ernie? You and your wife are the most remarkable couple I've ever met,' she added. 'I think what you and Doris have and have had for all these years is true love. You've both been very lucky.'

Maddie took her hand from Ernie's shoulder and placed it on to his hand as it held Doris's. 'You know what, Ernie? I bet you a fiver that Doris will be fine, and you'll have her out walking in Derbyshire in no time at all.'

Ernest lifted his head and turned to look directly into her eyes. 'What's your name, love? I can't remember it.'

Maddie looked back at Ernie. She could see his eyes were swollen and that he seemed to have aged overnight. 'I'm called Maddie. My boyfriend ... do you remember him? Well, he's called Jim. We've been talking, and next year I think we're getting married. We would like you and Doris to come. Jim hasn't got any parents. They're dead. We thought that we would like you and Doris to be his parents for the day. What do you think of that?' she said.

'Eeh, lass, that'd be lovely. Doris'd be in her element. I'll talk to her about it. That'll give her something to look forward to when she wakes up.'

'Well, if you're coming to my wedding I'd better give you a kiss.' She leaned across and kissed his cheek. 'I've got to go now. Just going off duty. Got things to do, washing and ironing … you know, a woman's work and all that stuff.'

Ernest looked at Maddie; she could see a tear in his eye.

'It's kind of you to come to see us. Doris will be pleased you've been. I'll tell her tonight,' he said, a smile of gratitude creasing his face.

'Right, I'm off. Goodnight. I'll call round again,' she said as she moved away and walked out of the ward and towards the exit from the hospital.

22

Red Watch sat around the table on the mess deck. Taff and Mick Young tapped their spoons on the white Formica table top.

'Why are we waiting, oh why are we waiting?' they sang tunelessly as they sat sipping their mugs of tea. Taff's mug sported the red dragon emblem of Wales. Mick's had a fire fighter logo stating that Firemen had longer hoses.

Jock's head emerged over the kitchen counter. 'Ifn yi dinni shut it, am gunna stick yi mugs up yer jacksey and ya kin drink ye tea from the other end dya ken?'

It was Jock's day as mess manager: today it was cheese and onion rolls, and he was behind schedule. The ritual continued. It was a rare event for any mess manager to escape the wrath of the boys. Even Mac, who from time to time would do the job, would get stick, only more so.

Mac smiled. He knew that if the crew sat quietly and behaved sanely, he would have to begin worrying that maybe things weren't right. A loud cheer erupted as Jock walked slowly from the kitchen with two dinner plates piled high with rolls filled to bursting with cheese and raw onions.

This had long been the watch's staple diet. Occasionally someone would do something different, maybe bacon or sausage, but generally it was cheese with something, to keep them going until lunchtime.

The conversation around the table was boisterous; as usual the subjects of women, football or the inadequacies of the other watches were the main topics.

Each watch was a rumour mill, where discussions would take place on the sexuality of the leading fireman on another watch. Maybe he'd been seen emerging from a gay club with a bloke from green watch, for example. Ninety-nine per cent of it was conjecture and the rest was imagination. This all served to create the view on the watch that the reds were the best, the rest were puffs by comparison. The fact was of course that all of the watches held the same view.

They'd almost finished their food and were in the final stages of surgically dissecting the performance of Tony at the morning's drill session, when the alarm sounded. Chairs screeched as they were shoved back from the table, accompanied by comments from the watch as they made for the appliance room. In seconds the mess deck was deserted, mugs of tea left steaming, the remnants of cheese rolls still waiting to be consumed.

The appliance flew around the ring road, lights flashing and horns wailing. Lines of cars were stacking up, and moving to make way for the emergency vehicles. The appliance was following an ambulance and both vehicles' sirens wailed, trying to get to the incident as quickly as possible.

'Right, pull in over there,' Mac said, motioning to Mick with his hand to go left. 'Get all the rescue kit off, lay out a couple of jets … hose reels will do … and the tool kits.

OK, Tony. See to it.' The crew dismounted the appliance, Tony shouting orders to the crew and directing where he wanted the equipment to go.

Mac sat quietly on the machine, watching the men getting the equipment sorted out. He took a minute to get straight in his mind what should happen next. He'd heard on the radio that two other appliances had been mobilised along with another more senior officer. Mac was happy with the progress of the crew.

'*Control from Alpha Zero One Zero. Over.*'

'*Alpha Zero One Zero, go ahead. Over,*' came the response from control.

'*Control from Alpha Zero One Zero, informative message.*'

Dan Brogan had been sitting in his office, writing appraisals for two hours: he thought were a waste of time, but had to be done. His phone rang. 'Right I'm on my way,' he called down the telephone.

Ian Blain was on his way by car to a council meeting, when he heard Alpha Three book mobile to a multiple vehicle accident on the M1 motorway. His radio crackled.

'*Alpha One. For your information we have mobilised three appliances to the M1 motorway. A report of a multi vehicle incident. We have informed ADO Brogan and he is mobile.*'

'*Control from Alpha One. Message received. Will you give me the first message? Over.*' Ian slowed his car. The route to the council offices was taking him away from the incident. The message was slow coming. He pulled into a lay-by and waited nervously, his mind going back to the promise he had made to himself the other day.

Mac quickly surveyed the scene: the crew were operating with their usual efficiently. He knew the first message should be accurate, but that he needed to get in with the boys and do the nitty gritty work.

Dan Brogan swerved and braked through the rapidly backing-up traffic, sounding his siren and cursing. He was feeling the stress of the race to maybe save a life. At least he knew Mac was there and that it would probably be sorted when he got there.

'*Control from Alpha Zero One Zero. Informative message from Sub Officer James, at M1 motorway northbound carriageway, south of Junction thirty two: we have collisions involving six vehicles, five cars and one heavy goods vehicle involved, make pumps four rescue tenders two. Over.*'

Dan was almost stationary, jammed in a mass of traffic. Some vehicles had tried to progress and had blocked the hard shoulder, and he was about two miles from the incident. He picked up his radio.

'*Alpha Three. I'm stationary in traffic, unable to proceed at present. Inform all other vehicles best access from the bridge at junction thirty-two southbound. Over.*'

Control sent a blanket message to all mobiles attending that the northbound carriageway was out, and they should try via the southbound carriageway.

'*Control from Alpha One. I am at junction thirty-two. The incident is visible from the bridge. Suggest all mobiles rendezvous here and proceed on foot.*'

Ian put on his high visibility jacket over his fire gear, grabbed his hand radio and began descending to the empty lanes of the northbound carriageway.

'*DC calling Sub Officer James. Over.*'

Mac had left the appliance and was running around the periphery of the incident, trying to work out the priorities for when the support appliances arrived. His radio crackled. *Damned bloody radio,* he thought. *Just what I need. Someone wanting a chat in the middle of this little lot.*

'*Hello Sub, DO Blain. I'm on my way on foot. Be with you in a couple of minutes. Anything I need to know?*' Mac smiled.

'*Well, boss. It looks like we've got about ten casualties … most not too bad, a couple serious, a couple trapped in the cars and the driver of the lorry believed trapped and serious.*'

'*Do we have any ambulances in attendance?*' Ian asked

'*Yes, sir: two. We're getting it sorted but need help. The job covers a wide area. Over.*'

The road looked like a battlefield: several vehicles, travelling at high speed, had collided. One car was on its roof with its driver trapped inside, steam and smoke issuing from beneath the bonnet, another car had slewed into the crash barrier and had been hit by a container lorry. The car was demolished, the occupant not immediately visible.

The driver of the lorry was trapped, his ankle broken and jammed between the pedals of his lorry. A further car had slammed into the back of the lorry and disappeared beneath the rear of the truck. The two people in the car lay silently amid the crumpled remains of the BMW which was belching out smoke and looked close to catching fire. Further away, two vehicles – a small convertible and a white transit van, both braking hard to avoid the incident in front – had skidded before colliding with each other. The occupants, having suffered only minor injuries, sat on the grass bank of the motorway being treated for minor cuts by an ambulance technician.

Mac spent time assessing the incident and in his mind he had prioritised the tasks for the crew. He clicked on his personal radio. 'Tony, get over here a s a p. I need a word.'

Within seconds, Tony appeared.

'Well you've had a look. What do you think?' Mac said, looking into his eyes. 'Wwwell, Mmmmac,' Tony stammered. 'It's a mess. Reckon we need a cccrew on each. I've got the lads having a go at the lorry. Shouldn't be too bad. The car under the back looks grim, ttthough.'

Mac looked at Tony. 'You're doing well. Settle down a bit, nice and calm. Don't want to wind the troops up. The DC will be here in a minute. You carry on. I'll brief him then we'll get this mess sorted out.'

Mac heard the sirens wailing as they approached the bridge a few hundred yards north. He knew the officers in charge would all have their personal radios switched on when they got off the appliances. He thought: *I need to get hold of them before that.*

'*Control from Alpha Zero One Zero. Over.*'

'*Alpha Zero One Zero. Go ahead. Over.*'

'*Blanket message to all appliances attending this incident: on arrival contact incident commander by radio before committing.*'

Ian Blain was sweating. The run south in fire gear was further than he expected and he was feeling tired. *Still, only a hundred yards to go,* he thought.

He heard Mac's message crackle from his radio. *Good idea, Mac,* he said to himself.

Dan Brogan's persistence was beginning to take effect. Cars were shunting and making space: he was now making slow but positive progress, and after a couple of hundred yards he emerged from a knot of vehicles and accessed the hard shoulder. *Phew. Thank Christ for that. Let's get to it.*

He pushed hard on the accelerator and powered north, passing vehicles and their occupants, most looking as though the world had come to an end. Dan knew just how they felt. He'd suffered it many times himself.

Ian arrived at the incident breathing heavily and sweating freely. He sought out Mac, who was crawling beneath the back of the lorry.

Brian Parks saw him. 'The DC's here,' he called to Mac beneath the truck.

Mac's voice emerged. 'OK, Brian. Tell him I'll only be a sec.'

Ian looked on. Only Mac's feet were visible. He could hear faint groans coming from the car stuck beneath the lorry and small wisps of smoke – or was it steam? 'When you've got a minute sub, need a word,' Ian said.

'Be there in a sec, boss.' A few seconds later, Mac began to shuffle out and soon emerged, his jacket covered in a mixture of oil and dirt kicked up during the collision.

He stood up and patted his jacket, knocking off some of the residual grit. 'Hello, boss. Glad you made it. Have you managed to have a look?' Mac said, a grim look crossing his face.

'Let's walk a minute, Mac.' They walked away a few yards. 'I got the message to oncoming vehicles that you radioed, Mac. I reckon we need all the hydraulic cutting gear and some of the heavy duty rams from the rescue tenders, plus airbags. What do you reckon?'

Mac replied immediately. 'I agree. Shall I contact them or will you, sir?'

'No you do it, Mac. I want to have a wander round, see how the lads are coping.'

Dan Brogan pulled to a halt close to Graveton's appliance. He could see Mac fifty yards away, and hear Mac's message to the other appliances to the north on the bridge.

'Hiya, Mac. How's it going?' Dan asked.

Mac turned to see him. 'Glad you got here. The last I heard you were glued up in the traffic.' He laughed. 'We're honoured today. Both you and the DC here. Reckon I can sit on the motor and have a snooze.'

Dan smiled. 'From what I can see from here there won't be much rest for anybody today. It looks a pig of a job.'

'The DC's having a quick look,' Mac said. 'I've briefed him. The lads are fully engaged. We're waiting for the other crews to arrive and then we can really get stuck in. I'm not too hopeful about the two people in the car under the back of the truck. Looks very dodgy to me. We're having to wait for the heavy gear so the paramedics can get under. I've heard some noises, but they must be well smashed up.'

'OK, Mac. I'll search out the DC; let him know I'm here.'

Jock was examining the remains of a Vauxhall Astra. A hose reel had been laid out to cover the possibility of a fire starting. He'd looked into the mangled wreckage and located the broken body of a young man wearing what had been smart clothes. His skin colour was white. Probably *a rep,* Jock thought to himself as he tried to find a pulse, first in his wrist then in his neck. Sadly there was no glimmer of life: he could feel the man's body beginning to cool. Jock couldn't get close enough to him to do anything about it. *Help the ones that can be helped first.* That was a philosophy he had been taught early on in his career. *No point wasting valuable time and resources on casualties who won't gain any benefit from your actions.*

Captain Phil Greening, increased the revs to take off speed, adjusted the rotor pitch and the helicopter rose swiftly, turning sharply and headed south. For the crew of two this would be their second call of the day. The first had been to a motorcyclist who'd run off the road below Owler Bar in the Peaks, suffering serious back injuries. They'd lifted him and taken him to hospital, where the trauma team were waiting to whisk him away for urgent treatment to his injuries.

The emergency doctor was Ricardo Garcia, an experienced doctor who'd worked with the emergency team for the past two years. He'd come to England ten years before, having qualified in Argentina. He'd moved to England to give him and his family a better life. Today, rigged in a flying gear with a large grey helmet or bone dome as it's sometimes called, he felt exhilaration as adrenalin was poured through his body. After this, how could he ever re adjust to normal medicine? He wasn't sure, but he was determined to get the most out of this whilst it was there.

Heading south, they cleared the city centre and followed the distinct line of the M1 south. It was a clear day and in the distance they could see the incident. Phil Greening spoke into the intercom. 'Can you see it, Ricardo? Looks like a good one.'

'I want you to listen to me mate,' Mac said, looking directly into the face of the lorry driver. 'Your feet are well stuck. I'll let the paramedic in to give you some gas: it should help with the pain, but were going to have to do something to get the pedals off your feet.'

The driver, a large man from the West Country, grimaced at the thought of what was to come. 'You do what you've got to do. Don't worry about me.' Mac admired the man's courage: he knew it would be painful, but also knew that it was vital that the trapped limbs were released quickly.

'Right, Taff. You and Brian get me the hydraulic gear, blocks and wedges, quick as you can,' Mac said, calmly.

They ran to the appliance to get the gear Mac needed.

'Right, mate, you can get in now,' Mac said to the paramedic, who'd been waiting to enter the lorry to check the driver and administer the pain-killing gas.

Tony and Jock had teamed up to gather the heavy lifting gear when the crews from the supporting vehicles arrived. Jock looked across at the lorry and the car jammed beneath it, he could see signs of smoke. This was a major worry. 'Tony,' he shouted. 'Get over here and get a jet in under the truck. Looks like something's cooking up.'

Tony span away quickly. They'd heard signs of life in the car, but hadn't been able to get a response from anyone. All they knew was that there were at least two people in the car. Suddenly the intensity of the smoke increased. Mac spotted it. He could see that Tony and Jock were in the process of dealing with it.

'Get in there, Jock,' Tony urged.

'Tell Mick loads of pressure,' Jock said, his voice betraying his anxiety.

Mick stood by the pump bay. He saw the flurry of activity and the smoke pouring now from under the truck. He saw Tony standing, arm raised above his head, signalling furiously for more pressure. He slammed the hand throttle down: the pump screamed, a stream of water was shot down the hose reel. The gauge on the pump was registering forty bars of pressure. He knew that the second Jock released the water onto the fire there would be a massive reaction from the water being shot from the nozzle. Jock turned the nozzle to produce a massive highly-pressurised spray of water and the branch recoiled like a high-powered rifle. He crawled quickly beneath the truck, opening the spray onto the flames now erupting from the front of the car, the spray so highly pressurised it emerged from the nozzle like highly pressurised fog.

Jock hit the fire hard, then turned the water off for a second 'Come on, yi bugger,' he shouted as he soon became engulfed in a cloud of boiling steam and smoke. His exposed skin tingled; he buried his face into the filthy tarmac hoping to find some clean air. He struggled for breath and was coughing, but also trying to hear for signs of life from the car. He listened in vain. As the smoke and steam began clear, he could begin to make out the shape of the car. Good, *that's got the bastard,* he thought.

Jock crawled out backwards from beneath the truck, coughing violently.

'What do you think, Jock?' Mac asked.

'I dinno, Mac. It dinni look to healthy to me.'

Mac looked at Jock's face: it was red and sore. 'When we've done here, get yourself to the pump, Jock. Get an ambulance man to take a look at your face. It's looking a bit red.'

The supporting crews were beginning to arrive. Dan Brogan assumed some control and had begun dispersing the crews and their equipment around the incident.

Ian Blain motioned to Mac to join him. They walked across to where Dan was standing. 'Right, this is what we'll do. ADO, will you oversee the action on the lorry? We've got to get the back of the truck up to get to the car. We need that urgent. Mac, you deal with the lorry driver. I'll get the other crews working on the other jobs. OK, any questions? None? OK, let's get to it.'

Mac was impressed. The DC was on the ball, and that was good news. 'Right, Jock, Tony. Come here. This is what we're going to do.'

The paramedic leaned into the cab of the lorry from the driver's side. 'Excuse me, pal. Do you think you can give the driver a whiff of the gas by going in through the windscreen? We need access to him from both sides. Do you mind?'

The paramedic moved quickly out of their way.

'Right, Tony. We're going to get the big ram in there and see if we can push the pedals off his feet. I want you in here with me. We're going to jack and block, I don't want that springing back onto his feet.' Tony lifted various sized timber blocks into the cab. 'Jock, are you ready with the compressor?'

The compressor was petrol-driven, used to pressurise hydraulic oil, forcing the oil down thin tubes, which in turn was fed into various pieces of cutting and spreading equipment.

Mac manhandled the heavy steel ram into position, close to the feet of the driver. Close inspection confirmed to Mac that the driver had two broken ankles: both feet were tangled up among the pedals. *This could be a painful experience,* Mac thought as he foraged around in the foot well, trying to find suitable spots to locate each end of the ram. 'Pass me a couple of small blocks, Tony.' Tony passed across two blocks of wood about six inches square and about two inches thick. 'They'll do nicely,' Mac said has he manoeuvred the blocks into position. 'OK. Mate,' Mac said, looking up towards the paramedic. 'We're going to start.'

'OK, pal,' the paramedic replied, as he held the mask supplying the pain-relieving gas over the drivers face.

'They're about to start, pal. It will hurt but we'll be as quick as we can,' Mac said, giving the driver an encouraging look.

The ram was controlled by a small lever on the pipe, close to the ram. Mac could control both the amount and speed of movement of the ram. It was important that both he and Tony worked together.

'OK, Tony. Starting now.' Mac slowly opened the valve, letting the fluid pour at pressure into the ram: it opened slowly. Mac could hear the tone of the compressor change as he opened the valve and the jaws of the spreader began to absorb some of the strain, he saw the blocks of timber shift slightly, adjusting themselves to the surface that they were being crushed against. He could hear the groan of metal being stressed. Mac closed the valve, 'Right, Tony. Another block.'

Tony slid a block about twelve inches long between the bulkhead and the floor. 'Well done,' Mac said and gave a sigh of relief. 'I don't think it'll take too much. We just need enough to get his feet out,' Mac said.

'Get ready with the next block.' Mac opened the valve, the ram spread another inch, the metal groaned as the heavy metal jaws of the ram forced the metal to bend, against its will.

Mac could hear above the noise of the compressor a muffled groan from the driver as the weight was removed from his feet and the blood began to filter back into his feet. 'Is he OK, mate?' Mac called up to the paramedic.

'Yeah, just keep going. He'll be fine,' the paramedic replied. Mac opened the valve again, and once again the ram expanded, an irresistible force slowly winning the battle with the twisted metal.

'Stop there, Tony. One last block and I think we're there.' Mac could see that the ram had exposed a route through which the driver's legs could pass. Tony carefully placed the block to reinforce the others inserted previously.

'OK, we can get him out now,' Mac said. 'Over to you' he added, indicating to the paramedic that he was now in charge.

Within five minutes the driver had been removed, placed on a stretcher and placed in the helicopter to be assessed by the Doctor.

Dan Brogan had moved the manpower and equipment around the incident to ensure that each section was covered. Crews of firemen were huddled on or around each vehicle. Ambulance crews were heavily involved in bandaging casualties or putting splints onto damaged limbs.

Doctor Garcia had jogged easily around the incident and had given treatment to the more seriously injured casualties. His main concern now was the situation beneath the rear of the lorry. He'd been told that at least two people were wedged beneath the vehicle and he was aware that there had been a fire, which was now extinguished. He considered they must now be the priority. Ian Blain agreed.

Ian contacted Mac and all junior officers by radio, telling them to meet him by the rear of the lorry. In a few seconds, they were all assembled.

'Right, boys, we've got to get to the car, urgent. All resources here, now. Let me have your ideas. No time to waste.'

Dan spoke up. 'I think, boss, given the time factor we just got to go for it, get the heavy jacks from the rescue tenders under the back, as many as we have. We haven't time to wait for heavy lifting gear, I think. Wedge the front to stop it rolling, heavy jack at the back, and pack as we go. If we move Graveton's motor to the rear of the truck, we can get the winch and chains on to the rear of the car and drag it out. I think that's our best bet.'

Ian Blain nodded his approval. 'Has any one got a better idea?'

The Junior Officers nodded their agreement that Dan's idea was the best in the circumstances.

'Right, let's do it,' Ian said, a note of urgency in his voice.

Mick Young disconnected the pump and hose reels and manoeuvred the appliance to the rear of the lorry; he removed the heavy winch from the locker and began connecting it to the heavy towing eye attached to the front bumper of the appliance. Meanwhile, men swarmed around the lorry. The situation was looking desperate. Officers shouting orders to their crews, equipment being manhandled into position. In seconds, the jacks had been positioned onto heavy blocks of wood. The wheels at the front of the truck had been wedged. Men were positioned on the long jack handles, ready to begin. Other men stood by with large wooden blocks prepared to place them beneath the chassis of the lorry as it was lifted from the car. The doctor stood waiting anxiously.

Ian Blain gave the orders. 'Is everybody ready?' He quickly looked around and got positive responses from all of the crews. 'OK, let's lift both jacks together. Mac, get your man at the pump to just put a bit of tension onto the winch cable.'

Mac signalled across to Mick, indicating that he should pump the handle of the winch to take up the slack.

Jock had busied himself pulling the hose reels around and reconnecting them to the pump. With all of the crews now synchronised into a single unit, the rear of the truck began to slowly rise, men worked furiously packing up the space with massive pieces of wood, ensuring that, in the event of either jacks slipping, the blocks would prevent the lorry falling back onto the car. Ian signalled to Mick to increase the strain on the winch. With the amount of weight now being exerted, using the winch handle was hard work. 'Keep going, boys,' Ian said to the men operating the jacks. 'I think we're almost there.'

Mick pulled now with all of his strength. The cable groaned at the tension it was being asked to apply. The rear of the truck was rising slowly. Almost imperceptibly the car began to move, the weight of the lorry having been removed from the roof of the car, and under the powerful force being exerted by the winch, there began a squeal of metal on metal emerging from beneath the lorry. Mac was concerned. There was a real danger that the backwards movement of the car could dislodge the lorry from the jacks and blocks. He moved across to Ian, who was peering nervously under the truck, and expressed his concern. 'Thanks, Mac. I'd thought of that. Get the boys out from under, just in case, but I think we've got to keep at it. It's their only chance.'

'We've got stacks of blocks in there, boss. If it does slip, hopefully they'll prevent it falling back too far.'

'Let's hope so, Mac. We've no time to rethink. There's no Plan B,' Ian said, his face etched with concern.

Mick strained on the winch handle. He could see that he was winning. Half of the stricken car was now visible, twisted and blackened by the fire. Water sprays were directed into the car in an attempt to reduce the heat for the occupants. Mick realised the winch was becoming easier: he could now see the car moving more freely. Men were swarming around the car. Mac and the DC were heading towards the car. Jock had just stepped back with the hose and Brian was turning toward him when a loud crash and a rush of hot air hit him in the face, followed in a millisecond by a blast – a wind filled with grit – that instantly scoured his face. Mick instinctively turned away, and then, realising he was unhurt, he wheeled around. He could see that at least ten men had been blown over by the blast. He could see movement among them but his mind couldn't compute the scale of what had just happened.

Mac picked himself up and looked around him. He had no sensation of pain and he could see other men getting to their feet. The DC, close by, was rolling over and examining himself, unsure of what had just occurred. Then a further bang erupted from the rear of the car, a mushroom cloud of blue flame came and went in a second, the car was by now engulfed in flame.

Mac shouted: 'Let's get a jet into it, sharp as you like.' The crews, now recovered, reacted instantly.

'Just a second, lads,' Ian said. 'I reckon that was LPG. Get a jet on it but stay low and behind cover.'

Two high-pressure hose reels were soon hitting the fire and creating vast clouds of steam. *The worry is*, thought Mac; we *don't know if it will pop again.*

The crews continued to pour water over and into the car, by now just a blackened shell. Mac knelt alongside the DC. 'Seems cool to me, boss,' Mac said. 'If we keep water going on to it for a while longer, I'll go and have a peek. What do you reckon?'

'Yeah, we'll do that. I'll come with you. I can't see the people in there could have survived that little lot.'

'Keep the water on it, lads,' Mac shouted. 'We're going to have a quick look.'

Ian braced himself. This was what he wanted: action, back to the basics of the job. 'OK, Mac, let's do it.'

They moved in quickly, keeping low. The car, almost completely freed from beneath the rear of the lorry, was a charred wreck. The roof had been crushed, making viewing the inside of the car almost impossible. The innards had been burned to charcoal, everything within that confined space was the colour of coal: the rubber, plastic, carpets had been incinerated Mac realised that there was no possibility of anyone surviving, but it wasn't his job to assume that. There was a doctor on site whose task that would be, if they could locate and identify the remains.

'I think we can safely say that rescue isn't an option, Mac. The car seems safe now. Look in the back there.' Ian pointed out the twisted remnants of two large LPG cylinders. 'I'm sure they were the cause of the explosions, so we'll get the boys in, get it opened up, let the doc do his job and then we can look to finishing this off.'

Within the next hour, all of the casualties were released from the vehicles, the fire had been completely extinguished and none of the crews had been injured, with the exception of Jock, whose face had been scorched by the steam earlier, and Mick, who in the explosion had received minor abrasions to one side of his face.

Ian climbed the grassy bank, stepping carefully over the debris which at the time of the collisions had become detached from the vehicles. He sat for a while reflecting on what had just been achieved. His admiration for the boys was intact and he felt he was beginning to win his spurs. He watched as the heavy wrecking vehicle reversed down the carriageway. He could see the crews clearing up the equipment and replacing it on the fire appliances. Mac and Dan Brogan appeared to have got things in hand, and were getting men back to their machines and back to their stations. He felt a glow of satisfaction. *Well, Ian, I think you've done OK*, he said to himself with a smile.

The helicopter rose gently from the roadway. The pilot, Phil Greening, spoke through the intercom. 'Another dollar, another day, Ricardo.'

Doctor Ricardo Garcia smiled. 'You're right. What a job. Those poor guys. I've not seen anything that bad before, can't think of a worse way to meet you're maker.' He could smell the smoke on his flying gear and had black stains across his chest from leaning into the car to check the remains of the victims. He felt sad. 'Take me home, Phil. I need a drink of something strong.'

The helicopter turned and headed towards the city, leaving behind the men who'd been toiling for two hours and would be there for hours to come.

23

6th July 1996. Jake was out of bed early. He'd dressed in casual clothes, not the usual jeans and tee shirt. Today he was wearing dark blue slacks and a grey short-sleeved shirt, he'd had his hair cut short, and he was ready. It was seven o'clock and today he was starting his career in the fire brigade. He'd been told to report to the Brigade HQ at eight thirty, and there wasn't a chance he was going to be late.

Jake had just started driving lessons: his mum had told him that if he passed his test she would buy him a car, and so far he'd been on two lessons. Other people might have made it look easy, but he now knew differently. He was determined to master it, though; the thought of having his own car was a big motivation.

His mum had got up with him and made sure that his hair was combed and his shoes were polished. She'd reiterated her point. 'First impressions count, Jacob.'

Jake smiled and thought: *Yeah, mum, but I'm eighteen now.* Of course, there was no way he would say that to her. She'd been his life: she'd always been there for him when he got into scrapes. He understood the pride she had in him, and he'd never do anything to hurt or embarrass her.

'You're right, mum,' he said, dutifully. 'How do I look?'

'You look great, son. Start as you mean to go on and you'll go far. Take care.'

Jake threw his jacket across his shoulder, kissed his mother on her cheek, picked up his brand new briefcase and walked out of the door. 'See you soon, mum. I'll give you a call to let you know how it's going. Thanks for everything. Love you.'

Jake's mum stood by the kitchen window, her hands stretched tightly across her mouth and watched her son – her Jacob – walk down the road to the bus stop. Her eyes filled with tears of pride. She knew this was what he was destined to do, and she was so happy for him.

Mark Devonshire pulled his car into the dirt car park to the rear of Brigade Headquarters. He'd driven up from Kent. The journey had taken him over three hours. It was now eight o'clock and he was in plenty of time. He walked up the road close by the car park and found a telephone box, tapped out a number and listened to the ring tone on the line. 'Hello, love, I've arrived OK.'

Trisha Devonshire was used to her husband disappearing. She'd been married to him whilst he was in the navy, so being away for a few weeks whilst he trained to become a fireman wasn't a problem. Besides, they would get together at weekends, so she was relaxed about everything. Her phone rang: it was Mark reporting in, a phrase they commonly used when he reported back to his ship when in the services.

'Hiya, Mark. How was the journey?' She stood and listened as Mark described the trip. 'OK then, love. You take care, and give me a ring when you can. Josh sends his love. Love you. See you soon.'

Mark replaced the phone on its cradle, picked up his sports bag, locked his car and walked back to the car park and then into the rear of the Headquarters Fire Station. He felt strangely nervous. The duty crew were out in the yard in overalls, washing the appliances; he heard a lot of laughing and could see men firing water across the yard trying to soak their friends. It seemed that they had been to a large fire. Across the yard lay several lengths of hose covered in oil and dirt, Mark carefully stepping over it as he traversed the yard. He felt excited: shivers of anticipation made his hair stand on end. He was sure he was precisely where he should be.

'Are ya all right, love?' a gruff voice came from the side. Mark didn't understand.

'I said: are ya all right? You one at new recruits that's starting today?' Mark strained to understand this strange language; he thought he could make out bits but the meaning of some words eluded him.

Mark turned to see a huge fire-fighter. He wore boots and black leggings held up by broad elasticised straps over his shoulders and a sweat-stained dark blue tee-shirt. 'I'm sorry, I didn't catch that,' Mark said trying not to look too worried.

The man beamed and gave Mark a knowing look. 'All right, son. Sounds as if you're one of them from down south. Are you a Cockney?'

Mark's ear was beginning to become tuned in to the language now, and he partially understood what the man was saying. 'No, I'm not from London. I'm from Kent. Just driven up. I'm starting a recruit course today.'

The giant looked at Mark. 'Well good luck. You'll find it hard, but it will be worth it. This is a good job. You'll love it. Good luck.'

Mark grinned: he wasn't used to this open and friendly approach. In his experience, people were usually more reluctant to speak. It seemed different, here.

'Looks like you've had a busy night?' Mark said.

'No, it's been pretty quiet. We'll soon be taking in washing to keep us going. We've only had about three jobs. Mind ya, the last one was a big one. We had an eight pump factory fire. It's a car park now. Couldn't get at it quick enough. Still, it's all part at job: win some and lose some. Just the way it goes.'

Mark grinned. 'Well, I'd better get in. It's been nice meeting you.' Mark laughed to himself has he walked in through the rear doors, to the sound of laughter and the splashing of water.

Jake entered Headquarters through the main entrance at the front of the building. On the wall of the foyer, he noticed the familiar black and white picture that he'd studied on one of his previous visits. A notice on the wall indicated that recruits should dial three on the telephone located below the sign. Jake picked up the phone and dialled. A young female voice answered and told him to go to the third floor conference room where he would be met and given instructions.

He climbed the stairs easily, looking through the glazed panels at each floor, seeing people, mostly in civilian clothes, busy at their jobs. He reached the third floor, soon finding the conference room and entering. He was pleased to see that he wasn't the first to arrive; there were already four other young men, seated and chatting between themselves.

Jake sat alone, apart from the others. A minute later the door opened and a familiar face entered the room. 'Good morning. I'm Sub Officer Porter. When the rest arrive, we'll make a start.'

During the next twenty minutes, more recruits arrived. Jake looked up each time, expecting Mark to come in, but each time he was disappointed. At twenty-five minutes past eight, the door opened and Mark walked into the room. He looked around and spotted Jake. They smiled broadly at each other. Jake took Mark's hand and shook it enthusiastically; they were both pleased to be there and in each other's company again.

'I was beginning to think you'd chickened out,' Jake said.

Mark grinned. 'No, I've been here ages. I had a chat with the duty crew in the drill yard when I arrived. Then had to make a dive for the toilet. Got a touch of the Delhi belly. I took the missus out for a curry last night and today I'm paying the price.'

Jake smiled. 'Well, you're here now. It's good to see you again.'

The last two recruits entered the room. Sub Officer Porter stood up. 'Right, gents and lady. Welcome to the South Yorkshire Fire and Rescue Service. We're all here now, so let's get cracking.'

The Sub Officer got up from his seat. 'In front of you there's a file. Inside you'll find a timetable for today, a sheet containing useful phone numbers and a list of the clothing you will be issued with. Can I remind you that whilst on duty between 0900 hours and 1800 hours, no phone calls, other than emergencies, will be allowed. Any questions?' He paused for a moment. 'Today is your first day. From now you're being paid. Already you're accumulating a pension. Later, we'll be going over to stores to get you rigged out with clothing.' He paused and looked around the room. 'After lunch you'll be given a talk by the FBU ... that's the union. You'll get the chance to join and I recommend that you do so.' The Sub Officer paused again. 'The Chief Fire Officer has expressed a desire to meet you all and give you a few pearls of wisdom. Then the Brigade Training Officer will want to tell you what to expect over the next few weeks, then, just to finish off, you'll be left to the gentle mercies of your course instructors, who, despite what the training officer has told you, will tell you what is really going to happen.'

'Right boys,' Mac said. 'Let's talk about the arrangements for Ray's retirement bash. It's only a couple of weeks away, so we need to get cracking on the arrangements.'

The watch were gathered around the table on the mess deck. 'We've got invites out to all of his old buddies from the horse drawn days. Most of them are coming. Some sent their apologies.'

Brian interrupted. 'On account of them being dead.' The watch laughed; Brian always brought humour to even the most serious subject.

'Taff, you were getting the collection up from around the Brigade. How've we done so far?' Mac queried.

'Well, not all stations have their money in yet, but it's good up to now. Latest count is two hundred and eighteen pounds. Some stations aren't putting anything in, though: they're going to buy him something themselves.'

Mac said: 'Well done, Taff. Keep chasing them. We'll have to decide what this station's getting him with the money.'

Brian chipped in. 'The catering is on track. The wives are getting together. They'll do the food. The money the social club have donated should cover it.'

Mac said: 'Well it all seems on track. I've got his axe mounted and the social club is giving him a tankard. Jock, can you sort out flowers for Mary?'

Tony said: 'I've got the music arranged for the night. Gazza Glenville off Blue Watch will do his disco and we're getting a two piece group in. It's all within budget, so no problems.'

After thirty minutes of discussion, all the arrangements were made. They were going to give Ray the send-off he deserved and Mac was delighted.

They were expecting a big turnout and the Chief and the DC were coming. Mac had already decided what he would say when he made his speech. He was also aware that others would also want to say a few words. Ray was very well respected: he deserved these accolades from his colleagues. Mac knew it would be a good night.

Tony was out with the crew, organising the station work routine. Mac sat quietly in his office reflecting on his life in the job. His time was coming. There was no way to slow the process down. Soon it would be finished and there was nothing he could do to change it. He felt a wave of sadness cross him, remembering his early days when the job required a lot less from its men, before health and safety and the litigious society invaded the life of the fire fighter. He knew it was progress, it was inevitable, but he longed for the carefree days of his youth, days when other people had the worry of responsibility, when all he had to worry about was going to work, fighting fires and having a good time.

He remembered the old hands, most of them long gone. They'd taught him so much about fighting fires, attitude, love of the job and about manhood. Sadly, he felt this type of role model no longer existed. He remembered his wedding day with the love of his life, the mother of his girls, the one person he had never had doubts about: Val. She always spoke her mind to him, but always in a way that wouldn't upset or anger him. He remembered them walking from the church, with his colleagues forming a gauntlet, all in uniform, holding their arms aloft forming an arch with their axes. He remembered his father, whom he loved and still missed: the man who had inspired him to join the brigade.

He recalled and recited in his mind the poem his father gave him on the day he joined the fire brigade.

Here's to one who took his chances in a busy world of men
Battled luck and circumstances fought and fell and fought again.
Won sometimes but did no crowing, lost sometimes, but did not wail
Took his beating but kept going, never let his courage fail.
He was fallible and human, therefore loved and understood.
Both his fellow man and woman, whether good or not so good.
Kept his spirit undiminished, never let down a friend,
Played the game till it was finished, lived a fireman to the end.

Mac knew it by heart. His father had said to him that he felt the poem epitomized manhood and hoped it would inspire him when times got hard in his life.

Where did the poem come from, dad? Mac had asked.

His had father replied: *D'ya know, Malcolm? We were in Bakewell one afternoon. It were flooded real deep. The basement of the Rutland Arms were five foot under water, so we were called. I noticed the poem. It were carved into the stone by the side of the main entrance to the hotel. It struck me as a nice poem, so I wrote it down and I've always remembered the words. It just seemed to me that it were the right words for you when you followed me into the Brigade. I just changed one word at the end.*

Mac sat quietly. He clearly remembered his dad saying those words. He'd been getting on in years and wasn't a well man. Thirty-five years of fighting fires had left his lungs in a sorry state.

Mac's father's death hit Mac very hard. After the funeral, he, Val and his sister, had sorted through his father's effects. In a drawer he'd found a folder which had contained a record of his dad's life. There had been old school reports, forms from years earlier, when he had joined the fire brigade, and a dirty crumpled piece of old exercise book, heavily stained with grime and on it written, in pencil, the words to the poem. This was the one thing that Mac insisted he kept for himself and it was now kept wrapped in plastic, safely stored to be passed on to his girls.

Mac was brought sharply back to reality when the office phone rang. 'Hello, Mac, DC here, how's everything at Graveton?'

Mac took a second to orientate himself. 'We're fine, boss. What can I do for you?' He noticed a tear running down his cheek and pulled his arm across his face.

'Peter Jacks. Your new man. All the paper work's done. I've just spoken to the Station Commander and he'll be starting with you first day shift next month, so you'll have a full complement. I've had a word with him and he's keen to start.'

'Pleased to hear it, boss. Thank you. By the way, the arrangements for Ray's retirement do are sorted. Will you be bringing your wife to the function? It will be nice to see you both.'

Ian Blain was beginning to loosen up, and at last feel part of the brigade; he went to lots of functions, nearly all formal events, many involving councillors. Retirement evenings were the type of function he enjoyed these days. The more relaxed atmosphere suited his new attitude to things. Certainly his wife preferred the new model husband and had told him so.

'We'll be there, Mac. I've got my speech written and we're looking forward to the event.'

24

The wards at this time of the morning were busy, bustling places, nurses scuttling around, caring for their patients, doctors – along with ward sisters and students – in gaggles, hovering around patients' beds. Shafts of bright sunlight streamed through the old Victorian windows. The ward was very warm. Ernest had come again to visit Doris and he mopped his brow as the sunlight added to the temperature.

'How are ya feeling today, my old love?' Ernie said, looking straight into Doris's eyes. Doris had regained consciousness a few days earlier and, despite feeling a bit weak and having little feeling down her left side, she was happy to see the smile on her husband's face. She could imagine the trauma this must have caused him, tough as he was: when it came to things regarding her, the kids or grandkids, he was as soft as butter.

She found speaking difficult. Some words she just couldn't get her tongue around. Ernest sat patiently while she struggled to say a few words. She knew not to worry; he always had enough words for both of them.

Doris looked back at him. She grasped his hand and gave it a squeeze. 'I'm feeling great. Can't wait to get out,' she said. 'Looking forward to coming home.'

Doris spoke slowly and deliberately. 'Doctors told me it won't be long. I need a bit of time to get some strength; then I'll be home and you can make me cups of tea.'

Ernie laughed.

'You know, it's about time I did something for you. You've carried me about for years, so I'll make you all the tea you want, and be glad to do it, just so long as you're all right.'

Maddie walked into the ward. Ernest had his back to the doors, so he didn't see her approach.

'And what's all this then, holding Doris's hand and chatting her up? It's not allowed,' she said. Ernest, hearing Maddie's voice, immediately recognised it. He let go of Doris's hand, spun around and laughed at her. 'What are you doing here again? Ya were here yesterday. A bet you're after her money,' he said, a wicked grin crossing his wrinkled face. 'Yer wasting yer time. I've got it all. I've put it all in some offshore bank account, so when she gets herself right, we'll be going on a cruise on the yacht I'm going to buy.'

Maddie smiled broadly. In the past couple of weeks she'd been in to see Doris almost every day that she'd been on duty. Often when she got there, Ernest wasn't there, so she would sit by her bed, hold her hand and chat quietly to her. They talked mostly about her and Jim, how they met and the walks they had planned, about the wedding that she'd invited them too. There were no plans for marriage. She'd only known Jim a few weeks: it was ludicrous to think they could be married, she kept telling herself. But, in the recesses of her mind, she wondered what Jim would think if she broached the subject. She knew if he came to visit them that Ernie would be bound to mention it, and then she would be in a quandary: what to do? Maybe she should bite the bullet and talk to him about it.

Maddie sat with Ernie for about ten minutes, chatting about Doris's progress and how he was managing to do the cooking and ironing. Ernie's view seemed to be: 'If you don't do the washing, you don't have to worry about ironing it.' Maddie smiled at the logic Ernie applied to his situation. She hoped he was looking after himself.

She looked at Doris. The stroke had been quite mild and although there was some paralysis to her left side, there was little physical evidence of it in her face. Only when she spoke was there a noticeable lack of control in her voice.

'What has the doctor said, Ernie?' Maddie asked

Ernie sat stroking Doris's hand. He looked at Maddie and replied. 'He says she's doing well, and if she keeps it up she'll be out and home soon, so we're looking forward to it, aren't we love?' he said, turning once again to look at Doris.

Doris smiled, weakly. 'We're going to be there, you know, Maddie, at your wedding. When I'm out, we'll get Ernest a new suit and I'll have to have a hat.' She smiled again. 'Do you mind if I go back to sleep now? I'm feeling a bit tired.' At that, she closed her eyes and drifted off.

'Right, Ernest. I'll get off now. I'll have the sister chasing me, if I'm any later. I'll keep popping in to see her. You take care, and get some washing done. If Doris finds out you're not looking after yourself, she'll not be a happy bunny.'

'OK, love. It's nice to see you. You get off to work and I'll just sit here for a bit.' Ernest sat on the armchair by Doris's bed, opened up his copy of the Daily Mirror, took out his well-chewed biro and began doing the crossword. Maddie laughed to herself as she looked back at the couple. She could really imagine that they were Jim's mum and dad.

Janet arrived at the Ranger Station early. She made a cup of tea for herself and the other rangers and waited for the boss to enter.

As he walked through the door, Stan Gregg scowled at the group sitting in the small room in the station. He was not happy, having been up most of the night, along with several other rangers and the Mountain Rescue teams from Edale and Buxton. A party of three schoolboys had failed to return to the youth hostel. Initially, they were mobilised to carry out what was expected to be a short search of the Kinder Scout plateau, but after a couple of hours and with the light failing, extra teams of police, rangers and other neighbouring rescue teams were sent up to assist with the search. In addition, two rescue dogs were deployed, one at each end of the plateau. Darkness soon fell and the situation had become serious.

At four thirty in the morning, the boys were found safe and well. They'd lost their bearings, descending from the featureless moor on its northern edge. Realising that they were lost, they had made their way back towards the top, and just below the summit they had pulled on their survival bags and bedded down for the night. They were found, all soundly asleep by one of the dogs, who, having discovered them huddled beneath a large gritstone boulder, began barking furiously, guiding the search teams to the group. The boys were then led down and returned to the youth hostel, embarrassed but unhurt.

'Right, folks, I hope you're all fit for the day that lies ahead. The forecast is for some bad weather, heavy rain and strong winds coming in from the west.' Stan spoke with a mock seriousness in his voice.

'I suppose this is rubbish being sent over from Lancashire,' one of the part-time rangers said.

'You're right. It is going to be rubbish, so keep your eyes open. Bad weather often brings problems with it, so let's be prepared for it.' Janet shuffled on her seat. She liked Stan, but sometimes his briefings were a bit tedious. She wanted to get going. He spent ten minutes speaking about issues on their patch, and then nominated the patrols for the day.

'Janet, I want you to do the Chatsworth circuit today. Take this young chap with you. It's his second training patrol, so be gentle with him,' Stan said, pointing to a youthful-looking man, who sported long hair and a somewhat ragged beard. Janet leaned forward and gave the young man a cursory wave of the hand.

'OK, head 'em up and move 'em out,' Stan said. 'I'll be listening out on the radio. Call in every couple of hours. I'd like you all back here by four thirty at the latest. Have a good day.'

Janet climbed into her car, inviting the trainee to load his rucksack onto the back seat, as the boot was full of animal feed.

'Hi, I'm Janet,' she said in her normal, friendly tone. 'Where did you do your first patrol?'

The young man looked a bit nervous. 'Well, I did a day at Fairholmes ... you know, over by the dams. We did a patrol up to Alport Castles,' he said in an uncertain voice. 'My name's Harry.'

'Nice to meet you, Harry. For the Chatsworth patrol, I drive us there. We do a circular walk then we drive back to Brunts. It's about twelve or thirteen miles, so not too bad.' Janet had trained quite a few recruits to the Rangers; she knew they had a lot to cover. 'What subjects do you want to do today?'

There was a syllabus to be completed before the trainee took examinations. The training was tough and required dedication on the part of the student. Often it also required determination from the ranger as well. Some rangers preferred not to get too involved with this side of the service, but Janet enjoyed it. She liked the variety of people she met. She remembered the help she'd been given when she'd started a few years earlier.

Janet pulled the car up on the front of Chatsworth House. At this time of day there were only a few tourists around, the car park was only sparsely occupied and very few people were evident around the grounds. *I bet they've heard the weather forecast and decided to stay home, sensible people,* Janet thought, as she looked for a steward to inform him what they were about to do.

This Chatsworth estate patrol covered a wide range of issues: people lighting fires, dogs running around affecting the estate's livestock, people swimming in the river. They would also do a more wide-ranging patrol, like the one Janet and Harry were to do today.

They hoisted their rucksacks onto their backs. Harry had his map and compass to hand. Now kitted up, they set off walking quickly eastwards along the riverside path. Soon they were crossing fields filled with sheep, then passing quickly through the village of Beeley. As they walked, they talked. Harry told Janet that he had recently left Sheffield University and was in the process of trying to find a job.

They passed through the village and began a steady ascent along a rough track. 'OK. Let's stop here for a minute,' Janet said. 'This is Hell Bank plantation. Look at your map and tell me how far it is to the top of this hill and how long it's going to take us to get there … and while we're at it, work out what the bearing between our position and the point we're heading for is,' she said, quietly pointing out the position on the map where she expected them to emerge onto the summit. 'We'll sit for a minute, get our breath and have a drink, if you like.'

The day was cool and with a strong breeze blowing. Harry struggled to open the map and then align the compass and do the calculations he'd been asked to do. He got frustrated with the map as it flapped like a flag in the breeze.

'Take your time Harry. You don't need the entire map. Turn your back to the wind and fold it so just the part you need is showing.' Harry looked flustered. He, like most trainees, found navigation the most difficult subject to master. It seemed easy in the comfort of your own dining room, but out on the hill, with the wind and rain, having to demonstrate your ability to another person made it hard to do the most simple things. Janet understood. She'd suffered just the same way a few years earlier, but she had to let him struggle. It was all part of the learning process. Her boss, Stan, had said to her when she'd complained of the difficulties and pressures of navigation: *Learn it now, under pressure, because when you really need to be able to do it, you'll be under even more pressure, and then you won't be able to make a mistake without there being a price to pay.*

So Harry got his head down and focussed on the task he'd been given. After several minutes, he lifted his head out of the map and, with a slightly cautious look on his face, said: 'I think I've done it!'

'OK. Let's see what you've worked out. Show me.'

'I think from here to there,' he said, pointing at the map.

'Where?' Janet asked. 'The end of your finger isn't accurate enough to work out a position on a map,' she said. Bending down, she plucked the stem of a piece of grass. 'Here, use this as a pointer. You'll find it will help you to be more precise when you're working out grid references and bearings.' Harry took the grass and, with Janet supervising, he readjusted some of his figures.

'Right,' he said confidently. 'This is what I think. From here to the top is twelve hundred metres, one point two kilometres. I reckon it will take us twenty-five minutes.' He checked his watch. 'I think we'll be at the top by about twelve thirty.' Janet looked surprised. 'You know we're walking uphill. Have you taken Naismith's rule into account?'

He looked embarrassed. 'No. I've heard about it, but I don't know much about it.'

Janet gave him a sharp stare. 'Harry, when you knew you were going to have to learn navigation you should have read up a bit. Naismith is integral to calculating speed over the ground. You must read it and I'm not going to go into it all now in detail, but learn it or you'll find it hard, OK?'

'OK. I will, sorry,' he said, looking sheepish.

'When you want to calculate speed over the ground, Naismith says, walking at three mph, add one minute to your time for every ten metres rise in the land.'

'Right. So I need to work out how much height we gain on this section of the walk?' he asked, a note of desperation in his voice.

'Exactly right,' Janet replied.

Brian began looking at the contours on the map, and after some difficulty, said: 'I think over this twelve hundred metre leg we're going to gain one hundred and twenty seven metres. At one minute per ten metres, I must add twelve point seven minutes to the time.' Harry looked relieved and grateful that he'd been given the information in a way he found easy to assimilate. 'Thanks a lot. I can see I've got a lot to learn.' An admiring look of gratitude now spread across his bearded face.

'Well done! Now keep up the reading. There's a lot to remember ... and what's the new time of arrival at the top?'

'It's now twelve fifteen. We should get to the top at twelve fifty-three, unless I've calculated it wrong.'

'Right. Let's make tracks. We've still a way to go.'

They donned their rucksacks and headed steadily up the dirt track, Janet speaking to him about the importance of pacing when calculating time and distance. Harry listened intently.

Over the past few weeks, Maddie and Jim had become close. Though nothing physical had happened beyond an occasional peck on the cheek, it could wait. They were both happy to just carry on the way things were, neither of them wanting to change anything and spoil what they had. One thing had developed, though. Maddie had given Jim her phone number and for the past couple of weeks, they'd spoken on the phone several times a day. The talk was mainly about their walks and the plans for the next weekend that they could get together.

Jim was in love. He knew it for absolute certain. Maddie was the sole subject of his thoughts and he had a constant ache in his chest. He knew she liked him, but wasn't sure if she loved him, at least not like he loved her. He wanted to tell her exactly how he felt, but something inside kept stopping him, because he wasn't certain of Maddie's feelings. He worried that if he told her, he might embarrass himself and then she'd be embarrassed, so he didn't say the words, even though everything he did was a way of expressing his feelings.

The early pangs and craving for cigarettes had vanished. He was proud that he'd managed to kick the habit, but in his mind, it was Maddie who got the credit. She'd done something to his head that gave him the desire to stop and the will to do it.

He noticed that he was beginning to put on weight. The trousers he'd been wearing for the past couple of years were now uncomfortable around his waist. Maddie had noticed, and had expressed her approval of the new Jim.

Maddie looked forward to her chats with Jim. She thought she loved him: in fact she was sure she did, but felt restrained. The experience of her past was holding her back. It had been easy at first, when they hadn't known each other very well, so she had felt somehow more liberated, probably because at first she had thought it was a short-term relationship that it wouldn't last, but as she'd got to know him better and her feelings had developed and the prospect of something more substantial had become a possibility, the situation had become more serious and she'd felt it required a bit more care.

Her mind drifted back to the events of a few weeks ago when Jim had lost the plot, and how skeletons had emerged from the cupboard. There were still things yet to be discovered and, despite her feelings, she wouldn't make the final commitment until she was one hundred per cent sure of everything; experience had at least taught her that.

'I popped in to see Doris again the other day and Ernie was there,' Maddie said. 'She asked about you and we had a nice chat.' Then she remembered the conversation with them about the wedding, as yet unplanned. At some stage she was going to have to tell Jim what had happened.

'What are we doing this weekend, mad woman?' Jim said with a cheerful laugh down the phone.

'I don't know. You're the navigator, so you tell me,' Maddie replied.

'There's a nice-looking walk down from Miller's Dale. It looks nice. Not too far. I reckon about seven or eight miles. Are you up for it?'

'Of course I am … you lead, I follow – the woman's role you know,' she said, a light giggle emerging in her voice.

'How about I pick you up, say about nine o'clock?' he said, confidant that the usual arrangement would continue.

'At the bus station? Will that be all right?'

'It would be all right, but it would be better if you came to my house and picked me up there, don't you think?'

James was surprised. They'd never really spoken about the place she lived. 'Well OK, but I don't know your address, so tell me. I'd love to come and pick you up.'

'I live in Totley, just off the main Millhouses Road,' she said, with a smile in her voice. She gave Jim her address. He promised to pick her up at nine o'clock.

Jim turned off his mobile phone and smiled, everything was going so well, all he had to do was survive without her until tomorrow morning.

The ground was rising steeply now, as they entered Hell Bank plantation. The density of the pine wood meant their eyes having to adjust to the change of light. As they walked at a constant pace, Janet was talking to Harry about the rules relating to dogs being kept on leads and other laws which he would have to become familiar with.

'OK, Harry. Stop and show me where we are on the map.' Harry fumbled with the map, laid the compass across it, looked at the terrain and guessed where they were.

'Not good enough. You need to keep track on the map so you always know within a little, exactly where you are,' she said, mildly rebuking the trainee. 'Right, let's work it out. We knew where we were ten minutes ago, we know how fast we walk. What time is it now?' Harry looked at his watch.

'It's now twelve twenty-seven. We've been walking for twelve minutes,' he said, fumbling with the compass.

'OK. Let's sit down, relax now. From that information you should be able to calculate where we are pretty accurately. Have a go. No rush, but I am getting cold.'

They sat in the gloom of the plantation on a damp grassy bank until, after a few minutes; he'd got his head around the mathematics of the problem and came up with an answer. 'I think this is where we are,' he said, pointing with a small stick to a position on the map.

'Right, I want you to pace it to the top, and let's see how accurate you are. In mist or darkness this could be really important.'

Once again, they set off for the top of the hill, over very rough ground, Harry counting his double paces under his breath. Janet was also pacing; she did it as a matter of habit, as it helped to maintain her skill level but also enabled her to check if the trainee was being accurate.

Jake sat at home in his bedroom. He had a mound of homework to do. His instructor, Sub Officer Blackett, had been with them from the start, taking them slowly through the early phases of training, teaching them the practical points of operating a fire pump, lifting water from a dam or pumping from a hydrant. They had spent a lot of time running hose and re-rolling it, something that Jake felt he was becoming good at, but still not as good as his instructor, who could still run the legs off the whole squad, despite being in his late thirties.

They'd spent a lot of time on ladders, learning the methods of extending and pitching them into the windows of the drill tower. They'd learned how to climb and descend a ladder safely, sometimes carrying hose. They were being taught how to tie various knots, an important skill the Fireman needs to know.

Life was busy; they had classes of theory on subjects ranging from legislation to hydraulics and chemistry, building construction and firemanship. There was so much to learn. There was never much time in the evening to socialise with the other students. Both Jake and Mark found that it filled most of their waking hours. Even when let off on a Friday afternoon to go home for the weekend they had tasks to fulfil. Jake would come home. His mum would make his tea then he would go off to his bedroom to study and write, cramming information into his head. Jake loved his life in the training school. The work was never a chore, it was just something he had to do. He would learn and he would pass and he would become a fire fighter. Only death or serious injury could prevent it.

Mark had to make the three hour journey home to his family in Kent, and then he would have to do his homework, as well as adapting back to family life after a week away.

During Jake's short time at the training school he'd got to know the other recruits. They were a good crowd, but he viewed Mark as his particular friend. They had a great mutual understanding, forged during that first day they met at the initial interviews. Jake viewed Mark almost as an older brother. Mark had a great regard for Jake, too. He'd seen a side of him during the tests to join the service that he could easily admire, and realised that, had Jake not pushed him, he would probably have failed the tests. In the evenings they would sit in one or the other of their rooms and discuss the trials of the day, over a cup of coffee.

Because of Mark's greater experience, he seemed to have a better grasp of the technical side of the training. Hydraulics were difficult for Jake, so Mark would help him through it until he finally understood it.

Jake excelled in the practical subjects. He found he could do the hands-on things easily. Between them they were doing well and gave each other support. They had a comfortable and mutual arrangement of help, something which, thus far, none of the other students had achieved.

Some of the squad struggled with the workload and the physical demands that the course made on them, but despite most of them being older than Jake, they looked to Jake as the main force on the squad.

The course instructors had singled Jake out as the probable winner of the silver axe, the prize given to the top recruit of the year and highly sought after. It was often seen as an indicator of a recruit's potential. However, with Jake, they saw it differently. None of them saw him as a fast track officer candidate: they saw in him something special. They saw a young man who appeared to have a natural instinct for the job; the practical training came easily to him. They could see in him an absolute determination to achieve his goal. However, on the weekly assessment interviews, the instructors were always amazed that his only ambition was to be a fire fighter; he had no presumption that he was better than anyone else or that his life in the brigade would be anything beyond a man in the back of the fire engine.

It was Jake who mentored several of the squad who were finding things hard. He frequently laid into his fellow recruits, whom he thought were letting the squad down by not giving everything during practical sessions, therefore bringing on the wrath of the instructors. Often the instructors would stand back and watch Jake verbally working over someone who failed, then picking them up and driving him on again. The net result was that Jake was almost single-handedly dragging the squad forward to better performances. He was seen as a one off. Mac was right to say to them *Keep your eye on him, he's a good lad. I'd like him to do OK.*

Janet and Harry emerged from the plantation. Along the way they'd met a few walkers and spent a little time chatting, which had put them behind schedule. Janet checked her watch: it was ten minutes past one. 'How was your timing?' she asked.

Harry was breathing heavily and sweating freely. He checked his watch. 'By my reckoning, it's ten past one. We were due here at seven to the hour. Crikey, we're seventeen minutes late,' he said, sounding surprised.

'Don't worry about it. We're late because we stopped and spoke to people. Had we been on a schedule where we would have to be accurate with timings, we wouldn't have stopped,' Janet said, trying to lessen the disappointment Harry felt. 'How was the pacing?'

Harry's face lit up. 'Well, I think I did OK. Over the twelve hundred metre leg, I counted for each one hundred metres and, when we got to here, I was on twelve hundred and seventy-five, so only seventy-five metres out.'

'Not too bad,' Janet replied. 'Why were you over, do you think?'

He scratched his head and creased his brow. 'I'm not sure. It's the first time I've done pacing on a rough track going uphill. Do you think that will have affected it?'

Janet smiled at him. 'Don't get stressed about it. When you walk uphill your pace stride is shorter … therefore more paces per one hundred metres, so you were bound to be out. You just need to practice and learn your pace over different ground, and then you'll be more precise with timing and distance.'

She began walking purposefully out of the plantation, with Harry walking along behind her. They emerged from the dense woodland onto a dry stony track which they quickly crossed. Then they climbed a high stone stile leading them onto open grassland high above Chatsworth Park. Taking a path alongside woods, after twenty minutes they walked onto another summit. Before them was open moorland, the heather just beginning to turn purple. The track slanted off to the left. Janet stopped. Across to their right was a grass covered mound.

'This is Hob Hurst's House,' she said. 'It's an ancient monument. It may just look like a pile of old dirt, but it's more important than that,' Janet said. 'Right, next test,' she said, smiling broadly, giving him a grid reference to another point on the map, then telling him to work out the route and take her there. Harry laid out his map on the rough heather, placed his compass on the heavily creased surface, found the grid reference, aligned the compass between the two points and soon calculated the bearing he needed. Looking very pleased with himself, he said: 'We turn right, walk for four hundred and fifty metres. It should take about six minutes.'

'OK, then. Lead on,' Janet said, impressed by his certainty and confidence.

The wide track formed an ancient route across the moor formerly used by traders with their mules in the sixteenth and seventeenth centuries, but now mainly used by farm vehicles and deeply rutted and dirty.

Walking on a bearing requires a sense of purpose, a need to walk exactly straight, frequently checking the compass to ensure accuracy. Janet walked comfortably along the edge of the path, carefully avoiding the rough boggy section. Harry, however, walked the track, unable to avoid the water and mud. Soon the lower half of his legs were encrusted in the sticky brown glue, and he was sweating heavily. After a few minutes a vertical stone post appeared amid the bracken.

'I think we're here,' he said, a triumphant note in his voice.

'Spot on, Harry. Well done. Do you know what this is?' she said, placing her hand on top of the post.

'Not really. It looks like some old signpost.'

'Exactly right. It's a Guide Stoop. They were placed at crossroads or junctions in the early seventeen hundreds, to help travellers find their way across tough terrain. There are a lot of them in Derbyshire.'

Harry looked fascinated. 'How come you know about them?' he said, his features displaying a thirst for knowledge.

'Well, as part of your training,' she explained 'you walk with people who know about history and plants and fungi and lots of stuff, so you pick things up. I learned about the stoops from a trainee who knew quite a bit about them. I found it interesting and we had a good day, although he struggled on the navigation as well, so you're not on your own.'

Mac braked heavily. The huge truck laden with tons of broken stone filled the road ahead, and it was not about to give way. Mac managed to pull the car into a field entrance a few yards ahead, before the lorry then thundered past, throwing up clouds of grey dust.

'Why is it that every truck in the area comes out on the road the minute we hit the minor roads?' Mac said, with a hint of irritation in his voice.

Val sat patiently at his side, smiled. 'Perhaps they knew you were coming. They missed you the last time, so they thought they'd have another go,' she said with a chuckle.

'I reckon you're right. Anyway, we're nearly there now.'

They rounded a bend and the view in front of them opened up. They loved the ruggedness of the Dark Peak, but the green, gentler prettiness of the southern dales also had a special place in their heart. Below and to their right sat the two most spectacular hills in the Peak District. Chrome and Parkhouse Hills; remnants of a long-lost limestone reef, often referred to as the Dragon's Back, each hill having a spiny ridge sitting like two huge Cornish Pasties in the centre of a lush green valley.

This had been a favourite area of Mac's and Val's for years. They'd walked extensively across this part of the peaks many times. Chrome Hill had always had a concessionary path across its ridge, but Parkhouse had been off limits to walkers for many years, unless there was a determination to trespass. Mac and Val would have loved to have walked its ridge, but neither was keen on falling foul of the farmer.

Mac negotiated the steep, winding road flanked by sheer, craggy cliffs and through the hamlet of Glutton Bridge, where the vast mass of the hills tower above the road. He guided the car slowly into the village of Hollinsclough and pulled the car into the side of the road, close to a row of neat stone cottages. Close by was a minute chapel and a village hall. It was quiet and peaceful with no sign of any of the locals. It was very still: a perfect day for a walk.

They started uphill and soon entered fields through a sprung gate. The path meandered along the side of a shallow valley, through which, at its bottom, a stream flowed amongst hawthorn trees and wild garlic. On the other side of the valley sat their target for later in the day. They passed a stone barn and walked carefully amongst the sheep. After a steady thirty-minute stroll, they arrived comfortably at the end of the first stage of the walk.

'Let's stop here for a breather, Mac,' Val said.

'OK, love. It's a good spot for a rest. It gets a bit steeper over the stream.'

This is a common place for walkers to take a break, with its serene location: a lovely shallow stream and an old packhorse bridge set among the hills, one of those special places at the junction of ancient packhorse routes and the confluence of streams.

They sat quietly, taking in the views. All around, the land climbed steeply. Only the route they had just walked offered relief to the walker.

'Can you imagine what it must have been like all those years ago, to find yourself in a place like this? It must have been a lonely old existence, just you and your horse,' Mac said.

'You know, we're lucky to have this on our doorstep. There must be people who've never been to a place like this. I just thank God we can get here so easily.'

Val looked at him. 'Since when have you taken up religion, then?' she retorted.

'It might sound corny or daft, but when I get out here sometimes, it does feel religious. You know me well enough. I'm not into that sort of thing, but to me this is almost like what I think some people get from going to church.'

'Are you all right, Mac?' This wasn't like Mac, hearing him talking in such sensitive ways. She'd noticed a few times recently that there'd been some subtle changes in his attitude. She thought he'd mellowed; he'd always been the rock of the family, someone they'd always relied on to keep cool when everything seemed tough.

During the early days of their marriage, times had been hard, the children had come along and she and Mac struggled for money. It was Mac who solved the problem; doing two extra jobs, sometimes working twenty hours a day without comment or complaint. When the children were older she'd got a job, allowing Mac to ease off a bit, but he'd been restless, and had set about building his own house. It had taken fourteen months of working every hour available to them, Val mixing all the cement and passing him up the tiles to finish the roof, mixing the plaster for him and doing most of the decorating while Mac had been at work.

'No, I'm not all right really,' Mac said. 'With Ray retiring soon, it's got me thinking about me, you, the job and what we've got coming. I don't think I'm going to find it easy, you know. The job's been a big part of our life.'

Val looked at him. 'You shouldn't worry, Mac. Everything ends sometime. It'll be another page in our book. It'll maybe give us a bit more time for things like this, or time with the girls. They're always complaining that they don't see enough of us. You've given thirty years of your life to the brigade, we've made good friends and had some fun, but your job's given me a lot of worry. I've always dreaded someone knocking on the door and telling me you were hurt or worse. Much as I've love you doing your job, I'll be a bit relieved when it's over.'

'Yeah, you're right as usual, I suppose. I'll be OK. It's just this thing with Ray: that's all. I'll miss him … and the boys.'

'You're joking! You won't be allowed to miss them. I reckon they'll be round at our house with the engine, tapping us up for tea and biscuits every week, and I reckon the hydrant in our street will be the best maintained hydrant in Sheffield.'

Mac sat quietly, staring up at Chrome hill. 'This should be a good walk, and, oh, while I remember, I was chatting to the training school instructors the other day. They tell me that Jake is the star man, best they've seen, probably set for the silver axe. That makes me really proud, the fact that we played a small part in him coming into the job.'

The breeze had died; the day was perfect, sunshine with just the sounds of sparrows squabbling in a nearby tree.

'Look there, Val!' Mac exclaimed, pointing back down the valley. They could see, a hundred yards away, a Heron flying slowly, ten feet above the stream. Fifty yards away, it landed and settled at the edge of the stream and stood motionless, waiting for an unsuspecting fish to swim by.

'Shall we make a move then?' Mac said, sounding almost reluctant to move from this delightful place. 'It's so nice that if we have a steady plod we can maybe have our lunch up on the summit,' he said, looking up at the top of the hill, with its spiked ridge topping a bright green flank. The sun shone and the occasional cloud cast its dark shadows on the lush bright hillside.

They got up reluctantly, having sat for twenty minutes; the location had simply taken them away to unseen places in their minds.

They were met immediately by a deeply rutted, steeply rising track, heavily eroded through hundreds of years of use by traders with their teams of ponies and donkeys. In more recent years, farmers had used the track to move stock and feed across the valley, initially with horses, but nowadays only tractors would cope with the depth of the gouged out track.

They moved slowly up the track, which was framed on each side by hawthorn bushes and high dry stone walls, built in the seventeenth century from local limestone, a material ready to hand and available in vast quantities. Both Mac and Val removed a layer of clothing, but were still sweating profusely when they reached the top of the track.

'Let's just stop here for a breather, shall we?' Mac said, between gasps. The hill had proved tough and in today's heat they both needed a rest.

They kept the rucksack on but leaned against a low wall.

An old black and white sheepdog bounded across the garden of a nearby farmhouse. It stopped short, letting out a low bark, wagged its tail and looked up at Val.

'Seems the dog's taken a fancy to you,' Mac said with a smile. 'I often wished that we'd had a dog, but we always seemed to have our hands full with other things. Maybe when I retire we'll get one.'

Val looked at Mac, it wasn't often he expressed regret, she thought.

They were about to walk on when a shabbily dressed old lady came out of the farmhouse door, into the garden. She saw Mac, Val and the dog and called across. 'He's not troubling you any, is he?' They looked at her and smiled; although she looked unkempt she had a soft warm smile.

'No, he just came across to investigate us, I think,' Val said. 'We just stopped here for a breather. It's a steep old track.'

The old lady hobbled across to them with some difficulty and mildly scolded the dog. 'He's a menace. Nearly everybody who walks up this track has to stop for a breather,' she explained. 'Old Trip here, he's used to it. One time someone gave him a piece of cake. Ever since, he's seen walkers as an alternative food supply.' She smiled. 'Come Saturday and Sunday nights, he's no appetite for his own food. You're a monkey, aren't you Trip?' The dog looked lovingly up at the old lady and leaned his body against her. She put her hand down and ruffled his ears. 'He's an old softy. You'd never think that he used to be a champion. He's been on 'One Man and His Dog' about ten times.'

Mac smiled. 'Doesn't he work now, then?' he asked, leaning over the wall and stroking the dog's head.

'No. When my husband died last year, I got rid of the sheep and quite a bit of the land. I couldn't manage it. So no, he's retired. We just take it easy, now, don't we, Trip? He doesn't work. He's just my pal … my only friend, in fact. If it weren't for him, I'd have nobody,' she said, a sad look crossing her wrinkled face.

'I'd had Bill, well we'd been married for fifty-one years and neither of us thought about it ending. We were always too busy with the sheep and the land. Before we knew it he'd gone. Now it's just me and Trip.'

Val could feel herself getting emotional. Mac began thinking about their life. Gone before we knew it: that's what she'd said.

'I don't suppose you fancy a cuppa, do you?' the old lady said.

Val chirped up before Mac could say anything. 'Course we would. That would be lovely.'

They sat on white plastic chairs in the garden. The lawn was bordered by roses of every colour and a sun dial stood in the middle of the grassy lawn. Mac wondered how long the shadows had been going around the dial. He noticed that the grass needed cutting.

'Do you do the garden yourself?' Mac asked.

'I used to. Now I just dabble a bit. My legs won't let me do too much.'

'If you like, while I'm here, if you've got a lawn mower, I'll cut the grass for you,' Mac said, almost immediately wondering what he was doing. They'd come out for a walk, the next thing he was gardening. He smiled to himself. *There are worse things to do than this, in a place like this,* he thought to himself.

Half an hour later, they were back on their way, the sun still hot and Mac sweating, after cutting the old lady's grass.

'Goodbye then … and thank you,' the old lady said, as Mac and Val set off along the well-worn track which would eventually take them to the base of the hill.

'You're welcome. It's been a pleasure. We'll pop in for tea the next time we're coming by,' Val replied, giving a flamboyant wave.

Janet and Harry were walking hard. Janet noticed a bank of cloud was appearing on the western horizon. Since their stop for lunch they'd made good progress. Brian was getting the hang of the pacing and becoming more confident with his compass. They headed north along a track across open moorland then

'Just for information, this is the stream that feeds the lakes at Chatsworth. We cut off left here. The path's not shown on the map, so don't worry about it,' Janet explained.

They descended steeply into a grassy gorge, the slope littered with boulders lying at crazy angles. A stream powered down the gorge, fed from the moor a hundred feet above.

'Take care here, Harry. Some of the rocks are pretty slimy.'

No sooner had she spoken when she heard a crash behind her, accompanied by a muffled yelp. She looked around, her heart pounding. Harry had slipped on a rock and lay laughing as he tried to get up, the weight of his rucksack stranding him like a turtle on its back.

Janet laughed. 'I told you to be careful,' she rebuked him, between giggles. She leaned forward. 'Here give me your hand. I'll pull you up.'

'Sorry about that,' he said, looking a bit embarrassed.

'No problem. Are you OK?'

'Yes, I'm fine,' he replied.

'OK. Let's get moving again.'

Harry began walking, feeling sore but not wanting to appear a wimp in front of a woman. They walked on, into the bottom of the gorge alongside the stream, slowly ascending the other side. Janet noticed that he was limping heavily. 'Are you all right?' she asked.

'Well, I thought I was, but I think my ankle's swollen. It's pretty painful. How far have we got to go?' he replied.

'About three miles. The terrain's pretty easy. Do you think you'll manage?' Janet asked, realising it was going to be difficult for him. 'Sit down, Harry. Take your boot off and let me have a look.'

Harry sat on the grass bank and, after a painful struggle; he managed to remove his boot. Janet gently examined his ankle.

'Can you move it at all?' she asked, feeling a little worried. He winced, but the ankle moved.

'Well, I'm no nurse but it seems it's not broken. If I strap it up tight and get you a stick, do you think you'll manage?'

Harry grinned as she removed a bandage from her first aid kit, and wound it around his swollen ankle.

'Here take this,' she said, passing him a painkilling tablet. 'I'll find a stick for you to walk with.'

In her rucksack Janet carried a Swiss Army knife, as yet unused. She selected a likely looking bough from a tree close to the edge of the stream and after a short, violent struggle the branch came away.

'Let's just measure this so you can use it as a crutch,' she said, smiling broadly. A few minutes later, the crutch was made and tested. It seemed to fit perfectly.

The rain began to fall, slowly at first, giving them time to put on their waterproof coats. Within minutes it became a deluge. Harry was managing well with the crutch and they were making good progress, albeit the rain managed to find its way inside their waterproofs.

'Are you OK,? We've about a mile to go?' she said as they descended through dense woodland towards Chatsworth.

'I'll be fine,' he said, through gritted teeth. 'The crutch is a godsend.'

The track became steeper. Harry was slipping and finding it tough. 'Can I take my rucksack off and leave it here, pick it up later?' He said.

'Yeah … Take it off if you think it will help.'

He slid the rucksack from his back and seemed more comfortable. 'That's better,' he said. 'I should be OK, now.'

Mac and Val had reached the base of Chrome Hill. They climbed a wooden stile and headed easily over lush grass sprinkled with limestone rocks. 'This is beautiful,' Mac exclaimed.

In front of them, the hill rose steeply. The track they were taking would lead them onto a steep, rocky ridge. It was a walk they'd done before and they understood the precarious nature of the ridge. Behind them, the rain clouds banked up. Mac was first to notice the change in the temperature. Quite suddenly the sunlight had gone and the sky became heavy with low cloud.

'Seems to me we don't want to get caught aloft, love, if that lot decides to deposit its contents on us. Shall we go back and go around the side?'

Val looked up at the clouds. 'Ten minutes ago it was as clear as a bell. Yeah, I agree. Don't want to be on top and get wet through.'

Reluctantly, they reversed their tracks and made their way around the side of the hill. Within a few minutes the rain began to fall and they were glad they'd made the sensible decision. They cut across a field, making their way back into the village.

'Tell you what, love. Weather permitting, let's do this walk again next week. I just love it up on the top.'

They got back into the car and set off back to Sheffield. The rain now heavy. Mac was happy that they'd got off the hill safe and reasonably dry.

During the drive back home Mac couldn't get the old lady out of his mind. He determined that they would go and visit again soon.

'Right, Harry. You go down ahead of me at your pace. I'll follow you,' Janet said.

He set off slowly down the track, his face indicating the pain he felt. Janet picked up his rucksack and threw it over her shoulder, the weight – now of two rucksacks – made walking more difficult. After a few minutes they emerged from the woods close by the Hunting Tower, a prominent landmark on the hillside overlooking the Chatsworth estate.

'Right, you wait here Harry. I'll leave the sacks here. I'll get the car and I'll be back in a few minutes,' she said as she jogged briskly down the steep track towards the car.

Fifteen minutes later, she drew her car into the space by the tower. Harry had heard her coming and was standing up, ready to go.

'Right, let's get you back to Brunt's,' she laughed. 'I don't know what Stan will have to say about this, but you can bet your cotton socks that he'll say something.'

25

Jim was wearing new boots and had a new rucksack slung across his slim shoulder. Maddie was impressed. 'Looks like we're going to be doing this a lot more, then,' Maddie said, beaming at him as he opened the door of his car to let her climb aboard.

'You may scoff, young lady,' Jim replied, lightly. 'I may change the car next week,' he laughed, his face betraying the delight he felt at being with her again.

'What's brought on this sudden rush of blood to your wallet then, Jimbo?' Maddie said, leaning across the car and patting the wallet which he had stuffed into the back pocket of his trousers.

'And just who do you think you're calling 'Jimbo', then? You should refer to me, in my new jacket as 'mister', or 'sir'. Yeah that's it: call me 'Sir Jim',' he said, attempting to look smug.

'I'll give you 'sir' - Get driving before I give you a clip round the ear. Take me away from all of this urban thing. Take me to the country they call 'The Peaks',' Maddie said, in her best royal voice.

'Right, milady. Where would one like to be taken? The car is primed and I, your chauffer, await your ladyship's pleasure?'

'Just drive, you daft bat,' Maddie giggled. 'Take me to another place, a place of beauty,' she said, mimicking the voice of old Ernie.

As always, the road was busy. Jim drove out of town and cut across country, leaving the busy main roads behind.

'Just look at that beautiful church,' Maddie exclaimed. 'We must come and have a good look at that sometime.'

'Tideswell's church, known as the 'Cathedral of the Peak', is at the heart of the village,' Jim responded, showing off his newfound but rapidly developing knowledge of the area.

'Pull up, Jim. I'd like to get a photo of it.'

Jim pulled into the side of the road, close to the village shops. While Maddie was away taking pictures, Jim went into the Baker's shop. In its window were displayed a vast array of cakes. After a little thought, he bought his own favourites cakes – two jam doughnuts and two custard slices – sure that they would enjoy them.

He got back to the car. Maddie was already back. 'Where've you been then? Off seeing some other woman, I suppose,' she jested.

Jim looked at her. 'I've been spending a small portion of my vast fortune on a special treat for you. Would you like to see?'

'Of course I would. They smell great.' They both laughed. Jim opened the cardboard box containing the cakes.

'Oh, yummy. Have I got to wait or can I have some now, Sir Jim?' Maddie said, fluttering her eyes wildly at him.

'You can have one now and one later. See how I look after my girls,' he said, grinning. 'Nothing is too much for the girl I love.'

Maddie grinned at him. 'Do you love me or is it just talk?' she said, flashing her eyes again.

Jim sat back in his seat. 'Saying things when we're messing about is easy, but if I try to get serious, then I get so I don't know how to say things. I think you're gorgeous. You're in my head all the time,' Jim said, lowering his head and looking at his feet, embarrassed by his own honesty. 'You're the best thing that's happened to me, Mad. I'm lucky.'

Maddie took his hand. 'I see you've started growing your nails,' she said, trying to lighten the conversation.

'We don't come out here every weekend to get too serious. Let's enjoy it. I feel just the same, so get driving. Take me to wherever we're supposed to be going,' she said, with a laugh in her voice.

'Well I will, once you've finished eating your custard slice. Get your seatbelt on and hang on,' Jim said, the serious side of him evaporating.

They looked at each other and laughed. Maddie looked into Jim's eyes and saw a troubled young man, despite the smile trying to cover it. Jim looked at Maddie and felt waves of emotion flowing through his body and into his heart. He just shook his head and smiled.

Jim parked the car at Miller's Dale station, now defunct and used as a briefing centre for the rangers, and a common place for walkers who wanted to explore this area to park their cars.

They walked east along the tarmac road which flanked the river as it carved its way down the dale. The water flowed swiftly, creating eddies beneath the limbs of trees that hung low over the river. Some sections, moving slowly, created a glass-like surface reflecting the sky and the clouds as they hung motionless above them. The shallows just covered the weed beds giving the water a green hue. Occasionally, a trout would strike and take an insect from the surface, leaving a circle of waves travelling rapidly towards the river bank. They stopped occasionally and watched as the fish lay almost motionless facing upstream, waiting for food to drift by, just the tail fin moving gently, like the rudder of a boat holding its position.

They crossed the river by an old timber footbridge and were soon climbing steeply to gain what was once part of the old railway line, now made into a track well-suited for walkers. They climbed again and cleared the trees, finding themselves on the steep open side of a hill which towers a hundred and fifty feet above the River Wye. Since leaving the car, they'd walked almost in silence, lost in their own thoughts. The path was narrow and a slip would send them plummeting down the steep grassy slope towards the river.

'This is a bit tricky, Jim,' Maddie said, nervously.

Jim looked back at Maddie, who looked scared. Jim had been walking on, unaware that she was finding it difficult.

'I'm sorry, Mad. I didn't realise. You go in front and I'll stay close behind. Just take your time and don't look down.' Maddie came past Jim, taking great care. The path was narrow and the ground very steep. She began walking gingerly along the narrow stony track. Up to the right a cluster of rocky outcrops stood out from the hillside, undercut at the base. This would afford some respite from the sun. 'Shall we stop and have a cuppa and a bite to eat?' Jim said.

Maddie was beginning to wilt in the warm sunshine, the steepness of the climb up on to the path having winded her. 'That's a good idea. Shall we go up there?' she said, pointing upwards to the rocks.

'Yeah, that's a good-looking spot.' They left the track and climbed, with some difficulty, up the steep bank, to the rocks forty feet above the footpath.

Jim took out a plastic sheet from his rucksack. 'Let's sit on this. It'll save you getting your trousers dirty. I'll pour the tea.'

'I've done us some egg and cress sandwiches and my mum gave me some flapjack. How's that sound?' Maddie said, between sips of tea.

'Sounds great. This is a good spot. Doesn't look like anyone's been up here for years.'

They sat eating, drinking tea and chatting, letting out an occasional laugh. There had been one small group of walkers who had followed the track since they'd climbed up to the rocks. Maddie and Jim were almost invisible in their lofty hide away.

'Shhhhhhush,' Maddie said, as the group passed below.

'Let's not let them know we're here,' they giggled, quietly feeling they had found a special place.

'You know what you said earlier, Jim?' Maddie said.

'What was that then?' Jim replied.

'You remember, in the car … you said you loved me?'

'Yeah, I did, didn't I? Hope you didn't mind.'

'Of course I didn't mind. Don't know what my dad would think, though. He gets a bit possessive when I have a boyfriend, but I'm glad you said it. Do you remember old Doris, and what she said to us in Padley Gorge that day? She said she thought that we were made for each other, just like her and her Ernest.'

Jim shuffled, unsure of himself. 'I'm glad you didn't mind. It was just that it was what I was feeling. It seems strange: we've only known each other for five minutes and suddenly everything's changed. Marvellous, isn't it … if the pub hadn't been so crowded, you wouldn't have needed to come and sit with me, and we'd probably never have met. It's very strange,' Jim said, shrugging his shoulders.

Maddie looked at Jim. 'If we hadn't met, it would have been a tragedy. I think it was fate.' She paused. Jim sat quietly listening. 'I think the pub was full just to make sure that we met. It's fate that we're together. I love you and I miss you when we're not together.'

Jim sat, not knowing what to say in the face of this sudden outburst. She seemed to feel as strongly as he did.

'I'm glad' he gasped. 'I'm so amazed, I could burst.'

Maddie shuffled up close to him and put her arm through his. She turned and kissed him gently on the cheek. 'I do love you, Jim. Believe me,' she said quietly, moving closer still. 'Do you fancy me, then?' she said, mustering a sexy voice.

Jim turned to her and said: 'You know bloody well I fancy you.'

Maddie leaned quickly against Jim and kissed him. Jim gasped. 'I think it's time to do something about it then, don't you?' she said, mischievously.

Jim put his hand on her shoulder. 'You know me, mad woman. You're the only one for me. I'd love to do something about it, but we'd better be quick or it'll be too late.' He slid his arms around her waist. 'I'm glad the pub was busy,' he said, as they lay back on the sheet, shaded from the sun by the overhanging block of limestone.

Maddie sighed as she looked into his face. 'Well, young fellow, I'm about to do just that. Teach you a lesson I don't want you to forget,' she giggled, as she pushed up close to him. 'Now, Jim, when I put my hand here, I don't want you to laugh,' she said, as she slowly unbuckled his belt. 'And when I do this, you'd better hang on,' she laughed, as she jumped on top of him, her hand foraging, lowering the zip of his jeans. Jim lay back, the tension in his body forcing beads of sweat to his brow, his heart thumped violently as Maddie lay pushing her body hard against his, her lips – soft and hot – moving across his shoulders and neck, her breath rapid and warm against his skin.

Forty feet below, a party of elderly walkers made their way carefully along the path, blissfully unaware of what was taking place just a short distance away.

Janet pulled the car to a halt at the Ranger station She unloaded their gear from the back seat of the car and then she gave Harry a hand, as he struggled to extricate himself from the passenger seat of the car.

Stan peered out of the station door. He'd seen Janet pull the car up onto the grass by the station and wondered why she appeared to be struggling to help the trainee out of the car. When he saw Harry hopping, he assumed, rightly, that something had gone wrong on the patrol.

'What have you been doing to him, madam?' Stan shouted across from the door of the station.

Harry, looking sheepish, spoke up. 'It was my fault. I was careless. I wasn't watching where I put my feet.'

'Where did this happen, then?' Stan said.

Janet looked at him and saw a smile just emerging from beneath his whiskered face. We were coming down the gully towards Dobb Edge. He slipped on a wet rock, but it's just a sprain. I think you'll be OK, won't you, Harry?'

Harry was worried that his mistake was causing such a stir with the boss; he would rather have drifted off home without anyone getting to know anything about it.

'It's fine. We had a good day and I've learned loads, especially on the navigation.'

Stan looked at Janet with mock severity across his face. 'You're supposed to train these lads, not kill them,' he said, chuckling aloud.

They helped Harry into the rest room. 'Put your foot up on that chair,' Stan said, pushing a black plastic seat across the floor. 'Are you going to be able to drive home tonight?'

'I'll be fine,' he said. 'I've got an automatic. I only need one leg and luckily it's my left leg that hurts.'

Jim was walking on air. They hadn't finished the intended walk. Instead, they'd stayed in their lofty perch for the whole of the afternoon. They'd sat talking, keeping close together and laughing, until the clouds gathered and the rain began to fall.

Jim walked in a daze. He couldn't believe how his life had changed. Today had been the highlight of his life. If ever he had had any doubts about him and Maddie and the reality of their feelings, they'd now been completely dispelled. In his mind he felt the equal of anyone. He'd become a man and he had Maddie to thank for that.

Maddie gripped Jim's hand hard as they strolled back alongside the river to the car.

'You do know you will have to marry me now, don't you … make an honest woman of me?' she said, laughing.

Jim put his arm over Maddie's shoulder.

'After today, I'd do anything. It's been the best day of my life,' he said, turning to face her. 'Marry you? I'd do it tomorrow, if I could. I still can't believe you want to go out with me, let alone marry me.'

'So you would like me to marry you? Is that what you're saying?' Maddie said, her face quizzical.

'It was you that said I would have to marry you,' Jim replied, his voice hoarse as they began walking again.

'So you want us to get married, is that right?'

'Well, yeah. Course I do.'

'That's good, I accept' Maddie said. 'It would have been very awkward if you didn't.'

'Why's that, then?' Jim asked, confused at the direction the conversation was taking.

'Well,' Maddie said, as if struggling to find the words. 'I've already invited Doris and Ernie to our wedding next year. They would have been really upset if there hadn't been one.'

'You did what?' Jim exclaimed. 'You've already got people invited? What if I'd said 'No' ?' he said, as he wrapped his arms around her and gave her a gentle squeeze.

Maddie looked serious again. 'I went to see Doris the other day. Ernie was there. We got chatting about things. The subject of you and me came up and I said we were going to get married next year and that I wanted them to be your family for the day. Hope you don't mind.'

'How could I mind? I think it's great. I've got nobody, so that would be brilliant.'

Maddie thought for a minute. 'D'ya know, there's not too many things I'm sure about in my life,' she said, earnestly, and pinched his chin with her fingers. 'But I'm sure about us. It seemed the right thing to say at the time. I thought it would give Doris something to look forward to, something to get better for.'

'I agree, but I think I'm going to have to tidy myself up a bit if I'm going to get married,' Jim said, suddenly feeling more confident. 'I suppose we'll have to get engaged first. Shall I meet your mum and dad, do you think?'

'Yeah, I think we should do it soon, but let's give it a couple of weeks. It's all happened so quick. I think we need a bit of time just to think it all through before we go home. I'm sure my parents will have a few questions.'

They strolled slowly back up the road, arm in arm, oblivious to the rain bouncing off their waterproof jackets. Maddie's hand jammed in the back pocket of Jim's trousers as they walked back towards the car, their heads full of thoughts and ideas, fears and excitement.

'Take me home, lover,' Maddie giggled, as she climbed into the passenger seat of Jim's car.

Jim turned his head, looked at her and winked, as he turned the key in the ignition and guided the car out of the car park, turning right down the hill past the ramshackle café and on toward the village. From their elevated position he could see across the valley. He could pick out the path they had walked earlier and he spotted the rocks they had spent so long beneath. '*That will always be our special place,*' he thought and smiled as he turned the car and headed steeply back up the hill towards Tideswell.

26

'Hiya, Mark. How's the homework going?' Jake had been thinking about Mark, realising that the travel, then having to reabsorb himself into his family was hard. They'd spoken about it. Mark had said that the schedule was difficult. As always, Jake had seen the positive side of it.

'You just hang on in, Mark. Not too long to go. This job's going to need you for the next thirty years. It'll be worth the effort. Just you wait and see.'

'I'm fine,' Mark replied. 'I've got the work done. I'll be setting off at about half past four in the morning, so I'll be having an early night tonight.'

'Glad to hear it. I've been struggling with the Chemistry, but I've just about done. I was going to go for a run tonight to clear my head,' Jake said.

Mark chuckled. 'You're a glutton for punishment. You do enough of that all week.'

'Yeah, I know. But if I sit too long, my legs go twitchy. Just a couple of miles does me a lot of good.'

'Well, you take care. Don't want you pulling muscles. That would be a disaster. Old Blackwell wouldn't be happy,' Mark laughed.

'OK then, Mark. I'll get off. I've still a bit to do. See you soon.'

'Yeah, see you then. Take it easy.' Mark hung up the phone.

It was just approaching nine thirty; Jake had finished his work for the night. He changed into his tracksuit and training shoes and tripped lightly down the stairs, while his mother sat in the lounge watching television. He leaned through the door. 'I'm off out for a run, mum. Shan't be long. I've got my key.'

His mum looked over her shoulder. 'OK, love. Go steady.'

Jake began running. The streets were fairly quiet, with just a few cars on the road. It was mild, with no breeze. He jogged gently towards the city, crested the hill at the end of the street and could see the lights of Sheffield laid out below him like a huge funfair.

He ran easily, and soon he was descending into Graveton. Passing the fire station across to his right, there was little sign of activity. The lights were on in the first floor recreation room and an office further along the building was lit, and he could see the outline of a couple of people but was unable to make out their features. He wondered if Mac was on duty.

Mac sat in his office, discussing the arrangements for Ray's party with Tony. The night had been quiet so far. Tony had taken the lads for a short session on first aid and then they'd had fish and chips for supper. The remainder of the watch were reading or watching television.

Jake dreamed as he ran. He thought about his course and what it would be like when he finished his training. He was looking forward to his mum coming to see him when he passed out. He ran along the heavily built up High Street and turned right up the hill at the mini roundabout. Lost in his thoughts, he hadn't realised that he was three miles from home. He was running along narrow streets with long terraces of houses, the only access to the rear of these houses being via narrow passageways.

Jake slowed, when he noticed a strong smell of smoke in the air. He looked around but couldn't identify the source of the smell. He felt the hairs on his neck stand up as he sensed that something was wrong and slowed to a brisk walk. He stood and turned around. Across the road, a mid-terraced house was in darkness, and he imagined that he saw a dull flicker of light through the curtains, so he walked over to the house. The smell was very strong and acrid, and he now saw wisps of smoke coming from around the bedroom window.

Christ Almighty, the house is on fire. Jake's thoughts began to spin. *What do I do?* He tried the door, but it was locked. *I know. Phone the Fire Brigade.* He ran to the phone box twenty yards up the street, its light illuminating the corner of the junction. With his hands shaking and his mind racing, he dialled 999.

'*Emergency. Which service do you require?*' the operator said in a slow, calm voice.

'*Fire Brigade,*' Jake shouted down the phone.

'*Hello. Fire brigade. What is the nature of your call?*' a young female voice asked.

Jake's heart was pumping fast. '*There's a house on fire. Peters Street, Graveton. I don't know if there's anyone inside,*' Jake said, anxiety making him rush his words.

'*Right, sir. They're on their way.*'

Jake stood peering up at the bedroom window. The volume of smoke was increasing. He saw the curtain move, the face of a young woman appeared at the window. She had a cloth pressed across her mouth and was calling, but Jake couldn't hear what she was saying.

'Well, Tony. Looks like it's all sorted. We'll just have to do a memo to the DC and let him know what's happening. Most of the invites are out now.'

There was a low thump. Both Mac and Jim stood up, as the light came on and the alarm sounded.

'House fire, Peters Street, Graveton,' Mick Young shouted, as he ripped off the sheet from the printer and handed it to Mac.

'Get your sets on, boys,' Mac called back to Ian and Jock. Taff drove out of the station, pulling the wheel hard right and gunned the engine along the High Street. The traffic lights were at red, so he negotiated them slowly: the traffic ahead, reacting to the siren, had slowed or moved to the side to let them pass.

The smoke in the bedroom was thick black and it impossible to breath. Tracy Jameson had fallen asleep on her bed; a wire in her computer had overheated and the plastic surround had caught fire. By the time she'd woken, the smoke was scorching her lungs. She could see that the smoke was almost to the floor, and she began to panic. Unable to breath, she pushed her face into the carpet and was vaguely aware that she was going to die. She craved fresh air, and, forcing her head up into the smoke, she pulled the curtain to one side, her brain functioning slowly as it became starved of oxygen. *'Maybe I can open the window,'* she thought. Then, as she glimpsed someone on the pavement below, she took a breath and tried to shout, but her brain closed down and she lost consciousness and crashed to the floor.

Jake heard the siren in the distance. It seemed to be taking forever. His mind was in torment. Two seconds ago, he'd seen a face at the window. He made a decision.

'Come on. Let's get a move on,' Mac said calmly to his driver.

'Doing my best, Mac,' Taff replied. He turned swiftly into East Street which was jammed with cars parked on both sides of the road, so that Taff had to drive cautiously, with just inches to spare on each side.

'It wants to be better than this at the job,' Jock shouted. 'If it's this tight we wilni be able to open the doors to get off the motor.'

Mac was concerned and angry. It was unlike him to get stressed, but this situation was getting to him. He realised that the address was only a couple of hundred yards away and that they could get there quicker on foot.

'Right, stop, Taff. Jock, Ian, get two lengths of forty-five mill and a branch, standpipe key and bar. Let's go.'

While Jock and Ian got the gear, Mac began running towards the address. As he turned into Peters Street, he could see that it was empty, and then, at the far end, he saw a dense cloud of smoke erupting from the bedroom widow of one of the houses.

Jake tried the door again. He pushed using all of his weight, but it wouldn't move. He remembered something he'd been told in class. *Often an entry through the back door will be easier. The doors are often weaker.*

Jake sprinted the twenty yards back along the street and found the passageway leading to a common yard serving several of the houses. There was no obvious sign of fire at the rear, Jake had counted the houses and knew he wanted the fourth one along. The house was in darkness. He looked quickly through the window, and then checked the door and felt it rattle when he shook it. *Come on, Jake. One chance.* He launched himself against the door.

The one securing latch gave way, the door flew open, and Jake stumbled, crashing into the kitchen table. The room was hot. He could smell acrid burning plastic and knew if he inhaled he would be disabled, unable to act.

He'd lived in a house like this for most of his life, so he knew that the downstairs had a front room and a back kitchen with the staircase rising between the two rooms; he knew the girl was at the front of the house upstairs. He quickly rehearsed what he had to do in his mind, then stepped outside again and filled his lungs with fresh air, taking several deep breaths.

Mac approached the house. Behind him, coming fast, were Jock and Ian with the equipment. He stopped momentarily. 'Get set into the hydrant and get a jet going. I'm going to have a look round the back.'

'*Keep low, be fast, upstairs turn right, don't breath. Come on, Jake.*

He got to the bottom of the stairs; the smoke ceiling had reached half way down the *staircase Come on. Do it. One chance,* he shouted to himself, feeling his heart pounding in his chest. He felt no doubt: he was certain what he had to do.

Jake climbed fast. He kept low, his face close to the stairs. As he entered the dense, black smoke, his vision disappeared, his eyes stinging and rivulets of tears running down his cheeks. He wanted to breathe, but knew he mustn't.

He moved quickly, hitting the wall at the top of the stairs. He felt his way forward. Unable to see in the blackness, he fumbled, fighting the desire to retreat. The heat forced him low and he felt his skin begin to dry, but ignored it. He was focussed on one thing.

Come on, Jake. Turn right. The desire to breath was overwhelming. As he tried to look, to gain his bearings, all he saw, through tear-filled eyes, was an impenetrable black fog surrounding him.

He crawled to the right, hoping he would hit the bedroom. He was blind, so he felt around with his hands until he felt the side of a bed. He could just make out a faint red glow to his right, so he scrambled around. *Find a wall, Jake,* he told himself. The weeks of training were kicking in. Searching a room for a casualty should be systematic, done quickly but thoroughly. Jake knew he didn't have time to be thorough; he just had to be systematic and fast. He didn't have a BA set, so the time he had was the time he could hold his breath. Already, his lungs were craving fresh air.

Mac entered the yard at the rear of the terrace. He ran to the back of the house and saw that the door to the house was open and thick smoke was issuing from it, he entered. He could feel the heat; the smoke was now at the bottom of the stairs and travelling along the ground floor ceilings. He heard the appliance approaching, so he darted back to the front of the house and saw that a few neighbours were beginning to emerge from their houses. He could see the smoke pouring from the roof above the bedroom. 'Mick, Jock. Get your BA tallies on the board, round the back, fast as you like.'

A neighbour approached. 'Is she out then?' he asked.

'Are you sure there's someone in there?' Mac said to the elderly man.

'Aye, she was in there an hour ago. I saw her pull the curtains across when I came back from taking the dog out.'

'Thanks a lot,' Mac said. 'Right. Looks like persons reported. Get in there, take the hose reel. I'll get a message off,' Mac said, as he ran to the appliance.

'*Control from Alpha Zero One Zero. Persons reported. Make pumps three,*' Mac said, not waiting for a response from Control.

Jake found the wall and, forced low by the heat of the hot smoke, he quickly felt his way around the wall until he felt something light brush his forehead. *The curtains,* he rationalised. His lungs were on fire. *Got to take a breath. Don't, Jake.* He was on the edge of panic, as he felt a soft shape and he quickly ran his trembling hands over it. He was sure he'd found her.

The BA crew entered the kitchen, dragging the hose reel with them. Jock could feel the heat, even through his anti-flash hood. 'Let's go, Mick,' Jock shouted through his face mask. Then he opened up a wide high-powered spray of water at the ceiling. He felt the water evaporate, and the temperature rose momentarily, then quickly subsided.

In the back of Jake's brain, he thought he could hear voices downstairs. He grabbed the bundle of clothes and, with all of his remaining strength, he dragged the girl back towards the top of the stairs. He had to breath. His lungs forced out the air which had sustained him. Jake gasped and inhaled: his lungs were choked by the smoke. He felt he was finished. As he reached the top of the stairs, he was coughing uncontrollably, mucus pouring from his nose and his mouth, his mind not working well. *Not far now, Jake. Just a few feet. Don't stop.* He reached the top of the stairs, his head swimming. He couldn't feel anything, only the bundle in his hands.

He knew he was at the top of the stairs. *Do or die, Jake,* he told himself. Grabbing the bundle close to him he launched himself into the smoke, tumbling, not feeling anything.

'Hello, sir. For your information, we have a reported house fire, persons reported, at 62 Peters Street, Graveton. One pump in attendance, Sub O James in charge. Two further pumps have been mobilised.'

Ian Blain had been sitting with his wife, watching the television.

'Book me out. I'm on my way,' he said, putting the phone down in its cradle. 'See you later, love,' he called, as he moved quickly, pulling his jacket on.

'Take care, darling,' his wife called. She always felt anxious when she knew he was going to a fire.

Jock and Mick were close to the stairs when they heard a low crash and two bodies landed at their feet. 'Bloody hell. That frightened the life of me,' Jock said as they glanced down at the two shapes barely visible through the smoke. 'Grab one each and get them out of here.'

The back-up appliance pulled up in front of the Graveton appliance. Mac grabbed the Officer in Charge. 'Get two men in BA. I want them in fighting the fire on the first floor.'

'OK, Sub. Consider it done,' he replied.

Mac ran around to the back of the house again, in time to see Jock and Mick backing urgently out of the house, each dragging an unconscious body. 'Put them over here,' Mac shouted, as they emerged from the kitchen door.

'Salvage sheet, oxygen, first aid gear: is it all here?' Mac said to the junior officer.

'Yes, Sub. I'll get a couple of my lads to see to them.'

'Yeah, quick as they like, thanks.'

Mac glanced at the two figures being laid on the ground; a flicker of recognition crossed his face. Mac shone the light from his torch onto the young male's face. 'Is that Jake?' he said, moving up close to the young man. 'Jake. It's Mac. Open your eyes.'

'In the deep recesses of Jake's brain, he felt something entering his consciousness. He could barely breath but he could feel a rubber mask being pushed onto his face. Someone was calling. His mind swirled. *Am I dead?* he thought. He couldn't feel his body, just his face. It was dark, but dull flashes of light flashed through his head. *Are we still in the fire?* he asked himself.

'Come on, Jake. I know you can hear me,' Mac called. There was no response.

'What do you think?' Mac said to the paramedic, who had just arrived and was dealing with Jake.

'Well, he's breathing on his own, but I reckon he's had a good dose of smoke.'

'How's the girl?' Mac asked the other paramedic. 'Is she OK?'

'Well, she seems pretty bad, but she's breathing on her own. I think they got out in the nick of time.'

Something stirred in Jake's mind. He could clearly hear voices and could vaguely hear sirens. Life seemed to be returning to his body: he could feel his hands, he could feel his shoulder. It hurt like hell.

'Come on, Jake. Open your eyes.' Jake heard that clearly. He opened his eyes. It was difficult to see, a bright light was shining into his face and he could make out a dark shape hovering over him, forcing a rubber mask onto his face.

'He's coming round,' the paramedic said, with relief in his voice.

'Come on, Jake. It's me. Mac. What've you been getting up to, then?'

Jake's mouth was dry, his throat was sore and he could heard a voice claiming to be Mac. He felt relieved.

'How's the girl?' he asked.

Mac knelt down alongside Jake. 'You're going to be OK, Jake. Just take it easy. They're going to get you off to hospital shortly. Everything's going to be fine.'

Jake tried to speak again, but his voice was a croak. 'I've got to be on duty in the morning … daren't miss … the Sub will give me a right bollocking.'

'Don't worry about him. We'll square it with him. We'll see you later.'

Mac turned to leave.

'Mac,' Jake said, through cracked lips. 'Will you let mum know that I'll be OK? She knows you. At least she knows about you. I'd like you to let her know. '

Mac looked at Jake. 'Yes, we'll do that. We'll just put this fire out and we'll drop in to see her on the way back, OK.'

The ambulance crews continued to administer oxygen to both Jake and the girl. Now she was responding to the treatment, the ambulance crew prepared to remove both of them from the scene and get them to hospital.

The fire in the bedroom had been extinguished, and the windows of the house opened to clear the smoke. Ian Blain had arrived at the incident after a difficult drive across town, encountering road works and at one point getting lost amid the maze of back streets. When he arrived, he contacted the crew and sought out Mac, finding him in the back yard of the houses, assisting the Ambulance crew to deal with the casualties.

'Hello, Mac. What's been going on here, then?' Ian asked.

Mac turned to see the DC. 'Hiya, boss. We had a small but very hot and smoky job in the front bedroom. The girl, the occupier, was rescued by the young chap, who just happened to be passing when he spotted the smoke. In the circumstances he did very well, but it almost killed him,' Mac said.

'Are they going to be OK?' Ian asked.

'Yeah, I think so. The ambulance crew reckon the girl will be OK. The lad just had a bit too much smoke. He'll be fine.'

'That's good then, Mac. A happy ending.'

'Yeah, in fact the boy's asked me if I'll inform his mum that he's OK. I said I would. Is that OK by you?'

Ian gave Mac a quizzical look. 'Why would he ask you to do that, Mac?'

Mac smiled. 'Well, it's strange. Do you remember me telling you about the boy on the moor who helped me when I came across the man having a heart attack?'

Ian thought for a second. 'Yeah, I think so.'

'Well, that boy joined the Brigade. He's in training at present. Well, it's him. We've just loaded him into the ambulance. It seems the training is what helped him survive the rescue.'

'Well, I'll be buggered,' Ian laughed. 'He's supposed to wait until he's got through training before we have the heroics.'

'Well, he's doing well in training. I've been checking his progress. I shouldn't think this will do his career any harm at all.'

'No, you're right. It will sure get him noticed,' Ian laughed.

They walked together into the house. There was an overpowering smell of burned plastic permeating throughout the small house. The ceilings of the ground floor were tinged black from the smoke, the bedrooms and staircase were blackened, and the lampshades hung like stalactites from their fittings.

They walked into the bedroom from where Jake had pulled the girl. Everything had been impregnated with a layer of black, oily deposit. The water from the fire-fighting had saturated the bed, and floor of the room was a mess. A small table in the corner of the room stood covered in charred plastic and the remnants of paper and books.

'This looks like the likely cause,' Mac said, reaching down among the tangle of charred wires. 'Some sort of problem in the computer, look. The adapter there is overloaded; it's got four plugs in it. It's a wonder that didn't catch fire.'

'OK, Mac. I'll make myself scarce. The boys did well. I'll leave you to it and I'll contact training school in the morning, let them know why the young man's not there.'

'OK, boss. Nice to see you. Did you get the memo about Ray's retirement bash? It's all sorted, so we'll be looking for a good turnout.'

'Well, you can be sure we'll be there. I think the ADOs are coming, as are the secretaries. I think your Leading Fireman grabbed us all to contribute to the leaving present.'

Mac grinned. 'I hope he wasn't too hard on you all, you poor officers, always short of a bob or two,' he laughed.

'No, he was fine. He seems to have fitted pretty well into the job. Seems a good lad,' Ian responded.

'Yeah, the boys gave him some stick at first, but he's settled in well. I'm quite happy with him.'

'OK, Mac. I'll be off.'

Ian walked to his car, put his fire gear into the boot and drove off, waving to the crew by the appliance as he left.

Mac stood alone in the bedroom and imagined the situation Jake had found himself involved in. It was clear that conditions had been difficult, but he'd shown that he had what it took to do the job. Mac felt proud. *Well done, boy,* he said to himself.

Jake sat in the ambulance. The oxygen had brought him back and, although his chest was clogged up with mucus and his face and hands were scorched, he felt fine. He was glad he'd seen Mac. He was sure his mum would be OK about it, if Mac was to tell her. He looked across the ambulance at the attendant who was still administering oxygen to the girl, but the signs were good. She was moving and he hoped she would be all right.

Oh hell, he thought. *The Sub's not going to be happy in the morning.*

'OK, Taff. Pull in here,' Mac said, as they pulled up outside Jake's house. 'I'll just pop in and see his mum.'

Jake's mother was sat watching television when the doorbell rang. *Who on earth could that be at this time of night? Oh, maybe Jacob forgot his key,* she thought, as she got up from her chair and made for the front door.

'Hello, Mrs Higgins. Nothing to worry about. Can I come in for a second?' Mac said, trying to alleviate her fears by smiling broadly at her.

'What's the problem? I haven't called you,' she said, looking confused.

They got through to the lounge. Mac sat down. 'I'm Mac. I think Jacob has mentioned me to you.'

'Mentioned you? He always seems to be mentioning you. You did him a great favour. He's joined the Fire Brigade because of you. I think you're his hero,' she said, smiling.

'Well, you mustn't worry,' Mac said, trying to appear casual. 'Jacob's been taken to hospital.'

'Oh, no. What's happened to him?' she said, panic spreading across her face.

'No, really. You mustn't worry. Look, Jake has been a little hero tonight. He saw a fire in a house, so he called the brigade and then went in and rescued a girl. They're both OK,' Mac said, attempting to be reassuring. 'Jacob will probably have to spend the night in the hospital, just under observation. I think the girl he saved will need a bit longer, but he did well. You should be proud of him. We are.'

'The little devil,' she said 'Wait till I see him. I always tell him to be careful,' she whispered to herself, now looking much calmer. 'I ought to get ready and go across to see him. Where have they taken him?'

'They've taken him to the Hallamshire. Look, if you put a coat on, we'll take you across now in the fire engine.'

'Control from Alpha Zero One Zero. Over.'

'Go ahead. Over'

'Control, for your information, we' will be unavailable for approximately twenty – two zero – minutes, re-stowing gear and topping up with water.'

'Alpha Zero One Zero received. Inform when back on the run. Control out.'

'OK, Taff. Let's go. Are you OK in the back there, Mrs Higgins?' Mac said, as they drew away from her house.

'I'm fine,' she said. 'This is very exciting … Phew, doesn't it smell of smoke in here?'

Ten minutes later they drew up outside the Accident and Emergency entrance of the Hallamshire Hospital.

'I'll just walk you up to the reception desk and then we'll have to get back. Tell Jacob that I'll see him tomorrow, and not to worry about Training School. It's all being sorted.'

'OK, Mac. Thank you all, and thank you for the lift,' she said, as she leaned forward and spoke to the young nurse behind the reception desk.

Jim sat in his flat. He'd dropped Maddie off at her parents' house, and she'd left him reluctantly. It seemed that the events of the day had somehow brought them even closer together. He began running the day through his mind, as he always did. She was his life: he thought of very little else. And to think they were now discussing marriage. Time had gone so fast, he no longer felt like the loser he'd been a few months before. He now knew what his life was for. Maddie. *Make her happy, make her proud, do something with my life*, he thought.

Maddie lay in her bed. Her parents were still sitting downstairs, listening to the radio. When she got into the house she'd spoken to her parents briefly, hardly able to contain her feelings. She desperately wanted to speak to her mum about the things she and Jim had discussed, but sense prevailed. She knew that a lot more discussion between her and Jim should take place, but the time would have to be right. This was going to be her big day. She didn't want anything to cast a cloud over it. She lay and remembered – with a great feeling of love – what she and Jim and done that day.

Clive Botham woke up. The sun shining through the bedroom window had pierced his eyelid and roused him. It had been a good night off, one of the three bank holidays that he was owed. Helen was lying next to him, still fast asleep. They'd been to the bowling alley in town and then on to an Italian restaurant. They were late getting in and, after sitting for an hour talking about the future, the baby, weddings, parents and dresses etc, before they knew it, it had been half past two. They'd announced Helen's pregnancy to their respective parents and said to them they thought it was about time that they got married. Thankfully, both sets of parents had been delighted.

So far, Clive hadn't told the watch, what with Ray's retirement do coming up soon, he'd decided it would be better if the watch weren't distracted by his and Helen's wedding plans. He did, however, realise that he would get some stick from them – when he eventually told them – for not informing them first.

Clive had never been one to lie in bed, through force of habit. He'd always got up pretty early to go for a run, and this morning was no different. He padded barefoot across to the bathroom and had a shower, the water quickly waking him up.

He put on his tracksuit and trainers, got a drink of orange juice from the fridge and sat eating his cornflakes at the breakfast bar. When he switched on the radio, Hallam FM News was just beginning. The newsreader began.

'*At approximately nine thirty last night, the fire brigade rescued a young male and female from a house fire on Peters Street, Graveton. They were taken to hospital suffering the effects of smoke inhalation. A brigade spokesman said that the young man, a recruit fire fighter, was passing, saw smoke and attempted a rescue. Both he and the young woman he was attempting to rescue were pulled from the house by fire officers wearing breathing apparatus. The Officer in Charge said that the cause of the fire appeared to be some sort of electrical fault, but this would be further investigated. He also stated that the young man had made a great effort to save the young lady and had almost perished in the attempt.'*

Clive stared at the radio. 'I don't believe it. Missed another bloody good job,' he said, banging his fist on the table.

Mac had got up and showered. The rest of the crew were still asleep as he sat in his office and began gathering the details of the Peters Street job to put into the fire report. Just then, the telephone rang. 'Hello. Graveton Sub Officer speaking.'

'Hiya, Mac. It's Clive. Seems I've missed another good one. Reckon I'm fated.'

'Well, it wasn't much. The fire was confined to one room. The smoke did a lot of damage, though. The main thing was the rescues. A lad had gone in when he'd seen the smoke.' Mac then related to Clive the whole scenario. Only occasionally would Clive come in with a 'bloody hell' or 'another soddin' job missed' or 'I'm never having another day off ... it's fatal.'

'Well, don't worry about it, Clive. Your day will come. How's everything with you?'

'Its fine. We were out last night. Had a late one, so I'm knackered today. Helen's still asleep,' he laughed. 'OK, Mac. Well, I'm off for a run. I'll see you next tour.'

Mac hung up the phone. *I think I'll just give the hospital a call,* he said to himself.

In the ward, the nurses pulled back the curtains, allowing the early morning sunshine to flood in. Jake woke up. All night he'd been dreaming fitfully about the previous night's attempted rescue. The night staff had cleaned him up, forced him to drink lots of water, and treated the minor scorching to his face and hands. He felt very well: fit enough to leave, he thought to himself. The nurse came over to him. 'Well, Jacob. Who's the talk of the town today then? How are you feeling? Do you fancy a cup of tea?' she asked, smiling broadly at him.

Jake was impressed. *How nice she was, very caring and pretty,* he thought. He'd worried last night. They'd allowed his mother to come in and see him briefly, and she'd become upset.

'You've got to stop it, Jacob. You can't go risking your life like that. You'll kill yourself,' she'd said, her voice choking with emotion.

She'd sat by his bed, holding his hand, something that she hadn't done since he was a little boy.

'I'm fine now, mum. I learned a lot from that and I'm glad I did it,' Jake had said, looking at her. 'I feel I'm doing some good now.'

Mac had almost finished the fire report from the previous evening's job; he'd had his usual breakfast of cornflakes and toast. He sat back and reflected. Not long ago he'd been bemoaning his future. The day of his retirement was now fast approaching: he'd miss all this. He felt that nothing could better what he'd had for nearly thirty years. Last night had made him think. He realised that his crew were very capable of surviving without him. Tony was doing OK and would for sure make a decent sub officer in time. Young Jake was the future of the service. He had the capacity to carry the flag forward. Somehow Mac felt better about many things.

He'd rung the hospital to check on Jake. The nurse said he was fine and would probably be discharged before lunch. Mac was relieved. *Time for a relaxing few days off,* he thought.

Next week was arriving fast for Ray and Mary. They'd planned their escape. After his retirement party, they were off on the ferry to Brittany, a few weeks away, to take time to relax and get used to the idea that he wasn't going back to work.

They'd drive down from St Malo to La Baule, a few days there and then they would just tour around as the fancy took them. Ray had always had an interest in the Second World War, so he hoped they would have time to look at some of the remnants of the German coastal batteries, built to protect the Submarine Pens at St Nazaire.

Mark Devonshire sat in the classroom of the training school with his squad – now a tight-knit bunch, forged out of hardship and some tough treatment from the training school instructors – their desks piled up with books and notes, their work done over the weekend. There was some discussion among the group about the news report that someone from training school was in hospital. As yet they had no idea who it was.

The classroom door opened. In strode sub officer Blackett.

'Officer present,' the squad leader for the week shouted. The squad jumped to attention by their desks.

'Thank you. Now sit down' the sub officer said. 'You will note that one of the squad is missing. For your information, Mr Higgins is in hospital. Last night at around nine thirty he got involved in the rescue of a young lady from a fire. During the rescue attempt, he shipped a lot of smoke and had to be rescued himself by the Graveton fire crews.' The sub officer paused.

'Is he OK, sub. What happened?' Mark asked, anxiously.

The sub officer thought briefly. 'I can tell you that he'll be fine. In fact, he'll be discharged later today. The girl he helped to rescue is also OK. However, she'll have to stay in for a few more days.' He stopped again. 'This serves to prove that fire is dangerous. That's why when we go into fires, we wear breathing apparatus, and why fire appliances have loads of water and equipment on board. We also have men to back us up. Mr Higgins had none of that. He came across a situation, made a decision and had a go. Whether he was right or wrong I couldn't say, but he saved a life, he could have lost his.' He paused again. 'It only takes a second. You know, because I've told you: one breath is all it takes, one breath and it could be you finished. He'll have learned a lot from that. You need to learn, also.' He drew a chair across to the front of the class. 'I've spoken with the Brigade Training Officer and suggested that I take you to the house before it's disturbed. Look at it, imagine what it was like last night and consider what you might have done. You may have done something different. What is important is that we look at it and learn something from it, OK.' A babble of noise went around the classroom. 'Right, folks. Go and get changed into you're fire gear. We leave in ten minutes.'

27

Mac pulled his car along the side of the road close to the hospital. '*Fantastic,*' he thought. '*Not often you get parked first time.*'

Jake sat up in bed. The nurse had come around a few minutes earlier, tidied his pillows and brought him a cup of tea. His throat was still sore from the night before. He was sipping the tea when he noticed a figure walking slowly down the ward. '*It's Mac,*' he thought, leaning across to his left and putting the teacup on his bedside table.

Mac walked around his bed, smiling broadly. Jake suddenly felt very happy. It was the first time he'd seen Mac since he and his wife had dropped him off at home after the White Edge incident.

'Well, young man. How are you this morning?' Mac said. 'Seems like you've been doing some realistic training while you've been off duty.'

'Hiya, Mac … I mean sub.'

'Forget all that sub stuff. Save it for training school,' Mac said. 'Glad to see you survived. Was your mum OK, last night?'

'She was fine, thanks to you. She gave me a rollicking for being daft, but she's great.'

'You did well. You definitely saved the girl's life. Just getting her down the stairs saved a few minutes … time in which she would have gone. Well done. I'm proud of you.'

Jake looked at Mac. The thought that Mac was proud of him overwhelmed him. Tears filled his eyes: they streaked down his face, still reddened by the heat from the fire. 'You know, there was a time in there when I thought I was dead. I tried to breathe. The smoke was so strong, I couldn't inhale. I thought I was going to die. I don't remember much after I found her near the window.'

They chatted for a while. Mac said: 'Look, Jake. They're letting you out at lunchtime. I'm off home to get changed, then Val and I will come and pick you up and take you home, all right?'

'That'll be great. I hope I can go back to training tomorrow.'

'Don't bank on it. I think the BTO will be popping in to see you this morning. He'll make a decision based on what the doctor tells him, OK.'

The training school personnel carrier pulled up alongside the house in Peters Street. Police and Fire Brigade cars were already there. The windows had all been opened but there were clear signs that there had been a fire. The brickwork above the bedroom window was blackened by smoke, the glass on the window was black and a smell of plastic hung in the air.

The recruits disgorged from the mini bus and stood on the pavement, looking with interest at the outside of the fire-damaged house.

'Right, lads. The fire investigator is about finished inside. When we go in, don't get in his way, and don't touch anything,' the sub officer emphasised.

The squad put on their helmets and followed the sub officer into the house. 'Look,' he said. 'This is where Mr Higgins got in. It looks like he broke the door down.' They entered the kitchen, immediately aware that the house was still warm from the fire and that the smell of the fire – a mixture of plastic and wood – was still in evidence. 'Remember what I've told you: heat rises. See how the smoke's been pushed downstairs and coated the ceiling. See how the heat the fire generated, even down here, has begun to bubble the paintwork on the tops of the window. That's why we tell you: when you enter a building, go in low, stay low, no need to give yourself more punishment than necessary.' He stopped talking for a moment and surveyed the kitchen.

'Smell that smell. Last night it would have been a hundred times worse than it is now. One breath and forget it. That's why so many people die in fires. They just don't wake up. The fire starts while they're asleep, the smoke creeps up on them and they never know there's a fire. If they did, it's unlikely that they'd survive, anyway.'

'How did Jake … er Mr Higgins survive, do you think, sub?' one of the recruits asked. He thought for a second. 'Well, you've all been learning for a few weeks now. He probably put some of the things he's been taught into practice. He'll have worked out a plan, kept low and gone for it, and, oh, he'll have held his breath.' The squad laughed, now beginning to realise the magnitude of Jake's effort and wishing that the chance for glory had come to them.

The staircase was dingy and hot, the carpets sodden from the fire fighting, the ceilings and walls coated in a viscous layer of oily, black deposit. In the confines of that space, the residual fumes from the fire attacked the back of their throats. They climbed the stairs. In the front bedroom was the fire investigation officer; he was packing his equipment away into a small leather case.

'Good morning, sir,' the sub officer greeted the officer. 'I'm Sub Officer Blackett from the Training School. I've got a squad of recruits here and we thought it would be interesting to let them see the impact a fire has on a building. Mr Higgins, the one who carried out the rescue last night, was part of this squad. I hope that's not a problem.'

The station officer pulled his gloved hand across his forehead, to wipe off the perspiration. The room was like a sauna: the heat of the fire had been absorbed by the walls and the water used in fire fighting had evaporated, making the humidity in that confined space very high.

'No, that will be fine. I've finished. Your man was very lucky, but he did well.'

Mark Devonshire spoke up. 'Excuse me, sir. Have you managed to work out what caused the fire yet?'

The officer smiled. 'The best guess is an electrical fault in the young lady's computer. If you look down there,' he said, pointing to the floor beneath the remnant of a small table on which was a crumpled casing of a computer, 'you'll see a load of wires and adaptors. She had a room heater, the computer, two bedside lamps, a radio, an electric blanket etc all plugged into one power source. Some of the plugs had fuses which were overrated for the appliances. All in all a very dangerous situation. She would have breathed fumes in before she woke up. She was very lucky. If your friend hadn't happened by, she would almost certainly have died.'

The recruits looked around the small bedroom. It was devastated: the heat had brought down plaster from the upper part of the room, and every last thing was black and stinking. 'Bloody hell. Old Jake was lucky to get away with it, wasn't he Sub?'

'He was. He did well, but it nearly cost him dear. Remember: smoke is deadly, if in doubt get a BA set on. Without it, you're useless,' the sub officer said, his face serious now. 'I brought you here to see at first-hand what a fire looks like at close quarters. Dismiss the idea that fighting a fire is an adventure or is glamorous. It's not. It's bloody dirty and it's dangerous, and that's what I want you to learn from this visit.'

The squad looked around the dirty, damaged room and imagined what Jake had done.

'Right, any questions from you lot?'

The squad stood in silence.

'Right, let's have you back downstairs and on to the van.'

Mary was awake early, so she got up from her bed. She'd decided that today, Ray would have his breakfast in bed.

'Good morning, love. Wakey wakey,' she called, whilst gently shaking his shoulder.

Ray stirred; the scent of freshly cooked bacon was permeating around the bedroom. *Smells lovely,* he thought as he tried to prise open his eyes.

Mary stood by the bed with a wooden tray, on which was his favourite breakfast of bacon sandwiches with brown sauce.

'Ooh, that looks lovely,' he said, hoisting himself up into a sitting position. 'I could get used to this.'

Mary passed him a mug of tea, then switched the bedside radio on. Brian Mathew was playing music from the sixties.

'It's about time they packed it in. It's a load of old rubbish. I prefer old Stewpot anytime,' Ray complained.

'Now, Ray. Stop moaning. You used to like it thirty years ago. Get your teeth round those sandwiches and drink your tea. It's a special day today.'

Ray momentarily looked sad. 'Yeah, I know ... the last day. I thought it would never come. Just get the retirement do over tonight, then off to France ... can't wait,' he said smiling gleefully.

Mac drove into the station. He could see that the day crew were well advanced with the arrangements for Ray's do. The appliances had been pulled out onto the front of the station and the crew had mopped out the appliance bays and laid out the tables and chairs.

'Hiya, Max,' he said as the sub in charge of blue watch came into the yard to meet him. 'How's it going?'

'It's nearly done, Mac. The florist's been, the music sorted. We just need everyone to turn up. How's Ray?'

'Saw him yesterday. He's got mixed feelings about it, but he's ready to go, I think.'

'Yeah, he popped in last week, just to check us out. He seems to have got his head around it.'

'Is there anything you need us to do, Max? It seems your lads have done a good job. Tell them 'thanks' from the Reds. We're grateful.'

Well, it's for Ray. Everybody loves Ray and he'll be missed.'

'Yeah, I'll miss him. We're from the same school. The changes in the job are hard to absorb these days ... not be long before it's our turn.'

'You're right. I think my missus is dreading it. She's already told me that I'll have to get a job, and that she doesn't want me under her feet, wrecking her routine.'

'OK, Max. Thanks again. I'll get off … see you tonight.'

Mac climbed back into his car and drove into town.

Jim was weary after his night shift; the patrols were becoming increasingly more mind-numbing. Since meeting Maddie, he'd changed a lot. He now thought about the way he dressed: the old bomber jacket had been thrown in the bin, he'd bought new trousers and leather jacket, he'd had his hair cut, everything had changed. He'd changed. He was going to marry the love of his life. He sat in wonderment, completely bemused at how his life had turned around.

I'm going to change my job. I can do better than this, he thought. *'I just need to figure out what I can do instead.* He began to run through his mind the jobs he would like to do, then the jobs he was qualified to do. The two mental lists he'd formed didn't tally. When it came down to it, he wasn't qualified for any job, other than jobs that required no qualifications. *This is not good. I'll talk to Maddie. I'll give her a ring tonight, see what she thinks.*

Maddie was tired. She'd done four of her night duties, all of which had kept her busy. She liked to be busy, but the cumulative effect of the nights was taking its toll and she was ready for a break. She'd give Jim a ring, later.

Ernie was sitting by Doris's bed. They'd got the news they'd been waiting for. Doris could go home today: she was much better, having regained most of the feeling in her body, and she could walk quite easily with a stick. Her speech was still a bit slurred, but they'd been informed by the doctor that it would improve over time.

'Right, my old love, are ya going to get yourself dressed or shall I give you a hand?' Ernie said, enthusiastically.

'Ernest, you never change, always wanting to see me with my clothes off. You sit there and I'll get myself dressed behind the curtains, thank you very much.'

Ernest looked disappointed. 'I thought that now you're something like right, that we could, like, ya know, start getting a bit, ya know.'

'Shut up, Ernest. Save that talk for the privacy of our house,' she said with a light-hearted laugh in her voice. 'I haven't forgotten that I still owe you a seeing too,' she said.

Ernest rubbed his hands together. 'I thought you would have forgotten about that,' he said, 'what with ya being poorly an all.'

'You know me, Ernest. I never forget a promise. I hope you've been taking your arthritis tablets.' There was a moment's silence.

'The doctor's said I have to take it easy. He never mentioned stopping.'

They both laughed, mostly from a sense of relief that Doris was OK, that she'd recovered and that their life could continue.

Maddie opened the door of the ward and could hear Ernest laughing. As she approached, she could see that the curtain was pulled around the bed and Ernie was sat outside, chatting to Doris through the curtain.

'Good morning, sir,' Maddie said.

Ernie turned to see Maddie. 'Good morning, love. She won't let me help her get dressed, so she's struggling on her own.'

'Hello, Doris. It's Maddie. Do you need a hand?'

'Yes please, love. I wouldn't let him in … a hand would have been what I got. I don't trust him,' she laughed.

Ten minutes later, Maddie drew the curtains from around the bed. 'Look, Ernest. She's all shipshape and Bristol fashion for you.'

Ernie was overcome with joy. There had been many times in the past few weeks when he'd had doubts about this ever happening. 'Eeh, ya look fit to eat, Doris. Let's get you home. Ya can get yer feet up and I'll make you a nice cuppa tea.' His face beamed.

Doris chuckled. 'Thanks, Maddie, you've been a great help. When we get home and settled, you and Jim must come and visit.'

She looked around the ward and walked gingerly across to see the nurses who had been caring for her. 'Goodbye, my loves, and thank you for sorting me out and putting up with this reprobate,' she said, looking at Ernie. The nurse put her arm around Doris and kissed her cheek. 'It's been our pleasure, Doris. Pop in and see us when you come in for your check-ups.'

Ernest fumbled in an old carrier bag; he pulled out a huge box of chocolates. 'These are for you, for looking after my Doris. I don't know what I'd have done if I'd lost her,' he said, his voice cracking. 'I'm right grateful, thanks.' Ernie turned away and wiped his coat sleeve across his face. 'Come on, mi old fruit, let's get thee back to our house.'

Maddie walked with them down to the car park. She carried Doris's suitcase, and helped her into the car.

'Have you got that heater fixed yet, Ernest? I don't want to roast on the way home,' Doris said, looking sternly at him.

'Give over nattering. Of course I've had it mended. Now sit back and listen to the wireless,' Ernie said, a smile breaking across his wrinkled face. Maddie's mind instantly went back to Padley Gorge, and to the first time they had met. *Some things never change*, she said to herself. She smiled and waved as they drove out of the car park.

The car park at the Hallamshire Hospital was busy. Mac managed to find a spot to park the car and walked the four hundred yards to the hospital entrance. Val had wanted to go with Mac but she was due at the Hairdresser's in an hour.

Jake was up and dressed, eager to leave. He'd had a busy morning. The Brigade training officer had been in to see him, and they had chatted for a while before, to Jakes relief, he had been told he would be able to re-join his squad the next day. The press and a photographer had also been to see him whilst the BTO was there. He had given a short interview and had his photograph taken. He'd felt uneasy about the incident, saying that if he'd thought about it too much he probably wouldn't have tried it, but that he was grateful to the firemen who rescued him and that he wouldn't advise anyone else to try it, that he realised how lucky he'd been.

His throat and chest were still feeling sore, his hands and face were reddened and had been creamed to reduce the soreness of the mild scorching he'd received during the rescue. He sat on his bed, his bag packed, looking forward to seeing Mac and his mum.

Mac walked into the ward. Jake, who had been expecting him, stood up and shook Mac's hand.

'Are you ready, young man?' Mac asked. 'Have you said your thanks and goodbyes to the staff?'

'Yeah, they've been great. A couple of the young ones have hinted that they'd like to go out some time and a couple wanted my autograph. Aren't they daft, Mac?'

'Come on. Let's get you home. It's my leading fireman's retirement do tonight, so I can't hang about, and your mum will be pleased to see you.'

The night was chilly. Ray drove the car knowing it would be an emotional night for him; he'd not stopped talking since they'd got into the car.

He drove through the town. As he looked at the offices and shops in the High Street, his mind wandered back to the times over the years when he'd been involved in fires in many of the buildings and had many good times with his pals. It seemed that the awareness that tonight was his last night in the service brought everything flooding back into his mind. He remembered his first fire in a local fish and chip shop where, in his enthusiasm, he'd sprinted into the shop and slid on the greasy floor, landing in an untidy heap at the feet of the shop owner. He remembered the night when he'd helped rescue a child from a burning house, a fire where he'd lost a friend. It had been a good and worthwhile life with the boys, but tonight a line was going to be drawn under it, tonight his service to Sheffield would become part of the Brigade's history.

Mac had got a table close to the front of the appliance room; he was sitting with Val, when Ray and Mary arrived. It had taken them an age to get across the room. Various friends and colleagues had grabbed them on their way across, and there was a lot of shaking hands and back patting, with Ray smiling broadly as he found his way across to Mac and Val.

'My God, Mac. I hadn't expected a turnout like this. There are people here I haven't seen for twenty years. I just met old Bill Brookes. He was my LF when I joined the job … he must be ninety if he's a day.'

Mac got up and shook Ray's hand. 'Come on, you two. Sit down and I'll get you a drink.'

The room had filled up with colleagues both past and present. The crossed conversations produced a loud drone which made hearing a conversation difficult. Mac noticed that the chief and Ian Blain had arrived with their wives, along with a gaggle of local councillors, who all sat chatting among themselves.

Mac banged an ashtray on the table in front of him, until the rumble of noise in the room slowly subsided. He spoke briefly about the agenda for the night. The crowd had become quiet.

Mac continued. 'Tonight, I find myself in the enviable position of being one of Ray's many friends. Here is our chance to pay tribute to a fine fire fighter, an excellent junior officer and a truly nice man.' Mac was ignoring the copious notes he had made for the speech. 'Ray and I have worked together for years. I think I know most things about him and I think he would say the same about me. Ray's always been a great servant to the service and to Sheffield. I think the turnout tonight gives some idea of what people think of him.' Mac paused and looked around the room. 'Ray's always been a man you could trust, and for sure I've had to trust him with my neck, on more than one occasion. He's always been there when he was needed, he never shied away from the difficult things in the job, he was the perfect fire fighter.' Mac turned towards Ray and grinned. 'I'll have the fiver now, if you don't mind, Ray.' The audience laughed. Mac wasn't one normally for making speeches, but tonight was a special night and he was speaking from the heart.

'Tonight, I'm sad to be saying goodbye to a special friend and colleague, although pretty soon I'll be following him into the sunset. There've been times when he's infuriated me … he can be an argumentative old sod, as many of you will know, and you'll have seen that from time to time.' Mac paused again. There were comments from the audience, such as 'too true' . They all laughed.

'We've shared some difficult times. His mate was killed in a fire some years back. We all struggled with that, but Ray just kept going. We've had some laughs and I'll miss those times, but be glad we had them. Ray, Mary, Val and me, we've had a life together and it's been great, but now it's time for the rest of his life, when they can both get off and do the things they want to do. It's been a privilege, Ray.' Mac paused for a second. 'The DC has asked if he could say a few words.'

Ian Blain got up from his seat to polite applause from the gathering. He took a card out of his pocket.

'Thank you, Mac, and thank you, Graveton, for inviting my wife and me to this very important evening. As you're aware, I'm sure, I've not been in South Yorkshire very long.' He paused and looked around the room. 'During my short time, however, I've observed some remarkable things, more so than anywhere previously. There seems to be a unique culture within this brigade. I've met men who are, I believe, the finest I've met. Some while ago I spoke to Ray and Mary about his forthcoming retirement. During our conversation, we spoke about the picture so proudly displayed in the foyer at Brigade HQ. At that time, I had little idea of the circumstances surrounding the picture and less idea of who the men featured in the picture were. I recently learned it was Ray and Mac. I then heard the story behind the picture.'

Ian stood quietly for a moment, his mind instantly back in Ray's lounge, where he had spoken to Ray about the fire, then continued. 'Ray has been a great servant to the people of Sheffield for almost thirty years. During his time he's seen many changes, but his standards – standards forged in his early days in the service – have always remained. He's shown an almost unparalleled love of the job, he's been a friend to many, a guiding hand to many more, and a rock when at the sharp end of a branch when things got tough, he would always be there, helping supporting, in fact doing exactly what a good officer or junior officer should do. Ian paused. 'I recently heard about an incident long ago where Ray was involved in the rescue of a child. He and his colleague, Dick Blackburn, risked everything to save that child's life. Unfortunately, Ray's colleague died in the attempt. Ray got an award for that and it was richly deserved. He acted in the best tradition of the South Yorkshire Fire Service, and we should all be proud and grateful for having Ray as a friend and colleague.' Ian paused and the audience burst into a spontaneous round of applause.

Ray looked down at his feet, wiping his eyes with the handkerchief that Mary had given him. Mac leaned across to Ray. 'I'll second that,' he whispered into Ray's ear.

Ian continued. 'Ray and Mary, would you please come up here to me?'

Ray got up, looking puzzled. *What's going on now?* he thought, as they walked across the room and stood by Ian.

'Ray, over the years you've never boasted about your exploits, but tonight we've living proof of one of them.' Ian paused again. 'Ray, can you remember the name of the child you rescued that night?'

Ray smiled. 'Course I can. I see her often, me and Mac. Well, we're her godparents. Her name's Jessie Turner. Is she here?'

Ian beamed. 'You're right, she is here. Come over, Jessie.'

A young woman emerged from the large group of people. She was carrying a small child and was crying openly, tears streamed down her face, as she walked across to Ray, falling into his arms and sobbing on his shoulder.

Ray tried hard not to get emotional also. He motioned across the room. 'Come over, Mac,' he called.

Mac got out of his chair and walked across the room. The people in the room were applauding. Mac walked up to Ray and Jessie and put his arms around them both.

Ray said with a voice cracking with emotion: 'Thank you for coming, Jessie. It's made my night.'

The applause subsided. Ian continued: 'We have one other special visitor. She insisted that she came. Please welcome Irene Blackburn, the widow of Dick Blackburn.'

Every person in the room was standing, applauding the small group of people who encapsulated everything the fire brigade stood for. Ian Blain put the card back into his pocket and joined in the applause.

Irene took the microphone from Ian; she coughed nervously and began to speak.

'To be here tonight means so much to me. It's many years since I lost my husband in the fire that Mr Blain spoke about. It hadn't been my plan to say anything at all, but having heard what everyone else has said, I just wanted to be here to say to you all that Ray is a very special man. Over the years, he's helped me in all sorts of ways, taken me shopping, brought me the Benevolent parcel round at Christmas, and he and Mary have even taken me on holiday with them. They are a lovely couple and they deserve a long happy retirement. I am proud to be a friend of theirs.' There was more applause from the audience.

Jessie took the microphone from Irene and looked up at Ray.

'When I lost my family in the fire I was only a baby, so I have no memory of the fire, only what I've been told. I want to say to Ray and to Mrs Blackburn, 'thank you' from the bottom of my heart for giving me and my baby a life.' She stopped and wiped her eyes with a handkerchief. 'Mrs Blackburn's husband died saving me and I can't find the words to express my feelings about it. I feel a mixture of love and gratitude for Ray and Mac, who have always been a great support to me, as have their wives, Mary and Val. I also feel pain at the loss of my family, but most of all I wish there was some way I could have known Dick. I feel the pain of Irene's loss. Her husband made a conscious decision to push his luck attempting to save a child he didn't know. I'm so grateful but so sad at the same time.'

Irene moved across to Jessie, put her arm around her, and stroked the baby's hair. Jessie continued. 'All of you firemen here, remember Ray and Mac and Dick and Irene. They did the ultimate. Be proud to be associated with them, as I'm proud to know men like you.' She handed the microphone to Ian and pushed up against Val, who put her arm around her.

The audience were clapping, and shouting 'speech, speech'. Ray looked at Mary and smiled. His eyes filled with tears, as he waved his hand to quell the applause.

'Ladies and gentlemen,' he said, 'my speech will be short.' A shout of 'thank God' emerged, followed by laughter and then 'that'll be a change' , coming from a group of firemen who clearly were having a good time.

'I never thought today would come. In all my service, I've never looked forward to retiring, I've loved the job so much. I love the work, going to fires and the stuff we all do day to day. It was more like a hobby than a job.' He paused. 'And now it's over, chapter two begins, off to do something different.' He paused and looked around, and then he put his arm around Mac's shoulder.

'There are three good things about the Fire Brigade. The work – dirty, horrible, stinking, sometimes dodgy, sometimes boring, but always different jobs we have to do, there was never a day when I didn't want to come to work.' Ray paused briefly. 'The second thing is the people you help from time to time. You remember them. The old biddy that lost her keys. So you scramble up a ladder, in through the bedroom window, and let her in just before she finds the keys in the bottom of her handbag.'

There was laughter. Everyone recognised the character. 'Then there's the casualties we drag out of cars, injured. They see us almost as a Messiah, exuding their gratitude. That's worth a lot. Do you think a bank clerk gets that? I don't think so. We're lucky, we get lots of it. And then there's Jessie, lovely Jessie. People like her, the lives you save that make everything worthwhile. Who needs pay when you get Jessie coming to see you on your last day?' There was more applause. Ray waved his hands again. 'Settle down, I've not finished yet.' Ray wiped his sleeve across his eyes.

'Then, thirdly, there are the mates. You lot,' he said with a mock snarl on his face. 'Yes, you lot. You make being in this job worthwhile, we all – well us old dinosaurs – complain about how it was better in our day. Well it was in some ways, but the blokes are the same. I'll take with me many memories of all of you. I'll think about you and wonder what you're up too, and yes, I'll miss you. I hope you all have the good fortune to meet and work with the type of men I've had the good fortune to work with, like good old Dick, and my buddy Mac, here. I must never complain about you modern guys, about your commitment. Why, only a day or two ago a young recruit, not yet out of training school, put his life on the line trying to rescue a woman from a fire just down the road from here. He learned that commitment from us; from the traditions we've carried on from our predecessors, and are now passing the baton on. Young Jake, that recruit showed he has what it takes to do the job alongside us, so don't let old fogies like me tell you they were better. You're as good as we were.' Ray stopped talking and the audience began applauding again.

'Anyway, young Jake came out of hospital this morning, and I say 'good on him, good on all of you'. I'm grateful to have shared your lives, thank you.'

As Ray put down the microphone, the audience erupted and cheered, while the families and friends flooded across the room, all wanting a piece of him.

28

Maddie's mobile phone rang just as she was about to get into bed. 'Hello,' she said, wondering who it could be, calling at this late hour.

'Hiya, it's me,' Jim said, picturing Maddie's face as he spoke. 'I just called to say I love you,' Jim said lightly.

'Did you now, James? Is that it, then?'

'No, I wanted to talk about us and me and what I should do.'

'What do you mean, what you should do?'

Jim was quiet for a second.

'Are you still there, Jim?' Maddie asked, wondering if he'd lost the line.

Jim was thinking how to phrase what he wanted to say. He knew that if he didn't think it out, it would all come out wrong.

'Well, Mad, I want to change my job. I think I can do better than I'm doing now. I thought you may have some idea.'

Maddie thought for a second. 'I'll tell you what, Jim. It's late and I'm on duty early in the morning. We need to talk properly about this, so how about we meet tomorrow afternoon, after my shift? We can have a drink somewhere and a proper chat, and it would be nice to get together anyway. What do you think?'

Jim laughed. 'Sounds good to me. Shall I pick you up?'

'Yeah, that'd be good. How about at my house, then we'll have a drive out into the Peaks ... and one more thing, mister.' Jim wondered what she was going to say. 'I love you, too. Now get off the phone and let this gorgeous nurse of yours get some beauty sleep.'

'OK then. I'll pick you up tomorrow, about half past three,' Jim said, a broad smile crossing his face.

Mac was never keen on starting a tour of duty on a Sunday. Sunday on a fire station is a strange day. Half of the day is spent cleaning the station, the other half of the day, the boys relax. Not the sort of day to get your teeth into anything.

Mac was in the Station Office having a conversation with his opposite number, Alan Wilson, the officer in charge of the off-going night watch. They'd had a serious house fire during the early hours of the morning and they were all looking a bit jaded.

'Yeah, Mac. Sorry we didn't get the gear cleaned up. Didn't get back till a quarter past five, so we just re-stowed, serviced the sets and sorry we left you the dirty work.'

'No problem. It'll give the boys something to do,' Mac replied.

Their conversation was interrupted when there was a knock on the office door. 'Come in,' Alan called.

The door opened and a fireman dressed in his working trousers and a dirty anorak stood in the doorway.

'And who might you be?' Alan asked.

The man – in his early forties with unshaven face – looked at the two junior officers. 'I start here today on Red Watch.'

Mac looked at the man for a moment. 'Red Watch, are you sure? We were due to get a bloke called Peter Jacks.'

The man looked confused, 'Yeah, that's me,' he said with a weak smile on his lips.

'Are you trying to tell me that you're in the Fire Brigade,' Mac said.

The man looked bemused. 'Yeah, that's me. I was told to report here today.'

'What station have you come from?' Mac quizzed.

'Halifax Road. I've been there ten years,' the man replied.

Mac turned to Alan. 'Do you mind, Sub? I think I need to have a word with Mr Jacks.'

The Sub Officer smiled. He had a notion of what was about to happen.

'Sit down there, Mr Jacks,' Mac said, directing him to a plastic chair, set in the corner of the room. 'Let me ask you why you wanted to come to this station and this watch.'

Jacks scratched his head. 'Well, it's nearer home and I wanted a change,' he answered.

Mac looked at the man he saw before him; the very essence of everything he disliked, a man with no pride in his appearance, who seemed to have no respect for the job and only wanted this transfer because it was nearer home.

'Well, Mr Jacks, I'm going to give you a choice.' Mac paused. 'If you want to be on this station, on my watch, things have got to change; you've got to change.' Mac paused again. 'Here's the choice. You either piss off back to where you came from, because I won't tolerate a person like you on my watch, we have a standard on this station and frankly you don't reach it – you're a scruffy individual …' Mac paused once more. 'On the other hand, the second choice … I don't mention this to any one, you go away for the morning, you get a wash, a shave, a haircut, you press your trousers and you turn up back at this station looking clean and smart. That's your choice. I won't tolerate someone in your state on my watch, do you understand?' Mac's voice cut through him like a razor.

'Yes.'

'Yes what, Mr Jacks?' Mac spoke, his voice steely but controlled.

'Yes, sub.'

Mac looked at him; it was plain that he'd never been confronted before. 'So, Mr Jacks, what are we going to do?'

'I'll go and get changed.'

'You'll go and get changed what, Mr Jacks?' Mac said, glaring directly into Jacks eyes.

'I'll go and get changed, sub.'

'That's much better. Off you go. Back here for thirteen hundred hours, OK?'

Jacks turned and left the office. Mac smiled to himself. *That will be a nice little job for Tony to get his teeth into*, he thought.

Jim pulled his car to a halt outside Maddie's house; there were a few neighbours out mowing their lawns, washing cars or generally tidying up their gardens. All morning, Jim had been checking his watch, anxious to go and pick Maddie up from her home. He thought to himself how different it was to the area he came from, where no one gave a damn about their property. He liked this place and felt that if he tried and worked hard, he could maybe buy a house like this in time.

Maddie was looking out of the lounge window. She saw Jim pull up outside and waved to him from the window. Jim saw her and waved back. Two minutes later, she walked down her drive and turned to wave to her mother, who stood peering out of the window.

'Hello, Jimbo. How are you?' Maddie asked, as she climbed into the car.

'I'm fine,' Jim replied, unable to control the massive smile on his face.

Maddie leaned across the car and kissed him. Jim could see her mother looking at them out of the window and wondered what she would think, their daughter going out with him.

He drove out of the city, keen to get out to the hills and to get to talk to Maddie. The road climbed steadily, taking them out to the open moorlands. The roads were busy, the peaks filling with people taking advantage of the nice weather.

'Where are we going, Jim?' Maddie asked.

Jim looked across the car at her. 'I thought we would go for a drink and a sandwich at the Yorkshire Bridge, and then have a chat and a gentle stroll by the dam. How does that sound?' he said.

They drove by Fox House and along to the Surprise View.

'Phew! You know, Jim. That view always impresses me. I don't think I'll ever get tired of looking at it,' Maddie said, as they turned the sharp bend overlooking the village of Hathersage. 'Do you think you'll bring me to see it when I'm old and grey?' she said, leaning across to him and ruffling his hair with her hand.

'You know me, my love. Your wish is my command ... and anyway, you won't be grey. I'll get you to dye your hair,' he replied, grinning at her.

They drove on through Bamford and pulled into the car park at the side of the public house. They could see that along the roadside there were dozens of cars parked, their occupants having left them and gone for a walk or just stopped for a few minutes to take a photograph of the reservoir and the surrounding hills.

'You know, Jim. Now that we are a sort of an item, we should do this a bit more often, maybe come out in the evening for a drink and a chat,' she said as they sat in comfortable chairs in the lounge bar. The pub had a warm atmosphere. Despite being a large building, it retained an intimacy: low lighting, and pictures on the wall depicting the Lancaster Bombers which practiced their flying skills over the Ladybower and Derwent dams, before going on their epic task of bombing the dams on the Ruhr Valley in Germany, during the war. This helped to create a homely atmosphere. The lounge was filled with families, many out for their Sunday lunch. Maddie sipped her orange juice and Jim was half way down a bottle of lager.

'I need to talk to you, Mad. I'd like you're advice,' Jim said, an earnest look on his face.

She noticed the look. 'What is it, love?' she said, unsure of what he was about to unburden.

Jim shuffled in his seat. Finding the words again was proving hard for him. 'Well, what with everything that's happened over the past few weeks, it's sort of given me a boost, you know, and I'm not sure I'm satisfied with my lot. You've made me realise that I could maybe do a bit better with my job, so I thought I'd ask you what you thought about it.'

Maddie took hold of his hand. 'You know what? I like you as you are, you don't have to push yourself to impress me. You know that, don't you?'

'Yeah, I know that. It's just that, since we've been going out, I've felt like I can improve myself, and that's down to you. You know, I've stopped smoking. Look, I've got some decent clothes now. If it hadn't been for you that would never have happened. Now I think I can do better in a job. I'm fed up with being a security guard. It does my head in. What do you think I could go for?'

'What would you like to do?'

'I'm not sure. One time, I fancied being a fireman. I tried three times and failed every time. Most jobs I fancy, I'm not qualified for,' Jim said, looking sorry for himself.

'It seems to me that you need to think about what you'd like to do, then find out what qualifications you need to do it, then go and get them. Nothing's easy. They don't give good jobs away on a plate. What do you think you'd like to do?'

'I fancy the idea of being a plumber or some trade in building.'

Maddie was a bit taken aback. This was a new idea. He'd never shown any interest in practical things. 'Why that, Jim? It'll be tough, but if you're serious, go for it.'

'I am serious,' Jim replied. 'Very serious,' he said, a determined look fixed into his pale features.

Red Watch had finished their work for the morning. Drill had gone well. It had passed without anyone getting too wet, they'd washed out the appliance room, cleaned the kitchen and recreation room, and now at thirteen hundred hours, they'd stopped for lunch.

Pete Jacks pulled his car into the station yard, but he was not happy. He'd gone about his business for years, and no one had ever spoken to him in the way he had been spoken to today. He took his bag and his fire gear out of the boot of his car and carried it across the yard into the rear of the appliance room. He walked up the stairs onto the mess deck; the crew were just about to sit down for lunch. Mac saw him come in and noticed that there'd been a marked improvement in his appearance.

'Come in, Mr Jacks. Take a seat. We've done you some shepherd's pie,' Mac said, looking carefully at the new man.

He was taken aback. He'd half expected that, after such a bad start, he wouldn't have been offered lunch.

'Thanks,' he said, sitting down quietly next to Jock.

Jock offered his hand. 'Welcome to Red Watch, the best watch in South Yorkshire,' Jock said, in his finest Glaswegian accent.

'Thanks a lot,' Jacks said and he set about eating his shepherd's pie.

Mac spoke. 'This guy is Pete Jacks, from Halifax Road. Make him welcome and show him the ropes, and what we require on this watch. And, Mr Jacks… at two o'clock my office please.'

Jacks felt that the sky was about to fall in on him. He wondered what the sub officer would have to say next.

Jake sat at home, bored and desperate to get back to his mates in the training school. His mother had cooked them a lunch of beef and roast potatoes, sprouts and gravy, along with her own version of Yorkshire pudding, with a few raisins in the mix. It was Jake's favourite. 'That was lovely, mum. Shall I give you a hand with the washing up?'

'No, you keep those hands out of hot water. They're still a bit sore. You know what the doctor said. You're OK, but take it easy.'

Jake picked up the local paper and was thumbing through the pages. He saw a picture of Mac and a group of other Firemen. He read the article, which spoke about a leading fireman who had just retired, and gave a short overview of his career in the Fire Brigade. On the next page he saw a picture of himself, sat up in his hospital bed, looking bewildered. The headline read: 'Young *Fire Recruit in Heroic Fire Rescue Bid*.' Jake was surprised to be reading about himself in the local paper.

The report gave statements from the brigade. One said: Recruit J. Higgins acted in the very best tradition of the Fire Service. A further report said Mr Higgins, after a valiant attempt to rescue a young lady from her burning bedroom, was overcome by the smoke and also had to be rescued by fire fighters from Graveton.

Only now was the enormity of what he'd done beginning to sink in. *I almost died. How bloody stupid was I?* He remembered the panic he'd felt when he knew he would have to breathe, knowing that if he did, he was beyond self-help. He'd made a mistake.

The elation he had felt previously disappeared. Suddenly he felt guilt. *I almost died. Mum would have been left alone. Stupid Jake, bloody stupid.*

Jake's mum walked into the room from the kitchen. She saw the look on his face. 'What's up, Jacob?' she asked.

Jake looked at his mother, his face twisted with pain. He spoke in a broken voice.

'I don't know, mum. I was fine. I just started thinking how stupid I'd been. It nearly killed me, mum.' He paused, took in a deep breath and gathered himself. 'It just seemed the right thing to do. I didn't think too much about the consequences if I didn't find the girl. If I hadn't found her so quickly, I'm sure I would have died. I kept going; mum, even after I knew I should have stopped. I was stupid.'

Jake's mother stroked his shoulder. 'If you want to know what I think, Jake,' she said softly, 'I think you were very brave and I'm proud of you. I'm sure your friend Mac's proud of you, too.'

'Did I hear you right, mum? Did you call me Jake?' he said in amazement.

'Yes, Jacob was my boy's name. You're not a boy now. You're my son, a man, so it's Jake from now on,' she said, a look of pride covering her features.

'Come in Mr Jacks. Sit down,' Mac said.

Jacks entered the office tentatively, not quite knowing what to expect. 'Come on in, sit there,' Mac said, gesturing to the chair opposite his.

Mac had taken off his jumper and tie; he sat, relaxed, in his chair. 'Right, Peter,' he said, 'that was a bad start to your time here, so let's talk. Tell me about yourself .Who's your family, what do you want, what are your interests, etc?'

Jacks sat uncomfortably in his chair, unsure of the sub officer's motives.

'Well, sub, I've been in the job for fifteen years, mostly at Halifax Road. I'm married with two kids, I don't have interests, I just do part-time work to make ends meet.'

'What about your wife and kids, Pete?' Mac asked, trying to create a friendlier atmosphere.

'I've been married to Trudy for nearly twenty years. I've got two boys, Luke and Jason. They're eight and ten years old.'

'And what do Trudy and the boys think about you being in the job?' Mac said.

'I don't know, really. I've never made much of the job. We've always struggled for money, had a few debts … it's been hard. Since her illness, it's been especially tough.'

'Oh, what was wrong with her?' Mac asked.

'She's got multiple sclerosis; she's in a wheelchair, and she can't do much for herself, nowadays,' he said. 'In fact that's one of the reasons I wanted to get closer to home. It will make things a bit easier for her if I don't spend so long travelling.'

Mac was surprised to hear this. He'd no idea of his circumstances at home.

'Right, Pete. Let me tell you about this place. Graveton is a great station, it has some great characters. What we all have in common is the standard. Clearly this morning you didn't measure up, and you're still not at the level I want, but it's better than before. There are lads on this station who, if you let them down, will probably pull your head off. On the other hand, you become one of them, one of us, the team, the best team on the best station, you'll be made, they'll do anything for you. The choice is there for you.' Mac got up, opened his office door and shouted: 'Brian, bring two cups of tea in here will you?'

'Well, Pete, which Pete Jacks do I get here? The one who blends in and enjoys his work, or the Pete Jacks who's life becomes a misery?'

'I want to be one of the watch, sub,' he replied, enthusiastically.

'Well, Peter. Welcome to Red Watch ... and by the way, call me Mac from now on.'

Maddie and Jim left the pub, having decided not to walk along the dam but take a short drive towards the city instead, then pull off and do a short walk on the moor.

Jim pulled the car onto an unofficial parking area beside the A 57 close by a bridge over a stream which deposited itself into the dam. Jim looked at the map, 'This is Cut throat bridge' he said, drawing his finger across his neck and grinning wildly, 'if we cross the road here over the stream cut left then it's a gentle rising walk and we should get a good view of the dams from the end, how does that grab you?'

'Sounds lovely,' Maddie replied. 'Let's get our boots on.'

The day was pleasant but not too warm; a slight breeze drifted gently across the moor as they climbed easily upwards along a well-worn track. After twenty minutes they rested and sat on rocks, alongside the track.

'What was the best day of your life, Jim?' Maddie asked, looking right into his eyes.

Jim replied instantly. 'The day we made love down Miller's Dale. I'll never forget it. Even after I'm dead, I'll remember it,' he said, emphatically, as he took Maddie's hand and softly kissed it.

'Oh no, that was only the second best day for me,' she said, mischievously. 'Now let me think,' she said. 'It's very difficult for a girl you know. I know ... it was definitely ... no it wasn't ... it was, errr, the day I met you in Edale.'

They both laughed. Jim put his hand on Maddie's shoulder and kissed her. The kiss lingered. They didn't notice the large group of walkers heading down the track towards them.

'The group of Clarion Ramblers, out on their weekly pilgrimage, saw the young couple sat by the track absorbed in each other and smiled, chuckling to themselves as they approached. Each one in turn said: 'Good afternoon' or 'Lovely day for a walk' as they passed.

Jim and Maddie pulled apart looked at the group of mainly middle-aged men and women and felt slightly embarrassed, Maddie blushing, Jim turning his face away.

'Don't mind us, love. We're all jealous,' one elderly lady said, with a broad smile etched across her weather-worn face.

'Aah, she's right. I wish I could get my missus to give me a snog while we're out walking. Good luck to ya both.' The group marched on, laughing as they went.

'You're a dangerous man, Jimbo. You keep getting me into these compromising situations,' Maddie said, giggling.

Jim laughed. 'Come on, let's get going or we'll not get to see the view before it gets dark,' he exclaimed, as he casually tried to arrange his trousers.

Maddie teased him. 'Are your pants too tight my love?' she asked.

Jim looked sheepish, but smiled. 'When I'm with you, my pants are always too tight.'

After an hour of gentle strolling and stopping to admire the views over the nearby hills and reservoirs, they finally reached the top of the long, sloping track. The pathway disappeared downward steeply, towards a vast wooded area. To the front was a superb panorama, the dam laid out before them, the huge mass of Win Hill and the Mam Tor ridge disappearing in the distance. Across to their right was the upper Derwent valley, with its steep sides heavily wooded and inhabited by hill farms and sheep.

They stood transfixed by the scene; the sun was dipping in the west, the reddening sun reflecting on the water, the smooth waters of the dam having a peach-coloured hue. Across the valley lay the twin peaks of Crook Hill and just below lay Crook Hill Farm, appearing to be glued to the hillside. It was quiet. There was not a soul in sight, just the occasional bark from a distant dog, probably from one of the farms scattered across the hillside.

'Let's stay here, Jim. Let's watch the sun go down. I think this is paradise. I don't want to move from here,' Maddie said, with a hushed voice.

Jim spread his coat on the ground. 'Let's sit here. Don't want to get your dress dirty.' They sat, Maddie leaning against Jim, he with his arm around her shoulder, waiting for the sun to disappear behind the distant hills.

29

It was five o'clock in the afternoon. Red Watch were beginning to think about getting ready for the end of their shift. Most of the boys were in the rec room, watching television. Mac and Tony were finishing off the paperwork for the day.

'Well, Tony, how's it going, do you think?' Mac asked.

'It's great. I'm loving it. It's not as easy as I thought, but the more I do, the more I enjoy it. The lads are good; they've made it easier for me, despite the occasional wind-up and soaking I get,' Tony replied, thoughtfully.

'Well, I think you've done well. The boys are happy, the ADO's happy with what he's seen so far. I spoke to the DC the other day, and he's happy as well, so no problem. I did speak to the DC about you. They'll be looking to fill Ray's job permanently within the next month. Just so you know, I've told him you should get the job. Obviously they'll need to consider others who're qualified, but I reckon you're the strong favourite.' 'Really, Mac? That would be great. I'm not that keen on moving to get this first promotion, although if that's what it takes, that's what I'll have to do.'

The station lights came on. A second later, the alarm system activated.

'Cat up a bloody tree,' Brian shouted, as Jock started the fire appliance engine. 'Just what we need. I've only just leathered the machine,' Brian grumbled. 'Number Thirteen, White House Lane. Hey, isn't that near Ray's place?' Brian said, laughing.

Ray and Mary sat in the lounge of their house, having spent most of the day packing the van, ready to get away on their extended holiday. They heard a short burst of an appliance siren. Ray got up and peered out of the window in time to see the Graveton appliance pull up outside his neighbour's house. The crew dismounted and looked across at Ray's house. They saw Ray standing in the window and waved to him. He smiled and returned the gesture, but showing only two fingers.

'I wonder what they're up to,' he said to Mary.

'Well, I suppose you'll have a wander across and find out,' she said, a smile crossing her lips.

'Oh right, I'll do that,' Ray replied, trying to appear nonchalant. Ray pushed on his slippers and walked slowly across the road.

Mac met the owner of the cat, who was very worried. 'We can't get her down. We've been trying for hours and we've even put food down for her, but she's not shown any interest,' she said, her voice tense.

Mac peered up into the branches of the huge Beech tree. The cat sat there, looking down at the activity below, completely unconcerned about the stir it was causing.

'You know what?' Mac said 'A few years ago, we would have pitched ladders up into the tree, we'd have taken risks to get your cat. However, there've been fire fighters killed attempting to rescue cats from trees. Nowadays, the policy is that we don't do that.'

The woman appeared surprised. 'I thought you did rescue cats,' she said, and then asked: 'What should I do, then?'

Mac looked up into the tree again. The cat had now settled down and seemed to have a belligerent look in its eye as it lay comfortably on a large branch.

'There's an old saying,' Mac said. 'You'll never find a dead cat up a tree. At some stage, she'll come down under her own steam. Cats are the most agile creatures. She's up there, not because she's stuck, but because that's where she chooses to be.'

'So you think I should leave her, then?' the woman said, looking slightly less upset.

'I'm sure of it,' Mac replied. 'If she's still up there in a couple of days, give us a call again, and we'll see what else we can do, but don't worry about her.'

Mac walked back up the garden to the appliance. He saw the boys crowded around Ray, who'd come out to see them.

'Hiya, you old fossil,' Mac said. 'Has Mary got the kettle on?'

As Mac said the words, Mary came across the road with a tray full of mugs of tea and biscuits. 'When we heard you arrive, I just thought you might fancy a cuppa,' Mary said.

The boys swarmed around Mary. 'Just look at them, Ray. You'd think they hadn't had a drink for days,' Mac said.

Ray looked at the boys, his friends. 'You know Mac; I'm going to miss this. Who's the new boy? His face is familiar.'

'Yeah, we got him today. He's from Halifax Road. He'll be all right, I reckon. We'll soon knock him into shape. His name's Pete Jacks. He's got some problems, but he'll be OK.'

Ray turned around and saw the new man. He walked over to him, offering his hand. 'Hiya. I believe you're new on the watch. I'm Ray Swift, just retired from this motley crew. You've just become a member of the best crew in the brigade. Don't let them down.'

Pete was taken aback, but took Ray's hand. 'It's going to be tough, but I'll be working on it,' he said, a friendly smile crossing his face.

After five minutes of banter, Mac said: 'Come on, lads. Let's leave these two to get packed for their trip. The shift's nearly over, so let's get back and get the machine sorted.'

At five minutes to six, the off-going and on-coming watches mingled in the appliance room, ready for the changeover. Peter Jacks had found himself in conversation with a couple of the watch.

'How do you like it then, Pete?' Clive asked

'I wasn't very happy about the way Mac spoke to me this morning,' he replied.

'Oh, why was that then?' Clive asked.

'Well, he was a bit aggressive. He sent me off to get myself cleaned up,' Jacks replied.

Brian hovered close, listening to the conversation.

'So, what did you say to him?' Clive asked

'Nothing. I just went home and cleaned myself up.'

Brian entered the conversation. 'I hope you're not criticising Mac for telling you to get cleaned up, are you?'

'Well, no, not really. He just took me a bit by surprise. He was just a bit aggressive.'

'Let me tell you something, mate. There's a lot of pride on this watch. We all support each other, so if you criticise one of us, we take it personally. If you've a problem with

Mac, see him. He's man enough to let you say your piece. And finally, if Mac hadn't dealt with you about the state you turned up here in, then we would have, and you wouldn't have liked that.'

Feeling slightly sorry for Jacks, Clive added: 'we're here to help you, but you have to come up to the standard we want, so don't make it hard for yourself.'

The officers of the night watch had gathered. The crews stood facing each other.

'Crews, crews. 'Shun.'

Both day and night watches came smartly to attention.

'Off-going watch, dismiss. Duty crew, stand at ease. The duties for the shift are as follows …'

Red Watch made a half turn to the right, then walked briskly away to change and then head off home.

The watch had all but left. There just remained Mac and Pete Jacks in the locker room. He had deliberately hung back, wanting the chance to have a final word with Mac.

Mac saw him hanging about. 'Are you all right, Pete?' he said.

'Yeah, I'm OK thanks, Mac. I just wanted to thank you for today, for putting me right. A couple of the lads have just reinforced what you said earlier. I just want you to know I'll change … I'll work hard. I'm not used to this. It was easier at Halifax Road, but I think I'll be happy here.'

'I'm glad to hear it, Pete. I've not mentioned anything about this morning to them. I'll leave that to you to tell them about you in your own time, and don't forget: I may be the boss, but I'm one of you. You got a problem; tell me, if it will help.'

Jacks looked relieved. 'Thanks, Mac. I'm looking forward to tomorrow now and it's a long time since I've been able to say that.'

30

The morning sunlight pierced the flimsy curtains of Jake's bedroom. Six thirty in the morning and Jake was awake. He hadn't slept much during the night. He'd tried, but each time he'd begun to drift, the image of the fire came back into his head and he found himself analysing what he'd done.

He got out of bed and was immediately aware that parts that his skin still felt tender. *'I'm fine,'* he thought to himself. He walked into the bathroom and prepared to have a shower. He could feel the tightness in his chest. His lungs were sore; as he coughed, a large lump of blackened phlegm entered his mouth. Jake spat it out into the toilet and watched the last remnants of the fire swirl around the water in the toilet pan. *That's better out than in,* he thought. He realised that his tubes now felt substantially clearer. He flushed the toilet. Maybe *I'll get some sleep now,* he said to himself.

Ray and Mary were in their campervan, heading south on the M1. The sun was bright, though still low in the eastern sky. Traffic was unusually light for a Monday morning.

'Ray,' Mary said, a look of contentment on her face, 'I've been waiting for this day for years. There was a time I thought it would never arrive. After you're illness, I was sure it wouldn't happen, so let's make the best of this time, shall we?'

Ray looked across at her. 'This is our time now, lass. Let's make the best of what we've got.'

The hills of Sheffield disappeared into the distance behind them as Ray drove south, heading for Southampton.

Pete Jacks was the first of Red Watch to arrive for their second day shift. He was in the locker room, polishing his fire boots. His shoes shone, his trousers were pressed and he bore no resemblance to the man who had turned up at Graveton the previous day.

'Hiya, Pete,' a familiar voice spoke, breaking Pete's concentration.

He turned his head. Coming into the locker room was a fire fighter from Halifax Road who'd been on the night shift on standby, giving cover to the night watch.

'What's all this then, Pete, cleaning your kit?' he said mischievously.

Pete stood up from the bench. 'Hiya, Ben. I just realised what a scruffy sod I was. Thought to myself: new station, new start. The watch is great, the lads are good, and the JOs are on the ball. I'm looking forward to being here.'

'I'll believe that when I see it,' he replied.

Pete smiled to himself. *Little does he know. I've wasted years ... Not anymore.*

Clive rode into the station yard and fixed his bike to the smokehouse railing. He had decided that today was the day he would tell the boys about the baby and the wedding.

He could see from the cars parked that most of the watch were already here. He would tell them at tea break.

Mac was in the office, talking to Tony. 'Right, Tony. I've got things to do today. You're in charge. Before I go, keep your eye on Pete. Keep him on the straight and narrow. It looks like he's trying, so let's make sure he's up to standard and help him if he needs it.'

Tony was delighted that Mac felt he could be left in charge. 'OK, Mac. I'll keep an eye out.'

'I'll be back about dinnertime. Just keep on with the basic drills and hydrants,' Mac said, 'but really do what you like. I'll leave it up to you.'

Jake arrived at the Training Centre. He looked at the building, glad to be back. The lads had got there before him. He smiled to himself. He could see their cars parked. He went inside, where the locker room was bustling, the recruits brushing their coats and polishing boots, standing and checking each other out, in preparation for parade at eight forty-five. As Jake entered the locker room, they realised he was there.

'Whoooah. Hiya, Jake. Who's a bloody hero, then?' The squad milled around him. 'How ya feeling, Jake?'

'We went to look at the house. You were a lucky bastard. What was it like?'

Mark found his way to Jake. As he put his hand on Jake's shoulder and took his hand, the recruits became silent, understanding the bond between the two of them. 'How are you, Jake?' Mark said, a look of admiration crossing his face.

'I'm great, now. Felt rough at first, but I got the last of the soot up this morning.'

'You did great. We're all proud, including the instructors. They've talked about it a lot.'

Jake stood a while and listened to the comments. 'You know what, boys? I only did what you'd have done. The fire was there, so I couldn't ignore it. You would all have done the same.'

At that moment, the instructor came into the room. He stood in the doorway; his uniform glistened in the morning sunlight.

'Welcome back, Mr Higgins. Glad to have you back. Right, you lot, let's have your gear extra smart this morning; the BTO is going to inspect you.'

Brian had turned up at work, his face a vision of happiness. Wait *till the boys hear this. They'll probably laugh,* he thought to himself, unable to contain the broad smile stretching across his face. He dumped his gear on the locker room floor and noticed that Pete was already there. 'Morning, Pete. How's it going?' he said cheerfully.

'Hiya, Brian. I thought I'd get in early and get myself sorted out.'

'Good idea. You don't want Mac on your case again.'

Pete was looking pleased with himself and said: 'When I came here yesterday, I was a mess, but Mac put me straight. For a little while I resented it, but having thought about it, he's right. This is a good job, why abuse it?'

'With that approach,' Brian said, 'you'll be fine here, and we'll be happy to have you on the watch.'

Tony called the two watches to attention.

'Off-going watch, dismiss. Red Watch, stand at ease. The night watch fell out and wandered back to the locker room to change and get off home, after a busy night.

'Right, guys. Duties for today are, myself in charge ...' There was a muffled gasp from the crew.

'And what's the problem with that then?' Tony responded.

Brian spoke with a pained expression. 'Well, LF. You've not been in charge before. What will happen if we have a fire?'

'What will happen is that if you don't bloody behave yourself, I'll chuck you on the bloody fire,' Tony responded, with a laugh.

'Right, boys. Brian, you're driver. Clive and Pete, BA. Taff, number five and watch room. As for this morning, Mac has to go somewhere, so it's up to me ... so, do the routines, a quick cuppa, then I thought we'd go up to the river and do a bit of open water pumping. After tea break at eleven, we'll go out and do a couple of visits. OK, any questions?'

'Squad, squad, 'shun,' the order rang out clearly across the drill ground. The recruits slammed their booted feet into the concrete. Jake smiled; he was back where he belonged and he was happy. The change in the quality of everything his squad did was easy to see. When they marched, they were together; when they drilled they gave everything. The mistakes they made were fewer, albeit the instructors wouldn't readily acknowledge the fact: it was their job to keep them on the ball, so they were constantly pushed to produce higher levels of performance.

Jake stood smartly to attention in the centre of the three rows of recruits. The Brigade Training Officer was inspecting them today, flanked by the squad instructors who were equally well turned out. In fact they set the standards of turnout that the recruits aspired too. The officer looked carefully at each man and made appropriate comments. 'This man needs a haircut' then 'You require more work on those boots.'

After several minutes, he stood in front of Jake. 'How are we today, Mr Higgins?'

'I'm fine, sir,' Jake replied.

'Glad to hear it,' the BTO said.

The BTO had finished his inspection; the sub officer stood before them, his face unable to disguise the pride he felt in his squad. 'Right, lads. When I give the order fall out, take a half turn to the right and double away to your locker room. I will see you in the classroom in your number one kit in five minutes. Squad, fall out.'

Jake and his squad sprinted across the yard at full speed.

'Wonder what's happening?' someone said. 'This period we were supposed to be doing ladder drills.'

The squad sat smartly in their usual chairs in the classroom as the instructor entered. 'Officer present,' the squad leader for the week shouted. The class sprang from their chairs and stood rigidly to attention.

The instructor stood before the class. 'Right, lads. We've changed the routine this morning for two reasons, and I have to say it's never been done before, but we think that it's necessary. Reason one: our colleague, Mr Higgins, as you are aware, got himself into a little difficulty the other day. The result is that he's still got a bit of a problem with his lungs.'

Jake spoke up. 'Excuse me, sub. I'm fine and my lungs are fine. You don't have to worry about me at all.'

'Thank you for that, Mr Higgins. Just tell me who's in charge here, will you?'

Jake looked duly remorseful. 'You are, sub,' Jake replied.

'That's right, Mr Higgins. I'm in charge, so if I say your lungs are a problem, then you'd better believe it.'

'Yes, sub,' Jake replied.

'Right. Now that we've established that me being in charge means that I'm right, even if I'm wrong, I'll continue, if that's all right with you, Mr Higgins.'

'Yes, sub,' Jake said, struggling with the overwhelming desire to smile.

'Right, Mr Higgins's lungs are not firing on all cylinders today, so we will be doing class work. He's also been a little bit cooked. You may have noticed the red ears, the red hands and the lack of proper eyebrows. This indicates to me, and remember I'm always right, that is until I get home to the wife, that Mr Higgins was close to being badly burned.' The squad laughed. The instructor smiled.

'Settle down, now. You may laugh, but being married is a serious matter. Today, or at least for the first period, we will discuss with Mr Higgins the fire he almost but not quite escaped from.' There was a loud outburst of laughter from the squad. They noticed the instructor laughing along with them.

'Right Mr Higgins, come and sit out front here with me and let's talk about the fire. Let us learn from you. Tell us what happened, tell us how you felt, tell us what it was that made you commit yourself into such a dangerous situation.'

Jake sat behind the desk alongside the instructor. He felt awkward.

'Right, Mr Higgins. The other day, you got involved in a fire. You helped to save a life, but you almost lost yours. Tell the class about it. Let's see if there's anything there that will be worth learning.'

Jake scratched his head. 'I don't really know what to say. I was out having a run, when I saw the fire, rang nine nine nine, then I didn't know what to do, but I saw a girl's face at the bedroom widow, and from then I just seemed to go on auto pilot. I remembered what the sub had said about the back door being weaker than the front, so I managed to break that down. I remember realising that I had to be quick, because the smoke was thick and acrid. I knew if I breathed it in, that would be it.'

'Tell the class what you were thinking and feeling.'

'I just remembered about keeping low, find a wall and be quick. I don't remember feeling scared.'

'So you got into the house and you went upstairs. Tell us, what then?'

I remember the smoke being halfway down stairs, and because the house was like my house I thought I could find my way quickly. I knew where she would be, so I got low and went upstairs pretty fast. In fact I smashed my head into the wall at the top.' The squad laughed again. 'I knew I had to turn right but it's amazing how fast you lose your bearings when the pressure's on. I got into the room and found the bed. I couldn't see anything, the smoke was killing my eyes and it was hot.' Suddenly Jake was back in the room: he spoke fluently.

'I found a wall, and then I saw the fire through the smoke. I crawled round the room and bumped into the girl. By now I was desperate to breath, but I knew I couldn't, so I grabbed her with one hand and followed the wall back out to the stairs. I still couldn't see, but I knew I was at the top of the stairs. Then I breathed, and the smoke just killed me. I knew I was finished, but I didn't care. I just jumped down the stairs with the girl. Fortunately, we survived the fall, and luckily, the firemen found us before it was too late ... and that was it.'

The instructor listened intently. 'What did you learn, Mr Higgins?'

Jake thought for a minute, wrinkling his brow. He could see Mark smiling at him.

'Well,' Jake said, 'I've thought about it quite a bit. I've learned that a lot of what we've been taught is right; the back door thing, how important it is to keep low, although it was so hot I didn't have much choice. Have a plan, don't just run in like a chicken with its head cut off. The main things though were the search. If I'd not been here, I wouldn't have tried, I'm sure wouldn't have found her and survived without what you've taught us, sub,' Jake said, looking with gratitude at the instructor, 'and I now realise just how deadly the smoke is, and without BA we're useless.' Jake went quiet. The other recruits sat in quiet admiration of their friend and colleague.

'Right, lads. A good first-hand account of what a fire is really like. Remember, it's not an adventure, it's not heroic or glamorous; it's very, very dangerous. What we teach you here isn't just a load of crap. It's lessons, like you've just heard; lessons learned through experience over many years. Listen to what we tell you, learn those lessons and there's a good chance you'll survive to collect your pensions.'

The instructor stood up in front of the class. 'Right, lads. You've heard first-hand what it's like. At some stage of your career you'll be in a house, on fire. When conditions are desperate, remember this: the key is to take care, and always use your BA set. It's your lifeline to the fresh air outside, so don't forget it.'

Mac pulled the station van into the training centre's car park at the rear of the building. He could hear the noise of fire appliances and lightweight pumps running, and he could hear orders being shouted above the clamour of the revving pump engines. Men were running, carrying aluminium ladders and slamming them into the windows of the drill tower. Some were running at pace up the ladders, with hose dangling from their shoulders, while others were tying lines around the hose. The scene was one of organised pandemonium. Mac smiled. He was reminded of his times in training all those years ago. He stood and watched for several minutes, the instructors seeing him and waving to him without apparently taking their eyes from the recruits under their charge.

'Come in,' the BTO's voice emerged from behind the door of his office. Mac went in. 'Take a seat, Mac,' the BTO welcomed him. 'What can I do for you?'

31

Red Watch had finished their drill session. Taff had made the tea and done the cheese and onion sandwiches, and now the watch were chatting happily.

'Listen up, boys,' Brian said. 'I've got an announcement to make.'

'Well, bugger me, so have I,' Clive said.

The watch all laughed. 'What's going on here? Some sort of conspiracy is it, then?' Taff said, in his finest Welsh accent.

'No, you go first, Brian.'

'No, after you, Clive,' Brian retorted, laughing.

Clive stood up at the table. 'Well, boys, I would like you all to drink a toast ... a toast to me and Helen. We're getting married at last, and further to that, we're going to have a baby. I'm going to be a dad. The wedding is on the tenth of next month, the Saturday, so obviously you're all invited. Invitation cards are in the post.'

The watch crowded around Clive, shaking his hand and offering enthusiastic congratulations. Taff sat back, happy for Clive, but deep in his heart he felt the pain of both his and his wife's on-going problem about their inability to conceive.

'Taff,' he said. 'How'd you fancy the best man's job, then?'

Taff looked up, a smile crossing his face. 'It will be an absolute pleasure and honour, boyo,' he replied, climbing out of his seat and shaking Clive's hand.

'Come on then, Brian, what's your announcement then?' Tony said, amid the noise of the crew talking.

'Well, my news is interesting, but nothing compared with Clive's,' he said, feigning humility. 'Well, it's just that, well, I've been chatting to Jane about taking Bill on holiday, and it's OK. The thing is though; it seems that we fancy each other again, so the three of us are off on holiday in a couple of weeks to the Isle of Wight.'

'That's great, Bry. What's Jill think about it?' Clive said.

'She's pleased as punch; we're all happy about it, so fingers crossed, eh?'

The watch chatted and ate their sandwiches. 'Right, lads,' Tony said, 'let's get tidied up and get out. We've got an inspection at the Clearwater Children's Home.'

Brian turned the appliance into the parking area at the back of the home.

'Right, Brian, we're off to have a look around. You listen out for the radio. We should be about forty-five minutes.'

The watch disappeared into the building, while Brian sat in the cab of the fire appliance, his face shaded from the sun. As he sat, gently dozing and thinking about the holiday he was soon to have with his family, he heard footsteps approach. Opening his eyes and peering out of the cab window, he saw two young children – a boy and a girl, maybe seven or eight years old.

'Hello, mister,' the boy said, in a confidant voice.

Brian looked down at them from the height of the cab and put his head out of the window. 'Hello,' he replied.

'Is this your fire engine?' the boy asked.

'I suppose it is. Well, actually it belongs to the Fire Brigade, but today I'm the driver, so it's sort of mine for today,' he said, lightly, smiling down at them.

'Shall I show you around it?'

'Yes please,' they said in unison.

Brian climbed down from the cab of the appliance. 'Hello,' he said. 'I'm Brian. Who are you?'

The young boy spoke enthusiastically. 'I'm Peter and this is my little sister, Alice.'

'Do you want to sit inside the fire engine?' Brian asked the excited youngsters.

'Yes please,' they replied, clearly keen to explore the appliance.

One by one, Brian picked them up and sat them in the front seat of the appliance. He told them about the controls, he operated the flashing blue lights and then he told them not to play with matches. The children were fascinated, as Brian explained to them about the breathing apparatus equipment, and how, without it, they couldn't do their job so easily. They both had on a fireman's helmet and were keen to see the rest of the equipment on the machine.

The radio crackled into life. *'Alpha Zero One Zero. Over.'*

Brian pushed the switch and gave a short burst on the siren.

'I'm sorry, but we've got to go,' Brian said, quickly lifting the children to the ground and ushering them away from the appliance. 'Bye. We'll come again soon.'

The crew, led by Tony, burst out of the building. They could see that Brian was talking on the radio. They began quickly getting into their fire fighting kit.

'Alpha Zero One Zero. Your message received, and proceeding to Hillside Farm, Graveton, Leading Fireman Ellis in charge.'

'What we got, Brian?' Tony shouted across the cab to Brian as he began to swing the appliance around to negotiate the school gate.

'Hillside Farm. Dairy Cow stuck, up to its neck, in a slurry pit.'

'Oh shit,' Tony groaned. 'Just what I wanted for my first job.'

'Oh shit, is precisely what you got. Enjoy,' Brian laughed as they raced towards the Graveton Road.

Slurry pits and cows don't normally go together, but when they do, it's a problem and usually culminates in the crew being contaminated by large quantities of smelly bovine waste.

Tony surveyed the scene, as he stood alongside the demented farmer. 'She's in calf, you know. It's due in about two days.'

'Don't worry, sir. We'll fix it for you,' Tony said, trying to appear confident.

The crew nodded. They knew these jobs were hard and often unsuccessful, but they attempted to look positive, standing well back from the slurry, none of them keen on getting too close. They thought the time was right for Tony to take the lead.

Mac was in the office, talking to the Brigade Training Officer when the BTO's phone rang. It was control. 'Excuse me, sir. Can we speak to sub officer James?'

Mac took the phone, listened carefully to the message from control.

'I'm sorry, sir, but I'll have to go. Young Tony Ellis has just picked up his first job as a JO. I think I'll go along, just to give him a bit of support.'

'OK, Mac. No problem. I'll keep in mind what we've just spoken about. Take care.'

Mac jogged easily across the drill yard, taking care not to get in the way of the recruits, who were running in all directions around the yard.

Jake sat in the classroom. He, along with his squad, were in the middle of one of the weekly written tests. This one was one of his favourite subjects: Hydraulics. He'd struggled a bit at first, but it had been fine since he and Mark had got together, and Mark had taken time to explain the maths of it. Once he'd got that, he'd found it simple and straightforward. He glanced out of the window and saw Mac running smoothly across the yard, watched him get dressed in his fire fighting gear and then saw him drive out of the yard, with the blue lights of the van flashing. *'I wonder what Mac was doing here?'* he thought to himself.

'Right, lads. A quick confab, please.' The boys gathered around Tony.

'It seems to me we've got a job on here. This is the plan to start: we've got to get the crap away from the cows face, because we don't want it to drown. Then we've got to somehow dig under it to put hose and straps round it. The farmer is going to bring his tractor and we'll lift the cow out. How's that sound?'

'Sounds a good theory, but let's hope the practise fits the plan,' Brian said, looking a bit doubtful.

'Right, lads. Let's get two lengths of seventy mill hose, the short extension ladder, and all the lines off the machine. Get on with that and I'm asking for another appliance. We'll need the manpower.'

Mac was driving swiftly now. He reckoned he was about ten minutes' drive away from the job, and he didn't want to get there too quickly. It would be good for Tony to have to make a few decisions for himself.

In the classroom, Jake's mind was wandering. Having seen Mac driving from the yard, obviously on the way to an incident, he began musing on what it could be he was going to in such a hurry … maybe a car accident or a fire in a factory.

'Mr Higgins,' a voice – delivered from a mouth less than six inches away – rang in his ear. 'I am sorry. Are we disturbing you?'

Jake was suddenly drawn back from his dreamlike state. He almost jumped out of his seat. 'I'm sorry, sub,' Jake said, earnestly, realising that there would be a forfeit to pay.

'Mr Higgins, it seems that you know everything about hydraulics there is to know, so why bother listening to what I – a mere instructor – have to say on the subject.' Jake felt the embarrassment cross his face.

'Right, Mr Higgins. Perhaps you can stand up and tell the class everything you know about water.'

It was now that Jake began to really wish that he hadn't let his mind wander away from the here and now.

Jake stood up. 'I'm sorry, sub,' he said, his embarrassment obvious.

'Thank you for the apology, Mr Higgins. The class await your pearls of wisdom on the subject of water.'

Jake's voice faltered as he attempted to remember the information he'd been told in a previous lesson, and that had been reiterated during the period of his daydreaming.

'Water is a clear odourless liquid and is virtually incompressible. It is used by the fire service as its main source of extinguishing medium because it's very efficient at cooling the fire and is in plentiful supply,' Jake recited, parrot fashion. Then it dried up, his face reddened and his voice faltered.

'Is it true that water can exist in three states, Mr Higgins … that one is as a liquid, one is as a solid and the other is as a gas?'

'Yes, sub,' Jake muttered, wishing that he were somewhere else.

'Is it true that water, because it can be delivered as fine spray, will attract more heat and therefore be more effective at cooling a fire, thus reducing the temperature of the material below that at which that material will give off flammable gas, therefore being very effective at extinguishing fires, Mr Higgins?'

'Yes, sub,' Jake responded, his embarrassment growing by the second.

'Is it also true, Mr Higgins, that water in its liquid state can't resist a change of shape and will always take the easiest line to the lowest point and isn't this a problem to the fire brigade because if we put out fires with lots of water, Mr Higgins, then that water often ends up in a cellar?'

'Yes, sub.' Jake was now wishing to be anywhere but here.

'Clearly, Mr Higgins, your mind needs a rest, so I want you to go out into the yard and do me twenty laps … and whilst you're doing them, maybe you can think of all of the other properties of water that we haven't yet covered.'

'Yes, sub,' Jake replied, as he moved out from behind his desk towards the classroom door.

'One more thing, Mr Higgins. Take the rest of the class with you, and I want you all back in here in five minutes. Now move it.' There was an explosion of noise, as chairs were scraped back and discontented voices could be heard.

'Bloody hell, Jake. Don't we do enough running around, without this?'

'Shurrup moaning'. He's helped you out often enough,' someone replied.

The squad began the steady run around the yard, Mark catching Jake up and jogging along by his side. There was a general feeling of hilarity and they were soon all laughing. 'You know, Jake, we covered that section on water while you were in hospital, so you did OK. Besides, this is great. I think we were all getting twitchy, sat there for so long. The exercise will do us all good.'

Sub Officer Blackett looked out of the window. He could see from the body language that the squad he had nurtured for these weeks were a team. Once again, young Jake had been the catalyst. He grinned broadly. Not long to go to their pass out and they were well on track, he thought, with some satisfaction.

The cow was stuck solid into the slurry, which had the consistency of thick porridge. This created an enormous amount of suction around the beast. Working was difficult, as there was only access to the cow from one side – the concrete hard standing – which was where all of the rescuers were located.

A second appliance had arrived from the city central station. This appliance carried ACROWS and heavy lifting gear. The leading fireman was happy to work with his crew, allowing Tony to remain in charge of the incident. Beyond the exhausted cow lay what appeared to be a sea of slurry. The crews had used spades and shovels to remove large amounts of material from around the cow's head, and had subsequently made progress digging down the side of the cow adjacent to where they stood. In the process, Taff had fallen in up to his thighs and had to be dragged out by the lads, much to their amusement.

'It isn't funny, you bastards. I'll stink for a month,' Taff had said, awaiting his opportunity to help someone else to share the experience.

Mac drove into the farm, following the water tracks of the appliances as they wove through the various farm buildings. He parked the van and walked the last forty yards, passing between low corrugated buildings which, years ago, had been painted black but were now showing signs of rusting around the edges. He emerged from between the building and could see, off to his right, a cluster of men working furiously. He saw that Tony was standing back and watching, keeping a general overview of the incident.

'How's it going, Tony?' Mac asked, as he approached from behind the crew.

Tony swivelled around, grateful to hear the familiar voice of his friend and boss.

'It's OK, Mac, but we're struggling a bit. It's difficult to get access to both sides of the cow, no hard standing on the other side.'

'Looks to me like you've done OK so far. I don't want to take over. I'll have a look around.'

'Thanks, Mac. I'd appreciate that,' Tony said, the relief clear in his voice.

Mac walked across to the group of men who were digging away from the one side, most of them covered in the slurry. He then walked off and spoke to the farmer. A few minutes later, he returned and took Tony to one side. 'This is what I reckon, Tony. I've seen the farmer. He's got stacks of pallets in the barn. You can use them to get around the other side of the cow. They'll float on top of the slurry, so we can use them as ramps to work from, and we can then dig around the cow from all sides. Then somehow we need a way to get the slings under the cow, so get your mind on that little problem. The farmer will help with his tractor. One more thing: ask for a vet. You might just need one.'

Ian Blain was on his way back to Divisional HQ, having just had a particularly frustrating meeting with the chief and the union regarding overtime working. Normally, these meeting were straightforward, but today, the union secretary had been particularly belligerent. He'd wasted time and been uncooperative, much to the irritation of the officers who were making serious attempts to apply some sense to what should have been a simple problem. Unable to come to an agreement, the chief was forced to finish the meeting and arrange for a further meeting after the union secretary had consulted his members.

Ian heard radio traffic regarding an incident with a cow trapped in slurry and decided he would take a look, since it was on his route back to divisional HQ. *This is something different,* he thought, seeing it as part of his operational education.

'What do you reckon now, Mac?' Tony asked, looking earnestly at Mac for some inspiration.

'It's your job, Tony. Think it out. Get a plan, talk to the crews, then do the job. It's as simple as that.' Mac said it with his tongue in his cheek. He realised this was an especially difficult job; he did, however, think that Tony was doing OK, and he saw it as an opportunity to have a look at him, to see how he coped.

'Right, lads. Let's have a quick chat. This is what I reckon we need to do …' After a couple of minutes of conversation with the crews, he concluded: 'OK, let's get to it.'

Mac smiled. He could see Tony was growing in confidence.

Ian Blain pulled his car up at the farm, next to Mac's van. He dressed in his fire gear and walked through the farm buildings. He spotted the crews some way off as he walked over to Mac. 'Hello, sub. How are things going?'

'They're doing well, sir,' Mac replied. 'Surprised to see you here, though.'

'I was on my way back to the office when I heard it on the radio … thought I'd come and have a look.'

Mac looked across at the crews. He caught Tony's eye. 'Come over here, LF,' he called. Tony jogged across, looking bedraggled, and smelling strongly of farmyard products. 'Tell the DC what you've got, LF.'

Tony pulled himself up to his full height and tried without success to look smart. 'Well, sir, we have a fully-grown dairy cow, in calf, buried up to its eyeballs in slurry. The problem was that we could only approach from this side. Then it was decided to use pallets to operate from all around the cow, to remove as much slurry as possible, one, to reduce the suction effect on the cow when we try to lift her, and two, to enable us to get the straps under her. Once that's done, we'll try to lift her using the strops, hose and the tractor.'

'Thanks for that very concise report, LF.' Ian turned to Mac and smiled. 'He seems to be doing OK.'

'Yes, sir, he's a good lad. I'm letting him get on with it. It'll be useful experience for him. I'll help if he needs it.'

There was the sound of a muddy crunch, instantly followed by laughter. Both Mac and Ian looked across at the bunch of men at the slurry pit side. Yet another of the crew had fallen in and was having to be forcibly extracted from the stinking morass.

'Shall we get up closer, Mac.? Let's see if we can help,' Ian said, enthusiastically.

Mac grinned. 'If you insist, boss. I'm sure the LF will be delighted to have your input.'

'How can I help, Tony?' Ian Blain asked.

'Well, sir, we're just about to try to get the hose and strops under the cow. We've managed to dig out around her, and hopefully the plan will work.'

'How do you intend getting the hose under her?' Ian asked.

'There's no easy way. Somebody's got to get into it. I thought if we tie lines around chimney rods, we should be able to thread the line under the cow, now that we've cleared away at the sides.'

'And how are you going to pick the line up on the other side?'

'Well, I figure once we feel the line has gone under, we can use the ceiling hook to feel around in the slurry and hopefully retrieve the line, then attach the hose and strops to the line and pull them under.'

'Well, that sounds fine. How about I give the boys a rest on the other side of the cow? I'll try to fish out the line with the hook.'

'Are you sure, sir?' Tony enquired; he, like all of the crew were not familiar with a Divisional Commander getting so involved.

Mac smiled to himself. He foresaw only one outcome, only part of which would be the retrieval of the line. He waited with interest to see if his instinct was correct.

Sub Officer Blackett stood at the front of the class of recruits. He felt proud. Over the preceding weeks he'd moulded this bunch of raw youngsters into a tight group of technically excellent individuals. The one female in the squad had performed well. Despite her lack of stature, she'd grown in strength and confidence over the weeks, and now, in the lead up the pass out, she'd leave training school qualified and capable of doing the job. That was the criterion he always applied; their colour or sex was irrelevant. Could they do the job? Would he ride with them to a fire with confidence? And with this squad, he could say 'yes', unequivocally, about them all.

He'd discussed the squad with the BTO and expressed doubts about some of the recruits during their training, but over the weeks they'd all improved and were now functioning as a team. They had all matured and grown into the job.

They'd discussed Recruit Fireman Higgins at length. He was exceptional, a natural leader, but always unassuming, never cocky or arrogant. He'd been the driving force of the squad. Many of the squad would have struggled, had Jake not cajoled and encouraged them to work harder. He often said things that impressed everyone, including the instructors.

Today is important, if you want to go on the beer, give less than the one hundred per cent the Sub Officer wants, you deserve to fail. Don't let yourselves or the squad down.

This was a message that Jake often delivered, but with venom and determination.

Since the incident of the rescue, Jake had become a hero to every recruit in the training school. The instructors, having seen what he did and respected the effort he'd made, also thought that, despite the self-inflicted danger he put himself in, he had done well. They'd discussed the top recruit award and decided that it was a very short list of one; Recruit Higgins would receive the silver axe at the pass out parade.

Ian was balancing on the pallet, which moved every time he shifted his weight. Across, on the other side of the cow, one unfortunate fireman, the youngest one, had been volunteered to be suspended, head down, into the slurry. He had the line attached to the chimney rods and was straining to push the lines under the cow. 'I reckon that's through, LF,' the young man exclaimed triumphantly through lips heavily stained by excrement.

'OK, well done, Ashley. Right, sir, can you manoeuvre the hook and try to fish out the line?' Tony asked politely, finding it hard to give his boss instructions.

Mac stood on a pallet adjacent to the DC and level with the rear end of the cow, and looked on in admiration as Ian, balancing precariously, pushed the hook into the dark brown oozing slurry. 'I think I've got it,' Ian exclaimed, triumphantly.

'Well done, boss,' Tony shouted across at him, genuinely relieved that his plan had worked.

The crews appreciated what the DC was doing. He didn't have to do this; it had never been known before.

Ian pulled on the hook and the line emerged from the slurry. 'If we've got the hose attached, I'll pull it through, LF,' Ian exclaimed.

'It's all connected, sir. Pull when you're ready,' Tony replied.

At first the line was taut, so that Ian had to exert some weight to the line to get it to move. It moved slowly at first, but then got easier. Suddenly, the line became taut again. Ian surmised that the coupling of the hose had caught under the cow's stomach.

'It's caught. I'll give it a tug,' Ian called, jerking the line. Initially it was taut, but without warning it was free from whatever had jammed it. The line slackened suddenly, and Ian's weight rocked violently to one side. Mac tried to catch him, but failed. In a second, Ian was stuck in the slurry up to his waist. The crew laughed momentarily and then went quiet.

'It's OK, lads. Get me out of here. I can't complain. I stood over there, laughing, when you fell in,' he said, trying hard to retain his dignity.

The crews gathered around and within a couple of minutes, Ian had been released from the clinging mess. He laughed at himself and, surprisingly, felt glad to be there with the lads from his division, going through what they had to go through. It felt good.

Thirty minutes later, the tractor had been brought in, the hose and strops passed under the cow were secured and the cow, exhausted but uninjured, was lifted from the slurry. The vet, who had arrived ten minutes earlier and had witnessed the scene, gave it a quick examination and confirmed that the cow, though exhausted, appeared to have come through the experience quite unharmed.

'Right, sub, let's get the lads together. Just a quick debrief,' Ian requested.

The crews had washed all of the equipment and managed to scrape and wash off the debris from their gear, but the smell would live with them for months.

'Right, boys, just a very quick debrief. I know you're all keen to get back to station and get showered. I know I am, so I won't keep you long. Today, you have done a brilliant job. It was rotten, the smell and the conditions were the worst I've seen, but you all got stuck in and you saved a very valuable asset for Mr Briggs the farmer. Well done to all of you, especially to the new LF. You did well, Tony.'

'Can I just say a word?' Mac had come to the front of the group. 'Just a couple of things. As a group, you all did very well. I didn't once feel that I needed to interfere. Well done for supporting Tony on his first job. Secondly, thanks to the DC. He could have driven in and straight out again … we've seen that before. I think the DC did well. Thank you, boss.'

'Right, lads, head 'em up, move 'em out,' Tony shouted to the crews.

The appliances moved steadily away from the farmyard. Mac and Ian stood for a couple of minutes talking about the incident. 'I think our Mr Ellis is going to be OK, Mac.'

'I reckon you're right, boss. Watching them today makes it easier for me to contemplate leaving. They did well. I know I'm going and leaving good guys behind to carry on.'

'You're right, and of course I hear good things about your protégé, young Jacob Higgins. It seems he impresses a lot of people.'

'Do you know what?' Mac said. 'The moment I met the lad, I knew he had something. I didn't know what, but he'll be great for the brigade, I think.'

'Just like his mentor then, Mac,' Ian said, slapping Mac on the shoulder.

32

25th September 1996:

Jake sat alongside Mark. They'd both looked forward to the end of the basic drills. Now they had two weeks of intensive training on breathing apparatus and road accident procedure to concentrate on. The rest of the squad sat there, nervously waiting for their instructors to enter the room to brief them on what the next two weeks had in store for them.

As Jake looked around the room, he saw the fourteen-strong group of recruits he'd spent the past few weeks with. They looked lean and fit and Jake had emerged from the group as the natural leader: it was readily acknowledged by them all that Jake was in a different class on the drill ground. He seemed to be able to draw the group together, especially when times got tough and some of the group were under pressure to perform.

The instructors were impressed. Even though Jake was the youngest of the squad, he carried himself in a confident but mature way. He was happy to fool around with the rest of the group, but he would do nothing that would impact on his performance in his training.

The door of the classroom swung open and the squad jumped to attention, as three instructors entered.

The head instructor wore his undress uniform, while the other two were dressed in heavily-scorched fire gear, lending them an image of toughness and authority.

'Right, folks, sit yourselves down. Welcome to the BA School. For the next week, you're going to be taught the basics of BA. You'll learn the theory of the equipment and the procedures that we use, and you'll spend a great deal of time over the next few days in hot and smoky conditions. It's going to be hard, but I guarantee you'll enjoy it.' He turned around and smiled.

'Now for the introductions. I'm Sub Officer Pearce; my colleagues here are Sub Officer Hardy and Sub Officer Randall. We're here to teach you, you're here to learn. How well we teach and how much you learn may decide if at some time in your career you live or die. Breathing apparatus is a vital tool for the fireman. Today, we can't do the job without it.' The sub paused and looked at the group of recruits. Like so many before, they all looked apprehensive.

'To begin, I'll be talking to you about BA procedures, how they developed into use and why. Then we'll look at the procedures in more depth ... boring, I know, but these are the safeguards that will help you at a fire. After tea break, the other subs will talk to you about the equipment, and then you'll get to take a BA set to pieces and reassemble it and also learn about the other gear we use in conjunction with the BA set.'

Jake and Mark stood together, along with the rest of their squad.

'I thought this morning's stuff was interesting,' Mark said.

'Yeah, but the practical will be better. Can't wait to get started,' Jake replied.

The squad stood in line on the outside of the smoke chamber, waiting for the instructors to arrive. They could smell the residual smoke from a thousand other fires in the building, and all of their hearts beat a little bit faster.

They saw the instructors walking across the yard, two of them diverting and disappearing from view. As one of the sub officers approached, the squad came to attention. 'Right, squad. Stand easy. This is what we're going to do. In a couple of minutes, we're going for a walk around the smoke house. You follow me, and one of the other instructors will follow and make sure that none of you gets lost. I'm just going in to check things are ready. You wait out here for me.' The instructor opened the door to the smoke house and disappeared inside.

The squad stood, casually chatting among themselves. They could hear the faint crackle of burning wood coming from inside the building and thick blue smoke began to squeeze out of all of the apertures around the doors and windows.

'Right, get your sets donned and started up, the way you were shown earlier,' Sub Officer Harding said, casually.

With a clattering of gear, the squad started getting rigged, some looking confident, others less sure. Out of the blue, Sub Officer Randall ran out of the door to the smoke house, panic in his voice. 'Quick, quick, hurry up. There's somebody in there, collapsed. Get in quick and rescue him. Quick quick. Don't hang about and don't bother fixing your straps. Get in. Come on, I'm ordering you get in. He might die, if you don't hurry up.'

There was a general air of panic, recruits milling around, trying to put on their sets and fasten their straps. Jake thought: *This is strange, they told us never to go in without tallies having been handed in. To hell with it. Let's get in.* The squad piled into the smoke house and instantly ground to a halt. The visibility was zero and they hadn't got lamps to illuminate the area, so moving around was difficult.

Jake shouted: 'Be quiet a minute. Let's split up. You lot do the ground floor, the rest of us do the top floor.' There was a general commotion before the groups sorted themselves out. Jake, finding himself in the lead, soon located the bottom of the concrete stairs.

'OK, lads. Let's get up there. Me, Mark and Judy go left at the top. Pete, Al, Fraser and Zak go right. Keep low. Let's be quick.' The squad made their way tentatively up the staircase. As they reached the top of the stairs, a Claxton sounded so loudly it made verbal communication between the groups impossible. They moved forward blindly, each sliding their feet along the ground and feeling in front of their faces to avoid walking into walls or doors. Jake heard a muffled yelp behind him, but continued his mind fixed on a forward path, still trying to locate the casualty who had been reported missing.

Clunk. The lights came on, and the instructors were shouting: 'Stand exactly where you are. Do not move.'

Huge fans began extracting the smoke, which was soon cleared, so that the recruits were able to see their surroundings. Jake looked around. He was alone. *Where are the rest of the lads?* he thought. *The bloody instructors have done us,* Jake smiled to himself, at the same time feeling a bit foolish. *I should have known better,* he thought to himself.

The three instructors stood before the recruits. Sub Officer Pearce smiled at them.

'What was the lesson from that exercise then?' he said, trying to look serious. 'I don't want you to worry about that. It was done on purpose to throw you off balance. The lesson is: you don't enter a building in BA unless all of the procedures are in place. Remember what we said this morning. Your BA set must have been checked by you. You must have filled in the tally. You only go where you're told to go. Your tally must remain outside on the board, and you don't go into an incident in a group like you did. Your entry must be organised and controlled.' He looked at the bedraggled group, all looking mildly shell-shocked.

'Why, you may ask. The procedures are there for your safety and survival. They were developed because of tragedy. Firemen lost their lives before we had these measures in place. The lessons of those losses were learned, so remember those points. You will be hammered on them this week. Now, off you go and service your sets.'

The recruits piled into the service area, Mark and Jake, alongside each other, began dismantling their BA sets 'How did you find that, Jake?' Mark asked.

'Brilliant. A lot easier than the last time I went into a smoky building. Just can't wait for the rest of it. Bring it on.'

27th September:
The crew sat on the mess deck, the overpowering smell of slurry still hanging around the station. Taff and Pete were in the kitchen, cooking breakfast for the watch. The usual eggs, bacon and tomatoes with a lot of fried bread. The mugs were filled with steaming tea and there was an atmosphere of calm around the mess room. The boys had cleaned the machine from the previous night and mopped the appliance room floor, so the station was ready for the oncoming day watch to take over. Red Watch were going off for a four day break.

30th September:
The breathing apparatus instructors had had a tough week. The course they were about to complete today had been a good course; the recruits had performed well and had relished all of the challenges put before them.

They were all more confident: they had been tested, but they'd just got stuck in to the tasks and given everything.

Today was to be the final exercise, one designed to challenge both their stamina and knowledge of procedures; if they got through this, they would go on to the next phase of road accident training.

The instructors had got together to discuss the recruits. In terms of ability and knowledge, they couldn't be separated. They were confident that all of the squad would pass and do well on the station they were being posted to.

They mustered, fully equipped with the breathing apparatus sets strapped to their backs and the control board close at hand. Their tallies had been checked and completed; their emergency distress unit had been checked. They knew this was a vital component of all BA operations and they were ready to go.

Sub Officer Pearce stood before them. 'Listen carefully to what I have to say. This is the final exercise. There are no tricks or stunts in this test. The job is what it is; it is as you find it.'

The recruits swallowed hard, wondering what the instructors had conjured up for them this time. Throughout the week they had been tested in all areas. They'd dragged twelve stone dummies over rubble through dense smoke in zero visibility; they'd pulled lengths of charged hose through the buildings, upstairs and through windows. They'd been shouted at and put under pressure in every conceivable way, but they were still nervous. No one wanted to let the group down. BA is a test of will and teamwork and they were desperate to do well.

'Before you is the ship 'Pride of Grimsby'. Previously, you may have thought it was the smoke house. Wrong, it is a ship. It is, as you can see, moored at the dockside, where you are standing. The ship is on fire,' the sub officer said in a serious voice, pointing upwards towards the roof of the BA complex, which was by now spewing out clouds of dark smoke. 'The crew of this ship have bravely attempted to fight the fire and failed. At least six of them are trapped in the engine compartment. Your job: first, locate and rescue the crew; second, extinguish the fire. Are there any questions?'

Young Ali, a lad from Barnsley, spoke up. 'Excuse me, sub. Where's the engine room?'

The instructor looked at him and smiled. 'Mr Hussein, the engine room in a ship is almost always at the bottom.' The crew laughed, nervously. Recruit Ali looked embarrassed 'Yes, sub,' he said, trying to seem dignified.

The instructor spoke again. 'For the purposes of this incident, I will operate entry control. Mr Devonshire, you will lead the first team. Miss Hines, you will lead the second team and Mr Higgins will lead the third team.' He paused for breath. 'Your entry point will be through the hatch on the main deck. One of the other subs will supervise your entry, and you will descend the Jacob's ladders until you reach the bottom.' The crews looked up towards the top of the building, which was by now almost invisible, wreathed in a vast cloud of dirty smoke. 'Remember what you have been taught. Speed is important, but so is safety. It's important that you rescue the casualties, but it's more important that you survive the experience. A dead fire-fighter is no use to anyone. Now, team one, get your sets started up, tallies checked and let's get to it.'

Mac and Val were in Sainsbury's, doing the weekly grocery shopping. 'How's young Jacob getting on, Mac? Isn't it his pass out, soon?'

'Yeah, just a couple of weeks and he'll be done. He's doing well. The instructors really rate him. He's on his BA course this week.'

33

Tony Ellis sat at the kitchen table writing his diary. In it, he wrote in detail everything he could remember about the job with the cow, and how he felt about his life in the brigade. He wrote: 'The last shift was a good one. Attended my first job in charge. I think I did well. We had a cow in a slurry pit. Everyone got covered in crap, even the DC. Mac helped, but he let me be in charge. I don't know if I'd been in his position if I could have stood back. A very satisfying day.'

Ray Swift was heading south through France, the sun was shining and he had his tapes playing his favourite Organ music, music from the shows. Ray had not missed the job for a second. Mary was with him and life was perfect.

Ernie and Doris were going out in the car for the first time since Doris had had her stroke. Ernie had decided they would drive to Monsal Head, sit in the car park, look at the view and have a nice ice cream cornet. They drove out of the city, the ground rising steeply above them. Doris said: 'I'm glad you've had the heater fixed at last.'

'Yep, I didn't want you getting too hot and me having to buy ya more than one cornet. I'm not made of money ya know, our Doris.'

Doris looked slowly around at her man. 'You're so good to me, Ernest, but I still love ya, you tight old sod.'

Ernie chuckled to himself and tried to hide the lump in his throat and the tear which threatened to slide down his cheek.

Maddie rang Jim's mobile number. He was in the middle of his final patrol of the shift, and he was happy with life. He'd written out his application, the first step towards him training to become a plumber.

'Hello,' Jim said, already sure that he knew who it was. Maddie had taken to calling him each night when he was at work.

'Hello, you. It's me. I just called to say I love you,' she sang the words to the tune of the same name. 'Mum's asked me to ask you if you'd like to stay for supper when we get back from our walk on Sunday.'

'That would be great. How've they been since you told them?'

'They weren't too happy at first, but I convinced them that you were the man of my dreams and they gave in. 'Just *so long as you're sure and you're happy,*' they said. That's why they want you to come on Sunday. They thought if I was to marry you, then maybe they should meet you.'

Jim stood, dreamlike, in the darkness at the back of the office block. Maddie's voice always raised his heart rate.

'I don't deserve you, mad woman.'

'Don't you start that again, Jimbo. It takes two to tango and you and me tango very well. Anyway, I'm off. I'll see you at the weekend.'

Pete Jacks unloaded the wheelchair from the back of his car, spent a minute assembling it and wheeled it around to the passenger side of the car. 'You all right, love? Do you need a hand?'

'No, just hold the chair and I'll hutch across.'

Trudy had noticed the change in her husband since he'd moved stations. He now seemed to be looking a lot tidier and he talked about the job, something he hadn't done for years.

'Come on, the let's go for a stroll,' Pete said, as he wheeled his wife along the tarmac paths which wound their way through the Botanical Gardens.

Ian Blain lifted the rarely used bag of golf clubs out of the back of his car. Today he was going to play Alan Carter at golf. A lot was at stake. For Ian, it was his division's credibility as a sporting entity. Alan was the Divisional Commander of 'C' Division, and this was an annual event played between all of the commanders. It gave them a chance to relax and mull things over between them.

Alan had walked over to meet Ian. This was Ian's first time, so Alan would guide him through the match.

'Phew, what's that smell?' Alan said, as he approached the back of Ian's car.

'That,' Ian said, 'is cow crap.'

'Well, I heard you went to the job, but you really shouldn't bring it home with you,' he laughed.

'That's nothing,' Ian retorted. 'My gear was covered in it. Div HQ still stinks. I'll think very carefully before I get that close again,' he laughed.

Ian had spoken to all of the DCs and told them of his change of heart, what he would now be doing, and the new emphasis in his life. They were all very supportive, but at the same time thought that he was slightly off his rocker.

'Come on, Ian Blain, let me show you how this game of golf should be played,' Alan said, grinning as he slung his battered golf bag across his broad shoulders.

Dan Brogan sat in his office. He was tired, heaving spent last night out on the town with Dorothy his fiancée, then finished the night off with a Chinese take away, a long, good night had meant he had only managed about three hours of sleep.

Dan had begun the process of packing things into boxes, ready to clear his office. He looked forward to retirement, which would happen in a month's time. It had been a long haul and he was finding it more difficult to recover from the stresses and strains of the job. He'd promised himself that he and Dorothy his long term fiancé would do New Zealand and Australia; he'd wanted to go there for years. And maybe he'd let her make an honest man of him. He knew it's what she really wanted. That would be his retirement gift to her.

Janet and Justin decided that today they would walk down and around Bretton Clough. This isolated deep valley had been uninhabited since the last farmer left in the thirties. They parked the four by four opposite the Barrel pub, which sits on the ridge overlooking Eyam to the south and the Clough to the north.

They were soon descending a steep track. The land fell away sharply to their left, the track winding downwards through dense shrubs and trees as they left the last remnants of habitation behind them.

'This is beautiful, Justin,' Janet spoke as the scenery took her breath away. The track soon became more eroded and uneven as it wound its way down into the depths of the Clough. Small streams crossed the track and soon they climbed a timber stile, the track then bringing them to a small rocky outcrop, where another stream rounded the base of the rocks. Then came to a series of junctions in the track, some descending, others contouring around the hillside, others climbing up the steep undergrowth-strewn hillside.

Janet stopped, the myriad of diverging paths confusing her usually good sense of direction. 'Let's just stop here a minute. I'll just check the map,' she said.

'OK. You're the expert,' Justin said, as he wiped the perspiration from his brow.

'We need to go over there,' Janet said, pointing to yet another stile. 'We should then descend about half a mile until we hit Stoke Ford. I've heard of it, but never seen it,' she added, enthusiastically. The warm day was making the atmosphere oppressive. As they walked, the sunlight hit small swarms of insects which buzzed around almost like shoals of herring, glistening in the bright sunlight.

They emerged from the trees and the landscape opened up before them. They were now at the base of the Clough. All around them were steep tree- and shrub-covered hillsides. Only the path along the base of the Clough offered easy walking. Soon, they found themselves on an elevated knoll, which overlooked the meeting point of several streams. There were old timber sign posts, and a bridge spanned the largest of the streams. A couple of fellow walkers sat by the stream, drinking coffee and eating sandwiches.

'Isn't this just lovely?' Janet said, pulling the peak of her baseball cap lower across her face, to shield her eyes from the brightness of the sun.

'Yeah. Shall we sit for a while and have a drink?' Justin said, looking as though he needed a rest.

The hatch door swung open and massive clouds of hot smoke poured out.

'OK, Team One. In you go,' said the instructor, nonchalantly. 'Search and rescue. Take care; it's hot in there.'

Jake stood back with the rest of his team; they could see Mark and his team engulfed by a dense cloud of grey smoke entering the building through a hatch in the roof. As the last of the team entered, the instructor closed the hatch above them.

Mark and his team descended the vertical iron ladder. The smoke was suffocating, and he could barely see the iron steps of the ladder only inches from the thick plastic of his face mask. He climbed down the ladder as quickly as the conditions would allow, and he and his group were soon standing on the concrete floor at the base of the ladder. He clipped his personal line onto a guide line which bisected a floor littered with debris, together with large pieces of wood and old furniture. He held the hinged hook of his personal line, which was in turn clipped to the fixed line in his left hand. He was moving forward blindly and could feel the heat in the smoke around the exposed skin on his neck. He slid his feet along, feeling for any sign of weakness in the floor. He felt something hit his shin. Feeling with his gloved hands, he surmised that it was a bed and when he felt further, on the bed was a clothed body.

Mark was elated. He turned round to his team. Unable to see them, he shouted: 'I've found somebody.' The team gathered round. 'Right, Ali, Bill, you grab the casualty. I'll lead us back to the ladder,' he called, his voice revealing his excitement.

'Team Two, in you go.' The Instructor opened the hatch and soon the second team were inside, descending into the smoke and heat.

Mark was leading his team, who were struggling to follow him and carry the heavy body over the rubble-strewn floor. They were breathing heavily. It was tough work, but they knew they had to move fast. Time was of the essence.

'Stop. Gauge checks,' Mark shouted to his team. They stopped, grateful for the chance to take a rest. Mark used his lamp to read their gauges. 'Ali, your air is lowest, so you lead us out. Let's move it and I'll help Bill with the body. They quickly reached the base of the ladder. The situation became confused; the second team had reached the base of the ladder, as Mark's team arrived at the same spot. Ali's low pressure warning whistle shrieked just as the second team reached the floor, causing confusion on the guide line.. Over the noise and confusion Mark grabbed Ali's shoulder and shouted to him: 'You go up and out, Ali. Drop the line for us to tie on to the body for it to be hauled out.'

'OK, I'll be quick as I can,' Ali shouted above the noise of the noise which reverberated around the room.

Judy Hines, having passed the first team, who were on their way out, was determined to get as far into the building has possible and constantly urged her team on. 'Come on, lads. Search quicker, keep low and don't miss the corners. The pre-laid guide line took them to the head of yet another Jacob's ladder, which descended even further into the base of the building. Visibility was zero and communication was difficult.

'Get on your knees, you're taking unnecessary punishment … Get down low under the heat layer.' One of the instructors stepped out from behind a low wall. He could see the team were moving but the search was erratic and they had missed three casualties. The instructor stepped back into the darkness and Judy's team pressed on into the darkness of the smoke.

BEEP BEEP BEEP BEEP, the piercing sound of a fire-fighter's distress signalling equipment pierced the already frantic scene being played out in the hot smoke.

All of the teams knew the procedure in the event of this happening. A DSU actuating had to be taken seriously; worst case scenario was that a fire-fighter was in trouble. The task now took on a different level of urgency. All teams began heading at speed for the sound.

Ali was out of the building and involved in pulling the body up the ladder, while Mark and Bill were still at the base of the ladder. Mark made a decision. 'Bill, gauge check.' He checked their gauges and saw that they both read eighty. This would give them time to look for the source of the actuating DSU.

'Right, Bill, let's go … no messing: direct and fast, OK?'

They both clipped on to the guide line and began once more crossing the floor, looking for the ladder which would take them to the man in trouble.

Sub Officer Pearce was standing close to Jake's team when the distress call went out. 'Right Team Three, emergency. Get started up and report to entry control on the deck.'

Jake's team buzzed with the sudden shock of adrenaline and were soon racing up the ladder on to the roof of the smoke house. After a brief input from the instructor on the roof, they sped down the ladder into the smoke, feeling the heat pour over them as they descended. With Jake leading, they moved quickly along the guide line, not caring to search, minds set on getting to the sound which told them that someone was in trouble.

Team One descended the second ladder, moving fast. The instructor stepped out and took hold of Bill and held him back. Mark was unaware that he was now on his own. The instructor took Bill and sat him behind the wall where he had been hiding. He pressed the button which set of the alarm on his BA set. Now two alarms were sounding in different places. Mark looked quickly at his gauge. It was reading fifty, so his low pressure whistle would blow in a couple of minutes. 'What's your reading, Bill?' There was no reply. Mark turned and saw that he was alone.

'Oh, bollocks!' Mark cursed.

From behind him the Instructor emerged and caught his arm.

'Sit down here and stay put. Entrapped procedure. If they find you, you're unconscious.'

Mark, now low on air, knew that he had to assume that he couldn't get out quickly. He must do everything in his power to preserve the limited amount of air he had left in his cylinder. That meant no panic ... relax ... shallow, slow breathing. His low pressure warning whistle began to blow.

There were now three alarms sounding and the conditions were still dire. The temperature remained high, quickly draining the recruits' energy, and the visibility was low. Jake made a snap decision.

'Stop a second. There are too many to get them all. Head for the nearest, then maybe if we can get one back to the ladder, we can see what else we can do. Gauge check.' Jake was thinking fast. 'Right, I'm clipped on the line. You clip onto me ... should be quicker.' They were soon at the head of the second ladder, which they descending rapidly, the sound of the various distress units causing confusion about where to go first.

Judy's team homed in on the sound. They found one of the instructors standing casually close to the brazier in which the fire burned. 'Well done, Team Two. Forget me, keep looking.' The instructor turned off his alarm. They now felt the impetus was with them and they soon located another alarm. It was Bill. He smiled at Judy. 'I'm not unconscious but I have to be assisted out,' he said, cheerfully.

Jake's team were closing in on an alarm; soon they came across Mark, who was doing a decent job of being unconscious. Jake got his team to do another gauge check. They all had around fifty atmospheres in their gauges. Jake checked Mark's gauge.

'We've got to be quick; he's only got ten atmospheres left.' The team struggled and scrambled and cursed as they dragged Mark, sometimes dropping him. They quickly arrived at the base of the ladder which would lead them up onto the roof. The overriding sound now was of low pressure warning whistles blowing, the efforts of all of the teams, having worked almost to the point of exhaustion, meant that the rescue teams were now in danger of running out of air themselves. Rescue lines were thrown down the ladder and the casualties tied in and hauled out of the smoke onto the deck of the ship.

Instantly, the massive extractor fans began to spin and large volumes of smoke were quickly driven out of the building.

'Well done, all of you. Get de-rigged, get a drink, service the sets and then – soon as you like – debrief in the classroom,' the instructor said, a broad smile splitting his face.

The squad sat quietly awaiting the instructors, who, they were sure, would be critical of the exercise.

'Right, what did we learn from that?' Sub Officer Pearce asked. 'Come on, don't be shy. You know there were balls ups. It's important that you recognise them. That's the first step to being a good BA man.'

Judy stood up. 'Well, sub, we got confused at the ladder when we crossed Team One. There were so many bodies milling about and the noise made it hard to think straight. It slowed us down quite a bit,' she said, ruefully.

'Anyone else?' the instructor asked.

Mark stood up. 'I think I made the biggest mistake. Firstly, going back to search with a low cylinder. Secondly, getting separated from my partner: that could have been fatal.' He said holding his hands out, as a gesture of culpability.

'I'm glad you recognised that, Mr Devonshire,' the instructor responded.

'How about your team, Mr Higgins?'

Jake stood up. 'Well, sub, we weren't started up when the DSUs actuated, so we were rushed and didn't have much chance to discuss things. When we got in, we decided just to go for it. Maybe we were in a bit of a panic and we may have been a bit more effective if we'd gone a bit slower.'

'OK, these exercises are designed to test you. We expect you to make mistakes. That's the idea. Make the mistake, then learn from it. In the real thing, you can't turn on a fan and clear the building, but you all worked hard and, despite the mistakes, you all did well. I'd be happy for any of you to be on my watch, as far as I'm concerned. That's it, you've passed. Well done and thanks for your commitment and hard work this week.'

Jake stood up. 'Sub, can we thank you and the other instructors for your effort in training us. We've all learned a lot and it's been really enjoyable.' Judy stood up and called 'hear hear.' The squad all stood and gave a round of applause to the staff of the BA School.

Mac pulled up outside the neat terraced house in Dronfield, Jake's mother was looking out of the window and saw them pull up. She grabbed her jacket and quickly walked down the path to Mac's car.

'Thanks for the lift. It would have been two buses to get me there. This is very good of you.'

'And how are you, Mrs Higgins?' Val asked, as she shuffled into the rear seat of the car.

'I'm fine. Very proud of Jacob, of course. I just hope I don't cry,' she said, looking very fine in her new outfit.

34

The squad were rigged in their best uniform; they were brushed, polished and pressed. Even the instructor, Sub Officer Blackett, was proud of them. These youngsters were one of his best ever squads and he was looking forward to showing them off to the senior officers and the families of the recruits.

'Listen now,' he said as the squad put the finishing touches to their uniforms. 'This is your big day. We start with you on parade, then the presentation, then back here, get changed into fire gear, then on with the display. Relax, you've practiced it, no problem, so let's get out there. They're all waiting.'

The squad marched out in three columns. Sub Officer Blackett called: 'Squad, halt.' They stopped perfectly together. 'Squad, left turn,' he shouted.

Mark and Jake were next to each other in the line, standing to attention. There was a crackle from the loudspeaker system. The voice came across to the visitors gathered at one end of the drill ground.

'Welcome to the South Yorkshire Fire Service Training Centre, and to the pass out of squad five ninety-six. Today is their big day. After many weeks of training they have all reached the high standard required for them to be accepted into the service, and have all been allocated posts on stations. They will begin their new lives at fire stations in the next few days.'

There was a brief pause.

'Firstly, just a brief résumé of the squad members …

'Fireman Mark Devonshire served in the Royal Navy and, before joining South Yorkshire Fire Service, he lived in Kent with his wife, Tricia, and baby Josh. He is twenty-nine years old.

'Ali Hussein is twenty years old and single. He lives in Sheffield with his parents and three sisters. Before deciding to become a fireman he was a student, studying chemistry at Sheffield University.

'William Peters, aged twenty-six, served in the British Army and did two tours of Northern Ireland. He is single at the moment, but hopes to get married later this year.'

Each description brought about a round of applause from the spectators.

'Judith Hines is single, aged twenty-four, and she has a child, Jessica, aged three. Before joining us, she was a driving instructor.

'Jacob Higgins is a former builder, the youngest man on the squad, aged eighteen and acquitted himself well when saving the life of a young lady from fire, whilst still in training.'

The anonymous voice over the tannoy continued giving a brief description of each recruit. When he'd finished, he said: 'The squad will now be inspected by the chief fire officer.'

Jake could barely contain his pride. His heart was thumping in his chest. He looked across the yard and could make out his mother, sat alongside Mac and Val, who was deep in conversation with a senior officer. Mark also looked across the yard. He'd spotted his wife and son, who were in the front row of the spectators. He'd been through something similar when he joined the Navy, but back then, he hadn't felt the same level of achievement he now did. He felt both proud and grateful. His head buzzed with anticipation. He would now have to begin looking for a new home for his family, and he looked forward both to a long career as a fireman and lasting friendships with his colleagues. He remembered back those few months earlier, when he and Jake had met in the room in headquarters before their initial interviews. He was astounded by the development of his friend, who'd gone from being a young man with little confidence to being the star. He'd become a man before his eyes. *'Yes, Mark, this has been a great experience,'* he said to himself.

Sub Officer Blackett stood two paces to the front of his squad. He felt great pride, as he always did, on these occasions, but these were a special squad. He knew this time that he had peaked; he'd really produced a good bunch of fire-fighters. He looked out of the corner of his eyes and saw the Chief and the Deputy, accompanied by the Brigade Training Officer. They marched smartly towards the group of recruits. Then, led by the Chief, they walked slowly between the ranks, each officer in turn spending time talking to each recruit.

Jake stood smartly to attention. He felt tense. He saw out of the corner of his eye the Chief, standing talking to Mark. The Chief shook Mark's hand and Jake heard him say: 'Well done, Mr Devonshire.'

'Well, Mr Higgins, we meet again,' the Chief said, as he stood before Jake. 'I see you made it all right.'

'Yes, sir, thank you.'

'I understand that you've had a very interesting time whilst you've been in training.'

'Yes, sir, it's been great. I've loved every minute of it.'

'Well done. You've done yourself proud, and I'm sure your mother is proud, also.'

'Thank you, sir. I hope she is,' Jake said, his chest feeling as though it would burst.

Mac sat among the spectators. He saw a movement to his left and glanced around: both Jake's mother and Val were wiping their eyes with tissue. The occasion was clearly getting to both of them.

Having finished the inspection, the Chief and his entourage stood at the front of the squad. The tannoy crackled into life and the voice rang out again.

'There is just one further task for the Chief Fire Officer to perform before the passing out display. That is the presentation of the Silver Axe …' The voice paused. 'The Silver Axe is presented to the recruit who, in the opinion of the instructional staff, has proved to be the best recruit during the year, the recruit who has shown outstanding qualities and most impressed the training staff …' There was another pause. 'The Silver Axe winner for 1996 is Recruit Jacob Higgins.'

The winner of the Silver axe was a closely guarded secret, only known to the staff of the training school. Neither Mac, Jake, Jake's mother nor the other recruits knew.

Jake, when he heard his name called, out almost fainted. He was stunned. Instantaneously, his squad broke ranks and gathered around him, applauding. Mac's chest almost burst with pride. Jake's mother and Val were both in tears as the applause rang around the drill yard.

'Squad, get back in line,' Sub Officer Blackett called. The squad quickly reformed into their three ranks.

They stood rigidly to attention.

Ian Blackett called out the order. 'Fireman Higgins, on the order, march. You will take two paces forward and stand to attention ... Fireman Higgins, forward march.'

Jake took two paces to his front. The Chief walked slowly towards him, and then he stopped and handed over the Silver Axe set on a mahogany plinth. Jake looked closely at it. The Chief spoke. 'Congratulations, Mr Higgins. I'm told that you have been outstanding throughout your training, and of course there was the small matter of the rescue you carried out. Be proud. You've done well. Keep up the standard.'

Jake was feeling overwhelmed. He shook the Chief's hand again. 'Thank you, sir. This is the best day of my life.'

Thirty minutes of sweat and effort now went into the practical demonstration. Ladders were thrown against buildings, water was flooded across the yard, the recruits driven on by bellowed orders. Soon the demonstration was completed and the recruits stood breathlessly – but proudly – in line, having given maximum effort to their display. They listened to loud applause from the large crowd of family and friends who'd come and watched their display with great pride.

The families gathered in the training school's recreation room, where they chatted among themselves, some in deep discussions with officers who had mingled with the families.

The squad had showered and changed and joined their families for a buffet, before leaving for home and then on to their designated stations the following week.

Jake walked across the room, accompanied by Mark and his wife and young son.

'Mum, this is Mark, a friend of mine, and his wife Tricia and son, Josh. Mark, this is mum, Mac and Val. They're the ones who gave me the inspiration to join the Brigade.'

Jake's mum put her arms around him and said: 'I'm so proud of you, son. Your dad would have been proud, too.'

Mac leaned across to Mark and shook his hand. 'You've all done well. Congratulations on getting through ... and you've joined the best team in the world.'

Mark stood with his wife and child looking very proud. 'It's been tough, but meeting Jake and having this new challenge makes it worthwhile. Jake's told me at great length all about you. I feel I've known you for a long time.'

35

Mac and Val had driven out to Hollinsclough. They'd parked the car and, in beautiful weather, they'd repeated the route they'd done a few weeks before, even stopping by the old farmhouse. They'd made a fuss of the old dog and chatted with the old lady and left her with the promise that they would visit her again soon. They meandered carelessly across the meadows leading to Chrome hill, where they stopped for a breather and Mac said: 'I love this area. It seems more beautiful every time we come.'

They walked steadily upwards over a grassy slope, which was littered with shattered limestone peeking out from the smooth, almost manicured grass. They passed small broken crags, all the time gaining height. They were breathless and hot, but they pushed on, eventually cresting the summit ridge. Mac and Val stood hand in hand, as the sun shone, with only a few wisps of cloud hanging motionless in the sky. They looked down the valley floor towards Parkhouse Hill, similar in shape but lower in height. From their vantage point, the vista was spectacular. 'This place is perfect, Mac,' Val said, with a hint of emotion filling her voice.

'You're dead right. You stand there, let me take a picture of my lovely girl, in the most beautiful place in the world.'

They descended the hill slowly, savouring the scenes around them, almost reluctant to end the walk. They came off the ridge into green fields, with just the occasional sheep standing there, quietly gazing at them. They chatted about life and love and Mac's imminent retirement.

'I know it's coming, Val. There's nothing I can do to change that, but I don't regret a second. These last few years on the Reds have been great.' They walked on slowly, ambling. Mac was quiet for a minute. 'I was sorry Ray left the way he did, but he's happy now and I'm pleased for young Tony. He'll do well, and I think Pete Jacks came to us just in time … and by the way, why don't we invite him and Trudy round for a meal one night?' Mac paused. The day they had just had seemed to have satisfied something inside him. He needed to talk. 'So much has happened recently. The DC's suddenly turned into a fireman, young Clive is getting married, Brian has got together with his ex and then young Jake … it's been a fantastic few months.'

'I reckon you're right,' Val replied. 'Are you OK, love?' she asked.

'Yeah, I'm fine. It's the fresh air makes my mouth go into overdrive!' Mac responded, with a laugh in his voice. 'I've got the perfect life. I've got you, the girls and the boys on the watch. What could be better?'

They walked along the gravel track which would bring them back to the car. Val jammed her hand through Mac's arm.

'You're right,' she said. 'You have the perfect life. You've got me, the girls and the Reds and, as you've reminded me on many occasions, you're much better Red than dead,' she chuckled, leaning across to him and tousling his hair with her hand. 'Let's drive up to the pub in Earl Sterndale, have a drink and see what that crazy dog's been up too.'

Mac chuckled to himself, thinking about Nipper, the legendary Jack Russell who lived at the pub, a dog with a liking for chasing tractors and fighting anything on four legs that ventured into his territory. 'Sounds good,' Mac said. 'I fancy a pint … and are there any of those sandwiches left? You know that damned dog will be into the rucksack after them, if you don't watch him.'

They climbed into Mac's old Volvo and drove almost reluctantly out of the village, taking a last look up at the spectacular ridge they has just traversed. 'Makes you glad to be alive, doesn't it,' Mac said, as he steered the car slowly along the narrow lane towards the pub.

The End